A MEASURE OF SERENITY

A MEASURE OF SERENITY

BRYAN PROSEK

CamCat
Books

CamCat Publishing, LLC
Brentwood, Tennessee 37027
camcatpublishing.com

Hardcover ISBN 9780744303629
Paperback ISBN 9780744303896
Large-Print Paperback ISBN 9780744303551
eBook ISBN 9780744303414
Audiobook ISBN 9780744303797

Library of Congress Control Number: 2021943219

Book and cover design by Maryann Appel

5   3   1   2   4

To my wife and kids, DeAnne, Luke, and Lucy,
for putting up with all of my late-night writing and their
support and encouragement to write.

And to my Aunt Jan and Aunt Bev for being such huge fans
and inspiring me to not give up.

PROLOGUE

My mind replays that night for me like a movie, whether I want it to or not. I can never erase an image, no matter how hard I try, especially not this one.

I was staring out the backseat window of our family car. The October night was as black as the cat on my Halloween T-shirt. The wipers intermittently creaked across the windshield, removing drizzle so my dad could see. I liked the darkness. I zoomed in on my reflection in the window—a ten-year-old girl with blonde hair and blue eyes trying not to calculate and count everything in sight. The mirror image helped me relax, and my eyelids grew heavy, my head dropped forward. My reflex jerked my head up and opened my eyes, just to repeat the process. It had been a long drive from New York City to Hancock, New Hampshire, but we were so close to Grandma and Grandpa's farm and I didn't want to fall asleep. I leaned my head against the glass. Wisps of fog skated over the window, adding an eerie tone to the darkness outside.

I had started to nod off again when my little brother's cry startled me. He was strapped into a baby carrier in the seat beside me. My mom unbuckled her seatbelt and twisted around to stroke his little arms and legs. "It's okay, Jona. Mommy's here. Go back to sleep."

Just as quickly as the crying started, it stopped. I leaned to my right to look through the windshield. The fog was lifting some, at least on that stretch of road. I could make out trees along the side of the road. I recognized the thickly wooded area. We were getting close. My stomach churned a little with excitement. I would have no problem staying awake now.

My mom turned back around to rummage through the glove compartment.

"What are you looking for, Mom?" I asked.

She did not answer but continued to search.

My dad turned his head to the right to look at me.

"How are you doing back there, Peanut?" he asked.

Peanut. That was his special name just for me. I loved it. So much more playful than Serenity, my real name. "Just fine. I cannot wait to see Grandma and Grandpa. I know we are close. How much longer until we get there?"

My dad looked at the instrument panel and then turned back to me. "We have twenty miles to go, and I'm driving fifty-five miles per hour."

"Twenty-one minutes and forty-nine seconds," I said without hesitation.

< 2 >

My mom laughed and shook her head as she looked up from the glove compartment, probably rolling her eyes at my quick math, when suddenly she screamed, "Look out!"

My dad swiveled forward, and his back and shoulders tensed up as he slammed on the brakes.

In the middle of the road, illuminated by the headlights, everything was distorted. The landscape wavered, moving as things seem to do when one looks at the horizon on a hot summer day. Except here, everything wavered within an area about the size of a double garage door. Objects inside it appeared to change shape, undulating while remaining recognizable. The road in front of us, the trees just off to the side, and a speed limit sign all wavered. And a slight haze covered everything, too.

I took in all of this as the car skidded on the blacktop. I heard the horrible screeching sound of the tires against the road. My dad turned the steering wheel sharply to the left. We spun. The sudden turn threw me into Jona. I felt myself turning upside down. The seatbelt pressed hard into my shoulder as it held my body weight. Then I felt myself roll again, stopping right side up. Jona's screams pierced my right ear. I looked at him. He seemed fine, still strapped into his carrier, which was fastened tightly to the seat. Then I looked forward. Mom was turned completely around with the back of her head resting against the dash, her legs on the seat, her back wedged against the open glove compartment. She didn't move, eyes closed, blood covering her face. She had not put her seatbelt back on after caring for Jona. I looked behind the steering wheel. My dad was no longer there.

I had to help my mom. But something I must have read somewhere popped into my mind—*save the youngest first*. That was Jona. But my mom was bleeding. My mind immediately jumped to another

< 3 >

thing—*help the person with the worst injuries first.* That was Mom. Like a computer caught in a feedback loop, my mind argued with itself. *Stop analyzing,* I tell myself every time I relive this memory, even though I know I cannot prevent what happens next, *stop analyzing and just act!*

The right side of the car began to waver just like the road and trees and sign. Even my mom's figure moved and contorted. I heard the sound of metal crunching. The front of the car was being crushed slowly, and the dashboard was moving toward me. I felt the back of the car pushing against me as well. The car was wedged crossways in the middle of the wavering area, and the force was crushing it as if caught in an industrial car crusher.

Get out, I thought. *I have got to get out of here, or I will be crushed.* I had to get Jona out, too. And my mom. But who was I to help first? I ran through the steps in my mind necessary to get Jona out of the car first, then return to help my mom. Based on all of the variables, I had a seventy percent chance of saving Jona and a twenty percent chance of saving my mom if I proceeded in that order. If I helped my mom first, then Jona, my odds of getting my mom out increased to thirty percent, but because of the time that would take, my odds of saving Jona fell to forty percent. Therefore, I needed to attempt to help Jona first. Those were the better overall odds. But then, I realized that I had not factored in the car being crushed. That made it a moving target. Why was I calculating all of that? I needed to move. But I could not. My mind would not let me. Not until I had weighed all the factors and run all the calculations. I hated my mind!

The car slowly caved in on itself. Jona. He was right there. No more calculating. I unbuckled my seat belt. The front seat started pushing against my legs. I reached over to unbuckle Jona's carrier, but

< 4 >

the buckle was jammed. I pressed hard with my thumb, then both thumbs. I tried to sit up to get more leverage, but my legs were caught. Thumbs aching, I pressed as hard as I could one last time, and the buckle popped open. I grabbed the handle of the carrier.

As I struggled against the weight of Jona and the carrier, I tallied the contents of Jona's diaper bag which were strewn across the back seat. Five diapers, eight different toys, and a spilled container of Cheerios. Forty-three Cheerios rattling on the seat.

Stop it!

Metal squealed around me. I gave up on trying to lift the carrier and unbuckled the safety belt instead as Jona screamed and squirmed. Finally, I got my arms around him. Numbing pain crept into both my knees. The front seat was now pressing hard against them. I could not lift Jona from this angle, so I dragged him out of the carrier onto my lap. My ears ached from the sound of metal being crushed and Jona screaming. I twisted around to the door, but my legs would not move. I had taken too long deciding what to do. Now I was pinned. I could not save Jona. I could not save my mom. I could not even save myself.

Suddenly, my door was wrenched opened. My dad's big hands reached in. One grabbed me by the upper arm, and the other grabbed Jona. A sharp pain shot up my leg as I was lifted out of the car and then heaved over my dad's shoulder as he ran.

The car exploded into flames behind us. The heat from the explosion stung my eyes, forcing them shut. When I opened them, the wavering had stopped. The road, trees, and sign were solid in the fire's glow.

"Mom!"

< 5 >

THE PROJECT

I love the feeling you get during the last class on a Friday afternoon. The small, rectangular window next to my seat is cracked open, just enough to let in the slightest chill. It cools my face. The classrooms are always overheated this time of year.

The trees are in full color outside. Everywhere I look, there is beautiful foliage, vibrant colors. Red, orange, and yellow leaves with a just hint of green. It is a perfect fall day to end the week. I focus in on one particular maple tree that has turned a brilliant shade of red. Its bright red leaves contrast against the deep blue sky. The beauty and peacefulness of nature help me to relax. And, more importantly, I do not count. Not the leaves on the tree, not the birds playing in the branches, not the white landscaping pebbles around the shrubs next to the building.

Everywhere I look, there is always something to count or calculate or analyze. Right now, I am relaxed. But I know it will not last long. It never does.

I can rarely find a place where, for any length of time, I am completely at ease—not thinking, not counting, not calculating, not analyzing, not hearing, not worrying. Not doing any of the things my mind does on its own. I wish I could always find that place. I wish I could be normal.

"Serenity?" The professor's voice brings me out of my trance. "You're the only one who hasn't given it a try. Can you save the class and give me the answer?"

He wants the answer. I did not even hear the question. I look around the room. Some classmates are looking at me, others are writing notes or typing on their laptops.

I look at the professor. "Could you repeat the question, please?"

He grins slightly from behind his desk and shakes his head but responds.

"One of the solutions to the equation x squared minus fifty-four x plus one hundred four equals zero is two. Can you find the other root using Vieta's formulas?" He stands up and walks to the front of his desk. "And as a bonus, if you get it right, the class is dismissed. You all can leave a little earlier."

The rest of the class suddenly becomes restless. Most of the students sit up in their seats, paying more attention now. The professor looks around the class and then repeats himself with emphasis.

"Only if Serenity answers it *exactly* correct. None of the rest of you did."

< 8 >

I overhear whispered conversations.

I can tell each person who is talking, even at a whisper. I have heard everyone in the room talk before, at least once, so I know which voice belongs to which person.

"She'll never get it right," Jasper whispers.

Andre replies, "Are you kidding? That's Serenity. Have you ever talked to that chick before? She's a stinking genius."

I hear multiple conversations at the same time.

"I think I know the answer."

That was Alex whispering.

"You just got it wrong yourself, you idiot," Marcus responds.

I hear Jasper and Andre again.

"That chick is only eighteen," Jasper says. "Kind of young for you. Plus, I hear she's quite the nerd."

"An eighteen-year-old senior at Harvard," Andre replies. "Who's ever done that before? And maybe I think nerds are hot."

The professor takes control. "All right, everyone. Quiet down so Serenity can answer."

I slide forward in my seat and look around the room again. Now, all eyes are fixed on me. I do not feel even the slightest bit nervous. I never do when it comes to academics. I have never seen this question before, and I do not recall ever studying or even reading about Vieta's formulas, but I must have skimmed over it at some point, speed-reading a textbook or research materials.

"From Vieta's formulas, we have negative, open parenthesis, x one plus x two, close parenthesis, equals negative fifty-four, so x one plus x two equals fifty-four," I say, trusting my voice to unreel what I saw. "We substitute x one for its value and get two plus x two equals fifty-four. Therefore, x two equals fifty-two."

< 9 >

The professor has a look of astonishment on his face, which quickly turns to a look of satisfaction, as if he is responsible for my answer. "That would be correct, Serenity. Excellent job."

Everyone in the class immediately starts to gather their things with a few soft shouts of "Yes!"

"Don't forget your homework assignment," the professor says, raising his voice over the bustle of people heading for the door. "It's on your syllabus."

The professor stops me as I walk by his desk. Everyone else files out of the door. A couple students give me a thumbs up or whisper "Thanks."

"Serenity," he begins as he leans against his desk, "how would you like to take part in a special project that the university is undertaking? We're selecting only three students for it. It'll look good on your resume when you graduate next spring."

"What does it involve?" I ask.

"It's a research project at a Harvard facility. The one where your father works."

Where my dad works? Maybe this will give me a chance to learn something about the "secret" project that Dad cannot talk about although it has consumed him for so long.

"What is the research?"

He straightens up. "I can't answer that myself, but Mr. Bailey is running the project."

"Dirk Bailey?" I interrupt, stepping back.

"Yes, is that a problem?"

Mr. Bailey brought my dad to Hancock, New Hampshire to work on a project the year after Mom died. I guess I should be thankful for that. Now, it's just a short drive to see Grandma and Grandpa on their

< 10 >

farm. When we lived in New York City, we only visited a few times a year. There was too much commotion for me in such a large city. Even if it did have some of the best neurosurgeons, neuropharmacologists, and therapists in the world, they had done all they could for me. So, moving us to Hancock was a blessing, but that was eight years ago, and Mr. Bailey still wants my dad to focus on that one project all the time. And whatever Mr. Bailey wants, Mr. Bailey seems to get.

I regain my composure and adjust my bookbag on my shoulder. "I just thought Mr. Bailey was pretty high up at the university to be leading a research project with a group of students."

The professor grins. "Well, I'll let him explain. Like I said, I don't know the details. He just asked me to see if you might be interested. His office is just down the hall. Why don't you stop by?"

I start toward the door. "Thank you, Professor."

"Good luck with it. And Serenity," he pauses, "excellent job in class today. For someone your age at the finest university in the country, you continue to amaze me." He gives me a genuine smile.

# # # # #

"Serenity," a voice calls from down the hall as I exit the classroom. I glance in that direction but do not turn my head. It is Shawn Patterson. I would recognize his tall, lanky frame at any distance. I look at my watch. I need to see Mr. Bailey *and* try to miss rush-hour traffic. I do not want to make my hour-and-forty-five-minute commute any longer.

"Serenity," he calls again, this time much closer.

I turn to face him. His blond hair bobbing with each step.

"You never returned my snap from this morning."

< 11 >

I hesitate, not sure how to respond. "I am sorry. I was in the middle of something for my dad and have not had a chance yet to respond." I did not lie. I was completing the app I developed for my dad's project so he can test it tonight. "I have had a lot on my mind lately."

His face softens. "I know. I understand. No worries."

"Is everything okay?" I ask. "Did you need something?"

Shawn shakes his head. "No. I had no special reason to . . . I snapped you because . . . I just wanted to say hey and see what you were up to."

I slide my bookbag off my shoulder, unzip it, and peer inside to see if I have to stop by my commuter locker to pick up any books for the weekend after I see Mr. Bailey before heading to my car. I need to make a quick getaway in order to beat traffic.

"Will you be at fencing club tonight?" Shawn asks.

Fencing is one of the few things Shawn and I have in common, besides our blond hair and being seniors at Harvard. He is a regular senior, unlike me, majoring in business to take over the reins of his family's medical supply business when his father retires. I am studying to do research in the field of medicine and have no idea where I will work or what I will do. He pretty much has everything handed to him, but he does not act like it.

"Sure," I say, zipping up my backpack and swinging it back onto my shoulder. "I will be there."

"Great." Shawn smiles. "Where are you heading? I'll walk with you. I'm done for the day."

I look at my watch, then at Shawn and nod in the direction of Mr. Bailey's office.

"Actually, I am just heading down the hall. I have to meet with someone."

< 12 >

Shawn's smile disappears. "Oh, okay, well, maybe next time."

I try to smile just enough that he can see I care about him as a friend but not enough that he will think that my feelings go any further than that. I do feel bad though.

He is my best friend outside of my family, and the one individual that I have not driven away by telling him everything he is going to do before he does it or because I cannot force myself to use contractions. The formality of my speech patterns makes me sound stuck up. But I cannot talk any other way. I cannot even think any other way. "Sure," I say. "I would like that."

# # # # #

The door to Mr. Bailey's outer office is open, but the chair behind the secretary's oak desk sits empty. Nobody is in the room, so I walk past two empty chairs and a large plant toward Mr. Bailey's door and raise my hand to knock.

"Yes, I can hear you clearly. Can you hear me?" Mr. Bailey says, apparently on the phone. "The connections are getting stronger. This is the first time I've been able to remotely form a connection through the facility. Go ahead and put him on." He pauses. "Hello, Mr. President."

Mr. President? President of what? The university? No, he would not call Angela Turner "Mister." I turn and look through the open door behind me. The hallway is empty. I hear nobody coming this way. But still, I should not eavesdrop. What Mr. Bailey says is none of my business.

"Yes, Sir. I will have Phil Ashdown working around the clock now until it's activated."

Dad?

< 13 >

I am certain it has something to do with the project he has been working on for so long. What does Mr. Bailey mean by "strong connections"? A connection through the facility?

I have heard enough. As I escape back toward the hallway, I hear Mr. Bailey's door open.

"Serenity, come on in! What brings you here—the new research project?"

Slowly, I return to Mr. Bailey's office. His secretary's small outer office pales in comparison to what sits behind this door. I cannot even take in the whole room without turning my head to scan it. I believe he has turned a former classroom into an office. And he spared no expense with his mahogany desk and floor-to-ceiling bookshelf on one wall.

The sun shines in through a wall of windows on the opposite side. On one wall is a framed picture of Mr. Bailey and Wes Masterson, President of the United States, jointly holding a plaque that I cannot read from this distance.

Mr. Bailey motions toward a leather chair facing his desk. "Please, have a seat."

I sink into the cushioning of the chair, my hands rubbing the soft leather of the arm rests.

Mr. Bailey sits in his tall chair behind his desk. "I haven't seen you in a while. How are classes going?"

"They are going well, thanks." I reply.

I am terrible at small talk. I never know what to say. I probably should ask Mr. Bailey how he is doing, but instead, I sit and wait for him to speak again.

"Your father says you graduate in the spring, is that right?"

"Yes."

< 14 >

"What's your major again. I think Phil told me, but I forget." He leans forward, folding his hands and rests his forearms on the desk.

I sit up straight. "Nuclear Medical Technology and Chemical Engineering."

He smiles. "A double major in two of the most difficult fields. Impressive. I believe you are perfect for the new research project I have."

"Thank you," I say, not looking at Mr. Bailey but rather, looking at his telephone. Something troubles me about the phone call I overheard. It was probably just something typical with my dad's work, but everything related to my dad's work troubles me. One thousand one hundred ninety-two books on the bookshelf. I look out the window. Forty-three students and six faculty members in sight, making their way across campus. I see the maple tree outside my classroom, now from a different angle. A sparrow is perched on one of the branches. Eighty-nine thousand seven hundred fifty-six. Just looking at the tree, I know the number of leaves.

"Serenity?" Mr. Bailey's voice brings me back to the conversation. "Are you okay? Can I get you some water or something?"

I blink my eyes and shake my head. "No, thank you, I am fine." I must have been completely ignoring him. "I am sorry, I was just trying to think what your project might be about." That is not true, but it is the best I can come up with.

He leans back in his chair and swings it sideways. "Have you heard of Doctor Friedrich Gruber?"

I nod. "Yes, he is a German scientist. He developed the quantum theory of astrological advancement."

Mr. Bailey smiles. "Of course, you would know all about him. I should have figured that. In other words, Doctor Gruber theorizes that time travel is possible."

< 15 >

I lean forward. Now that we are past the small talk and on to discussing academics, my mind turns on. I can discuss this with anyone forever.

"That is his *theory*," I say skeptically.

Mr. Bailey swings his chair back around to face me directly. "You don't agree with him?"

I clear my throat. "Mr. Bailey, I have read every book, journal, research paper, and note that I had access to that were written by Doctor Gruber and anyone else analyzing his work. I have run all the equations and did the math myself. No, I do not agree with him. I do not believe that his theory will work."

My intent is not to be confrontational with Mr. Bailey. I do not like confrontation with anyone.

But I cannot lie about something like this, and so I just state the facts.

Mr. Bailey grins. "That's exactly the attitude I am looking for, in at least one member on the team."

"Is the project to prove or disprove Doctor Gruber's theory?"

Mr. Bailey shakes his head. "No, not exactly. But it does involve Doctor Gruber's theory. It will be easier to show you than to explain. The other two students are meeting Professor Poiter at the facility Monday morning. Are you able to meet then as well? I understand that it's lab day for you. This would be in place of your lab." He pauses and shifts in his chair. "Professor Poiter is the on-site point person on the project. I believe you've had a class or two with him?"

I nod. "He is a very competent professor. And yes, I can be there."

Mr. Bailey claps his hands once and stands up. "Great! Once you see what Professor Poiter has to show you, I'm sure you'll be on board. I'm excited about it. And you students will get a lot out of the

< 16 >

project." He walks around the desk toward me. "I hate to run you off, but I need to jump on another call."

I look out the window at the maple tree as I stand up to leave. The sparrow has one thousand nine hundred eighty-two feathers.

< 17 >

EN GARDE

I bounce my legs to keep them from getting stiff as I wait my turn. Sitting on the cold, hard floor is not helping. Nor is leaning against the wall doing any favors for my back.

The instructor's feminine, yet bellowing voice brings me to attention, although I stay seated along with the rest of the club. "Remember, cell phones are permitted around the strip only to video your classmates, with their permission, for instructional purposes."

Charlene, sitting next to me, pokes my shoulder with her elbow as she raises her phone in front of her face, aimed at the two sparring students. I glance at her phone, but it is not set to video. She is sending a snap to someone called Pierre.

Charlene turns toward me and grins.

I match her gaze, crack a half smile, and shake my head. My own phone buzzes. Snapchat. I cannot resist. I hold my phone up matching Charlene's phone position and open the app. It is from Shawn. I look to my left and see Shawn with his phone hidden between his legs. He looks at me and grins. I grin back and shake my head slightly.

I keep my phone in front of my face and read Shawn's snap.

"You're only supposed to be videoing."

I do not look at Shawn for fear of laughing. My smile grows wider, so I position my phone to block the instructor's view of my face.

I look past my phone at the two students on the strip, their épées clashing. Looking past the sparring students, a young man in his early twenties catches my eye as he walks past the window. I have seen him before but not here or around campus. I saw him on the street back home in Hancock. I watch him as he approaches a white Chevy Impala parked at a meter on the street next to the studio. I saw an elderly lady park that car just ten minutes ago when this bout started. She was alone. I vividly recall her fumbling through her purse to find change for the meter. My mind spins uncontrollably as I recall every detail.

I watch as the young man reaches the empty white Impala and places two coins in the meter, then leans against the car as if he was waiting for someone. Is he waiting for me? Is he following me? No, of course not. Why would I even think so? The Impala has nothing to do with me. It belongs to the woman I saw before. He probably is waiting for her. It must be my dad's job and the secrets he keeps from me that are making me imagine such things.

I jerk and drop my phone at the sound of the instructor's voice. "Serenity!"

< 19 >

I grapple for my phone. How many times has she called my name? I was so focused on the guy outside.

She continues. "The bout is over. You can stop videoing now, if that's in fact what you were doing." She tilts her chin down and raises an eyebrow.

"No," I say. "I mean, yes. No, wait, I was not . . ."

The instructor saves me from continuing to stammer. "Your turn to bout, Serenity."

Charlene giggles as I get up. "It's okay. I've got your back."

I slip on my mask and step onto the padded strip. There is nobody new in the club, so it should be an easy night for me. I have seen everyone's moves. I know each person's technique, strengths, and weaknesses, male and female.

"Just my luck to draw your name for my bout tonight," says the voice from underneath my opponent's mask. "You seem to beat everyone these days."

It is Shawn. He has decent skill but is very predictable, even for an opponent like Charlene.

I hold my épée up and take the en garde stance. I like the sabre bouts better since you can score with strikes as well as thrusts, but I am just as comfortable with an épée. "Comfortable" is a relative term, however. I am not athletic at all, and my weekly fencing club is the only form of exercise I get. I do not like violence, but my dad "highly encouraged" me to take up some sort of self-defense class. Fencing seemed kind of like a classical sport to me, and it turns out that I am pretty good at it, provided I have time to study my opponent. Although, I highly doubt its usefulness in a self-defense situation, given that I do not carry an épée or sabre around with me, and attackers will not let me study them first.

< 20 >

"En garde! Prêts? Allez!" the instructor shouts.

Shawn and I advance toward each other. I parry his first thrust.

My counter attack is passé. I knew what Shawn's attack would be. I could have scored immediately on my counter, but I did not want to make him look bad.

We advance again. This time, our épées clash. I block right, left, right, left, over and over, retreating. Then, I move forward while he blocks my strikes. Right, left, right, left. I know each of his counters, so I keep him retreating until both of his feet are off the back of the strip.

"Hit, for Serenity!" the instructor shouts.

We start again in the center. This time, I let him score on a thrust.

"Hit, for Shawn!"

We approach the center again.

Shawn tips his mask up. "Don't let me score, Serenity. Give me your best."

"Okay then," I whisper to myself.

I take the en garde stance. I stare at him, focusing on his position. His lanky frame and long arms make it difficult to score on an initial thrust.

But he always leaves his chest open if he has to advance too far. He never maintains the proper form for too long. So, if I delay my advance and let him take four extra steps, the opening will be there when he is in range.

I do exactly that, and my thrust scores a touch.

"Hit, for Serenity!"

Shawn shakes his head as we walk back to the center of the strip. "How did you do that?"

I smile through my mask. "You told me you wanted my best."

< 21 >

I need just one more hit. I probably could do the same thing again, but he may have learned from the first time, so I will let him try to score first.

He backs me up, strike after strike. Then, I return the advance and back him up. But instead of forcing him off the strip, this time, I allow him to back me up again. That will give him confidence and lure him in. I parry each blow, waiting until the right moment for a riposte, when his épée is low enough.

Now. Shawn lunges, and I parry the attack, countering immediately with a feint. He goes for the fake, then I move in with a final thrust and score the touch.

"Hit, for Serenity!" The instructor steps onto the strip. "The bout goes to Serenity. Excellent job, both of you."

Shawn and I take our places along the wall to watch the next bout.

Shawn removes his mask. His blond, curly hair is flattened from sweat. "I remember once upon a time when I beat you. Twice as a matter of fact. Our first two bouts, when you first joined the club. Ever since then, you have had my number. In fact, you have had everyone's number lately. Why don't you go to any of the competitions?"

I do not compete because I would lose immediately. Unless I was able to study every possible competitor in practice or training, I would not make it out of the first round. I am not big. I am not fast. I am not strong. And I am not overly skilled. I win because I know what my opponents are going to do before they do it.

But that is not how I answer. I smile. "Thank you for the compliment, but I do not have the time. I am just in the club to get some exercise."

< 22 >

3

UNDER PRESSURE

There are four hundred fifty-three words on the computer screen in front of me. Thirty-two people here in the student tech room in Barker Center. Harvard's campus is packed today with men, women, and children. Why did Mr. Bailey have to pick family day to ask my dad to demonstrate his progress on the project? It must have something to do with that call yesterday. And why did my dad ask me to help in the first place? He always thinks I can do more than I can. On top of all of that, we waited to the last minute to perform the final tests. With a dead laptop and no charger, the media center is the only place on campus I can find a secure enough computer to update the app. My dad said that I cannot email the new app to him and sending it by any other electronic means is too risky, so now I have to finish downloading the app *and* run it across campus to my dad by 11:00.

I look at my watch. 10:30. I rub sweaty palms on my jeans. *Focus, Serenity, focus.*

A high-pitched girl's voice is to my left. "Did you see Jack's post on Instagram?"

Another girl's voice, this one with a New York accent. "Nah, did he post it on Facebook?"

"Facebook? For real?" The first girl laughs. "Isn't that for old people now?"

I startle as my phone vibrates in my pocket. When I pull it out, I see a message from Stella on Snapchat. "Serenity, where are you? We're all on Slack right now for our biology project. Remember?"

I feel my chest tighten. In my rush to finish programming the app, I forgot about my own project meeting. I look at my watch. 10:35. I shift in my seat. What is taking this app so long to download to the thumb drive? Somebody bumps into my back. This room is so crowded. I glance around. Now thirty-six people are in the room. Students showing their parents or significant others their projects on the computers and wall-mounted video screens. Most are probably media students.

I see a middle-aged, bearded man standing alone in the far corner wearing a Harvard baseball cap. I recognize him immediately. I saw him, minus the cap, in the checkout line in the grocery store near my house in Hancock. I recall his face perfectly, just like every face I see. First, the man at fencing club, and now, this guy. Am I just being paranoid again?

I send a snap in reply to Stella. "I am so sorry. I forgot. Tied up now. Will see you in class."

< 24 >

Stella replies immediately. "Are you okay? You never forget anything."

"I am fine," I deflect and shove my phone back into my pocket.

Why does my dad need a mobile app that connects directly with the program he is designing, anyway? There are a million apps out there. Does he really need another one? Yet he cannot tell me what the program is or what it does. Something about government policy and confidentiality. This is not the first time that he has asked me to help. And I am always in the dark. Apps are my dad's one technological weakness. He cannot program apps. Still, Mr. Bailey could have gotten one of his other servants to do something like this.

A sigh escapes me. I should not use the term *servant*, but that is the way he treats my dad—like a servant, not like his employee. And I have heard my dad talk on more than one occasion about the pressure Mr. Bailey puts on him and the unrealistic deadlines, with no explanation as to why.

I look at the monitor. The screen reads, "download complete." Next stop, my dad's presentation in the Science Center.

My brain instantly leaps to calculating the best routes. With a groan of frustration, I stand up and shove the thumb drive into my pocket. The man in the baseball cap is gone. My watch says 10:40. Impossible. How can I possibly make it on time? Why did my dad put this pressure on me?

No, it is fine. He needs me.

My phone buzzes. Another Snapchat message. This time it is from Shawn. A brief smile crosses my lips as I close the Snapchat app, put my phone in my other pocket, and push my way through the crowd and out of the room, then out of the building. There are way too many people on the campus. I just want to be alone in the peaceful

< 25 >

countryside or on Grandma and Grandpa's farm where I can focus. Two hundred twenty men in sight. Two hundred thirty-two women. One hundred fifteen children. I have to get moving. I raise my wrist. 10:45.

I need to cross Harvard Yard to get to the Science Center. I start to push my way through the crowd. I feel my armpits getting damp and beads of sweat forming on my forehead but not from heat. The fall air is cool. And it is not from nervousness. It is the closeness of the people.

My throat tightens. I feel like I am suffocating. I turn and catch a glimpse of the man in the baseball cap, I think. It is hard to tell through the people. Is he following me? No. Why would he be? I am just letting my mind wander again. I need to keep moving. I push forward, but the crowd is too thick. I see Widener Library to my left. I start in that direction. If I cut through the library, maybe I can avoid some of the crowd and move faster. I continue to move as swiftly as possible in that direction.

Widener Library is much less crowded than outside, but there still are plenty of people inside. I decide to take a side exit out of the library. It is a single side door facing Harvard Yard. I assume that there will be less people there than on the steps of the main exit. As I approach the glass door, I see the reflection of people behind me. It *is* him. The man in the baseball cap. I do not know why, but I believe he really is following me. I feel my chest tighten again. My heart races. Now, I have another reason to hurry.

I exit along with a small group of people down the old concrete steps. I look to my left. A toddler makes his way down the steps, clutching the spokes of the black iron handrailing to support himself with each step. The boy's mother is busy talking to someone as she

< 26 >

walks behind her son. I look ahead of the boy. Two steps down, a spoke is missing from the railing. At the same point, the concrete step is cracked and crumbling at the front edge. At his current pace, the boy will arrive at that spot in four seconds, at which point he will have to reach farther than he had been in order to grab the next spoke. That will cause his foot to extend to the front edge of the step. The crumbled edge will give way, causing the boy's foot to slip out from under him. He will fall backward, grasping for the missing spoke and hit his head on the edge of the third step up. He will bleed for sure, a possible concussion, maybe worse.

I do not mean to calculate it. I just happen to look to my left and see what is there.

Maybe I should not intervene. Let it go. Maybe I will stop noticing such things. Maybe that will set me free. But I look at that little boy, and I see Jona. Helpless. Whether it's a car collapsing in on itself or a concrete step, what's the difference when the numbers add up to something awful?

I bend down and reach out my hand to the left, opening my palm just above the edge of the step. A split second later, I'm cushioning the boy's head safely in my hand.

His mom gasps and picks him up. "Thank you," she says, wide-eyed. She hugs her crying boy, comforting him. But he only cries from the scare of the fall, not from pain.

That is why I had to do it. Somehow, in some way, the accident would have been my fault.

10:55. I continue down the steps. Since the crowd here is more dispersed, I easily navigate through it, running across the Yard, across the Plaza, and into the Science Center. I glance over my shoulder occasionally as I run, but I do not see the man in the cap.

< 27 >

In front of the Science Center, I bend over to catch my breath. Fencing is good exercise, but it sure does not keep me in shape for a sprint. I reach into my pocket for the thumb drive just to make sure it is still there, but it is the wrong pocket. My phone has three texts from my dad in the last ten minutes asking where I am and if everything is okay. I reach into the other pocket for the thumb drive and hold it firmly in the palm of my hand. The clock in the hall shows 11:00. I race to the computer lab.

My dad is standing outside the lab looking at his watch. I rush to him. "Dad, I got here as fast as I could."

My dad puts a hand on my shoulder. "It's okay, Peanut. Mr. Bailey just got here anyway." He smiles. "Thank you so much for doing this."

He must notice my frown, because his smile disappears.

"It would be easier to help if I knew more about the program that the app is to connect to. I wish you could tell me more." I pause. "Dad, does Mr. Bailey know I am helping you? He has to have other people who can design apps, right?"

My dad lowers his head. His eyes narrow. "Serenity, you know I can't answer those questions." He relaxes his face. "I need to get in there and show this to Dirk." He pauses again. "Love you, Peanut."

I trust my dad, but I like knowing all the facts. The lack of control makes things worse for my mind. And from what I know of Mr. Bailey, I am concerned for my dad and his job. As he turns away from me, I remember the man in the baseball cap. I want to tell my dad about my suspicions, but maybe I am just being paranoid. And now is not the time anyway. I know my dad needs my help, and as long as my dad needs me to help, I will do so. I already let my mom and Jona down. I cannot let my dad down too. I smile.

"I love you too, Dad."

< 28 >

4

NIGHTMARES

The full moon shines intermittently through the naked branches of the late autumn trees. The layer of fog covering the damp ground makes it difficult to see where to step. The sticks and plants of the forest floor poke my bare feet. The cold night air chills my skin. I look down. I cannot remember why I am wearing only a nightgown. But that does not matter now. I have to make my way to the sound of the baby crying. I can hear it in the distance. Each step takes me closer. Why is a baby crying in the middle of the forest? I do not know where I am or who the baby is, but I have to help the baby. I cannot tell if it is a boy or a girl. I stub my toe and stumble over a log but maintain my balance. I do not feel any pain in my toe though. As I continue walking, I begin to see more clearly now. The clouds are starting to dissipate, allowing more moonlight to pass through. So, I move faster. The crying becomes louder, more intense, as I close in on the baby. I have to help her. I have to save her from whatever is making her cry. My muddy feet slip on a rock as I walk more quickly.

I approach a small clearing in the trees, lit from the moonlight. The crying is coming from there. I slow down and cautiously approach its edge. In the middle of the clearing, I see a baby strapped into a car seat sitting on the ground. She is all alone and dressed in boy's clothes. I focus more intently on the baby. It is a boy, not a girl. I slowly enter the clearing. I have to help him. I have to get him out of the woods. I have to get him to safety, to his parents. As I get closer, I recognize the baby. It is not just any baby. It is Jona. But how can that be? Jona is now eight years old.

"Help me, Serenity," I hear from the far side of the clearing.

I look up. My mom is standing at the edge of the clearing. Blood streaks her face. The trees and ground around her waver, but she does not. A slight haze covers the area around her.

My mom reaches out a hand. "Help me, Serenity, please. And save Jona."

Jona's cries now pierce my ears. I try to take a step forward, but I cannot. I look down at my mud-covered feet. They will not move. I look around. Forty-eight trees are visible around the perimeter of the clearing. I try to step again, but my feet feel heavy. I look down, and I have sunk to my ankles in the mud. I look up. Eight hundred ninety-three stars are visible in the night sky. I am fifteen steps from Jona. I am fifty-one steps from my mom. I have to help them, but I cannot stop counting. I look down again. I have sunken deeper. The mud is now up to my knees, making movement impossible.

< 30 >

Jona screams even louder.

"Serenity, please," my mom begs. I look at her; the wavering area is growing larger, moving toward Jona and me. And my mom seems to be drifting farther away. Actually, she is not drifting into the forest—she is fading.

If I walk steadily, I can reach Jona in ten seconds, and I can reach my mom in thirty-five seconds. At the current rate of growth of the wavering area, it will reach Jona in twenty seconds. I have time to save him. I have to get him out of the clearing and to safety. Then, I can try to save my mom. But I still cannot move. I look down. The mud is up to my waist. The more I count and calculate, the deeper I sink into the mud.

Jona screams again.

My mom pleads, "Serenity, please. I need you." Her voice is barely audible now.

The wavering landscape continues to move toward Jona and me, and my mom continues to fade into the haze. I have to move. I try to will myself to move, but I am already too deep in the mud.

Jona lets out one final cry as the wavering landscape overtakes him and my mom disappears.

"No!" I shout. "Mom! Jona! No! Come back! I am so sorry. Please come back!"

"Serenity, Serenity," I hear coming from behind me. I feel a hand on my arm, gently shaking me. "Serenity, it's okay. It's just a dream."

I feel my arm shake more, and I slowly open my eyes. My dad is holding my arm as he sits down on the edge of my bed. I feel beads of sweat running down my forehead, dropping onto my pillow.

My dad smiles reassuringly. "You had the dream again?"

I nod. "More often than usual."

< 31 >

"Because of—?"

I nod. Because of tomorrow. The anniversary of the dreadful night eight years ago. I still blame myself. If not for my dad, my counting and calculating would have cost Jona his life. Jona lives, but Mom is dead. Not only was I unable to save her, but there was no time to say goodbye or a final "I love you." Just gone. And with no body to place in the casket, there was not even a chance to see her face one last time. But everyone said that was a gift. That we can remember her the way we have her pictured in our minds, which for me is easy. I just choose the picture I want and pull it up. Like pulling a photo album out of a drawer. I guess my mind is good for some things.

Jona's silhouette, dragging his teddy bear by the arm, appears against the hall light shining into my bedroom doorway. "Is Serenity okay?"

My dad turns. "Everything is fine. Just a bad dream."

"Did she see the boogeyman?" Jona asks.

My dad shakes his head. "You know there is no such thing as the boogeyman. Now, you hop back in bed. I'll be over in a minute to tuck you in again."

"Dad," I say, "do you ever have nightmares about that night?"

He never talks about that night, and I have never asked him about it. Until now.

My dad looks down and then slowly raises his head to catch my gaze. "I try not to think about it much. I don't like to think about it. And it's hard for me to talk about. I guess that's why I never do." He pauses. "Maybe if I was more open about it and talked about it, you wouldn't be having nightmares."

"Is that why you work so much? To keep your mind from thinking about it? And why you have me help you so much? So I will not think about it as much?"

< 32 >

My dad's forehead creases as he looks down again. I know that look. He wants to tell me something but does not know how. He is quiet.

He looks at me again. "No, it isn't why I work so much. I don't want to be away from you and Jona as much as I am, but I have to work. It's like I've said before, I just have to. And everything I ask you to do, I really need you to do."

This is the most he and I have ever talked about that night. I have always kept my questions to myself, but now I can't stop myself.

I sit up in my bed and lean on my elbow. "Do you know what we saw that night, Dad? Why was everything moving? What smashed the car?"

My dad's forehead creases again, and he pinches his eyes closed with his thumb and finger. Again, a long pause.

He opens his eyes but avoids eye contact. "I don't know. I wish I could give you answers, but I can't. I'm sorry."

I lay back. Which is it? He does not know or he cannot tell me? But I do not say anything.

My dad looks back at me. "I better go check on your brother. Will you be okay, Peanut?"

Part of me wishes he would not call me that anymore. It is a little embarrassing to be eighteen years old and still have your dad call you "Peanut," especially in public. But on the other hand, I love that we have such a good relationship, that he feels comfortable calling me that.

I nod. "I am fine." I do not believe that I am fine. And I am certain that my dad does not believe it either. But it is the best response that I have for now.

"We have to get up for church in the morning. Try to sleep."

I obediently roll over and close my eyes. But sleep eludes me.

< 33 >

5

SUNDAY DINNER

Sunday is my favorite day. Church and then dinner at Grandma and Grandpa's house. After last night's nightmare, I really need this. I enjoy everything about visiting Grandma and Grandpa. Especially the beautiful drive through the country to get there. Of course, one does not have to go far from Hancock to be in the country. I watch out the window as the hills pass by, perfectly painted with fall colors against a clear blue sky. I stare at the beauty, letting my mind wander and focus on something different. Even the dark red-and-brown grass growing over an old fence line is a picturesque sight. I relax, letting my mind wander off into the scenery. No worries, no fears, no need to focus on anything in particular.

"Come on, Serenity," Jona says, shaking my arm and bringing me out of my trance as the car stops. "Let's go."

I step out and look at the familiar sight of the old barn, its siding freshly painted bright red and set off by white trim. We park to the side of the detached garage, which is painted to match the barn. I follow my dad and Jona down the long cement walk leading to the large, white farmhouse. Overgrown bushes block the front room window and the summer house, which is just off the porch. My grandparents' homestead looks like it is stuck in the 1940s.

Halfway to the house, I jump at the sound of a sharp horn and turn at the sound of tires skidding in the gravel. A rusty, blue pickup slides to a stop in the driveway. Mr. Johnson—Grandma and Grandpa's neighbor to the north. I would recognize his truck anywhere.

Mr. Johnson waves his fist out of the truck window and turns up one side of his lip.

"Harold Stiner, your bull's in my field again," he shouts. "You have one hour to get him out before I shoot him dead. And you best figure out how he's gettin' through the fence and fix it. I'm a-warnin' ya. I'm fixin' to bring the law down on ya."

I look toward the house and watch as Grandpa starts making his way down the walk.

"Hold on there a minute, Jeb," Grandpa says, holding up a finger.

Mr. Johnson ignores the command, turns his head, and shifts his pickup into gear. His back tires spin in the loose gravel, throwing stones to the back and side as he speeds away.

"What was that all about?" my dad asks, looking at Grandpa.

"Oh, you know Jeb Johnson," Grandpa says. "He's been senile for years. And I've never met an angrier man. My bull's never been in his field. In fact, I sold my bull last week." Grandpa puts one arm around

< 35 >

me and one around Jona. "Now, how are my two favorite grandchildren?"

"We're your only grandchildren," Jona says, smiling up at Grandpa.

"Well, doesn't mean you're not my favorites," Grandpa says, looking down at Jona and me with his soft smile. A smile that only a grandpa can give. "I think Grandma's got quite a lunch a-cookin'. What do you say we go in and give her a hand?" He looks at Dad holding his laptop case in one hand and his brief case in the other. "I see you brought work, Phil."

My dad nods. "Unfortunately, yes. I'll have to take my dinner in the den. We're at a key breakthrough point on the project." His face is tight, his forehead wrinkled with tension.

My dad is worried about something. He has worked on Sundays before. It is not a totally new concept. But it has never bothered him like this before. What happened at his presentation yesterday? Was something wrong with my app?

I climb the stone steps, cross the porch, and walk through the front door. I love entering this house. Right inside the front door is the dining room table, already set for lunch. The smell of fried chicken hits me immediately. One of my favorites.

Yes, this is one of the few places where I relax enough to ignore the world and everything in it.

# # # # #

Everyone is quiet as we pass around the plate of fried chicken, a bowl of green beans, mashed potatoes, gravy, cornbread, and Jell-O salad. I bite into a crispy chicken leg. The meat falls off the bone and melts in my mouth.

< 36 >

"Are you going to watch the President's State of the Union address tonight, Grandpa?" I ask after I swallow.

Grandpa finishes off a fork full of green beans. "Wouldn't miss it for anything. We finally have a good president. Someone who's good with the environment, yet businesses love him."

Grandma looks at him and smiles. "Oh, Harold, you just like him because he's a Republican."

"Sixteen years of Democrats is quite enough," Grandpa says.

"I remember when we lived in New York. Wes Masterson was only a state senator," I say.

"From state senator to president," Grandpa replies. "Don't see that too often."

Grandma interrupts. "I fixed a plate for Phil. I'll take it to him."

I reach for the plate. "I will take it, Grandma. You have been working all morning. Relax and eat."

I open the door and enter the den. Dad's laptop is set up on the desk in the corner, and papers are strewn across the couch, but he is not here. I see him through the window, pacing back and forth in the yard, talking to someone on his cell phone. He must have gone out the back door to take the call or to make one. He must not want us to overhear.

A mathematical formula ending in a very complex equation catches my eye on my dad's laptop screen. It is something that I do not recognize. I have seen neither the formula nor the equation before. I set the plate of food on the desk and glance at the papers on the couch. I see notes related to the mobile app I developed and my work determining continuity equations for mass, energy, and momentum. I look out the window. My dad is not looking in, so I move to the other end of the couch and pick up a few papers. They

< 37 >

contain my work on quantum-geometry dynamics. I did this two years ago. My dad said that Mr. Bailey ended up not needing that work. But why does he still have my research results and calculations? And why is he apparently using them?

I look out the window again. My dad is still on the phone, so I move back to his laptop and sit in the desk chair. I slide the chair closer to the desk so that the angle from the window prevents my dad from seeing me. The call must have surprised him. He has left his work open. He never does that. His work is always secured with multiple firewalls. I lean back so I can see out the window. Still on the phone. I work the keypad trying to determine the purpose of the formula and resulting equation. My fingers slip on the keyboard from my nervous sweat. I should not be doing this. What if my dad catches me? He has gone to great lengths to keep the purpose of his work from me. And what is worse, he has kept the purpose of *my* work from me, too. But this is my chance to find out what the project is about. What Mr. Bailey has been doing that is so secret. And what *I* have been working on. I scoot forward in the chair and continue to search on the laptop. I find a description that encompasses all of my individual projects and some of my dad's work as well. It looks like the combined work has been used to derive the formula and then the equation I saw. I feel my heart beating faster. I glance out the window. Good, still talking.

I read the description. "Calculation of the probability of opening the universal continuum where mass and energy are intrinsic properties of preons and the number of preons needed to be acquired by a composite particle to maintain constant mass and energy regardless of speed." What are my dad and Mr. Bailey doing? I am so close. I just need to dig a little deeper. I lean back and look out the window. My dad is gone! Oh no. I start to close the files I had opened. I need to

< 38 >

get the laptop back to the formula and equation. I hear the back door close. Seventy-eight words on the laptop screen. Sixteen punctuation marks. Twenty-three numerals. I feel a bead of sweat trickle down my back. My fingers work the keyboard as fast as I can move them. Now fifty-six words, twelve punctuation marks, and eighteen numerals on the screen. My heartbeat quickens. I hear footsteps coming closer. Two more files. One more. The doorknob turns. The formula and equation pop up. I hop up and grab the plate of food.

The door opens as I turn and smile. "Dad, I brought you lunch."

He stands at the door expressionless. He looks at the laptop, then at the couch, then at me. He glances back toward the couch, then looks at me again and cracks a slight smile. "Thanks, Peanut."

< 39 >

THE FACILITY

The crisp, clear autumn Sunday has turned into an overcast Monday as I drive to the facility, near Peterborough. For the other students, the facility is a long way from campus. But for me, it is ideal. Hancock to Peterborough is a much shorter commute than Hancock, across the state line, and on to Cambridge.

The overcast sky is good, though. The sun always turns my skin pink, even in the fall. "You have such pretty, fair skin," my mom used to say. I say it is ghostly pale.

I try to call my dad's cell phone again, but it goes to voicemail. He must be in the basement lab—no signal. The staticky message he left last night just said that he had to work all night. That the project was nearly finished. When he left for the facility after we got home from Grandma and Grandpa's, he thought he would be home by eight or nine. He left a second message sometime during the night saying he needed to talk to me. That it was urgent. He sounded rushed. I wish I had checked my messages sooner, but I did not do so until I was in my car this morning. I keep playing Mr. Bailey's telephone conversation from Friday over and over in my mind. Who was Mr. Bailey talking to and what did he mean by "activated"? And I keep thinking about the formula, calculation, and description I found on my dad's computer. "The probability of opening the universal continuum." What does that mean? Then, there are the men that are following me. At least, I think they are following me. I have not had a chance to tell my dad about them. Something just does not feel right. I must find him as soon as I get to the facility. I will arrive early, so I will have time to look. But the basement lab has restricted access. At least I might find out what is going on. I turn onto the highway, and it begins to drizzle. A light coating of raindrops covers the windshield. Just enough to need the wipers on the lowest intermittent setting. My mind wanders again. I let it go.

"Your intelligence is a gift," everyone says. Wrong. It is a curse. I have heard "you are one of a kind" so many times, even I do not want to count. Maybe I am special, but it forces me to always be on my guard. It might start with a glance to the right, where I see cattle in the field and count them. And it escalates from there. Stars on a clear night, rows of corn in a field, words on a page, leaves on a tree, blades of grass. And then, there are the noises. The distinct sound of each car engine. Or the distinct sound of each cricket and katydid and locust on a warm summer's evening. It goes on and on unless I can make myself stop.

< 41 >

I hear the roar of a car approaching from behind. The engine is a six-cylinder inline. That particular engine is generally used in Jeep Wranglers. I look in the rearview mirror. Sure enough, a faded red Wrangler is gaining on me. A flock of birds, startled by the car, takes flight out of a stand of trees. I glance up. One hundred twenty-two birds. Stop. Calm down. Think of something relaxing and focus on that. I think about my dad, what he might be working on. That does no good.

Next, I hear eight motorcycles approaching from behind even before they are visible in the rearview mirror. As they slowly appear, I see that I am exactly right. Eight. Each engine has a unique hum. I hate the way my mind races off on its own.

There is movement in the field to my right. A deer. She is fifty yards ahead of me. My mind immediately takes over. It is not conscious. I immediately recall from my reading the top speed of a white-tailed doe. Thirty miles per hour. I glance down at my speedometer. I'm going fifty-five. I look toward the doe again. She runs perpendicular to me, straight toward the road. At that distance, running at top speed, the doe will reach the center of my lane two seconds after I do if I maintain my current speed. It takes me just a split second to calculate this. I do not slow down. The doe closes in as I quickly approach the spot in the road where she will be. I still do not slow down. Anybody else would. I am not nervous. I know my calculations are correct. They always are. I hate what my mind does.

For once, I want to be wrong and maybe all of this will stop. I want to hit the deer. The deer is six seconds from the road. I am four seconds from the spot. Three, two, one. The deer is right beside my car. Zero. No impact. The deer darts just behind my rear bumper two seconds after I pass.

< 42 >

I hate it!

# # # # #

I slow down when I see the turnoff to the facility. I try to call my dad again but get his voicemail. I almost come to a complete stop when I turn onto the one-lane road, which is engulfed on each side by trees. I continue to drive slowly, swerving slightly to miss the potholes, but it is impossible to avoid all of them. The narrow road winds through the trees, their thick leaves dressed in autumn colors. The trees hide the facility at every turn. My dad always says they want it to be inconspicuous. Why Harvard needs an inconspicuous facility, I do not know. It is probably a government requirement having to do with the type of research. But from what I have seen in helping my dad, it really is not Harvard's research—it is Dirk Bailey's research. And as my dad has said, while Mr. Bailey might be on Harvard's payroll, he certainly does not work for Harvard. He is a government man.

I make a final turn, and the tree-lined road opens into a twenty- or thirty-acre clearing surrounded on all sides by hills lined with colorful trees. I pull up to the large gate—the only opening in the black wrought iron fence surrounding the building. Through the fence, I can see the shiny silver of the new barbed wire chain-link fence, likely installed to reinforce the outdated wrought iron. And beyond that, the red brick building everyone calls "the facility." The entire setup looks like an old prison made secure with new fencing and a guardhouse. Although I know it has had many former uses, I do not believe that the building was ever used as a prison. It just looks like it.

I stop near the gate and watch as a man comes out of the guardhouse. His tan camouflage uniform blends in with the backdrop of

< 43 >

autumn foliage. A large handgun swings from the holster around his waist as he approaches.

"Hi, Serenity," the man says.

I recognize him when I see his face. "Hi, Winston."

Winston smiles. "What can I do for you? Are you here to see your father?"

I nod. "Sort of. Can I go on up?"

Winston looks at the small computer notebook he holds in his hand and makes a few swipes over it with his finger. "You're already on today's visitors list. You, two other students, and a Professor Poiter. Oh, you're part of the research group that I heard about. Sorry for the trouble, but if I don't mark you in and somebody else is here when you leave, I'm in big trouble. Head on up. Someone will meet you at the door."

I smile. "No problem. Thanks." I press the power switch to raise my car window, then stop. "Have any of the others arrived yet?"

Winston looks at his computer again. "Nope. You're the first." He starts to back up, then stops and looks at his computer again. "Wait, there's a note in here for you. It's from your father. It says to see him as soon as you arrive. It's marked urgent."

I lower my window again. "Do you know where I can find him?"

Winston shakes his head. "No, I'm sorry. Why don't you ask the guard at the door?"

I wait as the gate slowly opens, then I ease my car through. The drizzle has stopped.

It is easy to find a parking spot as the number of spaces far exceeds the number of cars I ever see here.

I pull into a spot in the second row. The newly painted lines are easily visible against the faded asphalt.

< 44 >

I make my way up the concrete steps. As I near the top step, I hear a click, and the large oak door slowly swings open. Just as Winston said, another guard greets me, dressed in the same tan camouflage uniform. I do not recognize him, but then again, I have stepped inside the facility only on the rare occasion that I came inside to wait for my dad.

The guard nods toward me. "Miss Ashdown, I presume? They called me from the guardhouse."

I do not answer immediately. Something feels odd, out of place. I have not been here many times, but I recall where every object was during my earlier visits and know where each one should be now. I look around the massive entranceway, now used as the lobby. I look toward the twenty-five-foot ceiling with its painting of English riders on horses led by hunting dogs. The riders are in a forest, all coming from different directions. And in the middle, a lone red fox looks as if it is trying to decide which way to go. If the painting came to life, the fox would not have a chance. Forty-three horses, forty-three riders, eighty-two dogs, one thousand four hundred seventeen trees, and one fox. Everything seems to be here, yet something is missing.

I slowly follow the ceiling to one of the thick wooden columns in the corner, then follow it down to the shiny marble floor, black swirled with white. In each of the four corners stands a pedestal. On each pedestal is the bust of a former United States president. Other than that, the grand lobby sits empty. Yes, the appearance is the same as always, but the place feels different. For one thing, it seems much quieter than before.

"Miss Ashdown?" the guard says, piercing me with his stare. "Are you all right? I'm here to escort you to the lab. It's just down this hall." He motions with his hand.

< 45 >

I glance at the guard and then look down the hall straight ahead. I wonder how to get to the basement lab. "Uh, yes." I nod once. "Yes, I'm fine. I, uh, I need to find my dad, Phillip Ashdown. The guard at the gate said my dad requested that I come see him. That message was marked urgent. I think he is in the basement lab. Can you show me where that is?"

The guard's face twitches underneath his thick black beard. "I'm sorry. That area is restricted." He offers no information, no alternative to finding my dad.

"Can you see if he is there? Tell him his daughter is here and wants to see him."

"I am sorry, but my orders are to escort you and the other visitors to the student lab." The guard steps to the side and holds out his arm to motion me down the hall. "This way please."

"But he has been trying to reach me," I plead. "I fear that something might be wrong."

The guard continues to look down the hall as if he did not hear a word I said. "This way, I said."

"Can you at least just see if he is here?" I ask as I start to walk. "Please," I add desperately.

I don't understand why the guard does not alert my father that I am here. I have the overwhelming sense that something is wrong. That he needs my help. That I should do something. But I do not know what. What else is new? All I do is think. Count. Calculate.

Without looking at me, the guard replies, "I will see what I can do."

Right. His lame promise does not convince me. Nonetheless, I walk down the large hallway, slightly ahead of the guard. The clang of his boots on the marble floor echoes, bouncing off the walls and

< 46 >

ceiling. We pass several dark oak doors. The facility's interior looks even more magnificent than its exterior. While the building is old, with its high mosaic ceilings, columns, and marble floors, it is very well maintained. And according to my dad, the labs and computers are state of the art. I examine the doors on the right and left as we walk past. None of them are marked. I count the number of marble squares there are from the front door as we walk without thinking about it. But there is no way to tell which door leads to the basement, if any even do.

The guard stops and turns toward a door on our left. "Here we are." He steps up and swipes his ID card over the electronic eye located on the wall beside the door. Next to it is an older model of a keypad security lock. They must have replaced the system recently. The lock clicks, and the guard opens the door, stepping aside to allow me to enter.

"I will be back with the others when they arrive," he says, reaching inside and turning on the lights.

I turn around when I am just past the threshold of the door. "And my dad, you will check on him," I say, half asking and half demanding.

The guard does not reply. He turns away, closing the door in front of me. There is another click as it locks behind him. This is my chance, before the others get here. My dad is missing. I need to find my him.

I will need access to the basement lab if and when I locate it. I think I have an idea. Hopefully, the old keypad security system is still operational as a backup, and hopefully it has one common passcode.

I go into the bathroom that is accessible from within the lab. I fill the toilet with toilet paper and flush, clogging it. Now, to mix a compound. I slowly look around the lab and against the side wall, just past the main workstation, my glance lands on the cabinet where the

< 47 >

nontoxic compounds are stored. I search the shelves and retrieve two bottles, one labeled "polyHEMA (2-hydroxyethyl methacrylate)" and the other "EGDMA (ethylene glycol dimethacrylate)." Perfect. These will work. I mix a small amount of each in a beaker. That should do the trick and create an anti-hydrophobic film.

I take the beaker and a small brush and open the door to the hallway. I look left, then right.

Nobody in sight.

I doubt I have much time. My armpits are damp with sweat. What does Harvard do to students who violate policy at the facility? Hopefully, nothing more than kick them out of the lab. I can live with that. Propping the door open with my foot, I brush the mixture over the electronic eye. After I rinse the beaker's contents down the sink, I exit into the hallway, allowing the door to shut behind me. I hear the lock click. I start walking toward the main lobby.

"Miss Ashdown," I hear from behind me.

I jerk, startled. It sounds like the guard. Of course, that is who I am looking for, but where did he come from? Did he see me brush the mixture onto the eye? Did he see me exit the lab just now? He was nowhere in sight when I walked into the hallway. He must have come out of another room.

"Okay, Serenity, keep it together," I whisper.

I cannot let him suspect anything. He could not have seen me. I was careful. At least, that is what I tell myself.

I turn around slowly, so as not to seem alarmed.

"Miss Ashdown," he says again. "Do you need something?"

"Oh, yes," I say. "I am looking for you. See, the toilet in the lab is clogged, so I came out to find another restroom, and I have locked myself out of the lab."

< 48 >

The guard stares at me, his lips tight, barely visible through his mustache and beard.

Why is he staring so long? He does not believe me.

The guard slowly turns and starts walking toward the lab door, his eyes still fixed on me. "All right, Miss Ashdown. I'll let you back in."

He swipes his ID card over the electronic eye.

Please work. Please let the compound work.

Nothing happens. No click, no anything. He swipes it again. Nothing. He rubs the card on his shirt and swipes it yet again. Nothing.

He holds the underside of his wrist to his mouth. There is a com device strapped to it. "Dionna, I need assistance at the student lab. My card isn't working. Can you bring yours down?"

A woman's rough voice comes through the com. "I'm tied up right now. I'll send you the backup code."

The guard pulls a handheld electronic device from his belt. He studies it for a second, then quickly punches numbers on the keypad. Two-five-eight-nine-zero-pound-two-two-five-five-five-seven-star. The door clicks.

I only need to see the numbers once.

# # # # #

I wait long enough for the guard to have left the hallway, then I leave the lab again. This time, I head in the opposite direction. There has to be a door that leads to the basement. Probably not off the main hallway, though. And there cannot be too many twists and turns. This is an old building, rectangular and box-shaped. I reach the end of the main hallway and turn left. A shorter hallway leads to another

< 49 >

wooden door that has no security pad of any kind. I slowly turn the knob. It is not locked. I continue to turn, and it opens. Enough light shines in from the hallway so I can tell it is a closet. I turn and head down the hallway in the opposite direction. There are a number of doors along this hallway, too, all wooden, but the one at the end, straight ahead, interests me the most. It is metal and looks very new.

When I reach the metal door, I try the handle. It is locked. It has an electronic eye as well as a keypad, just like the other doors. Without having to think about it, I quickly enter the code on the backup keypad. Two-five-eight-nine-zero-pound-two-two-five-five-five-seven-star.

The door clicks, and I slowly open it. Bingo! It leads to a descending stairway that is dark but for the light from the hallway shining in.

Now what? Should I go down? Yes, I have come this far. I have to find my dad.

I turn on my cell phone's flashlight and start down the steps. After two turns, I reach the bottom and dead-end into another metal door. Again, I enter the code on the backup keypad and the door clicks. As I slowly push the door open, light from within shines into the stairwell. As the angle of the opening door widens, so does the light. With the door partway open, I hear computers humming inside the room.

"Dad?" I say softly.

No reply. I slowly open the door all the way. My feet are frozen in place. What if somebody other than my dad is inside? What if I get caught? I force myself to move forward. I step gently, softly, almost tiptoeing on the pristine concrete floor. If nobody can hear me, then maybe I am safe. But I have already opened the door. If somebody is inside, they know I am here.

I step forward and look to the left. The bright ceiling lights make it easy to observe the room. The wall to the left is lined with a table

< 50 >

that stretches from one corner to the other, then turns with the contour of the wall and stretches along the entire back wall. The table is covered with computers of all sizes, monitors, keyboards, cameras, everything. Twenty-two separate computers to be exact.

I scan each computer screen. Every one shows a series of fixed numbers, all different. Every computer except one, that is. One computer runs a series of numbers that constantly change. I watch that computer for a while and notice the series eventually repeats. I wonder if my dad programed these computers. I think of the formula and equation I saw on my dad's laptop yesterday, but as far as I can tell, these numbers are not related to that. I wish I could have had more time to source the information on my dad's laptop.

Mounted on the walls above the computers are video screens in various sizes. Ten total. Each screen displays the same repeating number series that appears on the last computer. Against the remaining two walls are filing cabinets, some with drawers open and papers partially pulled out. More papers are strewn across the floor. There is a half-empty cup of coffee on one of the tables. Steam comes from it. Still hot. But there is not a single person in the room.

I turn my attention to the middle of the room. A large, circular metal object is bolted to the concrete floor. It stands about six feet high and is open in the middle, like a giant metal donut, a sphere. I visually follow each of the wires that run to it from the twenty-two computers.

Then I walk farther into the room so I can see directly through the opening in the sphere; the opening is about five feet in height from bottom to top.

The sphere is a good twenty feet from me as I move into a direct line of sight. Its opening is hazy, and I can barely make out the wall

< 51 >

behind it. Everything back there appears to be moving—undulating, wavering back and forth and up and down. My heartbeat quickens as I flash back to the night my mom died. I see it like it was yesterday, sitting in the back seat of our car, watching the road, trees, and speed limit sign waver. This is the same motion. And everything inside the sphere is covered in the same haze I saw that night. Whatever it is, it crushed our car.

As I walk closer to the object, I wipe my palms on the legs of my pants. A bead of sweat forms on my lip, just below my nose. Should I leave? Just get out of here? Of course I should. I have no business being here, that much is clear. But if this is my dad's work, I have to take this chance to find out what he is doing and if it has something to do with why I cannot locate him. I move closer to the metal sphere. In the center of its top arch is a computer screen with a fixed series of numbers on it, all different. I look back at the other computer screens, then again at the screen on the sphere. It must be an algorithm that results from combining the numbers on the other computers.

The sphere's opening is still hazy, and the wall behind it continues to waver. Looking through the opening, I notice there are no filing cabinets behind the object. When I step to the right and look around the sphere, the cabinets are there with papers pulled out, just like before. And they are solid, not wavering. I step back in front of the sphere. Now, I am only a few feet from it. I look through the opening again. The wall behind it is wavering and bare. No cabinets.

My heart pounds, and I jump at the sound of a door clanging shut.

"Miss Ashdown," the guard says. "Are you down here?"

Oh no! He is at the top of the stairs. I am caught. I quickly look around the room. No other doors, and, of course, no windows. Not

< 52 >

even a closet to hide in. What do I do? I hear the scrape of the guard's boots on the concrete steps, getting louder with each step.

"Miss Ashdown!" His voice is much sterner and loud. "You are not allowed down here. This is very serious. Let's get back upstairs. I'm going to have to contact the university, as well as Mr. Bailey."

He enters the room as he finishes his sentence. His eyes are squinted, the corner of his mouth turned up.

He mentioned Mr. Bailey. Not only am I in trouble, but I have probably gotten my dad in serious trouble as well. What do I do? Forty-seven pieces of paper on the floor! Four hundred twenty rivets in the sphere! The humming of the computers grows louder as I step toward the sphere and look into the opening. Still wavering.

"Come with me, Miss Ashdown," the guard demands.

I look at the guard. The humming grows louder. What do I do? I look back at the sphere. The haziness in the center is shrinking. I can start to make out the edges of the filing cabinets behind it. They are solid, not wavering.

There is a tight grip on my left arm. "It's time to go, Miss Ashdown." The guard stares deep into my eyes.

"No!" I yank my arm free. The sudden release of the guard's grip causes me to lose my balance, and I stumble backward. I quickly take one, two, three steps backward to try to stabilize myself, but I cannot. When I take a fourth step, my foot catches the bottom of the sphere. My feet go out from under me as I fall backward, through the hole in the sphere's center. I roll over onto the other side. I look up to see the guard's wavering, shrinking figure approaching. But before he can step through, the wavering stops, the computer stops humming, the guard disappears, and the sphere is gone.

< 53 >

HOME

gather myself up off the floor. When I rub my thumb and fingers together, I feel a dirty grit. My hand is covered with greasy dirt. As I look down, I see the concrete floor is cracked, uneven, and filthy, covered in grimy film. Then, I turn to the bare wall where the filing cabinets had stood moments ago. The lights had been bright white then, but they now give off a yellowish glow. The room is vacant but for some empty crates, barrels, and a couple of rusty, dust-covered metal tables.

I take a few steps toward the door, then look down. The dim yellow light highlights footprints on the dirty floor. I kneel and run a finger over one of the prints. It is fresh. I follow them to the door with my eyes. Three people. Two are sure-footed men, big. The third looks like someone who was struggling.

I make my way to the door and up the dirty concrete stairs leading out of the basement. The door at the top of the stairs is missing. Only the hinges remain. There are no lights on in the upstairs hallway, but the hall is well lit from the bright sunshine beaming through the windows. Sunshine. It was overcast when I went down to the basement.

I make my way back to the student lab, turn the knob, and push on the door. It is not locked, but it is heavy and tight. I brace my feet and lean into the door, opening it halfway. I look inside. There is no lab equipment at all. Instead, there are two large machine presses in the middle of the room. What is left of a conveyor system runs from the first machine to a small door on the far wall where the system has broken apart and fallen over. This cannot be. My heart quickens.

I walk into the hallway and toward the main entrance. The facility's pristine marble floor has been replaced by tarnished tile. My pace quickens as I approach the grand lobby at the entrance. But the large oak doors are now metal. And here, the marble floor has turned to concrete. The large wooden columns are now cinderblocks. I spin three hundred sixty degrees, then look up. A ceiling crane has taken the place of the beautifully painted mural. My heart beats even faster. My stomach churns. I feel nauseated.

"Hello?" I shout. "Is anybody here?"

I listen. Nothing.

"Hello?" I shout again.

Still no response.

I pull out my cell phone to call Dad, but the message on the screen reads "no service."

< 55 >

Movement through the window to the right of the entrance doors catches my eye. I move closer. Dull, gray grass and weeds have grown through the cracks in the parking lot, and the cars that were there when I entered the building, including my car, are gone. Instead, two dark green Humvees and two shiny, black SUVs sit alone in the lot. Eight soldiers dressed in green military uniforms carrying automatic weapons surround the Humvees, and four men in dark suits stand next to the SUVs. One of the men puts his finger to his ear, touches an earpiece, and talks into a small radio on his wrist.

Then, I look past the commotion, down the lane leading up to the facility. It, too, is overgrown, but I can see where the Humvees have plowed through, smashing small brush and breaking off tree limbs. The wrought-iron fence still stands in places, but most of it has fallen over. The gate is gone and there is no sign of a chain-link fence or guardhouse.

Nothing looks the same. What has happened? What should I do? Should I talk to the men outside? No, I have to avoid being seen until I figure out what is going on. The men look like they are gathering to depart. So, I walk down the hall to the left, careful to avoid the windows. While the building's appearance has changed, it still seems to have the same layout. Hopefully, the small door that exits near the woods is still there. That is the only other exit I know of.

At the end of the hall, I see the door. I grab the handle and push down on the latch button. Good. It is not locked. I slowly push it open to make sure it is clear outside and startle when a loud ring pierces my ears. My palms sweat, and my heart beats rapidly in my chest. The ringing is steady. I press my body against the door. I have to get clear of the building before the men out front swarm it. Can I make it to the woods? Can I sprint that far?

< 56 >

I look left, then right. All is clear. I take a deep breath, hold it, and dart across a small clearing. I feel like I have never run this fast in my life. Before I know it, I am in the woods. I stop behind a tree and turn back toward the building. From my angle, I can see the front of the building. Most of the men have gone inside, I assume to investigate the alarm. I look back at the door. It has closed, and I have made it to the woods unnoticed. I look above the door at the deteriorated building. Fifty-three missing bricks on the side wall, at least that I can see through the partially dead ivy that clings to the structure.

Until now, I had not noticed the trees. Their leaves are wilted. Not dry and colored from fall. They are dull and covered with a tinge of gray. The bushes look the same way.

I need to get to the main road and find a ride back to Hancock. I make my way through the woods quietly so the men do not notice me. I walk in a relatively straight line toward the road, keeping the grass-covered driveway in sight on my right. Once I reach the road, I start walking toward Hancock, toward home.

What is going on? What has happened to the building and the cars? What about the trees? I relax somewhat as I see that the road and its surroundings look the same, normal, except for the wilting, dull, gray-colored leaves, shrubs, and grass. Once I get back home, everything will be fine. Dad will be there. If something is wrong, my dad will go home to come get me and Jona. But why has he not tried to call? I check my cell phone again. Still no service. He probably does not have service either. This doesn't make sense. Nothing makes sense.

I hear a vehicle approaching. Judging from the sound, it is a truck engine, likely a 2001 or 2002 model year. I turn to look. I am right. An old blue pickup truck approaches, slowing down as it gets closer

< 57 >

to me. This could be good—a ride. Or it could be bad. A ride with whom?

When it reaches me, the truck comes to a complete stop in the middle of the road. The side window slowly cranks down. The driver is an old man wearing a faded red baseball cap pulled low on his forehead. Good. He is probably harmless. And I see nobody else in the vehicle.

"Hello there," the man says. "Are you all right? Did you break down someplace?"

Maybe I should ignore him, just keep walking. No, I cannot. He is right here in my path. And he sounds nice enough. In fact, he seems somewhat familiar.

"Something like that," I say.

"Can I give you a lift? I'm headed into Hancock to pick up a few things at the Five and Ten," he says.

What is the Five and Ten? I look him up and down, then glance into the cab of the truck. I still do not know if I can trust him, so I do not want to get into the cab with him.

His eyes follow mine as I look into the cab. He pulls his cap up and gives me a reassuring smile. "Tell you what. If it makes you feel more comfortable, why don't you hop in the bed? There's an old blanket back there to keep the wind off of you, and I'll take you on into town if that's where you're a-headin'. What'll you say?"

That seems safe. If he stops someplace that I do not like, I can just hop out and run. Even though I am not athletic, I am sure I can outrun him. And the man seems even more familiar. I give him a slight smile. "Okay then. Thanks."

He gets out of the cab, helps me into the pickup bed, and then hops back in the cab. The pickup moves forward, and the man shouts

< 58 >

back to me through the open window. "By the way, the name is Johnson. Jeb Johnson."

My heart skips a beat. Jeb Johnson? That is why he looks so familiar. But I have never seen nor heard of Jeb Johnson acting this nice and civilized. In fact, I have never heard Jeb Johnson say a kind word to anybody.

# # # # #

The pickup slows to a stop. I lean forward to look around the cab. We are at a red light at the edge of Hancock. That is odd. There was never a stoplight here. I look at the road signs. They are correct. Old Hancock Road running north-south and Main Street running east-west.

Mr. Johnson rolls down his window again to speak. "Is there someplace in particular that I can take you?"

I think for a moment. Should I give him my address and have him take me there, or should I just have him drop me off at the nearest intersection? Normally, I would never give my address to a stranger, not even in sleepy little Hancock. But this is not normal. And Mr. Johnson really is not a stranger. I will get home much quicker if he drops me off at my house.

I sit up on my knees and face the cab. "425 Bennington Road, out toward the school. If it is not too far out of your way."

"Not a problem at all," Mr. Johnson replies.

I lean back against the cab, pull the heavy wool blanket up to my chin, and huddle underneath it. Even though the sun is shining, the air is chilly. I see the reflection of the traffic light as it turns green, and the pickup proceeds through town. I recognize the street names but not the houses as we approach Bennington Road. When the pickup

< 59 >

turns onto my street, I feel a tingle down my spine and heaviness in my chest. I sit up on my knees and scoot to the edge of the bed. Laying my arms on the bed rail, I lean over the side of the truck to get a closer look. The landmarks are somewhat familiar, but what happened to the houses? Where are they? My beautiful street, which should be lined with large maple trees, is barren. Not even grass. And the small, quaint houses have been replaced by convenience stores, gas stations, and apartment buildings. This cannot be right. I look again at the street sign at the next intersection. It reads "Bennington Road."

I know of no other Bennington Road in Hancock.

The pickup slows and turns into a small parking lot leading up to a large, dark brick building. The facade is stained with streaks of black and green from what looks like years of neglect. In the center of the building hangs an exterior fire escape, reddish-brown with rust. I can see immediately from the uneven spacing that twelve rungs are missing. The bars covering the cracked and broken windows are bent and battered. The black numbers on the side of the building read "425."

Mr. Johnson steps out of the pickup. His eyes dart from me to the building and then back to me. He tilts his head to one side. "Here we are. 425 Bennington." He pauses. I do not look at him. "Are you all right? Is this where you wanted to go?"

I keep my eyes fixed on the building, trying to comprehend what is going on. "This is 425 Bennington Road?"

"Yes," Mr. Johnson says. "Is there someone here you want to see?"

"But where is my house?" I turn my head to look past Mr. Johnson and down the street.

"Do you live in that apartment building?" Mr. Johnson motions toward the building.

I shake my head. "No. I live in a house with a yard."

< 60 >

Mr. Johnson chuckles politely. "A house with a yard on Bennington Road? In Hancock? There never have been any houses with yards on Bennington Road."

I do not answer. I slowly climb out of the truck, taking Mr. Johnson's hand for support, and leave him standing there. I approach the building cautiously, fearing that some crazy person or savage animal will come pouncing out of the double-bolt steel door. I climb the steps to the front door and peer through the small square window in its center. I use my hand to shield the glare of the sun on the window, but the thick glass is stained yellow and is too opaque to see through. I put my face against the window. Still no good.

As I pull my head back, I see the reflection of a man looking at me from a distance. I pick up the colors of tan and black. I turn around quickly, but I only see Mr. Johnson. It must have been my imagination. I pull on the long door handle. It will not budge. I look on the left side of the door and then the right and find a voice com button. I press it and say, "Hello."

Silence. "Hello," I say again.

There is a long pause before a crackling voice comes back through the com. "What do you want?" It is the voice of an older woman.

I really do not know what I want. I know that this is not my home, even though it is my address. What I really want is answers, but I do not know where to get them. What can I do? Where can I go? Who can I talk to? I am lost and alone in a place that I do not recognize. But this is probably as good a place as any to start looking for answers. I feel a cold gust of wind against my neck. It reminds me that it is autumn. I pull my gray hooded sweatshirt up higher on my neck and shrug my shoulders. The crackling voice comes again. "Well, what do you want? Now that you've bothered me!"

< 61 >

I press the com button. "Do . . ." I pause, thinking of what exactly to say. "Do the Ashdowns live here?" I know the answer: No, they don't. But I have to ask. I have to start someplace, with some question.

The com crackles louder than before. I strain to hear the old woman's words over the crackling. "Unit 212."

No, impossible. This is not my home. Maybe it is a different Ashdown. "Phillip Ashdown?" I ask.

"Yeah," the woman replies. "But he's not here. He's never here. I see him stop by to get his mail, but he never stays."

"How often does he come by?" I ask. "Do you know when he will be back? I really need to talk to him."

"Don't know," the woman snaps back. "I just run the building. I'm nobody's personal assistant."

Another gust of wind cuts through my sweatshirt. I fold my arms and lean forward.

The com crackles again. "You can probably find his daughter if it's that important. I seen her on TV a lot. You know, waving guns around and shouting anti-government stuff. She's gonna get herself in lots of trouble. I suppose that's why her pop doesn't come 'round here no more."

I step back from the com. Maybe I heard her incorrectly through the crackling and popping. Or maybe she is talking about another Phillip Ashdown. Or maybe the woman is just crazy.

But I still do not know where I am, and now I have more questions than answers.

When I walk down the steps, my head grows light. I look up, but the sun blinds me.

I close my eyes for a few seconds and whisper. "Concentrate, Serenity. Focus."

< 62 >

When I open my eyes, I see a light brick building across the street. It grows dim as I feel myself wobble. Then I see a person on the sidewalk across the street in front of the building. Is someone following me? He wears a tan Carhartt jacket, black pants, black boots, and a black beanie. I see all of that in a second before I stumble forward. I feel the firm grip of Mr. Johnson's hand on my forearm, catching me. His other hand is on my shoulder.

"Easy there, Miss," he says. "Let me help you back to the truck."

Despite the aggravation and isolation that my mind causes me, it has always kept me one step ahead of everyone else. I always know what to expect, what is coming next, what to do. But not now. Now, I am lost. I have no idea what is coming, where to go, or what to do. I have no control.

The grip on my arm softens as Mr. Johnson leads me to his pickup. He opens the passenger door. I do not resist as he helps me get in.

I turn toward Mr. Johnson as he climbs into the driver's seat. He has a look of compassion on his face. "The man you're looking for, Phillip Ashdown—I know something about him. He's in the news sometimes. A smart man. Does government research. Sad, though. I understand he lost his wife and son in a car crash a number of years ago. He's just left with the daughter the landlord was talking about. Seems like they're estranged."

I do not look at Mr. Johnson, although I hear him. I look for the person who seems to be watching me. Apparently, that has not changed. Someone is following me, and it is someone different again. I look around the parking lot and then at the dark brick building that is 425 Bennington Road.

I turn toward the light brick building across the street, and then I look up and down the street. I do not see him.

< 63 >

Mr. Johnson starts the truck. "Can I ask what your name is, and where you're from? I would like to try to help you find whatever you are looking for."

Then it sinks in. Mr. Johnson said that Phillip Ashdown's son was killed too. "Did you say that his wife *and* son were killed in a car crash?"

"Yeah," Mr. Johnson replied. "Sad, isn't it?"

Something happened to my life when I went through that sphere. Everything has changed. Twenty-two potholes in the parking lot. Mr. Johnson pulls the truck onto the street. Fourteen buildings and six street signs in sight. Ten light poles. I need to focus on something. I need an objective.

"There's another place I need to check out," I say. "Harold and Maye Stiner's place on Loop Road." Hopefully, Grandma and Grandpa's farm has not changed and they will be home.

Mr. Johnson looks at me. "You know Harold and Maye Stiner? They were my neighbors. Their farm is next to mine."

"They *were* your neighbors, but their farm *is* next to yours. What do you mean? Which is it?"

Mr. Johnson turns back toward the road. "I'm sorry, Miss, but they died in a house fire a few years back. Their farm burned down. House, barn, garage, everything."

I sit silently for a moment. Shocked. It cannot be true. I had lunch with them yesterday. "What? How? That makes no sense."

"Well, they never found the cause of the fire, but it was pretty suspicious since every building on the property burned down. Probably had something to do with their granddaughter, the Ashdown girl, and her anti-government movement. It was bound to come back and haunt her or her family eventually. Anyway, the farm has sat deserted ever since."

< 64 >

I stare out the side window. I have nothing to say and no idea about what is going on.

"I'm sorry to have told you," Mr. Johnson continues. "I can tell that they must have been special to you. What can I do to help you?"

I look at Mr. Johnson. "I have to find Phillip Ashdown."

Mr. Johnson turns the steering wheel of his blue pickup, hand over hand, until the truck turns right at the traffic light. He glances at me.

"I think I know someone who may be able to help you."

< 65 >

MR. BAILEY

stare out the side window and stay silent as we drive through town to the east, trying to think of my next move. I know this part of town well. Or at least, I used to know it well. I recognize most of the road names and some of the houses. But there are additional roads going off Main Street that I do not know, and there are commercial buildings and stores I do not recognize. I do not understand why. But at least while I am focusing on the present situation, my mind is not wandering.

As we approach the city limit to the east, the pickup slows before coming to a complete stop. Traffic congestion. Cars are stopped as far as I can see. Fifty-four cars, I count, all stopped on the road in front of and behind us. Some cars turn around in gas stations and parking lots that, until now, never existed in Hancock. But that just makes the congestion worse as they cannot get back out.

A tan station wagon pulls into an Exxon station. It immediately makes a three-sixty to reenter the same road, trying to go the other direction. It slowly edges out, forcing its way into traffic, trying to cross the eastbound lane just behind us. But a Ford Explorer is not going to let the station wagon through. It is a standoff. The Explorer holds its ground and continues to edge forward. The station wagon continues to edge its way out until I hear the crunch of metal against metal. Neither driver has yielded. I have never seen traffic like this in Hancock.

"What is going on?" I ask Mr. Johnson.

Mr. Johnson rolls down his window again and sticks his head out, stretching his neck. I assume it is an attempt to see over the traffic. "Probably another protest."

I turn toward Mr. Johnson. "Protest? Here in Hancock? And what do you mean by 'another'? When has there ever been a protest in Hancock?"

Mr. Johnson takes his hands off the wheel and turns, resting his right elbow on his seatback. "Yes, there are protests all the time. And not just here. All over the world. Led by those anti-government out-siders. Where on Earth have you been hiding?"

The more I learn, the more I do not understand. Was the sphere some sort of time portal? Is that the project that Mr. Bailey was going to have us work on? No, time travel is impossible. I confirmed that myself. And, for the most part, Mr. Johnson looks like he did before I went through the sphere. He is just nicer.

"I have not heard about any anti-government protests," I say.

< 67 >

"I don't know what happened to you, young lady, but these outsiders have been protesting ever since the UR was formed," Mr. Johnson says. "And before that, they protested the US government. They're led by the daughter of the Mr. Ashdown that you're looking for. Mr. Ashdown, of course, is a government man. Probably cut into him like a knife when he found out his daughter was a traitor, opposing the very government he works for. It's all over the news, every day, everywhere."

I listen as Mr. Johnson rambles on, but I stare straight ahead, motionless. I absorb everything he says without thinking about it, but I do not process what he is saying.

He continues. "The protests have really picked up lately—rumor has it the government killed or captured the Ashdown girl. That news, if confirmed, will probably break the back of government outsiders all over the world. The Ashdown girl held it all together. I couldn't be happier, though. I say good riddance. Maybe now we can have some peace, get back to normal, and let the government get back to rebuilding everything from the wars."

The pickup starts to edge forward with the rest of the traffic but only by inches. The more Mr. Johnson tells me, the more questions I have. Phillip Ashdown's daughter?

I am Phillip Ashdown's daughter. And whoever he thinks is Phillip Ashdown's daughter is the leader of the outsiders? What outsiders? What is the UR?

What wars?

I don't want to hear any more from Mr. Johnson. I want answers, not more questions.

"Where are we going? Who are we going to see?" I demand. "Phillip Ashdown?"

< 68 >

Mr. Johnson cranks the steering wheel hard to the left. The pickup thumps over the curb and onto the sidewalk.

"We're going to someone that can take you to Mr. Ashdown." Mr. Johnson cracks a smile. "I usually don't drive like this, but I need to get you around this blockade."

After two blocks, we cut a sharp right across traffic. Blocks? There were never city blocks in Hancock before. A horn blows as we enter an alley. The alley opens onto an intersection, busy but not stop-and-go. Mr. Johnson forces his way into the traffic and turns right. Fortunately, we do not share the same fate as the station wagon. I look to my right and see a small park. Again, the trees are gray and wilted, and the grass is the same. Not greenish-brown from fall, but gray. Dead.

We turn left again. I lean to the right and look back. Protesters stand in the street. A military unit with soldiers dressed in green fatigues closes in on them. The group slowly fades from my sight as we continue eastbound once again.

# # # # #

I follow Mr. Johnson up the brick-paved walkway toward the front door of a large stone-and-stucco house on Antrim Road. The beautifully landscaped exterior is offset by the partly wilted and partly dead plants. Even the fall mums are dead. There have always been nice houses on Antrim, but I do not recall seeing this one before.

The feeling that I am being watched is back as we climb the concrete steps to the front porch. As we reach the top step, the house's front windows are blocked from my view by two large, beautifully crafted pillars, one on each of the porch's front corners. I turn around and see the man in the Carhartt jacket and black beanie dart behind

< 69 >

the house across the street. So I *am* being followed again. This man either wants me to know I am being followed or he is the worst tail ever.

I stand behind Mr. Johnson as he rings the bell, but I can still see the front door when it opens. I think I recognize the man, but he seems thinner, with darker hair than the man I am thinking of.

"Jeb Johnson," the man says. "To what do I owe the pleasure?"

"Mr. Bailey," Mr. Johnson says. "I have someone here who needs to speak to Phillip Ashdown."

I step to the side of Mr. Johnson. "Dirk Bailey?" I ask.

I have never been to Mr. Bailey's house, so I assume this is it. But other than his face, he looks different now. I do not understand. I just saw him in his office Friday.

Mr. Bailey steps onto the concrete porch. His eyes are fixed on my face as he moves. His stare does not leave me. His eyes are wide, his mouth open. "Serenity Ashdown?"

I look at Mr. Bailey. He is still staring at me. Then I look at Mr. Johnson. He is now staring at me as well and has a very puzzled look on his face.

I notice the cold breeze again.

"What?" Mr. Johnson says. "Serenity Ashdown . . . she is the outsiders' commander. I've seen her on the news." He turns to face Mr. Bailey. "How can this be?"

Mr. Bailey walks past me to the front edge of the porch. He peers to the left and then to the right, glancing around each pillar. His gaze is off in the distance. Then, he pauses for a moment, staring across the street. Did he see the Carhartt man too? Maybe I should say something about him. No. The less I say, the better. It will give me a better chance to figure out what is going on.

"Mr. Bailey, is something wrong?" I ask.

< 70 >

Mr. Bailey ignores me and turns toward Mr. Johnson. "Did you notice anyone following you here?"

Mr. Johnson cocks his head and squints, his forehead wrinkled. "Well, no, but I really wasn't paying attention. I never do. Why would anyone want to follow an old farmer?"

Mr. Bailey pats Mr. Johnson on the shoulder. "No reason. I'm just overly cautious these days. But to be safe, you better be getting out of here. Maybe go out of town a ways and then circle back. I'll take care of Serenity from here."

Mr. Johnson turns toward me. "Will you be okay? I think Dirk here has the best chance of getting you to Mr. Ashdown. I mean, your father, or whoever he is to you."

"Yes," I say. My eyes move from Mr. Johnson to Mr. Bailey and then back to Mr. Johnson. "Thank you," I say as he walks down the steps. Mr. Johnson has been so kind. I know a simple thank you is not enough. But that is the best I can come up with.

# # # # #

As I sink into the soft leather sofa in the beautifully furnished formal living room, exhaustion starts to overtake me. I had lost track of time. I had not realized how tired I was or that I had not eaten since breakfast. An orange ray of sunshine comes through the front window and hits my eyes as the sun partially pops out from behind a cloud, trying to hang on to the day as it touches the treetops and houses on the horizon.

I turn away, lean my head against the brown sofa, and take a deep breath.

I dare not close my eyes, although I long to sleep.

< 71 >

"Can I get you something to eat or drink?" Mr. Bailey asks as he enters the living room carrying a file with paper sticking out of the edges.

I want food, but I do not know Mr. Bailey well at all. My chest feels tight, and my stomach aches. Not so much from hunger but from worry. Worry about the situation, about my dad, and about being in Dirk Bailey's house. Mr. Bailey has been extremely nice, nothing like the Dirk Bailey I had come to know through my dad. But then again, since I passed through that sphere, nothing has been as I had previously known it. But the good thing is that the worry keeps me focused on the situation.

No time for my mind to wander off.

"Maybe some water, please," I say.

That will do for now. I can worry about food after I get some answers. Mr. Bailey leaves and returns quickly, handing me a bottled water.

# # # # #

"Thank you," I say.

I am too tired at this point for any more formalities. I just want to get right to the point. I open the bottle and take a drink. The cool water feels good on my throat. I take another long drink.

"You were thirsty," Mr. Bailey says with a slight grin. Then the grin turns into somewhat of a frown, and he shifts in his armchair. He opens his mouth to speak, then pauses as if he does not know what to say. "So, how did you get hooked up with Jeb Johnson?"

I ignore his question. I want my own answers. "Mr. Johnson said you can help me find my dad, Phillip Ashdown. Can you? And what

< 72 >

happened at the facility? I went there to work on *your* project, and suddenly, everything is different. Does all of this have something to do with your research project?"

Mr. Bailey shifts again in his chair and leans forward. "Well, it's a little complicated. Can you tell me how long you have been looking for your dad?"

Now, this is more like the Dirk Bailey I know. Avoiding questions and playing games. I am not going to let him lead me in circles. He is either going to help me or not. It is that simple. I sit up and try to raise my voice, although my loud voice is still no louder than most people's normal tones. "Can you or can you not take me to my dad?"

I hear two large vehicles in the distance that sound like Humvees. Probably very close to Antrim. I do not think Mr. Bailey can hear them yet, but he walks to the front window. He stands off to the side, pulls back the curtain with one hand, and looks right, then left.

Mr. Bailey steps completely clear of the window and turns toward me. "Okay, Serenity, I will level with you. Here it goes. At some point when you started to search for your father, things in and around Hancock became, well, a little weird to you, didn't they? They became different, as you said, right?" He pauses.

The answer, of course, is yes. I nod. "Go on."

I hear the vehicles getting closer. Definitely Humvees.

He takes a couple of steps toward me and scratches his head. "Right before that happened, were you in the building where your father works, maybe even in his lab?"

I nod again. "Yes, I said I was at the facility."

"Okay, yes, that's right. That's what they call it," Mr. Bailey says. "And, by chance, did you happen to pass through a large object, a sphere of sorts?"

< 73 >

I stand up. "Yes! What happened? What was that object? Was that your idea of a time portal or something?"

Dirk puts his hands on my shoulders. "Not my idea. And no, not a time portal. You are in the same time, and you are in Hancock, New Hampshire, United States, Planet Earth. But you're in a different place."

I look down and shake my head.

"Let me explain," he says.

Before he says another word, the Humvees round the turn onto Antrim. We both hear them now and go to the window. Two black Humvees stop in front of Mr. Bailey's house. Three men wearing green military fatigues and carrying automatic weapons hop out of the first Humvee and surround the second, taking a guard stance. A man in a dark suit and sunglasses gets out of the front passenger side and opens the back door. The sunglasses are odd, given that it is dusk, not to mention the military posturing. An older gentleman in a suit and black trench coat climbs out of the back.

I look at Mr. Bailey. "Who are they?"

Mr. Bailey leans his head forward so he is close to me. "I don't have time to explain any more. I work with these people, but you can't trust them. They aren't who you think they are, and don't believe anything they tell you. I'll explain more when I can."

The doorbell rings.

I do not trust Dirk Bailey, and he is telling me not to trust these men. So, does that mean I *should* trust them?

< 74 >

COI

I wake up when the Humvee turns off. I rub my eyes. My head aches from getting not nearly enough sleep. Even in a car full of strangers, I slept. Exhaustion had finally overtaken me. It takes a minute for my eyes to adjust to the city lights. I read the sign on the building in front of the Humvee: Marriott.

I must have slept through the entire drive from Hancock to Boston, where the older gentleman had said we were going. He introduced himself as Chase Franklin.

"James is getting a room for you and has taken the liberty of ordering you room service," Mr. Franklin says. "Eat what you like, and leave the rest."

I do not answer. I am too tired to think of all the questions I still have. One of the men in military fatigues opens the Humvee door and escorts me toward the hotel entrance.

I stop when Mr. Franklin steps out of the Humvee and turns to me. His stern face and perfect posture in his black trench coat make him look much more formidable than his short height and thinning gray-blond hair otherwise would.

"You get some rest," Mr. Franklin says. "We'll pick you up tomorrow and take you to COI headquarters where I think we can answer all of your questions."

"COI?" I say.

"Yes," Mr. Franklin replies. "You haven't heard of the . . .?" He stops himself. "Right. Of course you don't know what that is. We'll explain tomorrow. Right now, just rest."

I cross my arms, lean forward into the crisp evening air, and follow the military man.

# # # # #

I awaken to the sound of knocking on the hotel room door.

"Just a minute," I say. I climb out of bed and realize I slept in my clothes. I was too tired to change. But what would I have changed into anyway?

"Miss Ashdown," a man says from the other side of the door. "I have some clothes for you to change into."

Of course he does. They have thought of everything. Were they expecting me? I open the door, and the military man who escorted me into the hotel holds four large bags full of various clothing items. Shirts, pants, socks, sweatshirts, coats, hats.

< 76 >

He hands the bags to me. "I was told to tell you to pick out what you like and what fits and leave the rest."

I notice the circles under the man's eyes. There is an empty fast-food cup and wrinkled sandwich wrapper at his feet. The other man, James, from the first Humvee, stands across the hall, watching us. He wears another black suit, white shirt, and yes, sunglasses, even inside.

I look at the military man. "Were you outside my room all night?"

He straightens up, takes a step backward, puts his back against the wall, and looks straight ahead, not making eye contact. "I'm not at liberty to say, ma'am."

I shake my head. Of course he is not at liberty to say. Nobody seems to be at liberty to say anything.

I go back inside my room and sort through the clothes. They have thought of everything. Even clean underwear. A little while later, bathed and clean and dressed in a pair of loose-fitting jeans, a dark purple turtleneck, and a light white jacket, I head out the door with a renewed desire to find my dad.

James hands me breakfast to go. Then he, the military guard, and I head to the hotel lobby. When the elevator opens, the lobby is packed with people who stand shoulder to shoulder. I survey the room. Two hundred fifty-seven people, not counting the hotel employees behind the desk and assisting with bags or the guards in green military uniforms.

All adults. I pick out each distinct voice talking in different languages and accents. Fifty-one Americans, forty Chinese, eighty-six Russians, thirty-one Hispanics, fourteen Italians, eight Japanese, seven Cubans, six Koreans, and fourteen for whom I am not sure of their nationality.

"What is going on?" I ask.

< 77 >

"New government contingencies are arriving from all over," James says. "It's like this in all of the hotels in all of the big cities. Countries are knocking down the doors to get into the UR lately. UR support has really taken off. But Mr. Franklin will explain all of that, I am sure."

We exit the hotel and climb into the Humvee. The driver is waiting for us.

# # # # #

As we drive to what I presume will be COI headquarters, I notice that the buildings in Boston look different than I remember from the last time I was in Boston. They look newer, yet dirtier. They are not as tall but are more condensed, stacked side by side. More like Gotham City in the *Batman* movies.

"Are we in Boston?" I ask.

James, sitting beside me, looks at me, tips his sunglasses down with one finger, and peers over them. "Yes. It probably looks different to you. Again, Mr. Franklin will explain."

I want to ask more questions, but I can tell that James either does not want to explain anything or, more likely, does not have the authority to do so.

Our destination is a building similar to the others we passed in downtown Boston. But this one has no sign or markings.

The streets are crowded with people going about their business day, as in any large city. But as we enter the building, one person catches my attention out of the corner of my eye. I glance quickly to the sidewalk on the opposite side of the street. There, in the crowd of people, standing and looking at me and my entourage, is the Carhartt man in his beanie. Except this time, he is making no attempt to go

< 78 >

unnoticed. He just stands there watching us in broad daylight. I stare over my shoulder at him as I move forward, walking between James and the military man. So now I at least know that it is not these people who have been following me. But then, who has been? And why?

Inside the building is a large sign that reads "Center of Information" in English. The words are also written in Chinese and Russian. Oh, COI.

We pass through two large rectangular devices. One is a metal detector. I do not know what the other detects. Then, one at a time, we rest our chins on a retinal scan device sitting on top of a high counter. When I take my turn, a computerized voice says, "Serenity Ashdown."

# # # # #

I sit at one end of the large mahogany table and scan the conference room. I did not need to see which button had been pressed in the elevator to know that we traveled to the fifteenth floor. The elevator's speed and the travel time told me that. James stands just inside the door. The military man is gone. There are thirty chairs around the table. Twenty-one blue ink pens, nineteen black ink pens, and sixteen markers in the three baskets spread out along the center of the table. Fifty-six squares in the carpet pattern on the floor.

"Stop it," I whisper.

The door opens, and in walks Mr. Franklin and Mr. Bailey, both dressed in suits, followed by two more men dressed in dark suits and a fifth person I cannot see at first. Mr. Franklin walks along the table, which stretches from just inside the door to where he sits at the far end, his back facing the floor-to-ceiling glass window. This is the first

< 79 >

time I have seen him walk. He has a slight limp because his right leg is three-quarters of an inch shorter than his left. Mr. Bailey leans his hip against the credenza sitting to the left of the door. I still cannot see the fifth man. But when he steps out from behind Mr. Bailey and the other men, I see him. Dad! I jump up, run to him, throw my arms around him, and hug as tightly as I can. He squeezes me back. We keep our arms locked but pull our heads back so that we can see each other's faces. Unlike everyone else since I walked through the sphere, he looks exactly like he is supposed to, Phillip Ashdown, my dad. This is reassuring.

"Dad!" I say. "Oh, how I have been searching for you! You have no idea how worried I have been. Where have you been? What is going on?"

He smiles at me. "Serenity, I am so sorry. I have wanted to call you and let you know where I was, but I couldn't. I have been working on a high-level security clearance project for the government. But now that you are here, sit down, and we will tell you everything. In fact, we need your help."

My spirits sink a little. Not Again. "My help?" I say. "Dad, you know how I feel about that. Do you *really* need me?"

"Yes," my dad says. "We really do." He hesitates. "*I* really do. Let's sit down, and I will explain."

"Explain? Will you really explain everything?" I ask. "I mean everything. What this project is and what you have been working on all this time."

My dad looks a bit puzzled when he replies. "Yes, of course."

As we take our seats, I see half-forced smiles on the faces of Mr. Franklin and the two new men. Mr. Bailey has no smile at all. His lips are turned down, and he looks away, not even paying attention.

< 80 >

Then, I remember his words: *You can't trust them. They aren't who you think they are.*

"I believe you know Mr. Franklin and Dirk Bailey." My dad nods toward each of them as he says their names. "This is Gordon Conklin and Artemis Glenn."

He nods toward each of them in turn.

Mr. Conklin and Mr. Glenn each stand and extend a hand. "Miss Ashdown, it is a pleasure to meet you," Mr. Conklin says.

I shake their hands and force a smile.

My dad, sitting directly opposite from me, leans across the table. "Okay, so let's get you some answers. Where were you when you realized that I was gone? So I know where to start."

I put my forearms on the table and lean forward. "I was going to the facility to assist Mr. Bailey with a research project." I pause and look at Mr. Bailey. "Dad, you left a message sometime during the night before that you needed to talk to me. That it was urgent. Remember? And you left me a message at the facility's gate to see you. Again, it was marked urgent." I sit up, sliding my arms back, my hands still resting on the table. "But I could not reach you on your phone, and nobody at the facility would take me to you, so I started searching for you. I found my way to the basement lab. I thought you might be working there. And that is where I found it."

"Found what?" Mr. Franklin interrupts from the far end of the table.

I look first at Mr. Franklin and then back at my dad. I continue to address my dad. "The sphere. Or whatever it is. Is that what you have been working on for Mr. Bailey? Is that the project?" I glance at Mr. Bailey again and then back at my dad. "What is it? Why did you need to see me so urgently? Where did you go?"

< 81 >

"Was it active?" Mr. Franklin jumps in again. "Did you walk through it?"

I do not look at Mr. Franklin this time, annoyed by his interruptions. I wish I could just talk to my dad alone. I want to hear everything from him.

I want to ask him my questions and have him ask me his.

I lean forward toward my dad. "What is that thing? Some sort of time travel device or space-time continuum? Things are different in Hancock since I fell through it. People are different. They look a little different, and they act a lot different. Everyone except you and me."

Mr. Franklin stands up quickly, pushing his chair back and leaning on the table with both hands, palms down. He slaps the table with one hand. "So, you did go through it." He looks at Mr. Conklin and Mr. Glenn, who are seated at the other end of the table, nearest to my dad and me. "It stayed active longer than we thought. This just might work. We may be able to pass through."

Both men shoot Mr. Franklin a glare. My dad glances at the men and then at Mr. Franklin. What is going on? What did they mean by that? They knew it would have some effect. Why did they not shut it down? My dad and I both went through it, and we are the only ones who are the same as we used to be. Why?

I lean across the table, looking eye to eye with my dad. "Dad, what is going on? Please explain it to me."

My dad grasps both of my hands. "Okay, Pumpkin. I'll explain."

Pumpkin? He never calls me Pumpkin. It should be "Peanut."

"You are correct, Serenity," my dad continues. "We have developed a device to alter space and time. It is a government-funded project, the first step in trying to save the planet. You and I went through it relatively close in time, so to us, things seem different—but different

< 82 >

in the same way. If others go through at a later time, things will also seem different, but not in the same way as they seem different to us."

I lean back, pulling my hands away from my dad's. I look at Mr. Franklin. He looks at my dad with one eyebrow raised. I turn my attention to the other end of the table. Mr. Conklin and Mr. Glenn shift in their seats, looking at each other.

The explanation seems plausible, but something still does not seem to add up. How can different people see different things at the same time?

And Jona. What about Jona? And Mr. Bailey had told me the sphere is not a time portal.

I look at Mr. Bailey, who sits between my dad and Mr. Franklin. He has been quiet, almost motionless and expressionless. "Mr. Bailey, is all of this true? Have my dad and I changed the space-time continuum as we see it?"

Mr. Bailey looks at my dad, then at Mr. Conklin and Mr. Glenn, and finally at Mr. Franklin. Mr. Franklin gives him a nod. Mr. Bailey looks at me, still with a blank face. "Yes, Serenity, it is as your father has explained."

Before I can ask another question, my dad speaks again. "That is the reason for my urgent messages to you. We were so close and wanted to test it. I wanted to let you know what I was doing in case something went wrong. I'm so glad you searched for me."

My dad has never been the type of person to test something out without taking more precautions. Although, Mr. Bailey may have forced him to test it. But none of this explains the lady telling me that Jona was killed.

I look at my dad. "The lady who lives in the building at our address said Jona is dead. How can that be?"

< 83 >

"That's why I need your help," my dad says. "We have to go back through the sphere so things will return to normal for us."

"The sphere is gone," I say. "It just disappeared. How can we go through it again?"

My dad shifts in his seat, now facing Mr. Franklin but still looking at me.

"These gentlemen have built another one in a different location." He nods toward Mr. Conklin and Mr. Glenn. "And that's where you come in. The computer with the coordinates disappeared along with the transportal device, as we call it. Well, they didn't disappear. But they are gone in our new space-time continuum." My dad stands up and steps behind his chair, putting both hands on the back it. He leans toward me. "They have built the device, but they need the exact coordinates. Without them, you and I cannot get back home as we know it, and things won't ever be the same for us." He pauses, straightens up, and pulls the chair toward him. "I know you observed everything the moment you walked into the basement lab. And I know you remember everything you saw."

I close my eyes and rub them with my fists. I know what my dad is going to ask.

He sits back down, pulling his chair up to the table. "Can you tell us the fixed coordinate numbers on each of the computers and the sequence of numbers running on the computer closest to the transportal device? That computer had an algorithm running. There would have been a series of numbers, seventy-five to one hundred of them, eventually repeating." He places his elbows on the table and leans toward me. "We need to know the whole series, starting with the point where they repeat. That number sequence and the fixed numbers on the other computers are the only way to program the device to the

< 84 >

final coordinates shown on the screen on the transportal itself. You probably saw that too."

I shift in my seat. I start to feel warm, a little uncomfortable. I did see all of the computers, and I did notice the number sequence. And I watched until the series repeated.

"Yes, I saw them," I say. "But the sequence of numbers, you know that I cannot simply recall that many numbers changing that quickly."

Mr. Franklin interrupts yet again. He leans forward and looks at my dad. "But you said she has a photographic memory!"

I am puzzled. My dad would never tell someone that, especially not a complete stranger. Maybe my dad has changed, too. I look at him. He looks at me and then at Mr. Franklin.

"Well, Chase, that's not exactly what I—," my dad starts.

"It is not exactly photographic," I interrupt. "A photographic memory would not have a chance at recalling that many numbers changing that quickly. I did not say that I cannot do it. I said that it is not that simple. I need to see the sequence again. When I see it, I will recognize it."

Mr. Conklin finally speaks. "We have a program that will run every possible sequence of the numbers that could make up the coordinates. We would just need you, Miss Ashdown, to sit and watch them until you identify the right numbers in the right order."

That could take some time.

How can I possibly sit at a computer that long? How can I keep my mind from going crazy with so many numbers flashing in so many different orders? But it may be the only way to get my dad and me back to normal.

I look at my dad. "Is this the only way?"

He nods.

< 85 >

I look at Mr. Bailey for a sign, any sign. A nod or shake of the head, some sort of eye contact. I get nothing.

I look at Mr. Franklin and then back at my dad.

"Okay then. If it will get us home, I will do it."

< 86 >

SOMETHING IN THE ROAD

S trong wind in the morning air stings my face. Light snow flurries dance against the overcast sky. The jacket they gave me is a little large, so I pull my hands inside and wrap it around me like a cocoon. James opens the door of the black SUV for me, and I climb into the back with my dad. Mr. Franklin already sits in the front passenger seat. James climbs in to drive, and two green military Humvees follow us. The car is quiet during our drive through the city. The farther we get into the country, the more deserted the road becomes. That, along with the cold, dreary day, gives me an eerie feeling.

I break the silence. "Mr. Franklin, why do we need all of the protection?"

"Don't worry," Mr. Franklin says. "It's just a precaution. There are certain people who think what we are doing here is wrong. They would rather suffer and watch our planet die than try to fix it. But they won't try anything against our military escort. That's why I brought them along."

I look at my dad. He stares out the window at the countryside, not engaged in the conversation.

"How is your time portal going to fix the planet?" I ask.

Mr. Franklin turns and looks at me. "We are trying to go back in time, to a period before everything started to die. We want to isolate the cause. If we can prevent it from happening in the past, that should fix the present."

The more I think about time travel, the more I question it. Doctor Gruber's theory of time travel just does not seem like a plausible explanation for all of this.

"But Mr. Franklin," I say. "I have never seen a calculation that makes time travel possible. How can it be done?"

"Serenity!" my dad says sharply as he turns to look at me. "Mr. Franklin knows what he's doing. Now, stop with the questions."

I tilt my head and give my dad a puzzled look. He has never talked to me like that before. And he has never told me to stop asking questions. In fact, his motto has always been to ask as many questions as you can until you understand something, and then, ask more.

Mr. Franklin interrupts before I can respond. "It's okay, Phil. Your daughter is a sharp girl. Let her ask away. She has a right to know how it works. However, rather than me trying to explain it to you, Serenity, I'll show you as soon as we get to the site. While they are setting up the computers to run the algorithm, I'll show you on the portal's mainframe how time travel works."

< 88 >

My dad gives Mr. Franklin a glare. I do not respond as the sound of a car approaching from the rear, going very fast, catches my attention. From the sound of the RPM, its speed far exceeds the limit of fifty-five miles per hour. I listen as it approaches the last Humvee and then accelerates even more to pass our caravan. I look to the left, past my dad, as the car passes us. The driver is the Carhartt man in his black beanie. He turns and looks directly into our car. As soon as I make eye contact, he looks forward and continues past.

As the Carhartt man pulls back into the lane in front of us and quickly outpaces us, a flock of birds takes off from the brush at the edge of the woods ahead, off to the right side of the road. I see from the bend in the grass that they took off in the same direction as the wind. But birds take off against the wind unless they are afraid of something beneath them in that direction. I glance to the left and see the same thing. Another flock of birds takes off with the wind. And I notice the slightest movement in the brush near where they took off.

Mr. Franklin continues talking. "Oh, and one more thing—"

I interrupt him. "James," I say. "There's trouble up ahead. You better stop."

James looks ahead to the right and then the left and says, "Or speed up to get past it."

My head snaps back as the SUV rapidly accelerates.

I hear weapons fire, grenade launchers or rocket launchers or something. One on each side of us. I instantly calculate the spot of impact, assuming the weapons were aimed straight toward the road and were fired from where the birds took off. I do not know our exact rate of speed, so it is an estimate. But I know that we are not going to make it past the point of impact in time.

"Stop now!" I shout.

< 89 >

The SUV does not slow.

My ears suddenly feel like they will burst at the concussion and sound of an explosion. The SUV's tires squeal as James slams on the breaks. The SUV skids sideways. Dust and debris fly high and in every direction, coming from the middle of the road just ahead of us.

We skid to a sideways stop beside a large crater in the road. The first Humvee slams head-on into the driver's side of our SUV, pinning James and my dad. My head slams against the window. I feel a sharp pain in the side of my head, then blood trickles down onto my ear. There is another explosion behind our caravan, and the SUV jolts forward, turning on its side and skidding into the crater. Something smacks my left eye, and there is a sharp pain in my right side, up around my rib cage. I try to get my bearings, but I am light-headed. Everything is hazy. My dad is bloody, hanging from his seatbelt above me, but he appears to be conscious. I cannot see James or Mr. Franklin. When I try to say something, I cannot form any words.

Shouts come from behind us. I cannot make out all of the words, but they sound like commands.

I hear someone say, "Look out! Over there!"

Then gunfire.

Lots of gunfire. Odd-sounding weapons from behind us. Probably the military personnel in the Humvees. Rifles are fired from the fields and trees on both sides of us. But no shots hit our SUV or even come close. The shooters are targeting the back of the caravan. I try to think about what to do, but my head feels lighter and lighter. I fight to maintain consciousness. I try to move, but I am stuck. My head and side ache.

These must be the people Mr. Franklin was just talking about. They must want to kill us.

< 90 >

Just as the gunfire stops, I hear footsteps racing toward our SUV. I cannot focus my sight on anything. Everything is hazy and fuzzy, and my head throbs.

I hear a voice. "Is she in there?"

"Yes, I see her," says another voice.

The first voice replies, "Is she all right?"

"I don't know. She looks pretty banged up."

"What happened? How did her car get hit? It wasn't supposed to be touched!"

"Sorry, boss," a different voice says in a heavy Japanese accent. "I had the trajectory perfect, I'm sure. But they sped up at the last minute and got too close. I don't know why they sped up. I'm sorry."

"It's okay," the first voice says in a tone that is a little calmer. "Let's just get her out."

Then I hear a deep, husky voice. "What about the others in the car? They're still alive."

"Leave them. We don't have any time. I'm sure the soldiers in the Humvees called for backup. They'll be here any minute."

I raise my head and turn it toward the voices, but I can only see people from the waist down—no faces. They wear dark military-style uniforms. A trickle of blood runs from my forehead into my one good eye. The other eye is already swollen shut. Moving my head sends it spinning even faster. A dark, blurry face bends to look inside the SUV, then a hand reaches for me. After that, there is nothing but darkness.

< 91 >

SUDDEN EVACUATION

I open one eye. Everything is a blur, and my other eye will not open. Reaching a hand to my face, I wince at the pain as I touch the swollen tissue. I rest my hands on a firm mattress. The sheets feel stiff, like in a hospital. I push on my hands to sit up, but a sharp pain pierces my right side. I grab my side with my hand and fall backward.

"Take it easy there." I can hear an older man's voice from somewhere nearby.

Through my one open eye, I see a blurry figure leaning against the wall. I try to talk.

"Where am . . ." My mouth is too dry, and my head feels light. I stop.

Footsteps come toward me. "You took quite a spill," the voice says. "You need to rest. Here, this will help."

The figure's hand is on my back, trying to help me sit. My vision starts coming into focus. I am right. It is an older man, probably in his seventies, with white hair, a white mustache, and wiry glasses. He wears a long, white coat. I grab my side again as the pain stabs me.

"This will help with that, too," the man says.

He holds a cup to my mouth and helps me drink. It tastes fizzy and thick. What did I just drink? But it seems to have helped my mouth and throat already.

I cough and clear my throat. "Where am I? What happened? Where is my dad? Who are you?" The pain shoots through my side again. I grimace.

"You are in Hancock, New Hampshire," the man says. "As for the rest of your questions, they can wait. I'm a doctor. And you need to rest. I'm sure all your questions will be answered once you're up to it. For now, rest. And by the way, the name is Sam."

I lie back down and sigh as the pain in my side subsides.

My eyelids are already growing heavy. I want to know more, right here and now, but I cannot formulate another question. I am exhausted, and whatever the doctor gave me must be working. I feel relaxed, pain-free. I give in to sleep.

# # # # #

It seems like only seconds later when I hear a door creak. I open my good eye. My vision is in focus, and I feel much better. Much more rested. I turn my head slightly and see the doctor, Sam, entering the room with a tray of food. The smell of french fries fills the air. I am starving.

< 93 >

"How long was I asleep?" I ask.

Sam smiles. "Since I gave you the medicine, it's been fourteen hours. I was coming in to wake you before we lost you forever." He chuckles.

I try to sit up, but the sharp pain shoots through my side again.

Sam sets down the food and grabs me. "Hold on now. It's going to take more than fourteen hours of sleep to heal those bruises. Nothing's broken. You just took a good shot to the ribs. And another good one in the face. You have quite a shiner. Don't worry, though. No permanent damage."

Sam leaves me alone to eat. The food is delicious. Simple but good. A hamburger and french fries. A cold soda would wash it down nicely, but all I have is water. I hold the glass up to the light and swirl it. All clear. No additives this time. I look around the room as I eat. I cannot figure out where I am. I am definitely not in a hospital or clinic, at least not any like I have ever seen before. It does not even look like a doctor's office, and there's no smell of medicine. It has all the equipment you would see in a hospital room, but the feel is quite different. For one thing, there are no windows. The floor is tile, and the walls are covered with soft blue-and-gray-striped wallpaper. There are eighty-five stripes of each color on the walls and four hundred three tile squares on the floor. It seems like an office that has been turned into a makeshift hospital room. I reach into my pocket and pull out my cell phone. I have to try again. I dial my dad's number.

Nothing but silence.

I try to remember what happened. I had finally found my dad. I was going to help us get back to our time period. We were going to drive to the site of the sphere to do so. Then we were ambushed. But by whom? The man in the Carhartt jacket was with them. But I did

< 94 >

not see any of the attackers' faces. It happened so fast. Who has me now? If I was being held by the government, my dad would also be here. So, the attackers must have me. But why? How do I get back to my dad?

Footsteps approach the closed door to my room. Three people. They stop at the door and talk. I doubt that they know I can hear them. Two males and one female. They are discussing a fight. And shooting. They have just returned from a gun fight.

The door opens without a knock, and three people walk in. I start pulling the bedsheets up to my neck and notice I am still wearing the same clothes the military man gave me in Boston. They are a bit torn and bloodstained, but at least I know they did not undress me.

I look at my three visitors. They all wear the pieced-together military-style uniforms the ambushers wore. They really do look like they just came from some type of a fight. Their skin is shiny with sweat and streaked with dirt and grime.

One of them steps close to the side of my bed. He looks solidly built and ruggedly handsome, probably in his twenties. A chain tattoo circles his left bicep. Except for his light brown hair, he looks familiar in the same way that Mr. Johnson did.

He stares at me, looking deep into my eyes. He looks as if he has seen a ghost. Tears well up in his eyes.

"What?" I ask.

He turns away quickly. "It's her all right. Minus the shiner."

"It is who?" I demand. "And who are you people?"

He rubs the back of his hand across his face and turns back toward me, ignoring my questions, his eyes now red. "How do you feel?"

It is a simple enough question, but it irritates me. Where do these people get off asking me questions and talking to me like I have been

< 95 >

with them forever? I am the one with the questions. When are they going to start giving me answers?

"I would feel a lot better if someone would tell me what is going on," I say.

I glare at the man who stands over my bed and then at a man who leans against the far wall. He is African American, tall and muscular. I do not think I have ever seen someone this big in person. He wears a black combat vest stuffed full of what looks like various handguns, grenades, and whatever other weapons he can fit in that will shoot, burn, or explode.

"All right," the man by my bed says, his voice cracking. "Fair enough. Let me see. Where to start?"

He is interrupted by a woman standing just inside the door. "Do you think it's a good idea? Telling her now?"

The woman is average-sized, seems very athletic, and has a gun slung over her shoulder.

She has a dark complexion and short brown hair that looks like she cut it herself with a razor. She probably looks a lot less like one of the guys when she isn't covered in grime.

"How do we know she's not already working for them?"

I look at her and grit my teeth. "For whom?" I demand. "What are you talking about?"

The woman's face tightens as she takes two steps closer to me. "Look, girl. Don't get mouthy with me. If it was my decision, we would have already fed you to the wolves."

The man by the bed quickly turns toward the woman. "It's not your decision. Now back off!"

The large man leaning against the wall grins and shakes his head.

< 96 >

The man by the bed speaks. "You deserve an explanation." He nods toward the large man. "This is Isaiah Burton." He turns toward the woman. "Your friend here is Danica Eubanks."

Danica rolls her eyes.

The man continues. "You are in Hancock, New Hampshire. Just not quite the Hancock, New Hampshire, you know. Oh, and I'm Shawn Patterson."

As the name "Shawn Patterson" registers in my mind, and before I can reply, the door bursts open, and a small Japanese man runs into the room, dressed in the same makeshift military fatigues as the others. The man looks at Shawn and pants for a moment, catching his breath, then speaks in broken English. "They found us! They know we're here! They're on their way! What do you want us to do?"

Shawn turns quickly to face him. "Okay, Takeo. We knew this could happen. They must have followed us. Contact Massachusetts. Tell them we need an immediate evac to HQ. Round up everyone and head to the tunnel." He looks at Danica. "You get Fancy and grab the laptops and com equipment. I'll get a couple guys, and we'll grab the guns and ammo. Isaiah, you help Serenity. We'll all meet at the tunnel in ten."

Danica pulls her automatic weapon off her shoulder and steps up to Shawn. She tilts her head toward me. "We should leave her behind for them. I told you we should never have brought her here. She's going to get us all killed."

Shawn's face goes blank. "She might just be the only person who can *save* us."

I catch myself staring at Shawn throughout the commotion. I now realize it is and is not Shawn Patterson—my Harvard schoolmate, my fencing partner. His hair is different, and he is more mus-

< 97 >

cular, but it is Shawn. How can this be? How can any of this be? As Shawn and Danica leave the room, I sit up, put my feet on the floor, and start to stand. It feels like there is a knife stuck in my ribs. I grab my side and double over.

Isaiah walks to me, kneels, puts his arm around my back, cups his forearm and hand behind both of my knees, and scoops me up. "I've got you, ma'am."

His voice is deep, yet gentle. Too gentle, it seems, for the giant of a man that he is.

"Wait," I say. "Why should I go with you people? Who's coming? Is it my dad, coming to rescue me? Leave me here."

Isaiah looks at me with compassion. "I know how confused you must be. But you have to trust me. You really need to come with us. Shawn will finish explaining everything when we get to Massachusetts."

Isaiah is going to take me with him whether I want to go or not, so I put an arm around his neck to brace myself. I glance at his face. His expression is guileless.

I still do not know who to trust. I just want to find my dad and go home. And I do not know who "they" are or what "they" want. But on the other hand, Mr. Franklin seemed very demanding regarding his agenda. And why would my dad call me Pumpkin? Then, there is Mr. Bailey's warning that they are not who I think they are. And so far, these people are treating me fine. Except Danica. And they are taking care of me. Besides, at the moment, I do not have much of a choice.

I look at Isaiah. "Why not just go to the police?"

Isaiah looks at me. "They own the police."

# # # # #

< 98 >

saiah carries me down four different hallways, all with doors along either side, some open and some closed. I look into the rooms with open doors. They look like offices of various sizes that have been repurposed. More hospital rooms, a communications room, a computer room, a lunchroom, and most noticeably, a number of bedrooms. Isaiah looks at his watch. His pace picks up, and so does the bounce in his step. With each bounce comes a jab in my side. I have to keep quiet. It cannot be easy for him to carry me. And I know the pain would be so much worse if I was walking.

"What is this place?" I ask as I bounce in Isaiah's arms.

"Home," Isaiah answers, still breathing easily.

At the end of the last hall, we go through a door and descend six flights of stairs. Through another door, we enter a large, damp, dimly-lit storage area. The air smells stale. Probably the basement of whatever building this is. Or was. I notice twelve filing cabinets against the wall, some old computers on tables, and outdated dresses, scarves, and other women's clothing hanging on numerous racks throughout the room. I can see twenty full racks in what little light there is.

I guess that we are in some type of office building that has been turned into a safe house. Isaiah walks us to the back of the room. Takeo is already there with a large group of men and women. Fifty-two people. Some are dressed in the black combat outfits, others are dressed more like doctors or nurses, and still, others are dressed in street clothes. It is quiet, considering how many people are in the room. Takeo breaks the silence, barking orders to five men, who remove concrete blocks from the back wall.

Danica arrives with a redheaded woman who looks to be in her forties and has a large scar on her left cheek. I assume this is Fancy. She, too, wears combat gear. They each carry two large, unzipped

< 99 >

duffel bags stuffed with laptops and assorted tech equipment. Shawn and two other men follow them. Between the three of them, they carry two large trunks. Must be the ammunition and extra weapons. Finally, Doctor Sam enters the room, pushing a wheelchair.

"All clear," Takeo says loudly.

Isaiah sets me in the wheelchair and pushes it forward. They have opened up a hole in the wall leading into a dark tunnel. A few people pull out flashlights. Shawn and his two men go first, followed by Danica and Fancy, then Isaiah and me. Everyone else follows us, with Takeo taking up the rear, carrying an assault rifle almost as large as he is. Everyone is quiet and falls into place perfectly. I am quite sure they have either been through this before or have practiced the drill many times.

The tunnel is damp and smells musty. When the occasional flashlight shines on the wall or ceiling, I see concrete. Dark, moist concrete blocks. The tunnel is tall enough for everyone, even Isaiah, to stand up straight.

"Where are we going?" I say quietly, leaning my head back toward Isaiah.

"Massachusetts," he says.

I am learning quickly that Isaiah is not much for words. I decide not to ask him any more questions.

The end of the tunnel is blocked by a round metal slab. Shawn and the other two men set down the trunks. They each grip a spot on the large plate and try to push it. The veins in their arms and necks bulge, and their faces tighten as they grunt and groan. The plate barely moves.

"It's stuck," one of the men says.

Isaiah flips the wheelchair brake. He steps up, motions for one of the men to move back, and takes his place. The three of them push

< 100 >

again. Isaiah never makes a sound. He just grits his teeth and lowers his head. The plate screeches, scraping the block edges until it falls over in a loud thud. Shawn and the other two men stand for a moment, hands on their knees. Isaiah slowly walks back over to me, folds his arms, and stands straight.

I hold out my hand. "Let me walk for a bit. I feel better." I want to try to get a look outside the tunnel to see if I can tell where we are . . . and who the people are that are evacuating us. And if I do not like what I see, maybe I can sneak away. Although, in my condition, I doubt I can get far, and I need to better understand the situation before I know where to go. What I need right now is information.

Isaiah does not say anything. He just holds out his arm to give me support.

We move up by Shawn, Danica, and Fancy. Two men step forward as well, their automatic weapons at the ready.

The tunnel opens out of a hillside and into a field. I do not recognize the place. It is hard to see in the moonless night. I cannot see anything above or behind us due to the hill. A slight hum comes from behind us, over the hill. Helicopters. Two small ones. They'll need more than two helicopters to transport this many people.

I look at Shawn. "What are the Massachusetts people sending to evacuate us?"

"Helicopters," Shawn replies.

"I hear them," Danica says. "Come on. Let's go." She motions to the group behind her.

"Wait," I say. "How many will they send?"

Shawn raises an eyebrow. "Five. That's typical evac procedure for a group our size."

"Will they send them together?" I ask.

< 101 >

"Always," Shawn says.

"But there are only two small helicopters coming," I reply. "Small rotors for maneuverability. Probably fighters."

Danica shakes her head and curls her lips. "I hear them as well as you. If you hear one or a hundred helicopters, they sound the same. And there's no way the Feds know about this tunnel and that we will be coming out here." Danica turns to me with a glare. "You just want us to get caught. Like I said, you're probably working for them." She turns back toward Shawn. "Now let's go before the Feds locate our birds."

Shawn looks at me. "What makes you think there are only two?"

Just like all of my calculations and computations, I do not know how I identify the sound of two helicopters as opposed to three, four, or five, nor do I know how I recognize the type of helicopter. I just know.

I look at Danica and then at Shawn. "I cannot explain it. I just know. There are only two helicopters coming over that hill."

Shawn looks at me, then at Danica, then back at me. Then he looks outside the tunnel. He stands there. The whirl of the helicopters grows louder.

Danica pounds the stock of her gun against the ground, grits her teeth, and tightens her face, putting herself nose-to-nose with Shawn.

She shouts, "Don't think I don't know why you're giving her the benefit of the doubt like this, there are a lot of lives at stake here. I've fought beside you every day for the past three years. We've held family and friends in our arms together as they've died for our cause, and you're going to ignore me and trust this Blondie, who you didn't even know until yesterday? You know she's a different person." Danica shakes her head. "How could you?"

< 102 >

Shawn glances at me one more time with a troubled look, then looks away. "You're right." He turns back to the group and yells. "Let's move out!"

I look at Isaiah. "Isaiah, I know that I am right."

Isaiah stares at me, frozen where he stands. The entire group pushes past us until only Takeo, Isaiah, and I are left at the edge of the tunnel.

Takeo looks up at Isaiah. "Let's go, big guy."

Isaiah still does not move.

I see the flash before I hear the air-to-ground ballistic missile strike the ground. I have to close my one good eye as the blinding light illuminates the tunnel entrance. I try to stay on my feet, but the momentum of the blast knocks me to the cold, hard floor of the tunnel. I go deaf for a moment from the concussion of the explosion. Everything seems to move in slow motion. Isaiah stumbles and falls over backward. Takeo, too, falls to the ground.

As my hearing returns, I hear muffled sounds. Sounds of screams and shouts. Over and over, I hear, "Get back to the tunnel! Get back to the tunnel!" I do not know who is shouting or how many people are still alive to scream. Then, I hear machine-gun fire from the helicopters. I lay on the ground, unable to move, and watch as what is left of our group races back toward me and the tunnel. Most of them are mowed down by the gunfire. I want to help them, but I am helpless. Blood spurts from arms, legs, and heads. People fall. Some try to crawl the last few yards to the tunnel or try to get back up, just to be hit again. I close my eyes. I have never seen carnage like this before, not even on television, let alone to be living it. Who is doing this? And why? It certainly is not my dad's men trying to rescue me. He would never be part of something like this.

< 103 >

There is another explosion. This one is in the sky above the hill. The sky lights up. Then a second explosion and another flash of light. Then the gunfire and screams are replaced by the whirl of helicopters. This time, five of them.

< 104 >

HQ

Only two of the five helicopters are needed to transport what is left of the group. I sit quietly in my seat. Everyone is silent, with blank stares on their faces. Like me, they are probably recounting the horror we just lived through.

I stare out the helicopter window, watching the sunrise. I am able to see slightly out of my bad eye, orange and yellow breaking over the distant hillside. I have always loved to watch the sunrise over New Hampshire, how it slowly lights up the trees and grass, the entire countryside. But this is the first time I have seen it from this vantage point, in the air. I try to forget, for the moment, where I am. I let my mind wander back to the brightly-colored fall trees that I had observed just two days ago. I lean closer to the window and look down. The sun is high enough now to light up the landscape. I blink a couple of times to clear my vision. But it is still the same. I close my good eye for a few seconds, then open it. The landscape still looks the same as it did moments earlier. I lean farther forward. That cannot be. This is not the tree- and grass-covered landscape of the New Hampshire that I know. A lot of it is barren. The hills are still there, but many of the trees are gone. Those that remain are dead or dying. They have the same look that I had seen earlier, up close, but from this viewpoint, I see it on a much larger scale. The grasslands look dead as well, mostly gray or completely dried up. Maybe it is just the altitude. But no, the woods around the facility were the same, and so were the trees and grass in town. I am seeing correctly. Everything I see, everyone I meet, makes me long for my dad and for home. This is one long nightmare.

I look across the helicopter at the others. Only Isaiah and Takeo are without injury. The tunnel spared them . . . and me. Danica sits with a blood-soaked wrap around her thigh. She stares at the floor. Fancy is a few more people away, bent forward holding her side. She is pale, very pale. At first, I cannot see the wound. Then, when Fancy's hand moves slightly, I see her blood-stained shirt.

Shawn is seated next to Danica. He lifts his hand and touches a large cut on his forehead. He grimaces as he looks at me. "How did you know?" He pauses and takes a deep breath. "About the helicopters?"

When he lowers his arm, I see a wrap on his bicep. Blood is starting to seep through.

The volume, the differences in the whirl of the blades. Like so many things, I wish I did not know. Then, I would not feel responsible. I should have been more insistent with Shawn, with the others.

< 106 >

But how do I explain all of this to him? I shake my head feeling the frustration building inside me.

"You would not understand." I look back out the window.

"Even the most seasoned combat veteran, with years of training and field experience, wouldn't have been able to do that," Shawn says.

I turn toward Shawn. "I did not ask to be here. You drag me along without any explanation as to who you people are or why you have me. I tried to help but you ignored me. Now, all those people are dead. I want information, but you give me nothing. I owe you no explanation!"

Shawn starts to respond but is interrupted by the pilot speaking over the com.

"Hang on back there. We're heading in to land."

The helicopter descends, and wind rocks us back and forth until we land atop a rocky cliff overlooking the ocean. The waves crash against the rocks below. I have been along this coast before. We are in Massachusetts.

As we exit the helicopters, I am chilled by the cold breeze. Shawn quickly exits, so I guess our conversation is over. He waits outside the helicopter to help the injured exit. As I approach the opening, Shawn holds out his hand. I look at him, then turn and take Isaiah's arm and step down.

Other than a small wooden building, I see nothing but rocks and dried, wilted grass. I estimate the square building to be twenty feet by twenty feet. It looks like an abandoned shed or the last remaining structure from a farm. I hold Isaiah's arm to support my aching side as Shawn leads the group of survivors toward the building. Everyone is silent. Once we are inside, the door closes and a computer panel lights up on the wall. Shawn presses a few buttons on the panel that

< 107 >

sends us into a fast, jerky descent. The building's entire interior is an elevator. With one final jolt, we reach the bottom. I grab Isaiah's arm to keep my balance.

One side of the elevator opens into a large room with gray cinderblock walls, many computer stations scattered throughout, and a large computer screen that covers almost the entire front wall. It shows a map of the world with small yellow dots scattered all over and a lesser number of larger red dots.

One hundred twenty-two yellow dots and thirty-three red dots. There are people everywhere in the room, some in street clothes, some in the same makeshift military fatigues that I saw before. Many are busy working at the computer stations, but others congregate in different-sized groups standing or sitting at the numerous tables at the center of the room.

Still, others enter and leave the room through the various connecting corridors.

Shawn turns to me. "This is Massachusetts HQ. You'll be safe here."

I glare at him as I step away from Isaiah. "Safe! I still do not have an explanation for why you kidnapped me from the people you refer to as 'the Feds,' let alone an explanation for the attack at the tunnel. I am still blindly following you people, mainly because that is my only option at the moment. But I plan on changing that."

"Look, we saved your life by getting you away from the Feds. And I told you I would explain everything, and I will. When have I ever not kept my word?"

This is not like me. I never get angry. I take a deep breath to try to calm down, but it does not work. "Oh, I would not know, Shawn. I just met you last night!"

< 108 >

Turning away quickly, I lose my balance. An older lady whose graying hair is dyed a bluish shade catches me and guides me toward an empty wheelchair. She is dressed in street clothes.

"So, you're Serenity? Looks like I got to you with this chair just in time." She holds out a hand. "So nice to meet you."

With one hand on the wheelchair for support, I shake her hand and force a smile, still trying to calm down. How does this lady know my name? How does everyone seem to know my name?

"I'm Marlene," she says. "But most people here just call me Ma. Come on. I'll show you your room and where you can clean up and get something to eat."

I glance at Isaiah. He looks at me, then at the wheelchair, and then back at me. He nods. I do not know why I look to Isaiah for confirmation, but there is something about him that makes me trust him more than the others. So, I climb into the chair.

The place is a maze of well-lit corridors. After leaving the operations room, as Ma called it, Ma pushes me through another large room. It is about half the size of the operations room and is set up as a cafeteria. Next, we pass the men's and women's bathrooms and shower rooms. All of the hallways look the same. They have white, tile-dropped ceilings, and bright fluorescent lights contrast against the gray cinderblock walls and yellowish tile floor.

"Here we are," Ma says as we come to a junction with four new passageways that shoot off from it. "These are the sleeping corridors." She points down one hall. "The men's corridor goes that way." She points down another. "The women's, that way. And families stay in those rooms." She points down the third hall.

Then Ma points to the fourth hallway. "Down there you'll find the laundry room and a place to pick up new clothes, a toothbrush,

< 109 >

soap, whatever you need. And if you can't find what you want or need, just ask whoever is working there. We have people getting things from the stores in town daily."

On top of my anger and exhaustion, I feel overwhelmed. This is a whole other world. Things just keep getting crazier by the minute. Why do all these people live down here? They must fear the government, or "the Feds." And why is everyone being so welcoming? Like I should feel safe here with them, like a protected refugee. Anyway, I do not pay much attention to the last part of what Ma is saying. I have no intention of staying here long enough to need anything.

"Oh," Ma says. "And medical is down there as well." She nods toward the last corridor. "You might want to get that eye and your side looked at again."

That makes me think of Doctor Sam, who treated me. "The doctor, Sam," I say. "Did he make it?"

Ma smiles. "He's fine. A few cuts and scrapes, but, yes, he made it."

Ma helps me to the shower, then shows me to my room. It isn't much. A perfect square with more gray cinderblock walls, a white dropped ceiling, fluorescent lighting, and yellowish tile floor. It is furnished with a bed, a small closet, a trunk for belongings, and a small nightstand with a brush, mirror, and clock on it. Very institutional looking.

I then realize how hungry I am. But even more than wanting to eat, I want to sleep. I down most of the bottle of water that Ma had given me and then lie down on the bed. Sleep instantly overtakes me.

This time it is a restless sleep. Nightmares consume me. But not my usual dream about my mom and Jona. Instead, I dream about men and women who are outside the tunnel and get shot by machine-gun

< 110 >

fire as they hopelessly try to make it back to safety. There is blood everywhere.

"Don't go out there! Don't go out there!" I wake myself screaming. Cold sweat soaks my clothes and sheets. I sit up and take a drink of water. I should have done more to stop them from leaving the tunnel.

I look at the clock. 4:00 p.m. More sleep isn't going to come, so I might as well satisfy my hunger. I make my way to the cafeteria. Even after seeing the maze of corridors just once, they are imprinted in my mind. The people all walk quickly from one place to another. Each one has a preoccupied look on his or her face. They all walk with a purpose. Everyone must have a job to do in whatever this place is.

Shawn sits alone in the cafeteria, eating a sandwich. It is time to get some answers. I grab a tray, pick up a sandwich and drink for myself, and look for a place to pay. Not that I have any money on me, but I figure I can explain myself to the cashier. But I cannot see a cashier. People seem to be picking up whatever they want, sitting down, and eating, so I follow along.

I head straight for Shawn. His back is to me, but I can see that his head has been treated. It is bandaged and looks much better now. His arm also has clean wraps on it. He looks at something on a computer notepad lying on the table in front of him. I approach quietly and see that he is looking at a digital picture. A picture of a woman. I draw closer. It is not just any woman. It is a picture of me! But in the picture, my hair is short and dark red, my eyes are green, and my complexion is darker. I am also more physically fit, my body more toned. And I have the same chain tattoo around my left bicep that Shawn has. But the face in the picture is mine. No mistake about it. What is up with these people? The people I recognize are different. Different

< 111 >

in appearance, like Shawn. The Shawn I know is not built like that. And different mentally. The Mr. Johnson I know is never that nice.

And what is up with Shawn, *this* Shawn. He could have digitally enhanced a picture of me to change my appearance? That is kind of disturbing. And why would he do that? Or is that a picture of another me? What is really going on here?

Shawn quickly turns and flips the pad over, slamming it face down on the table. "What do you think you're doing, sneaking up like that?"

What right does he have to be upset with me? He is the one with a picture of me.

I step around to the other side of the table, drop my tray on top of it, and before I sit down I retort, "I did not sneak up on you. You were just too enthralled with that picture. And what are you doing with a picture of me anyway? And why do I look like that in it—so different? Why does everyone look different?" Now, I have these questions on top of all the questions I already want to ask him. "You promised me answers."

Shawn takes a deep breath. "Okay, okay, I'm sorry. You're right. We've dragged you through two states. You've been shot at and beaten up. And we haven't given you a single explanation." He motions to the seat across from him. "Please, sit down."

I stand there for a moment contemplating whether to sit down or leave. I came over to him to get answers, but he makes me angry. Why do I get so angry around him? I hardly ever get angry. But I am also afraid.

Scared that I will never see my dad again or Jona. That I will never get home. But I cannot let Shawn know that I am afraid. I cannot let these people think that I am weak. I do not know what their intentions are. I decide that my fear and the opportunity to get some

< 112 >

answers outweighs my frustration with Shawn, so I slowly pull out the chair and sit, but I do not scoot up to the table. My bottled water and cold lunchmeat sandwich will have to wait.

"Okay, I am listening," I say.

"I'm not sure where to start," Shawn says. "It would be more like you to ask the questions and lead the conversation."

My eyes narrow. "More like me? What do you know about me? You know nothing about me. At least not about the real me." I look at his notepad that sits face down on the table.

Shawn rolls his eyes and shakes his head.

"Do you know a Phillip Ashdown?" I ask.

Shawn takes a drink of water and pushes the remainder of his sandwich to the side. "Yes, but not the Phillip Ashdown you know. Not the Phillip Ashdown who is your father."

"What do you mean?" I ask as I fold my arms to hide my shaking hands. "I was just with my dad when you people took me. Or at least, I presume it was you who took me since I woke up in your hideout. Not to mention the fact that you almost killed me, and for all I know, you did kill my dad."

Shawn looks at me. "First, everyone else who was in your vehicle is fine. Second, your vehicle was not supposed to crash or get hit. We had it planned perfectly to force your vehicle to stop without hitting it. But your driver sped up at the last minute for some reason, throwing the timing off. Our surface-to-surface should have hit the road far enough in front of your vehicle to allow for a safe stop." He pauses, looks down, shifts in his seat, then looks at me again. "And third, that was not your father."

"But—"

He holds up his hand. "Let me finish."

< 113 >

"No," I interrupt. "What do you mean he was not my father. Do you think I do not know my own dad?"

Shawn grins. "Now you're acting just like her."

I pull myself closer to the table but keep my hands underneath it.

"Like who? What are you even talking about?" I stop myself. "Wait! Stop changing the subject. Do you know where my dad is?" He is the most frustrating person I have ever met. Or maybe it is this whole situation. It is really getting to me. I feel a lump form in my throat, and my eyes start to water. No way, I tell myself. No way am I going to let him see me cry. I take a gulp from my bottled water.

Shawn holds out a hand, palm down. "Relax, I'll get to your father."

Relax? Who is he to tell me to relax? But he is right, I do need to calm down. Patience, Serenity, patience. I take a deep breath and another drink of water. "Fine, continue."

"A couple of days ago, you walked through some sort of constructed device, a sphere-shaped metallic structure, am I right?"

I fold my arms again and nod. How does everybody know that? And why is that always the lead-in for their explanation?

Shawn continues. "And everything seemed to change for you, didn't it?"

"Maybe. What do you know about it?"

"Well, I know whatever the Feds," he pauses, "I mean, whatever the people that were holding you told you about it isn't true. What did they tell you it was, a view into an alternate future or something?"

I do not like his tone. "Mr. Franklin, Mr. Bailey, and my dad," I pause for emphasis, "explained that it was some sort of time portal, and the timeline I was living in got altered. But I suppose you are going to tell me that they are lying about that too."

< 114 >

Shawn leans, forward placing his elbows on the table. "It's not a time portal. And everything that I'm telling you is the truth. You have to believe me."

"Why should I believe you? You have not given me a better explanation for everything that has happened."

Shawn shakes his head. "Maybe if Isaiah told you, you would believe it."

"And just what is that supposed to mean?"

Shawn leans back and looks down. "Nothing. Never mind." He pauses then looks up. "Okay, so their explanation must have been something like everyone and everything you know looks a little different because you're in a different time or you changed the space-time continuum. Something like that. Am I right?"

I hesitate. Why am I the one giving the information? "And my dad went through too. That is why he and I look the same as we always have."

Shawn sits there. He seems hesitant to tell me again that it was a lie. "And what did they say you need to do?"

Is he playing me? Maybe he doesn't have an explanation and he is using me for his fishing expedition, trying to gather intelligence on the Feds. Maybe I should stop answering and start asking. "What do you think they want me to do?"

Shawn sits up. "I don't know exactly why they need you to do so, or how, but I think they told you they want you to help them get you and your father home, back through their time portal. Am I close?"

Again, the frustration builds. But am I frustrated because I am not getting any closer to any answers, or am I frustrated because he is right? "Well, programming their time portal is just what I was going to do until you and your people came along."

< 115 >

Shawn leans forward, elbows on the table again. "Okay, don't go getting all Serenity on me, and just hear me out."

I do not even know what he is talking about, but it is insulting. I am used to insults but usually from people jealous of my mental abilities or people who do not understand me. But Shawn is being much more personal. I feel the lump rising in my throat again, but I will not cry. I do not talk for fear of losing it.

Shawn continues. "Those guys you mentioned work for the government. The Feds, as we call them. Well, all but Mr. Bailey. I'll explain that later. What they told you about a time portal and a new timeline is what they want you to believe. If they tell you the truth, they know that you won't help them."

I shake my head. "My dad would never lie to me." But I have to admit to myself that he might not tell me the whole truth. "Fine. For the sake of argument, if they *are* lying to me, how about you tell me the truth?"

Shawn straightens in his seat. "When you walked through the sphere, you didn't change any timeline—you entered a parallel universe. Another universe with another Earth and a duplicate of every person. That's why you recognize people and places, but they all look a little different, act a little different, and have different personalities. And someone might be athletic in one universe but not in the other or really smart in one universe but not in the other. Back in your universe, there is another me. You may not have met me, but I bet I look and act a little different. Everyone in your universe is also in this universe—or was, at least. People can die at different times."

I hesitate. Now what do I believe? What is more plausible—altering time or a parallel universe? I have disproved Doctor Gruber's theory of time travel. It does not work. But what if there is another

< 116 >

way, another theory that does work? That would have to be a more plausible explanation than a parallel universe. And that would mean that Shawn is wrong about my dad. Maybe I can find a hole in Shawn's parallel universe explanation.

"Okay, but why does my dad look the same?" I ask. "And why has nobody in my universe ever heard of this?"

Shawn takes a drink of his water. "They made our Phillip Ashdown look exactly like your father in order to trick you. And people in your universe do know of this. At least, certain people do. Do you know Dirk Bailey in your universe?"

My spine tingles thinking of my encounters with Mr. Bailey and what he has put my dad through. "Yes," I say. "My dad works for him. What is your point?"

"He actually works for our government, the Feds," Shawn says. "There are a few others in your universe that we believe work with him, but we don't know how high up it goes."

"Okay," I say. "For the sake of argument, assuming this is true, how high up in your government does it go?"

Shawn leans forward again. "All the way. All the way to President Masterson."

I shake my head. "No. I still do not believe you. If all of this is true, why did they make your Phillip Ashdown look like my dad? And where is my dad? And why do they need me?"

"You've noticed our landscape, right? How everything looks like it's dead or dying?" Shawn asks.

I adjust myself in my seat. "Yes. I thought it looked a little unusual."

"Well, every country on our planet has been engaged in constant war," Shawn says. "We have developed weapons far beyond the capabilities of weapons in your world. Because that's all we have focused

< 117 >

on, at the expense of the people and the planet. There is no quality of life anywhere in the world. Unless you work for the Feds, you have nothing. And ever since the United States, the Soviet Union, and China combined to form the United Republic, there's no hope of any other country overtaking the Feds, let alone the entire UR."

"The UR?" I say.

"Yeah," Shawn says. "And Wes Masterson is the president of it all."

"So again, assuming you are right, and I am not saying that I believe you, who are the Feds?" I ask.

"That's what the Resistance called the US government and military prior to the formation of the UR. And at least here in the US, the name still sticks, although they're technically the UR now. But the bigger problem we have is the environment. With all the vegetation dying, soon the wildlife and livestock will start to die."

I interrupt him. "And then the people starve."

"Right," he says. "Then, we have chaos."

I dab beads of perspiration from my forehead with a napkin. The environmental conditions in this place have been almost perfect, until now. Now I feel warm, too warm. But it probably has more to do with the conversation than with the temperature.

Shawn continues. "Think back to when you talked to your father—I mean, our Phillip Ashdown. Did he say or do anything uncharacteristic of your father?"

I cup my hands over my face and place my elbows on the table. I remember that he called me Pumpkin rather than Peanut. That was odd. But I do not want to let Shawn know that yet. Not until I am convinced that his explanation is correct. And not until I know what he and his people want from me, so I just shake my head. "If the Feds, as you call them, do not want me to help them program a time portal,

< 118 >

what do they want me to do? And what do you and your people want with me?"

When Shawn leans forward, his eyes light up. It seems like these are the questions he wanted me to ask. "They do want you to help them program the sphere, if that's what they told you. Whatever the reason they said, a time portal or whatever, it doesn't matter. Because you're not programming a time portal. You're programming the sphere for their purpose. The Resistance doesn't know what that purpose is yet, but we know the Feds have been working on it for a long time. The details are being kept at the highest level within the Feds." His hand moves, bumping my water bottle. It wobbles but stays upright. Shawn glances at it and then looks back at me. "They needed their Phillip Ashdown to convince you to do it. But they don't care whether you get back home. They don't care if your father does, either—he's in our world, too, but you haven't seen him."

I stare intently at Shawn, not wanting to break his flow of information. I do not know whether to believe him, but at least I am finally getting some answers. I nod so that he will continue.

"Anyway," he says, "whatever the Feds are up to, it isn't good for the Resistance, this world, or you and your father. And we, the Resistance, are trying to stop them." He leans back. "We have pockets all over the world. Ultimately, we'd like to overthrow our government—the Feds. But we know that's unlikely anytime soon. What we really want to do is save our world from dying, which means stopping the wars, stopping the focus on weapons, and stopping the destruction. It also means focusing on sustaining what is left of the environment, building an economy, giving the people hope and a way of life." He leans forward again, grabbing my water bottle and flipping it from hand to hand as he talks. "And our more immediate

< 119 >

concern is to stop the Feds from doing whatever they are up to with the sphere." He looks at my water bottle, sets it down, and then looks at me. "Sorry."

I ignore the water bottle. "Okay, assuming all of this is true, what does your Resistance need with me? I am sorry for all the problems you are dealing with, I really am, but this is not my fight. I just want to find my dad and go home. If home is through another sphere, whether a time portal or another universe, then I am all for helping to program it and going through it with my dad."

Shawn drops his head slightly and lowers his gaze toward the table, toward the notepad where the picture of the girl—of me—had been.

He speaks solemnly. "What does the Resistance need with you?" He looks up to make eye contact with me. "We need you to lead us. To keep us united."

I have no idea what he is talking about. "What? I thought that you are the leader. Or that you have someone leading you."

"We did have someone." He looks back down at the notepad and turns it over. The redheaded, combat-looking version of me is on the screen. "Her."

It instantly clicks. "Your Serenity? She is the leader of the Resistance?"

"She was."

I can tell that he does not want to talk about her. She must have meant more to him than an ordinary leader does, but I have to push him on this. I have to know.

"What happened?"

"She was killed a couple of days ago in a skirmish. It was just a simple mission to recover some documents from the Feds. I was

< 120 >

supposed to lead the team, but I got tied up on some other, unimportant matter. At the time, I didn't think anything of it because it was a low-risk mission with a very low probability of any casualties. But I should have known that she would go if I wasn't able to. They met heavy resistance. Somehow, the Feds knew what we were doing."

Instinctively, I reach out and touch his hand, but he jerks it back. Realizing what I did, I pull my hand back, too. We both look at the table where our hands were, but we say nothing about it. I speak softly. "I am sorry. I can tell that she meant a lot to you. But what are you expecting me to do?"

"The Feds don't know she was killed. She was out in front with Trent Bassani, another member of the team from California HQ. Too far in front, according to the rest of the team. When the rest of the team caught up, they found Serenity critically wounded and Trent gone—captured, we figure. She never regained consciousness to tell us what happened." He shakes his head slowly. "Why would those two have gone out of sight of the team? Anyway, the Feds have a suspicion that she's dead, but no confirmation. And so, there hasn't been an announcement to the world yet. Only the HQ Resistance fighters know. If word spreads through the Resistance and the general population, the Resistance will be finished. Serenity was the Resistance. She is the one everyone follows. She is the sole reason we continue to recruit people. Without her, I fear—we all fear—that we are done."

"And you want me to be her?" I ask.

Shawn nods. "The idea came to us when we heard that you came through the sphere. Otherwise, we would never ask. If we can make you up to look like our Serenity and show the world that you—that she—is not dead, then we may have a chance. And in the process, we can help you get home."

< 121 >

"I am sorry, but even if I wanted to, I am not your Serenity. I do not even know how to hold a gun, let alone shoot one. Or any weapon for that matter. And fight? I study fencing, but only as a hobby. That is not fighting. I very much dislike violence." I shake my head. "No, I am sorry."

"You wouldn't have to shoot or fight or anything. We just need you to look like you can. We would make you look like our Serenity and show you to the rest of the world. That's all."

I shake my head again. "Shawn, I truly am sorry, but even if I believe everything that you are telling me, I do not want to get involved in your world. I simply want to find my dad and go home. Now, where is my dad? Do the Feds have him?"

Shawn reaches across the table as if to take my hands in his, but he does not.

"Yes, the Feds have your father, and they'll use him as leverage to get you back. Like I said, they need you to help them for their purpose. But I think we may be able to use the sphere to get you and your father back home through it." He pauses, looks down at the table, and then looks up at me. "Serenity, I will never make you do anything that you do not want to do. The decision is yours. And if that decision is to get your father back and go home, I personally, and the Resistance, will do everything in our power to help you do that. Just think about it. Please."

< 122 >

CHESS MATCH

As I am leaving the cafeteria with Shawn, we walk by Isaiah playing a game of chess with a rail-thin young man. Isaiah's forehead is wrinkled as he studies the board intently. It must be his move.

The other man looks up as we start to pass. "Hey, boss. President Masterson will be on bright and early tomorrow. It's his national address, as we suspected. I'll have him lit up in ops. I have some prep work I need to discuss with you just as soon as I finish off Isaiah here. Can we meet?"

Before Isaiah can voice his protest, Shawn comments, "I believe Masterson's going to try to put the Resistance in check."

I raise an eyebrow at Shawn.

Shawn looks at me and grins slightly. "Ops is the large screen in the main operations room. The room you first came in."

The man looks at me, and then back at Shawn. "That's what I just said, boss."

Shawn holds out his hand toward me. "Todd, meet Serenity." He moves his hand toward Todd. "Serenity, meet Todd. You'll have to excuse him. He likes military jargon."

Todd stands up. "Wow, you really *do* look just like you. I mean, just like her. Well, but for the hair." He stammers. "Glad to have you on the squad. Now, you'll have to excuse me. The chess king has to finish off his latest opponent."

Isaiah just grunts his disapproval as I take in Todd's full appearance. He is tall and steps clumsily in his large shoes. That—along with his bony arms and shoulders and his long, slender face—makes me think of Goofy.

Shawn turns toward me. "Todd here is not only our anything tech guy but also our resident chess champion. He's never been beaten."

Todd interrupts, smiling. "Make that Resistance chess champion. My chess skills and reputation go far beyond HQ."

I look at Isaiah. His gaze has not left the board. Then, I look at the board. I have never played chess, but I read the rules. Isaiah is two moves from being checkmated.

My mind calculates every possible move and countermove for both Isaiah and Todd. Isaiah still has one shot at winning if he makes every move exactly correct. If Todd is as good as he says, then I know every counter move that he will likely make. I calculate all of this in an instant.

Isaiah finally looks up at me shaking his head. "Got any suggestions?"

< 124 >

Todd chuckles. "She's new here. I don't think you want to put her up against the champion so soon, and especially in a match that you're about to lose."

Isaiah and Shawn both grin and shake their heads.

I want to help out Isaiah. He was so kind to me earlier. I look at him.

"Move your knight back to f-three."

Isaiah does, and Todd, still standing, counters as I anticipated.

I step behind Isaiah. "Now your queen to g-six."

Isaiah makes the move.

Todd looks at me. His smile is completely gone.

He sits down and scoots his chair up to the table. He counters again as I anticipated.

I direct Isaiah for four more moves, and Todd moves in turn.

"Move your bishop to b-three," I say to Isaiah.

Todd stares at the board. "This can't be. How?" He continues to stare at the board until finally making a move.

Good, he made one of the two moves that I thought he would.

I step to the side of the table next to Shawn, who is still watching. "And finally . . ."

Isaiah interrupts me before I can finish. "Queen to h-seven." He moves the queen. "Checkmate." Isaiah stands up, barely cracking a smile, and walks past Todd patting him on the shoulder.

Shawn is now grinning ear to ear.

Todd looks up at me, wide eyed, shaking his head. "So, I take it you are some sort of chess champion in your universe?"

I do not smile. I do not want to gloat at all, but I have to tell him the truth.

"This was my first match, but I read the rules once."

< 125 >

# # # # #

The operations room is packed and noisy with chatter, even more so than when I arrived here yesterday. Standing room only. I always thought Grandpa was the only person crazy over President Masterson. Nobody in my Hancock stops what they are doing to hear a routine presidential address.

I make my way farther in, positioning myself where I can see the large screen that covers the far wall. A few people stare at me. They seem to be sizing me up. I try to just smile and move on. The map on the screen goes dark, then it lights up with a live television feed. I count twenty-two people in the room on the screen. They sit in rows facing President Masterson, who is behind a large desk with his hands folded on the desktop. He looks like the President Masterson that I know, except solid gray hair on this president's head has replaced the light brown hair of the president I know. Two guards stand on each side of the president. They are dressed in green military uniforms and have automatic weapons over their shoulders. That is different. That is not a typical Secret Service look.

I had counted the people in the room with the president. Until then, I had not been counting, calculating, thinking like I usually do. Before I can think through why, the president begins to speak.

"My fellow citizens of the United Republic. I would like to start by saying that this is a great day to be alive. We are about to embark on a journey that will change our nation forever. And not just our nation, but the world. I know you have had to witness much global disaster over the years. But with the combined nations of the United States, the Soviet Union, and China now operating smoothly, we are ushering in a new era of world peace. And your government is working on a

< 126 >

plan that will restore our nation, our planet, to what it once was. You will all benefit from this change. You just need to stay the course for a little while longer. I will remove the heavy burdens that have been placed on you. Everyone will have jobs, resources, and food aplenty!"

The chatter in the room picks up again with sounds of disgust and disbelief. People murmur among themselves.

They finally quiet down when the president continues to speak.

"And now, I need to address those of you who have become known around the world as the Resistance and those who support these criminals. You may not be aware yet, or your people may be hiding this from you, but your leader, Serenity Ashdown, was eliminated by government forces three days ago."

A picture of their Serenity, in full combat gear, poised for action, appears in the upper right corner of the screen.

The president continues. "She was killed by government military personnel who acted in self-defense. She and others in the Resistance were attempting to carry out yet another criminal attack against government property. Our hope for the peace and prosperity of which I just spoke hinges on those of you left in the Resistance laying down your arms and joining me, the United Republic, and the rest of the world in an effort to make life better for all of us. With your leader gone, the Resistance is at an end. So, I implore you to stop fighting and join us in peace. There will be no retribution against you. No punishment. We just ask that you stop your fighting and stop the attacks against government resources. It is a simple request with a huge reward for everyone. Peace." The president pauses. "So in conclusion, people of this great nation, I implore you, do not be discouraged. Your government is working for you. Your lives are about to change as we pass through to a new hope."

< 127 >

My mind races as I listen to the president. "Your lives are about to change as we pass through to a new hope." I have heard similar words elsewhere since I fell through the sphere. When I was in COI headquarters, Mr. Franklin said, "This just might work. We may be able to pass through." I think about all of the individual pieces of research that I did for my dad's work. Mass, energy, and momentum research. My work on quantum-geometry dynamics. The mobile app to connect with the culmination of my dad's work. Then, there is the formula and equation I saw on my dad's laptop at Grandma and Grandpa's house, described as the "calculation of the probability of opening the universal continuum where mass and energy are intrinsic properties of preons and the number of preons needed to be acquired by a composite particle to maintain constant mass and energy regardless of speed." My mind connects the dots instantly.

I know exactly what President Masterson plans to do.

< 128 >

THE PLAN

Minutes later, the ops room is emptied of almost everybody. Isaiah motions for me with a jerk of his head and moves over to make room between Takeo and himself at a long, rectangular table toward one side of the room. Fancy sits across from me, with Shawn at one end of the table and Todd, the skinny techno whiz, at the other. I immediately notice Danica's cold glare.

What did I ever do to her?

I do not recognize the other four who are seated around the table, but Shawn is ready for that. "Serenity, I don't think you've met Max, Horace, Rodney, and Sheila." He motions toward each of them as he says their names. "They're from here in Massachusetts."

Each of them nods and gives me a hello grin. I nod back but do not smile. Shawn's explanation of what happened to me and where I am now has to be correct. The pieces are starting to fit into place. From my research and Mr. Bailey's project in my world, to Mr. Franklin's comments and their President Masterson's speech. I know what President Masterson and the Feds are planning. They are not planning on restoring this planet and its resources. They are planning on taking the resources of my planet. They want to use the sphere to invade my universe.

But I do not know the true intentions of the Resistance. Maybe they want the same thing for themselves on their own terms. I want to tell the Resistance what I know, but I need to know what is at stake for them first. I need to be able to trust them.

Instead of the President's video feed or the map with yellow and red dots, the main screen shows a live feed of groups similar to the group seated here. I presume they are gathered at different headquarters around the world. Each group is shown in a separate section of the screen, with its location captioned at the bottom: London, Moscow, Yemen, California, Chile, Saskatchewan, Sudan, Mumbai, Beijing, Tokyo, Sydney, and Israel.

"I don't have to tell you how urgent everything is right now," Shawn says to those around the table. "Our next move is critical and must happen quickly." He looks into the camera mounted on top of the large screen and presses a button on the remote. Our image pops onto the screen with the caption "Massachusetts." We have just joined the video conference.

"All right," Shawn says still looking into the camera. "Let's get to it. Before we get into the President's speech, I want to report that we still have no word about Trent Bassani. The Feds have not made any

< 130 >

demands for us to get him back, and our contact has not seen him nor heard where they are keeping him or anything." He pauses and turns toward the table. "I'm afraid we have to assume the worst. I know that he's never even been here to Massachusetts HQ, but I believe that all of you have been on Massachusetts-California joint assignments with him at one time or another and knew him pretty well. I'll contact his wife in California, but we don't have the luxury of time to mourn." He moves his gaze back to the screen. "We know the president's speech yesterday was a farce. All propaganda to end the Resistance. We also know that no member of the Resistance will walk away if we turn ourselves in. We will simply disappear." He leans forward, resting his elbows on the table, and looks around at everyone. "But he is correct about one thing. Once people inside and outside of the Resistance are convinced that Serenity is dead, it will be the end of our movement." Shawn pauses, leans back, and looks at the screen again. "And that means there will be no hope of any future life in this universe . . . and no peace. And the UR won't stop fighting until every country has joined it, willingly or not." He slowly turns his focus back to the table, shifts in his seat, and then looks at each person sitting around the table. "And Masterson made the move we all thought he would in order to put us in check. He announced Serenity's death. We have to counter his move quickly or it will be checkmate."

Fancy scoots her chair closer to the table. "We can't keep fooling people much longer. We've been broadcasting that she was injured and is recovering, but people want to see her."

Horace, barely able to reach the table with his hands due to his large frame and huge belly, slaps the table. Beads of perspiration form on his bald head. "The people have to see through him. Everyone's hungry. No jobs, unless you work for the Feds. And the planet is

< 131 >

dying everyplace you look. Masterson can't let things go on like this, with or without a Resistance."

"But what does he care," Danica interrupts, leaning forward. Her face is tight. "That doesn't matter to him. All he really seems to care about right now is getting the sphere programmed."

Finally, something I recognize and something I want to talk about. The sphere.

That involves me and my dad.

Shawn looks at me. "Serenity, I wanted you to meet the core of the Resistance. These are the people the Feds want out of the way in order to end the Resistance. The people around this table, and around the tables you see on the screen, cannot hold the Resistance together without Serenity." He pauses and looks again at each person, stopping at me. "The Resistance isn't a formal organization that a person joins, and it doesn't elect its leadership. It's a cause made up of everyday people from around the world." He clasps his hands and lays them on the table. "Sure, there are people that spend their every moment working for the cause. Those are the Resistance fighters—all the people you see here and in the HQs around the world. But there are also Resistance supporters out there that help in ways we don't even always know about—providing food, clothing, and other resources and support." He pauses again, looks down, and then looks back up at me. "And in every cause, there is one common thread that weaves everyone together, no matter what their role is. In this cause, that thread is Serenity Ashdown." He pauses. "That thread is *you.*"

Everyone is silent—everyone in the room, everyone on the screen.

I break the silence. "I told you before, Shawn, I cannot do it. I cannot be the leader of a cause I barely understand. There must be

< 132 >

somebody, anybody, out there who can rally people to this cause better than me. Besides, it takes more than one person to start a movement, to mount a worldwide resistance. And you have a great team here. You do not need me."

"You're not wrong," Shawn says. "It does take a team. But that team needs a leader. The people need a leader. And not just any leader. One that isn't afraid to stand up to the opposition, to the Feds. One that can rally the team and the people behind her. That was our Serenity. Her fearlessness and optimism were one of the few remaining sources of hope in this fight. There is nobody like her. And even if there were, there isn't enough time to build the people's confidence in a new leader. You heard the president's speech. He's planning something, and it likely involves the sphere."

I look directly at Shawn. "I believe everything you told me earlier, and I want to help. Just not like this. I told you that I am not a fighter. I am not strong. I am an intellect. Maybe I can help in some other way. There must be some way to continue the Resistance and stop the Feds without Serenity Ashdown."

I look around the table and then up at the screen. In each person's face I see both disappointment and a heartfelt understanding. Well, in every face but one.

Danica gives me a wry smile. She continues to look at me while addressing everyone else. "I told you she wouldn't do it. I knew from the second I saw her that she didn't have it in her. She's no Serenity Ashdown. I told you this was all a waste of time. And now, Masterson has us backed into a corner, and we don't even have a plan."

Sheila, an athletic-looking African American woman in her twenties, leans forward. "But we do have a plan. Our original plan before we knew Serenity came through the sphere." She nods toward me.

< 133 >

"Right." Rodney, a short, stocky man with a crew cut, chimes in. "Let's stick to the original plan."

Danica shakes her head. "You all want to explain it to me again? Cause I think we have nothing!"

Shawn nods, a satisfied look on his face. "If it works, it will get Serenity and her father home and destroy the Feds' sphere." Shawn turns toward me. "But in order to get you home, we're going to need your help."

I am reluctant to agree, but they are doing this for me. So, I need to hear them out. "Okay. What do I need to do?"

Takeo smiles at me, showing his white teeth. "Those Feds don't have a chance with you helping us."

Shawn looks at Todd. "Todd, why don't you explain how the sphere works. Once Serenity understands that, she will better understand why we need her and what we need her to do."

Todd straightens up and attempts a commanding facial expression, which fails miserably with his Ichabod Crane appearance. "The universal connection cylinder operates on an algorithmically calculated continuum between the two parallel moving universes until a quantum time overlap is detected and maintained."

Shawn holds up a hand to interrupt him. "In English, Todd—in English."

Todd's eyes dart back and forth. "Oh. Sorry, boss. Of course. Said another way, what you refer to as 'the sphere' is a doorway between the two universes. But the door only opens when and where the two universes connect, which is random. But when they connect, people and objects can pass through to the other universe. There have been situations where the two universes connected, and by luck—or unluckily—someone or something accidentally passed through. For

< 134 >

example, a hot spot in your universe," Todd motions toward me, "is what they call 'the Bermuda Triangle.' Ships have randomly disappeared without a trace. They disappeared from your universe only to end up in ours. Another example is Amelia Earhart." Todd looks at me. "Your people have no idea what happened to her, right?"

I nod.

Todd looks back at the others around the table. "She passed through a connection and lived out her days in this universe." Then he looks at me again. "And vice versa. There really is an unidentified aircraft being held in your Area 51. But it's not a UFO, as your people like to call it. It is one of our aircraft that passed through a connection. Its technology is too advanced for your world to figure out, even though it's very old tech for us. It's the result of this world's obsession with bigger, better, faster weapons."

I stare at Todd, trying to take everything in. Trying to comprehend everything.

"And there have been incidents on both sides where people or things are caught in the connection point as it closes. Those people and things are truly the unlucky ones. They don't make it."

My mind races back to the night of the car crash when I lost my mom. I can still see it like it was yesterday. Could this explain the phenomenon I saw that night? The undulating landscape? The same wavering I saw when looking through the sphere? Our car being crushed by seemingly nothing? I want to know, yet I do not.

I lean toward Todd. "These random connection points. Do they create a distortion in the sky or landscape? A distorted appearance if someone witnesses it?"

"Yes, exactly," Todd says. But without asking how I know that or even missing a beat, he scoots up in his seat and anxiously continues.

< 135 >

"Early on, the government on both sides developed devices to communicate through soft spots along the universal continuum. These spots are more prolific and easier to detect. Unfortunately, it was our government, the Feds, and a government-funded research group at your . . ." He looks at me, then looks away again. "A research group at your Harvard University that discovered the communications. To the knowledge of the Resistance . . ." he glances at me again, "your government is unaware of these communications. A Dirk Bailey in your universe controls the information on that side."

I perk up at the sound of that name. "Yes, Shawn told me about Mr. Bailey's involvement with the Feds."

That explains a lot about Dirk's secretive nature, his treatment of my dad, and why he kept my dad out of the loop. Dirk had used him.

"But how do you know all of this about Dirk Bailey and the people on my side?" I ask.

Todd continues. "Because our Dirk Bailey is with the Resistance and is on the inside."

That explains why he tried to help me—and warn me. And he must not know the Feds' plan to invade my universe. Their Dirk Bailey must not be as high up the chain of command as the Dirk Bailey in my world.

Todd waves his arms. "But getting back to the explanation; in the other universe, only people at Harvard had the resources and knowledge to develop a device that allows physical transport between the two universes. And that knowledge was passed by their Mr. Bailey to our Feds, enabling the Feds to build a sphere. But physical transport can only occur at points of a hard connection, which, as I said, occur randomly in terms of both time and location. Although, as I said, they tend to occur in certain locations more repetitively."

< 136 >

"Like the Bermuda Triangle," I say.

"Precisely," Todd nods. "And in a particular abandoned building in Hancock, New Hampshire."

I look at Todd. "The facility."

"Yes, I believe that is what your side calls it."

More and more, the dots are connecting. Not just the dots since I passed through the sphere, but the dots of my entire life. Starting with my mom's death.

Todd takes a drink from his bottle of water, then continues. "The hot spots for repeated connections are usually close in our universes but not in the exact same location due to slight time differences and other variables. The hottest spot on land in both universes was found to be in Hancock. In your universe, the spot happens to be inside the facility that your Dirk Bailey secured, using Harvard grants, to house his research. Here, the connection point is in the middle of a forest. And the Feds have spared no expense in constructing a well-armed fortress around it. Once the Feds discovered these hot spots, the trick became trying to accurately predict when a connection would occur—or, better yet—forcing a connection." Todd turns toward me. "This is where your father comes in, and now you. Your father developed a software program with a particular algorithm that can do just that—force a connection. He programmed it into the sphere that he and Mr. Bailey built on your side so that he could pass through. We also know that it's not enough for just one side to be programmed. In order to pass through, both spheres must be properly programmed. You can pass through only when both sides' connections are open. Your father, and you, timed it right based on rough calculations and a lucky guess as to when there would be a random open connection on this side. That's why the opening didn't last. We don't know what

< 137 >

exactly the Feds are planning with the sphere. We have some details from our Dirk Bailey, but we haven't been able to put it all together yet. We just know it won't be good."

Listening to Todd, the final piece of the puzzle falls into place. I now know why the Feds need me to program the sphere. Why they cannot do it on their own, or why they cannot do it on their own quickly enough. But before I tell the Resistance what I know, I have to know where they think my dad stands in all of this so I know that I can trust them.

"No." I shake my head. "My dad would not do all of this knowing the consequences. He would not have come over here on his own to program your sphere."

Shawn leans forward. "I know." He pauses. "We all know he would not do that on his own. We are certain that he was lied to and deceived on your side and was coerced into coming through to this side."

"Coerced? How?" I ask.

Shawn looks down and sighs. I am starting to learn when he knows something that he does not want to tell me.

"I can explain that later—privately," Shawn says dodging my question. But at least I got my answer regarding my dad. Shawn's eyes light up as if something just dawned on him. "You said that your father wouldn't do all of this knowing the consequences. What consequences? Like we've been saying, we don't know what the Feds are planning with the sphere."

I sit up straight. "I do."

All eyes turn toward me. I clear my throat and continue. "President Masterson's speech was not a farce. He was not lying when he said that everyone will have jobs, resources, and food."

< 138 >

Sheila interrupts. "But how? At the rate we're going, the planet will be dead soon."

"He wasn't talking about *this* planet. He was talking about mine." The people around the table continue to look at me. Those on the screen start to mutter among themselves and then turn their attention back toward me. "The Feds are planning to invade my world, and with the superior weapons that you say exist over here, they are not going to kindly ask to borrow anything."

It is Danica that interrupts this time, with a smirk. "You don't know that."

I ignore her. "The project that Mr. Bailey in my world has been working on has been to develop the software program that will open a connection on both sides, as Todd said. My dad successfully developed the program, and it worked on my side. Also, as Todd said, my dad passed through, unwillingly I am sure, in order to install the software and program the sphere on this side. Once that is done, the Feds will be able to open the connection whenever they want to and keep it open."

Shawn nods. "Enabling them to pass into your world at will."

"How could you possibly know all of this, Blondie?" Danica blurts out.

I look her in the eyes. "Because I helped."

Danica glares at me again but has no response.

Todd looks at Shawn.

"Boss, that's consistent with the fragments of information that Dirk's been getting. He's not high up enough to be in the loop, but he feeds us what he can find." He turns toward me. "And based on a few pieces of Dirk's information, when Serenity's father passed through the sphere, it wiped his laptop."

< 139 >

"That makes sense," I say. "The same technology that runs the sphere would erase any electronic data that passes through it. So, that is why they now want me to help."

Fancy raises her hand slightly. "Wait, why do they need you? What can you do?"

Shawn nods. "That's a question that I've been asking myself as well."

Todd responds before I can answer. "Don't you get it, boss? It makes perfect sense now that we know the Feds' purpose. They need Serenity's father to recreate the program from memory, from his memory, since his laptop with all the data was erased. That could take years. He would have to develop the software program all over again. And given the state of this planet, they don't have that much time. The Feds want to move into Serenity's universe *now*."

Shawn shakes his head. "Even I figured that much out. But why her?" He glances at me. "What can Serenity do to make that happen any faster?"

I clear my throat rather forcefully. "I am still right here." I pause. "They want me because I can program the sphere."

Shawn looks at me wide-eyed. "From memory?"

I raise an eyebrow and nod.

Shawn leans back in his chair. "The helicopters."

Todd's eyes grow wide. "The chess match."

Isaiah nods at me and grins.

"So, when you passed through the sphere, they hit the lottery," Horace says.

"I guess you could put it that way," I say. "But what I do not understand is how they knew I could program the sphere? And why do they not have my Mr. Bailey just give them the information from the computers connected to my world's sphere?"

< 140 >

Danica turns up her lip in a smug half-smile. "Because they've been watching you practically your whole life. Do you think your Dirk Bailey spent so much time with your father and asked so many questions about your father's family because he cared? I don't think so. They've been watching your family for years."

Shawn interrupts Danica. "And our Dirk Bailey never reported to us much about you. We had no idea. We thought the Feds were only focused on your father."

So, I was not being paranoid.

Those guys really were following me. They probably switched out the trail every now and then so there would be less chance that I noticed.

"As for your other question," Todd says, "since the connection on this side was just random, by chance, rather than the sphere being programmed, it probably closed shortly after you passed through. And when the connection closed, the information would have disappeared from the computers on your side. But if the computers are properly programmed here, the connection will open on both sides because your side's sphere is already programmed . . . unless and until someone changes the programming."

Shawn looks at Todd, puzzled. "You just said that the information disappeared from the computers in Serenity's universe, but that the sphere in her universe is already programmed. Which is it? If the sphere retained the information, then that Dirk Bailey should be able to retrieve it and provide it to the Feds."

This time, I speak before Todd can respond. "It's both, right, Todd?" I look at Todd and then turn toward Shawn. "The information would have disappeared from the screens, but the sphere's mainframe would have retained the programmed data."

< 141 >

"Right," Todd says. "The data will activate the sphere again when this side is activated, either by random chance like when Serenity and her father passed through or when the sphere on this side is programmed and activated." He leans forward. "The data can't be retrieved. The data has to be programmed in again or activated in order for the sphere to create an opening." He pauses and shifts in his chair. "As I said, it takes an opening on both sides of the universal continuum to form a connection point to pass through. Each universe's opening on the universal continuum reacts to the opening in the other universe when and where a connection is made."

Danica stands up and looks me up and down while addressing everyone but me. "So Blondie here could hurt us as easily as she could help us. The Feds are going to stop at nothing to get her to program the sphere for them, which she'll do just to get home. They need her alive. We should get rid of her while we can."

My heart races and a bead of sweat trickles down my back. Isaiah looks at Danica and starts to rise but stops when Danica holds up her hand, palm toward him. "Relax, big guy." She jerks her head toward Shawn. "He isn't going to let anything happen to his Serenity." She plops down into her chair.

Shawn looks at me. "Danica," he looks at Danica and then back toward me, "does not speak for the Resistance. We need you to make an appearance as our Serenity, but if you won't, we will still help you find your father and return home. That's what we're about. But we will need you to help us help you get home. You're going to have to program the Feds' sphere one way or another. It's the only way for you and your father to get back home." He pauses and looks at Todd and then at me again. "But just know that if you don't help us stop the Feds and save our world, you may not have a home to go to."

< 142 >

Shawn's words make my heart race again. Fifty-six stripes on the shirt of one of the men in Chile on the screen. Eighty-seven flowers on a woman's dress in Mumbai.

Someone from the Sudan headquarters addresses nobody in particular. "So, what is the plan to counter the President's speech? What's our next move?"

Shawn looks at the video screen and then around our table.

"We go with the original plan, but first, we locate Serenity's father and get Serenity and him to the sphere so she can program it and return to her universe."

The room is silent. Everyone on the video feed is silent.

I finally speak. "What happens then?"

Again, silence until Isaiah, the man of very few words, speaks. "Then we destroy it . . . sphere, program, everything, and cut off the connection for good."

I roll onto my side and flip the covers back. The air is warm and stale. I am unable to fall asleep. The harder I try, the more that races through my mind and the more awake I become. I look at the clock. 3:00 a.m. I keep replaying in my mind everything that I heard at the meeting. I roll onto my back and stare at the ceiling. I immediately know exactly how many rectangular sections of the dropped ceiling are in my room and how many little holes are in each section.

As much as Danica rubs me the wrong way, she is probably the most honest person in the group. At least she says what is on her mind. No sugarcoating. She probably says what everyone else here is thinking. That I have let them down. Just like I let my mom and Jona

< 143 >

down. These people put their hope in me, and I have disappointed them. But how can I help them? They are just like my dad, expecting too much of me.

I cannot lie here and think anymore. I have to get up and move around. As I make my way to the cafeteria, I see a light at the end of one of the long hallways. It comes from the last room on the left—the laundry room. I might as well check it out and see who else is up at this hour of the night. But given that this seems like some sort of around-the-clock barracks, it would not surprise me if the room was full. I hear the washing machine running as I get closer. I know from the sound that only one machine is running. I step slowly and softly, careful not to make a sound until I see who is in the room. I peer around the edge of the open door. Like in all the rooms, the lights in the laundry room are a bright white. The tension immediately leaves me when I see Isaiah. I stand for a few minutes watching him as he sits, facing the washing machine, his back to me, reading something on his computer notepad.

His face buried in his notepad, he does not turn even the slightest. "Can't sleep?" Isaiah asks.

I grin even though he is not looking. "You do your own laundry?"

He turns his head and looks at me. "What's the matter? Never seen a six-foot-five black man carrying an automatic weapon and ammo belt doing laundry?" Then he grins.

I feel a little bad, like I insulted him. But I know he is not upset. "No, that's not what I meant. I mean, I thought you would have people down here to do it for you guys." I probably just made the insult worse.

He chuckles. "There are no other people. Everyone down here has a job to do that furthers the Resistance. We even take turns in the

< 144 >

kitchen. All the other personal necessities of day-to-day life, we each handle on our own. We aren't the UR military."

I change the subject. That might be my only way out of the verbal conundrum that I am in.

"Can I ask what you are reading? Or is it confidential?"

Isaiah holds out the notepad. "*The Lion, the Witch and the Wardrobe*. The Narnia books are my favorite reads. I've read them each a dozen times at least. Helps take my mind off of things."

I walk toward him and take the notepad. Sure enough, that is what it is. I have read the series a couple times myself. I like the books as well. But I had not taken Isaiah for a reader. Particularly *The Lion, the Witch and the Wardrobe*. The moment I met him, I stereotyped him as a gun-slinging brute. And here he is doing laundry and reading a classic novel. I can't help thinking about Shawn. Even now. I want to trust him. I want him to be on my side. But I cannot let my guard down. Shawn might be using me just as easily as he could be helping me. Why do my thoughts keep coming back to Shawn anyway? All he sees when looking at me is their Serenity and what I can do for the Resistance as her. At least I have Isaiah's friendship.

"Do you have any family? A wife? Kids?" I ask.

Isaiah gets up immediately and walks to the washing machine. He looks inside as if checking to see if it is still running. The noise alone says that it is. He glances at me and then turns his head back toward the machine. The blank look on his face shows that I struck a sore spot. But I did not mean to do so.

"I am sorry," I say. "I did not mean to pry."

Isaiah, still looking at the washing machine, slowly shakes his head. "No, that's fine. We seem to know so much about you. It's only fair that you learn something about us."

< 145 >

Isaiah puts both of his hands on the washing machine and turns his head to look at me. "I had a family." His voice cracks and his eyes tear up.

I stand silent, attentive, listening.

He continues. "A leak in our gas stove, ignited by a candle, the fire inspector said. Blew up the entire house. But I did my own inspection. I found explosives. There was no gas leak. The Feds did it." He turns back to the washing machine, puts his full weight on his arms, and hangs his head. "It was meant for me. Either to kill me or send me a message."

"But why?" I ask.

Isaiah keeps his head down. "The Resistance was new. I had just joined, and the Feds knew it. The Resistance didn't have bunkers like this. We had no real protection. We were easy pickings. I wasn't the only one. There were others who lost everything. That's when we started the underground network."

My eyes start to water and a lump forms in my throat. I think about what Mr. Johnson said about my Grandma and Grandpa in this world. They were killed by the Feds in the same way and for the same reasons, for being their Serenity's grandparents. I feel awful for Isaiah and awful that I made him relive it.

"I am sorry."

He stands and slams his fist on the washing machine. It jolts.

"I should have been there! I should have died instead of them!"

I want to go over to him, comfort him. But I hardly know him. And he seems to be angry more than anything else right now.

"It was not your fault," I say. "You could not have known."

I am starting to understand more about how things work in this world, but it raises more questions as well.

< 146 >

"So, the government over here kills its own citizens?"

Isaiah walks over to a chair and sits down again. "Yes, those in power will do anything to protect that power and survive. The military, well . . . they just follow orders. They have been told—and each one of them truly believes—that the Resistance is trying to overthrow the government just for its own power. A civil war of sorts."

I believe everything Isaiah tells me. His emotion makes him so believable.

And if everything he says is true, then everything Shawn said about Serenity Ashdown, *his* Serenity, is true, too.

I step toward Isaiah. "You said that they will do anything to survive. Do you think that I am right—that they really will move into my world and do the same things to people there that they have done to you here?"

Isaiah stands, looks into my eyes, and nods. "That's why we need to end all of this here and now. That's the only way to protect your world."

"I have to ask this. Why does the Resistance care about my world? Why would the Resistance not want our resources and a fresh planet to live on as well?"

Isaiah takes a deep breath. "We care about your world and want to protect it because that's the right thing to do. The Feds will destroy it like they have this world. And if we are going to stop the Feds and retake this world, we can't let them gain a foothold in your world. That will make them too powerful. They won't simply leave this world behind. They will want to control both. That's why we need to keep the Resistance together."

I look up at him. "And you think that I can keep the Resistance together?"

< 147 >

Isaiah nods his head and looks away. "Shawn thinks so. And there are a lot of others who think so. They believe in you. But that's a lot to put on one person. I don't blame you in the least for saying no."

"Do you believe I can?"

Isaiah turns toward me. "I believe that you are a lot stronger than you think you are. And from what I have seen of you, I believe that you can do just about anything if you put your mind to it. To lead the Resistance and stop the federal government, you're the only person who has to believe you can do it."

< 148 >

THE RESCUE

I am awakened by a knock at the door, and Fancy walks in, red hair glistening.

"Can I talk to you for a minute?" she asks.

"Sure," I reply. I sit up and scoot to the edge of the bed. "Where is everybody? I walked around earlier but could not find anyone . . . Isaiah, Takeo, Todd, Shawn."

Fancy pulls out the chair from the nightstand and sits down across from me. "That's what I want to talk to you about. Shawn didn't want anybody to tell you until they had left on the mission."

"Mission?" I ask. "What mission?"

Fancy hesitates. "It's about your mother."

"You mean the other Serenity's mother?"

Fancy reaches out and takes my hand. "No, the other Serenity's mother and brother in this world really are deceased, and so are her grandparents. But your mother, your real mother from your world, is alive. She's been in this world ever since the car crash. In fact, that crash is how she got here."

My heart races, and my palms become sweaty. I jerk my hand from Fancy's. This cannot be true. Yet another lie told in this world. The Feds lie, the Resistance lies. Everyone lies to get what they want. Is there nobody I can trust?

I shake my head. "No, that is not possible. I saw her die. I saw the car explode."

"Did you?" Fancy asks. "Did you really see her as she died? Did anyone see a body? Even in explosions and fires, there is some remnant of a body. Your car got caught in a random connection point like Todd described the other day. Your mother was knocked out of the car and into our universe just before the car exploded. That's why there was no body. She never died."

Considering everything I have learned about the two universes, this makes sense. I am starting to believe her—but no, I do not want to.

I do not want to believe, learn that it is not true, and lose my mom all over again.

I stand and start to pace. "If this is true, how come Shawn or Isaiah or anybody else never said anything before?"

Fancy turns in her chair toward me. "Because it would have been too much for you. Look how hard it has been to convince you of the truth about the parallel universe and the motivations of the Feds. Throwing this news in right away would have sent you over the edge.

< 150 >

You would not have believed a thing. It was Shawn's call, and he wanted to give information to you slowly. It was the right call."

I turn away, face the wall, and run my fingers through my hair. I am angry at Shawn, and at the entire Resistance, for not telling me. I am frightened by everything that I am learning and everything I still have not learned. And I am excited that my mom may still be alive. That I might be able to talk to her again. I do not know what to say or think.

I turn back toward Fancy. "Where is she?"

Fancy looks down at the floor and then back at me. "Well, that's the thing. The Resistance was just in its infancy when your mother passed through, so the Feds got to her first. They have had her ever since. We believe she is the leverage they are using against your father to help them build the spheres. And it was working for them until their timetable got pushed forward due to the state of our planet. Now, they need you."

So, that is why my dad kept the details of the project to himself. He did not want me to find this out and have me get hurt all over again.

I sit down on the bed again. "So, what is this mission? Why are you telling me this now?"

Fancy leans forward. "This mission is to recover your mother and your father for you and to secure the sphere site so you can all get home."

I shake my head. "For me? Why would they do all of this, risk their lives, for me?"

Fancy takes my hand again. "Because it's the right thing to do. These are good people. The Resistance was formed not only to stop the Feds but also to aid those that can't help themselves. And helping you get home puts the Resistance one step closer to achieving the first goal, and it helps you and your family."

< 151 >

I hang my head. Nobody outside my family has ever done anything like this for me. And certainly, nobody has been willing to risk their life for me.

Fancy continues. "Serenity, everything you have been told since you have been with the Resistance is the absolute truth. We have no reason to lie to you."

I nod. "I know."

Fancy and I sit for a moment. We do not speak until the silence is broken by the sound of boots running outside my door.

Then comes the shouting. "Hurry, hurry! They're coming in!"

My eyes connect with Fancy's. We both know this means Shawn and the others have returned from the mission.

"Mom," I say. I burst out of my room ahead of Fancy and race down the hall toward the ops room. That is where the elevator will bring everybody down, including my mom and dad.

"Get the Doc!" someone yells.

Another voice shouts, "Quick! Out of my way! Get a security detail out there in case they've been followed."

"Where's Doc Sam?" I hear as I enter the ops room. "There are multiple casualties. Bring the stretchers!"

The room is full of people, both those returning from the mission and those who stayed behind. It looks like total chaos, but I know that it is not. I can tell they have been through this before.

Through the crowd, I see men and women being supported by their comrades on either side. Some have bloodied wraps around their heads, others have a leg they cannot walk on, their pant legs shredded and soaked in blood. Still others have to be carried and laid on stretchers. Are they even alive? It looks like something out of a war movie.

< 152 >

I see Isaiah. Then Takeo and Danica exit the elevator. They are sweaty and dirty, but they look uninjured. But there is no sign of Shawn. The elevator closes and goes back up.

Danica has a snarl on her face as Takeo talks to her. "I saw you kill fifteen Feds at least, on your own. Why are you so upset?"

Danica slams her gun on one of the tables. "It wasn't enough!"

"Here. Hold this," an older man demands, handing me an IV bag. "No, hold it up high." He pulls my arm into the air. I look down at the bloody, battered person on the stretcher. The older man sticks the IV needle into the person's arm. The sleeve has already been torn off. The older man shouts, "Sam, better get to this one quickly. He's in bad shape."

A short girl, probably in her teens, takes the bag from me. She wears a blue nurse uniform. A couple of boys, also in their teens, wheel the stretcher out of the room.

I turn toward the elevator, and I come face to face with another man. He has a big gash down his cheek, and there is dried blood on his face. I step back quickly. It is Horace. I move backward until the elevator opens again. Someone shouts, "This is the last load!"

More injured, bloodied bodies emerge. I cannot believe the carnage. And all to help my mom, my dad, and me.

I see Shawn and run to him. "Shawn!" He does not appear to have any visible injuries. His expressionless face is caked with dried sweat and dirt. "My mom and dad. Did you get them?"

His face remains unchanged. No emotion whatsoever. Something bad has happened. He was not able to rescue them.

"I am sorry, Serenity. We did everything we could." Shawn looks down and shakes his head. "They have fortified the site with AI weapons, and your father wasn't where he was supposed to be. Everything was messed up. Dirk's intelligence was all wrong."

< 153 >

My anxiety makes me talk quickly. "And my mom. What about her? Fancy told me everything."

Shawn shakes his head again and looks up at me. "I am so sorry." He turns his head and nods toward a stretcher behind him.

I look and my heart races. No, no. I run to the stretcher. Doc Sam is already working on her, inserting an IV. She moves her arm slightly. The blood-soaked wraps around her abdomen appear blurry through my tears. I look past the cuts on her face, smeared with dirt and blood. She is my mom. Despite all the years since I have seen her, I know without a doubt that this is Mom lying here, broken and suffering. I look into her eyes, my mom's eyes. Eyes that shed tears of pain for me when I was hurt and tears of joy when I was happy. My heart aches for her.

I hear Isaiah's voice. "They shot her, Shawn. We had her out safely, and when they knew it, they shot her just so we couldn't have her. I saw the man take aim."

"Mom!" I shout through the sobs. "Mom." I kneel beside the stretcher, take her hand in mine, and put my face next to hers.

She tilts her head slightly toward me and gasps for air. "Serenity," she says softly and then gasps again. Her lips turn up in a soft smile. She talks slowly. "My Serenity. Let me look at you. You are so beautiful. I have missed you so much."

Tears from my watering eyes drip onto my mom's face, and my throat tightens. I can barely get any words out. "Oh, Mom. I have missed you, too. I love you. Please do not go. Please do not leave me. I cannot lose you again."

She reaches up and touches my hair, stroking it like she used to when she brushed it for me. She gasps again. "It'll be okay, Serenity. These are good people. They will get you and your father home."

"But Mom, you have to go with us. You have to go home, too."

< 154 >

She cups my face in her hands, looks into my eyes, and takes a deep breath.

"I love you so much." She pauses, lowers her hands, and gasps for another deep breath. Her voice is soft. She says, "Tell your father and Jona that I love them."

Her head rolls away, her eyes look to the ceiling, and her breathing stops.

I lay my head on her chest and sob. "No, no."

I hear nothing but my own sobs. I am removed from the chaos around me, as if my mom and I are alone in the room and time is standing still. My fear has been realized. I got my mom back only to lose her again. Because of my mental so-called gift, I could not save her eight years ago, and despite my mental gift, I cannot save her now. It hurts so much. Seconds feel like minutes. Minutes feel like hours. Then my senses start to return. I hear the noise around me and feel a hand gently touch my shoulder.

I hear Isaiah's words again: *They shot her just so we couldn't have her.*

My sadness turns to anger. This confirms what I already knew. The Feds lied to me. The Feds took my dad. The Feds *killed* my mom. And they want to take over my world. I have never really been angry at anyone, and I have certainly never hated anyone. But as I kneel beside my mom, holding her hand, her life drained by the Feds, the anger burns inside me. I hate the Feds.

I lift my head, look up, and turn toward Shawn.

"I will be your Serenity. Tell me what you need me to do."

< 155 >

THE MAKEOVER

hawn is quiet as we enter the ops room together, walking toward Todd who sits behind a computer in the corner with his back to us. I thought me agreeing to be their Serenity is what he wanted, but he has hardly said a word to me since I said I would do it. His expression is full of both fear and anxiety. I guess I understand. My emotions ran wild when Fancy told me my mom was still alive. I am certain that Shawn has similar feelings about seeing his Serenity again. But I am *not* his Serenity. I am only going to look and act like her.

I look straight ahead as I talk. "Fancy said that Todd will walk me through everything I need to know about this world's Serenity. Is that right?"

Shawn does not answer until we reach Todd. "What did you say?" He pauses. "Oh, yes. Todd will tell you everything you need to know."

Todd remains seated but turns around. "Hey, boss, Serenity. Good timing. I'm all set."

I stand behind Todd and look at the computer. A picture of their Serenity appears on the screen. I still cannot believe how identical we look, especially in the face. All except the red hair and dark complexion. It does not seem real. It is like I am looking at one of those programs that manipulate a computerized image of yourself and change different features to see how you would look. Shawn stands beside me. His eyes are fixed on the screen. His face has no expression. He just stares, not saying a word.

"Okay," Todd says. "Are you ready, Serenity?"

At the sound of Todd's voice, Shawn shakes his head. "I have to go," he says as he turns and quickly walks away.

I take a seat next to Todd in front of the paper-thin monitor. He pulls up a file on their Serenity. I read where she was born, what she did growing up, where she went to school, where she took her weapons training. I stop reading. Weapons training? That is not going to be easy to pull off. I will have to cross that bridge later. I keep my eyes on the monitor, reading.

"He loved her, didn't he?" I ask.

I glance at Todd. His eyes grow large, and he pulls his head away from the monitor. He looks at me. "What? Who? Who loves whom?" he stammers.

I continue to read and talk at the same time. "Shawn. He was in love with your Serenity. I can tell by the way he looks at her picture."

Todd pulls his hands off the keyboard, folds them, and looks down. He adjusts his position in his chair, puts his hands back on the

< 157 >

keyboard, looks around the room, and then glances at me. "Um . . . well . . . I wouldn't know. I think . . . well . . . I mean . . . I try to stay out of things like that. You know. I just work here."

I look at him and smile.

Todd is a genius with computers and technology but not so much with the social game. But then, that is not unlike me.

"Well, they probably did not let you in on their Snapchat conversations," I say.

Todd gives me a puzzled look. "Snap what?"

"Snapchat. You know. You can get the app on your cell phone."

He stares at me. "What is a Snapchat? And an app? Is that what you said?"

"Okay, you are the technology wizard. Do you not have Snapchat or Facebook or Instagram in your universe? Twitter? Any social media?"

"Did you say Twitter?" Todd shakes his head. "Never heard of any of that."

I pull out my cell phone and turn it on. The apps light up. "I have seen people talking on cell phones. Mine, of course, has no service here. And the battery is almost dead anyway."

He takes my phone as his eyes widen. "This is your cell phone?" He pulls his flip phone from his pocket. "This is the latest in our cell phone technology."

"I guess you guys do focus all your research on weapons. Maybe my world could teach you a thing or two."

Todd smiles ear to ear. I think I struck his geek chord.

His eyes stay fixed on my phone. "Can I have your phone to dissect it? I could reverse engineer the technology and move our culture ahead light years."

< 158 >

I wrinkle my forehead. "There is probably some universal law against interfering with the natural advancement of a society." Then I smile.

Todd looks at me and grins. "Yeah, the prime directive." He pauses. "We do have *Star Trek*."

I take my phone back. "I still might need this."

I turn back to the computer and return to reading the files, memorizing each bit of information.

"She had military training," I say.

"Yeah," says Todd. "She was a UR Marine before joining the Resistance."

"A Marine? But she is my age, right?"

Todd nods. "With all the wars in this universe, the governments start training their soldiers and sending them into combat at a much younger age than I'm sure they do in your universe."

"It says here that she has a couple of blemishes on her record for unruly behavior and failure to follow orders. That does not sound like me."

Todd looks at me. "Personality-wise, she wasn't anything like you. I mean that as a compliment to you. She was quite rebellious, and her sarcasm, *wow*. That came out no matter who she was talking to, even the opposition. Almost got her shot on more than one occasion."

I continue to read. My eyes dart back and forth across the screen, faster and faster as I focus more and more.

"Faster," I say to Todd.

"What?" he replies.

"Here, let me do it." I pull the keyboard from underneath his hands and start advancing the screens myself. I click faster and faster

< 159 >

with each screen. I glance at Todd as he turns toward me with a puzzled look on his face.

"You're flipping through these pretty fast," he says. "But I guess you don't need to know anything about her childhood. I mean, who's ever going to care where you were born or where you grew up or what your favorite food or color is?"

I keep my gaze focused on the monitor, reading the current file. "She was born in Grand Rapids, Michigan. Moved to Chicago when she was five because her father, an engineer, was transferred there with his job. She later moved with her family to Boston at the age of ten when her father took a job with COI. That's where she grew up and graduated from high school. Her favorite food was oysters. Her favorite color, purple."

Todd sits back and stares at me, his mouth open, a blank look on his face. "How? What? How do you?" He shakes his head. "Oh, that's right. Like with chess, you read the rules, once."

# # # # #

I sit on the edge of Ma's bed, staring at the blank concrete wall behind the nightstand as Ma works on my hair. She has turned the little mirror around so I can't see myself. Her room is the same as mine. Concrete walls surrounding a bed and a few essentials. Nothing more. Ma has a picture of their Serenity open on the computer notepad that sits on the nightstand.

I touch my face. The bruises are all gone, and Doctor Sam gave me a clean bill of health earlier in the day. I feel fine, physically. But I still have trouble believing that all of this is true, that all of this is really happening. A whole other world that I have been in for seven

< 160 >

days. Duplicate people. My mom was alive, and my dad and I are here. What can he possibly be thinking right now? Does he know where he is and what happened with my mom's escape attempt? What have the Feds told him? Does he know that I am here with him? There is so much to think about. But it keeps my mind from wandering, from counting, from torturing me.

And then there is Shawn. He wants to help everyone . . . the Resistance, this world, me, my world. But is he changing me so I can help, or is he changing me so he can have her back? Whatever the reason, my thoughts keep coming back to Shawn. He is so aggravating. And I have to keep a clear head. Now, more than ever, I need my wits about me if I am going to pull this off and get my dad and me home. Now, I actually need this mental burden I have carried my whole life. The ability to calculate, hear, notice every detail, think, remember everything. Here, in this world, I am going to need that detailed memory.

Ma pulls my hair tight and breaks my train of thought. I have not seen myself in the mirror yet, and I wonder what two hours in the shower room made me look like. Ma dyed my hair, supposedly dark red, and covered me with some sort of tanning solution. She wouldn't let me see. She told me I probably would not like the look, so there was no use agonizing over it until she finished.

Can Ma really make me look like the image on the computer notepad? I look down at the dyed red hair, which falls to the floor as Ma continues to work her scissors. I think of my long blonde hair, how my mom used to brush it when I was little. How my mom used to tell me what a pretty girl I was with my blonde hair and blue eyes. Then, my mind goes back to my mom stroking my hair while she was on the stretcher. What would my mom think of me now? Transforming myself into someone else. Some soldier woman.

< 161 >

Someone taps on the door, and there is a high-pitched voice in the hall.

"Is everyone decent?"

Ma shouts, "Come on in, Charles."

I turn my head slightly toward the door. In bounces a young, thin African American man with curly black hair. He looks completely out of place in this military-style compound with his red-and-yellow checkered shirt and leather pants. The bright light reflects off his silver earrings. I have to force myself not to laugh.

"Serenity, this is Charles," Ma says sharply as she continues working on my hair. "Charles, meet Serenity."

"It's a pleasure to finally meet you, Miss Ashdown," Charles says in the same high-pitched voice. "I've heard so much about you. I've been wanting so much to meet you. I think it's wonderful what you're doing for our cause."

"Nice to meet you too, sir," I reply. Ma presses against my head, forcing me to look forward.

"Miss Ashdown," Charles says. "You can call me Charles. I'm here for you. Whatever you need, just let me know."

"Do you have the rest of the stuff?" Ma asks, her face inches from mine, making her final snips with the scissors. "I'm almost finished with her hair. Then you can do your thing."

Oh, great, I think. *What could his "thing" be?* The short red hair and tan should be enough.

"Sure thing, Ma," Charles says. "I have the tattoo and contacts right here."

Ma turns me toward her and steps back. She tilts her head side to side, looks at the photo on the computer, then looks back at me. "Good. I think that's it. That's the look."

< 162 >

What look? It is killing me not to see myself in a mirror.

"Charles here will put a chain tattoo around your arm like our Serenity had," Ma says. "That's the only distinguishing mark she had. And whenever you go out as her, put in the contacts. We have several pairs. They have no prescription and will look clear to you, but they will color your eyes like hers—Wilson green."

"May I start now, Miss Ashdown?" Charles moves closer to me.

I am not sure. I have no desire to have my arm tattooed.

"Um, well . . . I guess so," I say.

I feel odd having Charles call me "Miss Ashdown," but I am too preoccupied with everything they are doing to say anything.

"Oh, don't worry, Miss Ashdown," Charles says, rolling up my left sleeve to expose my bicep. "This isn't permanent. It'll last for a few weeks, give or take a day or two, depending on how much you perspire and how often you shower. We'll reapply it after that. And it won't hurt a bit."

Reapply it after a few weeks?

How long do they expect me to be their Serenity? I plan on making a public appearance for the Resistance, getting my dad, and being home within a few weeks. But I need not say that to Charles and Ma.

"Okay, great," I say.

"I'll leave you two for a minute," Ma says. "When Charles is finished, you can change into the outfit in the closet. It's a full bodysuit. The suit looks the same as the one our Serenity used to wear a lot, except, this one has been modified to give you some added protection. It will deflect conventional bullets. Not plasma, so stay clear of plasma weapons. And it is fireproof, with a little fireproof hood you can pull out of the collar if you unzip it. I figure we'll stick with the

< 163 >

long sleeve, long pants outfits to cover up the difference in muscle tone between our Serenity and you."

I laugh to myself and make a mental note to hit the gym after all of this is over with.

"Why the tattoo then, if I am always going to wear long sleeves?" I ask.

"It's a just-in-case," Ma says with a slight smile. "You never know when someone's going to want more confirmatory evidence."

# # # # #

After Charles finishes the tattoo and teaches me how to put in the contact lenses, he leaves so I can change. Slipping into the black, tight-fitting, full bodysuit makes me wish again that I had worked out, at least a little. It pokes and squeezes me everywhere. I wiggle and squirm until I get into it, and then I zip it up. The zipper goes all the way up the collar, which wraps around my neck. I jerk my head back and forth and pull at the collar with my finger to loosen its grip on my throat.

Now, I have even more incentive to finish this whole thing quickly. I will not be able to survive if I have to put this suit on too many times.

Another knock on the door. It is Ma's voice. "Can we come in?"

I do not know who "we" is, but I am dressed, so I reply, "Yes, come in."

Ma and Shawn step through the door. I turn to face them.

"So, what do you think?" I ask.

Ma clasps her hands together. "Perfect!" She walks to the night-stand and turns the mirror around.

< 164 >

I turn toward it. I cannot believe what I am looking at; *who* I am looking at. I look exactly like the pictures of their Serenity. Exactly. I just stand there, trying to find my old self somewhere in the person looking back at me. But I cannot.

I turn toward Shawn. He stares at me. He has not moved or spoken since he and Ma walked in. His face looks shocked, and I can see the pain in his eyes. He reaches out and gently touches my face. He is looking at the woman he loves—she is alive and real again. What did I expect? I feel a slight ache in my chest. Why? I try to ignore it, to not let it matter to me. But it does matter. I fear I am jealous of their Serenity. If Shawn loves their Serenity, how can he ever truly care for me? But that should not matter. I do not care for him in that way—I cannot. He is not even part of my world.

Ma breaks the silence. "Shawn, what do you think?"

Shawn's eyes start to water. He looks at the floor and then looks again at me. His eyes penetrate deep into mine. Then he turns and quickly leaves the room.

< 165 >

TACTICAL TRAINING

have not been in this corridor, so I follow Isaiah and Takeo. The tactical vest is heavy and rubs my shoulders through the sweat suit Ma gave me.

"Where did you say we are going?" I ask.

Takeo smiles and says something in his heavy Japanese accent.

I look at Isaiah, raising an eyebrow. I could not understand Takeo.

"We call it the gymnasium," Isaiah says. "For lack of a better term."

"That's what I said," Takeo says. "Gymnasium."

I grin at Takeo.

Isaiah pushes the double doors open and flips several light switches. The bright lights reveal a huge room, much larger than the ops room. The ceilings are tall like a gymnasium, but it is set up more like a training facility. We enter on one end.

"This way," Takeo says.

We walk past various workout areas and an obstacle course with a floor-to-ceiling rock climbing wall at one end. I feel the cushioned floor as we cross a sparring area and enter a shooting range at the far end of the room.

I look at Isaiah. "Who built all of this, and why?"

"The whole complex was built as a safe house by several local governments during the Third World War and was used again during the Fourth."

My eyes open wide. "You have had four World Wars?"

Isaiah nods. "All of this was funded by the US federal government before the UR with funds they thought were going toward weapons research. The US government never knew it existed. And the Feds still don't. This room is designed to withstand an antimatter bomb."

I look at Isaiah again with a raised eyebrow.

"Fifty times more destructive than your nuclear bombs," he says.

Takeo interrupts. "Enough talk. Time for weapons training."

I turn to Takeo. "I thought I did not have to use any weapons."

"Use? No," he replies. "But you have to look like you know how to use them."

Takeo walks over to the wall and pulls down a large automatic machine gun, similar to the one he carried earlier, and hands it to me. As he lets go, the weight of it immediately causes the gun's stock to slip through my hands and clank on the floor. I manage to hang on to the barrel as it spins around to face Takeo.

Takeo jumps out of the way, shouting, "Look out! Careful!"

Isaiah grins and does not move at all.

< 167 >

Then he takes the gun and hands me a smaller one that he has pulled from the wall. A submachine gun with a retractable stock. I am able to hold it with the stock retracted, making it shorter, but the weight of it makes me feel awkward. I know that I am hunched over and probably could not aim it even if I wanted to.

The awkward feeling is verified when I see Takeo shaking his head.

"Zettai damé," Takeo says. "Maybe a pistol?"

Isaiah takes the gun. He extends the stock to its full length, holds the barrel in one hand and the stock in the other, raises his knee, and, in one swift stroke, slams the stock against his knee, snapping off the retractable extension. The blank expression on his face never changes. There is not even a slight grimace.

He hands the gun back to me. "Lighter now."

It does feel lighter, and I do not feel as awkward holding it.

I put in the earplugs Takeo hands me, and he points me toward the targets on the far wall. He positions the gun correctly against my shoulder. "Hold it like that. Aim through here." He points to the sight. "With the dot on the target. Flip off the safety." He points to the safety. "And squeeze the trigger."

That seems easy enough. I do everything exactly as he said. I take careful aim, closing my left eye and barely keeping my right eye open, then grimace in anticipation of the noise and pull the trigger. The gun pops, and I feel a sharp pain in my right shoulder. The kick of the gun pushes me backward. I try to catch myself but am unable to. I stumble and fall backward onto the floor.

Takeo runs to me. "Are you okay? Are you okay?"

I slowly nod. Everything seems to be in place and working, except for the pain in my shoulder.

< 168 >

Isaiah walks over, does not say a word, and holds out his hand. I grab it, and he pulls me up.

I rub my right shoulder. "I am sorry. I have never fired a gun before." I shake my head. "This is not going to work, is it?"

"It takes time," Isaiah says.

"Time is the one thing we do not have," I say.

"Let's try something different," Takeo says. "Hand-to-hand combat. Our Serenity was very good at that. Especially knives and swords." He starts walking to the sparring area. "Follow me."

On the wall in that area are various knives, swords, hatchets, ninja stars, and just about anything else that can be used to cut someone.

Takeo takes down two swords and rubs one of the blades across his arm. Nothing happens.

"Practice swords," he says. "They're blunt. Won't cut or stab."

He hands one to me, and I examine it. I give it a few awkward strokes. It is not what I am used to for fencing. It is thicker and heavier, but it is not unlike my fencing sabre.

"Have you used a sword before?" Takeo asks.

"I have done some fencing in a club at Harvard," I say.

"Hold it like this." Takeo places my hands in the proper positions on the hilt. "Stand like this." He demonstrates the proper stance and proceeds to scoot my feet apart with his. "Better."

He takes up his sword and takes the fencing en garde stance. "You ready?"

I nod.

He comes at me, slowly spinning his sword, then moves it side to side. I intently watch his every move with the sword, his every step. He slowly strikes. I raise my sword and block as I retreat. He strikes again. Again, I block and retreat. He speeds up his advance and

< 169 >

strikes. Two more strikes and he stops short of what would have been a fatal blow to my neck.

"You have to move the sword faster so it looks real," Takeo says.

I glance at Isaiah standing off to the side of the mat. His arms are folded, watching intently, no expression on his face.

I nod toward Takeo.

He advances again, this time at a faster pace right from the start. I retreat intentionally to observe his moves, and I block when I can in order to see his counters. I know he has much more in his repertoire, but if I can learn his basic instincts, that may be enough.

Again, the duel ends with what would have been a fatal stab to my abdomen.

"You need to try harder," Takeo says.

"Okay," I say. "Ready."

He advances quickly, wielding his sword in a circular motion, striking much more quickly. I am able to block a couple of strikes until he spins his sword in a roundhouse motion with the tip against my hilt. He flips my sword out of my hands and stops with the tip of his own sword against my throat. Even though it is blunt, I freeze.

Takeo shakes his head, lowers his sword, and looks down. "It's no use. I don't know any weapon you can look good with. I don't know how we can convince the people you are our Serenity." He turns toward Isaiah. "We better talk to Shawn."

"Wait," I say. "One more time."

I know I have all of Takeo's basic techniques down, and even a couple of his more advanced moves.

Takeo shakes his head. "No, it's no use."

I tense up. A little bit of anger swells inside me. I want one more chance.

< 170 >

"One more time," I say again. I look to Isaiah, still standing at attention, expressionless. "Please," I plead.

Isaiah stares intently into my eyes without saying a word. Then, still looking at me, he speaks in his normal deep tone. "Go again, Takeo."

Takeo shakes his head but raises his sword to the ready position. I do the same. He comes at me hard and fast. He looks determined. Probably determined to finish me quickly and prove he is right. He swings repeatedly and quickly. Right, left, right, left. I block each blow. He is setting up for the slice to my throat. I recall each and every move. But this time, when he goes in for the kill, I am ready and block his sword, thrusting it upward. I know what his counter will be. A fake to the head, and then the abdomen stab that he finished me with the second time. I anticipate and block the thrust downward.

Takeo steps back. His eyes are wide, and his face is tight. He comes again, circling and spinning his sword. He is going for my hilt again. I am able to time it perfectly. As he goes for my hilt with the tip of his sword, I pull my sword back, catching the tip of his on the back of my blade. I twist in the opposite direction. He is not ready for that, and the force of the change in direction yanks his sword from his hand.

I immediately step forward, putting the tip of my sword against his throat. He stands motionless, beads of perspiration running down his face.

"You're a fast learner," he says. "I'm sorry. I underestimated you."

I lower my sword. The anger I felt while kneeling by my mom's lifeless body returns in full. "They have my dad, and they killed my mom. I will not go down easily."

I glance at Isaiah. He grins.

< 171 >

"Nice job," I hear from across the gymnasium. I turn and see Shawn standing there.

"How long have you been here?" I ask.

He grins. "Long enough to see you take out Takeo."

< 172 >

SHAWN

I have to carry my dinner tray in my left hand. Any use of my right hand causes pain to shoot through my shoulder, which still aches from the kick of the gun earlier today. I look around the cafeteria for a place to sit. My eyes catch Shawn sitting by himself in the back corner. He motions for me to come, so I do.

"Have a seat," Shawn says.

I set my tray on the table across from him and sit down. I pick up a piece of fried chicken and take a bite.

"How do you like the chicken?" he says.

I shrug, then wince. I had forgotten about my sore shoulder. "It is not like my grandma's."

Shawn nods and smiles. "Hey, I want to apologize for the way I acted in Ma's room. You know, when I first saw you looking like . . ." He stops for a moment. "You know, looking like . . ."

I interrupt him. "Like her. Your Serenity."

He nods. "I'm sorry. It's just that . . . well . . . I never got to say goodbye. She was here one minute and gone the next. And then seeing you looking exactly like her . . . well . . ."

I interrupt him again. "It is okay. Apology accepted. I understand. She must have meant a lot to you."

"I guess you could say that." Shawn uses his fork to stir the food that is left on his plate, a few lima beans.

I want to apologize too, for being jealous of their Serenity. But Shawn does not even know that.

I take another bite of chicken and a drink of water. "You lost someone really close to you," I say. "You have a right to be upset."

"That's no excuse. Everybody down here has lost somebody close, including you. That's a big reason that we all are here. Why we all are doing this. But what really bothers me is not knowing what happened. I mean, I know the Feds killed her, but she never would have become detached from the team on her own. I don't know why she did that. And I should have been there. It was supposed to be me."

I set down my chicken. Maybe if I change the subject, it will get his mind off of it. "Do you have any family?" The question comes out before I really think about it. I immediately wish that I had not asked, after what happened with Isaiah. After he had to explain his loss to me.

"I lost my parents when I was five. Not due to the government, though. My grandmother raised me and my two older brothers. She passed a couple years ago. Natural causes."

< 174 >

"Your brothers, are they around?"

"My oldest brother was killed in the latest war, fighting for the Feds. The other one was one of the original Resistance members, but the Feds took him out. We didn't have the underground system back then. That's when I joined the Resistance. When they killed him. So, to answer your original question, no, I don't have any living family."

"I am sorry," I say.

He shakes his head. "Don't be. Like I said, everybody down here, and in the safe houses around the globe, has a story like that."

I take a bite of lima beans. "I cannot imagine living like you all live. Constant war and fighting, mistrust, corruption, few jobs."

"Yeah, it's just war after war. One country rises to power, only to be taken out by the next. And then they get taken out by the next. And so on. Then throw into the mix a world war every now and then. It's all about who can build the bigger gun, the stronger bomb, the more lethal chemical, or biological weapon. That's where all the resources go. That's where all the jobs are. And you have seen what the fallout of all of that is doing to the planet."

"Is the atmosphere like this everywhere?" I ask. "I mean, is the planet dying in other countries too?"

Shawn sets down his fork and leans back. "Yes, for the most part. It's worse in most places."

I wonder what he means by "for the most part," but before I can ask, Shawn continues.

"But enough about this world," Shawn says. "Tell me about you. I know a lot about your Earth from the reports we get. Based on the reports of your weapons, they are way behind ours, so your people must not spend every last resource on weapons development. What's it like in your world?"

< 175 >

I take a drink of water and lean forward, my forearms resting on the table. "Well, we have our share of war, fighting, and crime, but no, most countries have a balance between what resources are spent on defense, as we call it, and what resources are spent on trying to make life better. There is still a big disparity between the wealthiest people and the poorest, and the wealthiest countries and the poorest. But for the most part, every person and every country tries to help out every other person and country. The vast majority of the people are generally good. We still complain. But after seeing your world, we should be quite thankful."

Shawn nods. "So, what about you? If you don't have to worry about war and fighting, what do people do? What do you do with your time? Do you have a job or what?"

I chuckle. "I am a bad example of what people do. I pretty much spend all of my time studying. I will graduate from Harvard this spring. Well, I will if I ever get back to my classes."

"Harvard! Wow, that's impressive, assuming your Harvard is as highly regarded as ours."

My face heats up. Compliments embarrass me. I take a drink of water and try not to think about it.

"Wait." Shawn quickly moves close to the table and leans forward. "You are the same age as our Serenity was, eighteen. And you're graduating from Harvard? What are you studying to be?"

I wondered how long it would take him to figure that out. And I was afraid he would. Now, the questions go deeper. I need to answer and then shift the topic away from myself.

"I am double majoring in nuclear medical technology and chemical engineering. I want to do advanced technological medical research."

< 176 >

Shawn shakes his head slowly and smiles. "I read the few reports there were about you, but I had no idea you were that smart. And now, I've seen it first-hand."

I frown. "They have reports about me?"

Shawn must have noticed my frown. "I'm sorry. That had to sound terrible. Like we have been studying you or something. I meant it as a compliment."

"It did kind of sound like I have been some sort of specimen."

He holds up his hand. "No, no. Dirk just passed on the information the Feds obtained on you when they were watching your family. We were focused on your father. We weren't studying you or anything like that. I mean . . . well . . . you know what I mean. Don't you? I'm just making things worse, aren't I? I'm terrible at casual conversation."

I lean back in my chair and grin. "It is okay. Yes, I know what you mean. I am not good with conversation either, especially when it is about myself. And I thought I was being watched. I saw different men following me." I pause. "Shawn, why do you do it?"

Shawn's eyebrows narrow. "Do what?"

"How do you stay so positive? I know you do not like the Feds, but with the constant fighting, seeing your friends and loved ones dying, watching your planet die, why do you fight the Feds so hard for your universe?"

He smiles. "Can I show you something tomorrow? Actually, two things. Something in town, Manchester. And something on the coast. It'll help answer your question."

I would love the chance to get out of this underground city.

Get some fresh air.

See the sun.

And of course, I would love to *see* an answer to my question.

< 177 >

"You mean that we can leave this place without being on some sort of mission?"

Shawn smiles. "Yes. How do you think we shop for everything we have down here? Or . . . I shouldn't use the term 'shop.' Resistance supporters on the outside pretty much provide everything we need. We just have to go to the stores and shops to get it. But we have to be very discrete about it so we aren't seen coming or going and to protect the supporters on the outside. You never know who might be a Fed sympathizer or even where the Feds might have someone undercover. We go out in groups of no more than three so that we don't attract attention. And each group tries to leave and return at about the same time so that we aren't constantly coming and going. But we have it easier than most HQs. Our entrance is in a remote location. Some HQs are in the heart of a city. Our biggest issue here is transportation to town. We can't just leave a car parked outside."

I stretch my arms and wince. I forgot again. "Yes, I would love to go. Oh, and I keep meaning to ask you. The man who was following me not long after I passed through the sphere—he is not with the Feds, is he? He is with the Resistance, right? He always had on a Carhartt jacket and black beanie."

Shawn nods. "Yeah. That's Diego. Diego Sanchez. You haven't met him. He's with the Resistance, but he doesn't live underground. He stays up top and performs a lot of surveillance for us."

I hear footsteps.

When I look up, I see Fancy and Todd walking toward us. Their heads are down, and they look dejected.

"Boss," Todd says. "Did you hear?"

Shawn turns toward them. "Hear what?"

Todd and Fancy look at each other.

< 178 >

Fancy shakes her head. "The UR found London HQ. It's gone. They destroyed every square inch of it."

Shawn looks at Fancy and then at Todd, as if Todd might give him different information. Better information.

Todd lowers his head. "There were no survivors. Dirk says General Chen was the one who carried it out."

I lower my head and close my eyes. My heart is broken. Those poor people. All they have known is war. And now war has taken the life from every one of them. And their families. There are children living down here. Whole families. London had to be the same. How sad. How ruthless is the UR? How ruthless are the Feds?

< 179 >

WHY WE DO THIS

slip on a black hooded sweatshirt that I got from the supply room and grab my sunglasses, also from supply. Shawn said we need to cover up as much as possible. As I leave my room, I stop and look in the little mirror on my nightstand. I still do not recognize the person looking back at me. The tan, the green eyes, the short red hair.

I meet Shawn at the elevator. He wears a collared jacket and baseball cap pulled low on his forehead. We ride the elevator up and are careful to make sure nobody is around before we exit the shed and hurry across the grassy field to a thicket of dying trees. In the thicket is a moss-covered wooden building about the size of the elevator shed. Shawn opens the door. Inside is nothing but two dirt bikes.

"This is our transportation?" I ask. "I have never ridden any type of motorcycle before."

"No worries," he says. "I'll drive." He pulls one out and climbs on. "Hop on. Sorry, we have no helmets."

I climb on and we take off. The cold wind stings my face, and my hood blows back. I want to pull it back on and secure it, but I am too afraid to release my grip from around Shawn's waist, so I bury my face in his back.

The drive to Manchester seems especially long in the biting cold. When we reach the outskirts of town, we park at a small store. The faded sign beside the door reads, "Calvin's."

"I need to pick up a few things," Shawn says. "The owner here is a Resistance supporter."

"The owner is Calvin?" I ask.

"No, Nadia. I have no idea who Calvin is, or was." He laughs.

Shawn pulls his cap low, and I pull my hood up and put my sunglasses on, even though it is cloudy.

The store is small but packed with anything you need—groceries, automotive supplies, hardware, toys. Just about everything except clothes.

Every bit of space is utilized.

Shawn points to some small stuffed animals. "Grab six or seven of those." He then picks up some bags of candy.

"These are going to help us against the Feds?" I ask.

"No, they're for where we are going. What I want you to see."

"Okay. If you say so."

Shawn walks down every aisle and looks around every corner, then walks up to the counter. A Lebanese woman stands behind it.

She smiles. "It's okay, Shawn. We're clear."

< 181 >

"Good," Shawn says. He lays the candy on the counter, takes the stuffed animals from me, and then lays them down, too. "I scrounged up some cash, but I may be a little short to cover these."

She smiles again. "You're heading over to see the kids?"

"Yeah."

"You owe nothing Shawn."

Shawn nods. "Thanks."

"Just make us safe, please." She leans around and looks past Shawn toward me. She squints. Then she looks at Shawn. "Is that . . . is that Serenity?"

Shawn nods again.

I remove the sunglasses and step forward. Clearly, Shawn is not trying to hide me from her.

The woman puts her hand on her chest, looks at me, and sighs. "Oh, bless you. You *are* alive. I am Nadia. I don't believe you have ever been in here. We've been hearing rumors, and then when we watched the president's speech the other day, we thought for sure you were dead." She looks at Shawn. "People around here are losing hope. They think she's gone."

"I know. We're going to fix that. Very soon."

The door swings open, and an older gentleman enters the store. I quickly put my glasses back on, and Shawn pulls his cap down. Nadia bags the items, and we leave without saying another word.

I stretch my legs a little and then climb on the bike behind Shawn.

"Well, you passed the looks test," Shawn says.

"Is that what you wanted me to see? People recognizing me as your Serenity?"

Shawn turns around and grins. "No, that was an added bonus to the trip."

< 182 >

He starts the bike, and we go farther into town. The farther we go, the more run-down the houses and buildings look. This seems like that area in every town where you do not want to live. That you want to avoid. We finally stop in front of a building that resembles a medical clinic. There is a medical cross on the door, but the sign is partially broken off.

What is left of it is covered with graffiti.

I hesitate to get off the bike.

"Come on," Shawn says. "Keep the glasses on in case there are any strangers in here."

There are five mothers in the waiting room, each with two or three children. Some kids sit on the stained carpet floor, and others sit in their mothers' laps. Still, others look very sick. They sit or lay in chairs, coughing and sneezing.

We walk past the waiting patients, and Shawn raises his cap slightly to the receptionist.

She nods and says, "They're waiting. You can go on back."

We exit the waiting room through a side door.

"Why are we at a clinic?" I ask.

We walk down a long hallway, lined on both sides with small rooms, each containing two beds that sit side by side. The sheets and covers on all of the beds are rumpled, but the beds are empty.

Shawn looks at me. "This is much more than a clinic. This is a children's hospital. It's all the hospital that these people can afford. And it's overflowing. And this is just a small hospital in a small town. Every town and city in the world has these, all packed with kids. Kids that are dying. The atmospheric contamination that's killing the vegetation is also killing the children. So far, adults aren't affected. The children in the few families fortunate enough to be able to afford a

< 183 >

real hospital are able to get proper treatment. They aren't cured, but at least they aren't dying. But for everyone else, this is it."

I cannot believe it. All of these rooms, all of the kids that must use them. And the suffering looks on the faces of the children in the waiting room. This is horrible. This nightmare keeps getting worse and worse. Why did Shawn bring me here?

"These rooms are all empty," I say. "Where are the kids?"

"You'll see."

We reach the end of the hall. Shawn opens a closet door and pulls out a large bag full of stuffed animals.

"We've been stocking up on these," he says, smiling. "You can only carry so many on a dirt bike."

We proceed through the double doors at the end of the hall and enter a large room where a group of children sits in the center, all as sick-looking as those in the waiting room. Adults, presumably the children's parents, as well as nurses and doctors line the walls. The children and parents wear faded, ragged clothes.

The children's eyes light up when they notice the bags of stuffed animals. A nurse in a blue uniform approaches us. She does not use any names. She simply smiles and says, "Thanks for coming. They're all yours."

We walk to the center of the room and sit on the floor. The kids quickly huddle around us. They still look ill, but now they show some excitement. Not excitement like a child on Christmas morning— these kids are too sick to feel that excited. It is more like the simple excitement of a bright moment in their day.

I fill each eager, open hand with a stuffed animal, and Shawn does the same with the candy. There is enough for every child to get both. As sad as their condition looks, it makes me feel good to see the

< 184 >

twinkle in their cloudy eyes and a slight sparkle on their pale cheeks. We clearly have made their day and probably their week and month. Maybe even their year. But my heart aches for these children and their families. And it is like this all over the world? These are very poor families in a poor community, likely with little hope of improvement.

When I start to stand, a boy throws his arms around my neck. "Don't go." His hand catches my sunglasses and pulls them over the back of my head. His hand and the glasses catch on my hood and pull it back, completely exposing my face and hair.

One of the parents stands. "Serenity Ashdown," he says calmly and quietly.

One by one, the other parents, nurses, and doctors stand and nod. They all stare at me. None of them are smiling or excited. They are reverent. Like when you stand and look at the flag for the national anthem. I do not understand. I do not want such attention. I do not like such attention. It is completely silent in the room. Even the children are quiet.

A woman breaks the silence. "We thought you were dead."

A man says, "You're alive. There is still hope." A tear runs down his cheek.

I stand and look around the room at the parents. They all stand, as if in awe, still staring at me. Shawn places his hand on my arm and leads me toward the door. First the children, then the adults step aside so we can leave. The room is silent as we exit.

We walk down the hallway toward the waiting room. Shawn looks at me.

"You asked why we are at a clinic. I wanted you to see firsthand, in its simplest form, what we are fighting for. What *you* are fighting for. Not to convince you to join us. I wanted you to make that decision

< 185 >

on your own first, which you did. There are a lot of reasons the Resistance exists, a lot of reasons we fight. But perhaps the most important reason of all is that we fight for our future, for the lives of our children. If our world does not change—and change quickly—our children will die. All of them. We need to get them the proper medicine and food, and clean air to breathe. None of that will happen as long as the UR controls the world." He steps in front of me, stops walking, and turns to face me. "Serenity, do you now see how important you are to making that happen?" He points down the hall toward the room we just exited. "These people had lost hope until they saw you. There are millions of people all over the world just like them. Without hope, they are finished. And without them, the Resistance is finished. You are the key."

I do not respond. I do not know what to say. I want to help, but I do not know if I have the strength.

# # # # #

I do not notice the cold as much on the ride back toward HQ. The sun is starting to peek out from behind the clouds. My mind is still on those children. We are taking a different route back, one that I do not recognize, at least not in this universe. But Shawn did say he had two things to show me. We must be heading to the second.

The landscape flattens as we approach the coast. We have not passed a house for miles. The paved road turns to gravel and then to dirt. Dust clouds my vision. I want to spit the dust out of my mouth, but spitting into the wind is a bad idea. As we leave the last of the trees in the landscape, Shawn turns the dirt bike off the dirt road. I look behind us. The tires leave a line in the soft grass, snaking around the

< 186 >

rocks. We are high above the ocean on a rocky cliff. I can see water all the way to the horizon as we ride parallel with the coast. I cannot hear the waves crashing against the rocks below over the roar of the dirt bike's engine, but I can feel a light salt mist in the air. It is refreshing after tasting dust for the last ten minutes.

Shawn turns the bike sharply toward the cliff and shouts over the engine.

"Hang on!"

I feel my heart pounding in my chest. I tighten my grip around Shawn's waist. We are heading straight for the cliff. Has Shawn lost it? Is he going to jump us off the cliff? This is a rocky coast, but whether we land on rocks or in the water, the eight-hundred-foot drop will kill us. Should I jump off? I might break a couple bones, but at least I should survive. We are thirty yards from the cliff going at least fifty-five miles per hour.

Surely, Shawn has a plan. I have to ride it out. I am too afraid to jump off the bike anyway. I look over Shawn's shoulder, my eyes tearing up in the wind, which is cold and bites my cheeks. Ten yards away. We continue straight toward the drop off. I close my eyes and bury my face into the back of Shawn's jacket. I cannot watch. My stomach churns as I anticipate the weightlessness of the free fall toward the rock-lined shore below. The anticipation is awful, but the weightlessness never comes. Suddenly, my face smashes harder into Shawn's back. My entire body lurches forward against Shawn. I look up over his shoulder again. We are going down. But not falling. We are driving down a steep incline. Very steep. It has to be at least a forty percent grade. The cliff is rising higher and higher on each side of us. The path we are on is a narrow opening cut into the cliff, just wide enough for the bike.

< 187 >

My insides jar as we bounce over rocks and crevasses. Shawn has slowed down significantly, but the steep downward grade pulls at us. I can see green at the bottom. Bright green, not the blue ocean that I expected. I can no longer see the ocean at all. Everywhere I look, the green is surrounded by the steep rock cliffs. We are driving into a giant hole in the rock. There is nothing like this in my Massachusetts, at least nothing I have ever seen. While the path down is narrow, the opening we are riding toward is huge. As we near the bottom, I see that the green is grass. Beautifully green like in the springtime in my universe. It is a giant meadow with palm trees around the edges next to the rock cliffs, which form a perfect circle around the meadow. I estimate that it is at least a mile across the meadow to the trees and cliffs on the other side.

As the bike levels off, Shawn drives us between a few palm trees and out into the meadow past the shadow of the cliffs, into the sunlight. He slows to a stop and kills the engine. My heart is still racing. I take deep breaths trying to calm my nerves.

Shawn steps off the bike and smiles. My shock must be written all over my face. He raises an eyebrow. "You okay?"

I nod slowly and take one more deep breath. "I believe so. My heart is definitely still beating." I grin. "That was a bigger thrill than the Kingda Ka roller coaster at Six Flags."

Shawn's forehead wrinkles. "What's Six Flags?"

I smile wider and shake my head. "Never mind. I forgot that you do not have theme parks in your universe." I pause and look around. "What is this place? It is beautiful."

Shawn looks around as well. "It's one of the few remaining spots on the planet unaffected by all of the pollution. We're well below sea level even though we're right beside the sea." He turns and points

< 188 >

high up toward the cliffs on the opposite side of the meadow. "The ocean is clear up there."

I look to where he points. "Wow, that drop was even further than I thought."

I pull off my hoodie, spread my arms, and tilt my head back, exposing as much of my body to the warm sunlight as possible. The warmth of the sun feels so good.

I lower my arms and look at Shawn. "Of course. Being so far below sea level keeps it warm."

Shawn nods. "Yep, but never too warm. It's between seventy and eighty here year-round. Even when it's snowing up there," he nods toward the top of the cliffs, "the warm air turns the snow into rain down here." He looks at me. "And the vertical cliffs encircling the area cause the rising warm air to move upward constantly in a reverse whirlpool motion."

I nod. "Sort of like a tornado."

Shawn smiles. "Exactly. And that prevents any of the pollution, chemicals, and everything else emitted up there from coming down here."

I turn my head toward the trees. "How did all the palm trees get here?"

Shawn grins. "I have no idea."

I sit down on the soft grass, rubbing the palms of my hands over it. A slight breeze moves the tips of the grass. "You said that this is one of the few remaining places that is not dying. So, there are other places like this?"

Shawn takes off his jacket and lays down beside me on his side, leaning on his elbow. "None in the former US. But I've heard there are a few places around the world. I've never seen any. And very few

< 189 >

people outside the Resistance know of this place. We just stumbled upon it. You can't see it from the ground or water, and from the air, it just looks like another coastal cavern filled with water because it's so deep."

I lay on my back, folding my hands behind my head for a pillow. I let my pale skin soak up the sun. I just want to bask in the warmth. Here, alone, with Shawn, in a green meadow that reminds me of home, I feel safe, comfortable, and I do not count or calculate. But my mind wanders back to the kids we just saw. I think how they are missing their childhood. Missing playing in a meadow like this. I am sure this is too small a space to aid in any capacity.

I roll onto my side and face Shawn, leaning on my elbow like him. We are only a foot apart, face to face.

I smile. "Thank you for bringing me here. I love it. It reminds me of the countryside back home in my world." My smile grows. "Minus the palm trees."

Shawn's expression fades into nothingness. "This is why I do it."

My smile leaves. I stare at him and tilt my head. He has answered my question from yesterday, twice. First with the children and now this place. He has shown me the answer.

"I do it for the kids we saw, for kids like that around the world. And I do it for this." He motions all around us with his arm. "I want to see this world look like this again."

I stare deep into his eyes. I have never known anyone like him. Nobody with such passion. It is not a passion to fight or a passion to kill, but a passion to save. A passion to pursue what he believes in. I feel Shawn's eyes penetrating mine. Our heads move closer together. I feel a tingle up my spin. I have never had such feelings before. I want to kiss him. Does he want to kiss me? And if he does, is it me he

< 190 >

wants to kiss or his Serenity? I start to move my head closer when a hawk screeches overhead. We both look up, then at each other. Shawn shakes his head as if coming out of a trance. I want to prolong the moment. I do not want to leave, but Shawn is standing up.

He looks across the meadow, now completely covered in shade. "We better get back to HQ."

I know he is right. I know we need to go. We can never be together in that way. We are from different worlds.

< 191 >

20

PUBLIC APPEARANCE

saiah helps me into the back of the white unmarked van parked outside the HQ shed. It is all I can do to step high enough to get into the van while wearing this full bodysuit.

"You ready?" Takeo asks.

"I do not think I will ever be ready," I say. "But we have to do this."

This is to be my first broadcasted public appearance. Hopefully, it will convince everyone their Serenity is still alive.

Takeo hands me a small automatic weapon. "We found a small one for you with a short stock. And the clip is empty to make it lighter. So, you won't be able to shoot."

I nod. "Thanks."

An empty clip is fine. I probably could not hit anything even if I had ammo. Or, more likely, I would hit one of my own.

The van starts to move. Shawn drives, and Rodney, Isaiah, Horace, Sheila, Takeo, and I sit on short benches along the sides. Fancy is in front with Shawn. I believe Danica is driving the other van, which is loaded with more Resistance fighters.

Takeo reaches underneath the bench and pulls out a sheath. He hands it to me. "Here, this is for you."

I take it, grab the hilt, and pull out a shiny sabre.

"In case you get into trouble. I know you know how to use it. We found it just for you. It's solid like a full sword but smaller and lighter, like a sabre."

It feels good in my hand. Light, yet sturdy. But I have only used any type of sword or sabre in a controlled bout. Never have I fought someone who was trying to harm me, or even worse, kill me. Do I really want this sabre? I do not think I could use it in a real fight. Then, I think about what the Feds did to Isaiah's family, to Serenity's grandparents, and to my mom. The Feds killed my mom just so the Resistance could not rescue her. Having a weapon handy might be a good idea, so I decide to take it. I put it back in the sheath, and Isaiah helps me strap it on my back.

I turn to Isaiah. "Thanks." I know I have a worried expression on my face . . . because I *am* worried.

Isaiah nods. "It'll be okay. Stick close to me."

I know there is supposed to be no opposition where we are going, but I keep thinking of Shawn's warning to Isaiah and me last night. He said he had kept the information within the circle of people going on the mission. Nobody else at HQ except Todd, and nobody in any other HQ worldwide, knows where or when we are going. But Shawn

< 193 >

said we should still stay alert. The Feds seem to know our every move, from the ambush that killed their Serenity to the location of the Hancock safe house. The Feds must have a mole within the Resistance. That makes sense. After all, the Resistance's Dirk Bailey has infiltrated the Feds.

Even though we have kept knowledge of the mission within a small circle, I worry that the Feds still know what we are doing. The mole could be within the circle.

By the feel of our speed and the length of time we have traveled, I know we are now reaching the outskirts of Manchester. We are on the same route that Shawn and I took on the dirt bike. Our target building is in the middle of town. I pull out my computer notepad, open the diagram of the target building, and once again go over the plan in my mind. I do not really need to see it on the notepad. I can picture it just as clearly in my mind. But it gives me a sense of security seeing it on my pad, knowing everyone else sees the same thing on theirs. I run through the plan again. Team one, in the other van, will approach the target building from the south, the rear, and enter. Team two, in our van, is to secure the front but will not enter the building until we are certain it is clear. According to intelligence reports, the building is unprotected, but if there is any opposition, it should be against team one, so I am supposed to be safe.

Supposed to be safe.

It is too quiet in the van. I try to strike up a conversation to relieve my tension.

"Why is this building our target?" I ask.

"It's a Fed outpost where they gather information on us, the Resistance, trying to locate our HQ," Sheila says. "They know it's nearby."

< 194 >

"Why is it not protected if it is a Fed outpost?" I ask.

Horace responds in his deep voice. "They don't want to draw attention to it. It's disguised as an office building, with a travel agency and a shipping company, I believe. They don't know that we know about it."

"But what if our intelligence is wrong?" I ask. "We will have attacked innocent businesses." My body wobbles as the van bounces over a few potholes.

Rodney leans forward, his helmet completely covering his crew-cut. "We aren't wrong. Diego conducted the surveillance, and I gathered the intelligence myself. But even if we are, it won't matter. We aren't going in, guns ablazing. Nobody will get hurt, and we'll figure it out soon enough."

Shawn yells back at us over his shoulder. "We have a last-minute pickup to make that I think you'll all like. Trent contacted me this morning. He's out. He didn't have time to explain how. He just needed transportation to HQ so he can contact his HQ. I didn't have time to explain to him anything about Serenity, but I explained about the target we're going to hit. I told him to get to the route, and we'll grab him on the way."

"He's going to be in for a real surprise when he sees Serenity." Sheila laughs, and everyone in the back of the van nods and smiles.

The van stops and there's a knock on the back doors. Rodney opens them and holds his hand out to a husky Italian-looking man with long, dark hair. He hops in, and the van continues.

"Trent!" everyone says almost at once. There are hugs and pats on the back all around and even kisses on cheeks from Trent. Even Isaiah gives him a solid hug, although Trent stops short of kissing him. They have truly found a lost comrade. As Isaiah sits down, Trent's

< 195 >

eyes catch me for the first time. He freezes and stares. Not a glaring stare but an I-just-saw-a-ghost stare.

He shakes his head. "You . . . you're still alive?"

"Don't worry, Trent," Horace says. "We'll explain later."

Something about the way he is looking at me does not feel right. I am not sure whether to embrace him as the other Serenity would, explain who I really am, or just sit here. As I think about my response, my eyes are drawn to his military green socks. The same socks that all members of the Fed military wear. I have not seen any other Resistance member wearing them. He is also very clean.

Too clean for a prisoner.

But maybe the Feds treat their prisoners very nicely. Showers and clean socks!

Before I can say anything, the van stops. Shawn turns around. "This is it. Showtime! It's o-nine-hundred on the dot. We enter at 9:10. Team one should have everything secure by then."

Shawn looks at me. "Remember, Serenity, Fancy has the camera, so stay near her. This is going to be a live feed. Dirk has arranged for Todd to cut into every television station live at exactly 9:15. Whatever is on Fancy's camera will stream directly to Todd at HQ and then live to the world." Shawn looks around the back of the van. "Everyone, look sharp. Remember, the sole objective here is for the rest of the Resistance, and the world, to see that Serenity is alive and the Resistance is intact. And remember, complete radio silence. We don't have any frequencies jammed, and the Feds monitor everything. As soon as we talk, they'll know we are here."

"Wait," Trent says. "I was able to grab some updated intel after you told me what you are hitting. They recently armed this place. Not heavily, but there'll be a little resistance. I would send this team in as

< 196 >

well, just to be safe. I have been watching the area since I got to town, so I can take the front perimeter."

"Good thing you caught up to us then," Shawn says. "Okay then. Trent has the perimeter. The rest of us will go in." He looks at Isaiah and me. "But Isaiah, you and Serenity hang back behind us a bit. Close enough to be on camera but far enough just in case."

"On camera?" Trent asks.

"No time to explain," Shawn says. "We have to go—now!"

My stomach churns, and my palms sweat with nervousness.

I whisper, "Stay calm, Serenity. Focus. You do not have to do anything except be videotaped." Fifty-six rounds in the submachinegun belt slung over Takeo's shoulder. Six hundred seventy-two holes in the corrugated plywood sheet leaning against the van's inside wall, behind the opposite bench. "Stop it, Serenity," I whisper to myself. "Focus."

The double doors at the rear of the van open, and Shawn and Fancy are waiting.

I lean to the right and see the target building across the street. The street itself is empty. Nobody in sight. That's odd for any downtown on a weekday morning. I look at the businesses on either side of the street. They are empty. Nobody inside. And most are dark. Shawn takes my hand as I step out of the back of the van. I look at the rest of the team. They all glance at their notepads or scan the target.

I whisper to Isaiah, "It seems quiet."

Isaiah nods slowly and answers as he surveys the landscape. "Yeah, too quiet. It doesn't feel right."

"Fancy, roll the camera," Shawn says. "Keep it on Serenity and the building." He turns toward Trent. "Trent, you find a good observation point against one of those buildings." He points toward the east end of the street.

< 197 >

I take up my empty gun. Fancy puts the camera on me and then on the building as she walks forward with the rest of the team. They start to cross the street toward the target. Isaiah and I hang back by the van.

"We'll start across once they reach the curb on the other side," Isaiah says.

Something about Trent is not right. I feel it. I know it in my mind. What is it? Something about him seems too . . . *familiar*. I start replaying in my mind everything that has happened since I passed through the sphere. Mr. Johnson, where my house should have been, the Carhartt man, Mr. Bailey's house, the ride to the Marriott, leaving the Marriott for COI. Wait, the Marriott lobby—all of those people. Two hundred fifty-seven of them. Fourteen Italians. I saw each of their faces. One by one, I scan the room again in my mind. There! There he is. In the corner, near the edge of the counter, Trent talks to one of the military guards and points as if he is giving directions. That is it! He is with the Feds.

He must be the mole.

That explains why he was not shot with Serenity and why she disengaged from the rest of the team. He set her up.

Then he had to either get shot himself or be captured. Anything else would have drawn suspicion from the Resistance. It explains everything else, too. He probably told the Feds about the Hancock safe house. He would have been there, as they would have launched the joint assignment from there. But he could not warn them about the Resistance's ambush plan to get me because he was out of play then. And that is why Mr. Bailey knew nothing about Trent's whereabouts after Trent was supposedly captured. Trent probably avoided Dirk then and any other time he was with the Feds, which means the Feds

< 198 >

know Dirk is with the Resistance. That's why Dirk had bad information when the Resistance attempted to rescue my mom and dad—another mission when Trent was out of play. Even with Trent as a mole, the Feds have not taken out Massachusetts HQ. But that makes sense because Trent has never been there. He does not know where it is. The Feds would know where California HQ is, but taking it out could blow Trent's cover, and his intelligence on Massachusetts HQ movements is probably more valuable since the sphere is here. It all fits together.

I whirl toward Isaiah. "Isaiah, Trent is with the Feds."

Isaiah gives me a puzzled look. "What?"

"I saw him not long after I came through the sphere, when he was supposedly captured. He was giving orders to a guard. He was no prisoner. I do not have time to go into the details, but it explains everything that has been going wrong for the Resistance since I came through the sphere."

He looks at me. "Are you sure?"

I lower my chin and raise an eyebrow.

"Right," he says. He looks at me with his normal, expressionless face, and then he looks at the building. He looks at me again and then at the others who have just reached the other side of the street in front of the building.

"Stop!" Isaiah shouts.

The group stops. They all turn and look around. Even I know that they are sitting ducks if something is wrong. They are in a low position, in a wide-open space.

Isaiah ignores Shawn's last directive by pulling out his radio, turning it on, and breaking the silence. "Team one, this is team two. We need confirmation that everything is clear."

< 199 >

Danica's scolding voice comes through the radio. "Team two, what are you doing? We are to have radio silence. Get off the com!"

Isaiah replies, "A slight change in plans. Is your team safe?"

"Yes," comes Danica's response. "They are in. I have the perimeter. But they report that nobody is inside. The place is empty."

"Get them out!" Isaiah shouts into the radio. "It's a trap!"

He raises his hand toward the rest of the team and frantically motions them back. "Get back here!"

As the last word leaves his mouth, I am deafened by the sound and concussion of an explosion. The glass shatters. It blows out of the front door and the windows on every floor of the target building, followed by bright orange flames. I lose my balance and fall backward near the front of the van. I look, and Isaiah lies beside me, shaking his head.

Flames and smoke continue to bellow out of every window and door. Everything is spinning. I feel like I am in slow motion. I look toward the rest of the team. They were blown back into the middle of the street, but they are all moving, at least a little. My hearing starts to return with the faint sound of vehicles coming down the street from the east. I focus in on them. There are two. Humvees. I force air into my lungs with two deep breaths and shout toward the team in the street, "The Feds are coming!"

A hand takes hold of my arm, and I look up. Trent is trying to help me up. I yank my arm away from him.

Isaiah motions Trent toward the team in the street. "Go help them! Get them off the street!"

Trent gives me a puzzled look and runs into the street toward the others.

Isaiah and I make our way to our feet. My head finally stops spinning, and I get my bearings. The sound of the vehicles grows louder.

< 200 >

Two green Humvees roll toward us, quickly. One pulls up about a hundred yards away. Three troops in military fatigues hop out. They start firing their odd shiny guns, which have unusually large barrels. Some sort of energy blast blows chunks of asphalt from the road and into the air in between where Isaiah and I stand beside the van and the rest of the team.

"What are those?" I ask Isaiah.

"Plasma rifles! The Feds' primary weapon. We can't afford them. They always have us outgunned."

Isaiah puts his hand on my shoulder and pushes me to the ground beside the van.

The plasma blasts do not come close enough to injure the rest of the team, but with each blast, they are forced toward the buildings on the other side of the street, away from Isaiah and me.

I hear Danica's voice over Isaiah's radio. "Is anyone out there? Is anyone alive?"

Isaiah picks up the radio. "This is team two. We are all alive but under fire. Stay where you are. Did your team get out?"

"Negative. I'm the only one left," Danica responds.

The men from the first Humvee keep the team pinned against the buildings on the far side of the street. I assume they would be dead already if Trent was not with them. If there had been any question, there is not now. The Feds do not want to kill Trent. The team fires back, but their inferior weapons do little more than keep the Feds in the Humvee from coming any closer.

The second Humvee stops sideways in the road about thirty yards from our van. Three more Fed troops climb out and huddle behind the Humvee. I peek around the van just as a plasma blast rips into the asphalt beside me. I jerk back. Two more blasts strike the van. The

< 201 >

men from the second Humvee fire at Isaiah and me. But they are not just trying to pin us down. They are trying to hit us. Isaiah returns fire, hitting the Humvee.

"Why are they trying to kill us?" I ask. Stupid question, though. I already know the answer.

"Because they're the Feds," Isaiah replies.

The three troops from the second Humvee start to move forward, spreading out to flank us. The first Humvee still has the rest of the team pinned down. Isaiah stands up and fires. The Fed in the middle drops his gun and crumples to the ground in a heap. Then a plasma blast comes from the left and blood spurts from Isaiah's thigh. He grabs it and falls to the ground behind the van. He does not say a word.

I take off my sweatshirt and start to wrap it around his bleeding leg.

He shakes his head. "It's okay. We don't have time."

Another plasma blast from the left and Isaiah's shoulder bursts open, blood splattering my face. The Feds have flanked us.

Isaiah roars and spins on the ground, gripping his automatic weapon in his right arm as his left arm hangs limp. He fires over and over along the front of the building from which the last plasma blast came. The Fed stumbles out of the door and collapses.

Two more Feds climb out of the second Humvee. They just keep coming. Three of them are still coming toward Isaiah and me. My nervousness had first turned to fear, and now, it is turning to hopelessness. I look at Isaiah. He breathes heavily and is bleeding badly from his thigh and shoulder.

"Isaiah, what can I do to help you?"

He shakes his head. "Nothing for me. But if the rest of us get taken out, don't fight them. They will take you alive if they can. They

< 202 >

think you are our Serenity. She is worth more to them alive than dead, for propaganda. Once they find out who you really are, they may let you go. At least you'll have a chance. The Resistance will come for you when we can."

I nod. He is right. If I give up, they probably will not shoot me. And if I give up now, they might just leave and let everyone else live as well. So, that is what I have to do. I drop my empty gun, hold up my hands, and step out from behind the van.

"Not yet," Isaiah says. "We can still try to get you out of here."

I look down at Isaiah. "No, I have to."

"Hold your fire!" one of the Feds shouts. They stop firing, as do the Resistance fighters.

I slowly walk toward the second Humvee. When I get to within ten yards, I hear screeching tires. I turn and see Danica driving the other van, coming from the west, accelerating toward the second Humvee. I jump out of the way, as do the three Feds. They toss their guns as they dive. Danica turns sideways, skids, and crashes the van sideways into the Humvee. She climbs out holding a long knife, jumps on one of the Feds, and stabs him. A second Fed is on her quickly. He has a knife as well. They wrestle, rolling on the pavement, each one holding the other's knife hand. The third Fed has a cut on his forehead and is slow to get up.

I turn toward Danica and the Fed. He has her pinned and knocks the knife out of her hand. He sits on top of her, using both of his hands to lower his knife to her throat. Both of Danica's hands are on his wrists, trying to hold him off. She is stronger than I thought. The knife is barely moving, but it is moving. She is losing. His knife comes closer and closer to her throat. I calculate the rate at which the knife is lowering and the distance to her throat. The knife will pierce her

< 203 >

throat in five seconds. I do not think. I instinctively run as quickly as I can toward them. As I approach, I reach over my shoulder and pull my sabre from its sheath. Striking his left forearm will relieve just enough pressure for Danica to force the knife up and to her right. She can then roll him and take the knife, reversing their positions.

I count down in my head—five, four. I reach the target. Three. I raise my sabre. Two. I strike the Fed's left forearm. Exactly as planned, his arm gives way. Danica rolls him to her right and ends up on top of him with the knife in her hand, pressing against his throat.

What have I done? I just cut a man with my sabre. But I had to or Danica would be dead right now. At least that's what I tell myself.

"Stop!" The voice comes from behind me.

I turn. The third Fed aims his plasma rifle at Danica's head. She turns and stares at him for a moment before releasing the pressure on her knife. The Fed on the ground immediately rolls her off of him, jumps up, and shouts, "Kill her!"

Again, without thinking about it, I step between Danica and the Fed's plasma gun.

Danica shouts, "What are you doing? You're gonna get yourself killed!"

I look at Isaiah, who still lies unmoving behind the van, blood all around him. Then I look at the team members who are still huddled against the building—the Feds from the first Humvee still have their plasma rifles trained on them. I look at Danica lying helpless on the ground. I have to try to save the team. They have become my friends. Especially Isaiah and Shawn. I have to do whatever I can.

I hold my sabre to my throat and look down the barrel of the gun at the Fed whose finger is on the trigger. "Let them go. All of them. And you can have me alive. I will be a bigger prize than your superiors

< 204 >

ever hoped for today. Serenity Ashdown. Alive and in the Feds' hands. Think of the publicity that the Feds can do with that to end the Resistance."

The Fed gives me a wry smile. "And if I don't let them go?"

I narrow my eyes and stare directly into his. "If you do not let them go, then I cut my own throat. And then it is the Feds' word against the Resistance's word as to how I died. Not to mention, you risk making me a martyr, which could make the Resistance even stronger."

I remember Fancy's camera. If she is still recording this, it is being aired live. If the team can make it out, that video should be enough to keep the support for the Resistance alive and well regardless of whether I live or die. But if he calls my bluff, can I actually kill myself? I hope they let them all go and take me so I do not have to face that decision.

The Fed whose gun is on me looks toward the first Humvee and yells, "General Chen!"

Qiang Chen, one of the UR's top generals. I remember his name from reading about their Serenity's history. She had several conflicts with him. Todd said he carried out the attack on London HQ.

I turn and look. A short, stocky Chinese man climbs out of the Humvee and walks toward us. He is not wearing the military fatigues that the others have on. He is dressed in a plain green uniform. He tips his cap and wipes his bald head as he walks. He will expect me to know him. I have to fake it. I have to convince them I am their Serenity, at least until they let the team go. That means I need to talk and act like she did. Oh my. I have to be sarcastic and rebellious. Even mouthy. Can I do that? I have to pull it off for the team. And contractions. I have to use contractions. I cannot talk so perfectly. I mean, I *can't* talk so perfectly.

< 205 >

General Chen first approaches the Fed with the gun, and they whisper to each other. He then turns to me and smiles. I can barely see his lips underneath his thick, dark mustache.

"Well, well. Serenity Ashdown. So, you are alive. You, my dear, are a difficult one to kill. I thought I hit a vital organ. My aim must have been slightly off. But that's okay. I like the hunt." He clasps his hands behind his back and paces back and forth in front of me. His cheek twitches regularly. "What, no smart comeback? No challenge for me? Maybe we've finally knocked the fight out of you."

Come on, Serenity. I need to say something. Think. What would their Serenity say? I finally blurt something. "Oh, you big bully. Let my friends go."

That was all I could come up with?

General Chen stops and looks inquisitively at me. "That's the best you could do? You have weakened. Maybe you're weak enough to take me up on my offer? It still stands. Join the Feds. You and I would make a perfect team, if you know what I mean." He grins.

That makes me angry. I think of my dad still being held by the Feds. I think of my mom lying on the stretcher, lifeless. I can picture her as clearly as if I had a photograph.

Enough. I have to convince him. "The only time I want to be close to you is when I'm throwing your dead body in the hole I force you to dig right before killing you, which I *am* going to do!"

He steps back. "Now, that's more like the Serenity I know. My man here explained to me your offer. Intriguing, I must say. But why would I want to let all these Resistance fighters walk free?" He motions toward the rest of the team.

I try to stay angry. That helps me be their Serenity. And I still have my sabre next to my throat. "I already explained why to your *man.*

< 206 >

And if you do not—don't take my offer, you're stupid. But I wouldn't call you stupid. That would be an insult to stupid people!"

I think I struck a nerve. He turns to me sharply. His smile is gone, and his face is stern.

"All right, Miss Ashdown. I'll let your precious friends go and take you alive in return. But when President Masterson and Mr. Franklin are finished with you, you are all mine." He takes two steps toward me, and I jab my sabre so that it touches the skin of my throat. He stops and narrows his eyes. It is all I can do not to break down and cry, but I have to hold it together. "And I am going to kill you ever so slowly. You will wish that you were never born."

My hands start to shake. I hope he does not notice.

He turns quickly toward the guard with the gun. "Let them go. Then take her sword." He points to me. "And bring her to me."

Danica gets up. She shoots a cold stare toward General Chen and whispers as she walks past. "We'll be back for you."

I whisper back, "Trent is with the Feds. Tell him nothing."

She gives me a puzzled look and continues walking.

I turn and watch my team—*my team,* I cannot help thinking, like I really belong with them—load Isaiah into the van. I cannot tell if he is dead or alive. Everyone gets in except Shawn. He walks to the driver's door and looks toward me. My eyes catch his. We stare at each other for a moment. I am terrified at the thought of what lies ahead for me. But staring into Shawn's eyes, I see only peace. A tear runs down his cheek. In that moment, I know he will do everything humanly possible to save me.

< 207 >

INTERROGATION

I tug at the neck of my bodysuit. I have had it on for far longer than I expected to. I rub my wrist where my watch had been. My notepad is also gone. I look around at the four concrete walls, concrete floor, and concrete ceiling of the dank smelling room, then walk to the metal door and look out the small, thick window. I cannot make out anything. Then I sit down on a stool in the corner. I do not know exactly where I am. The Feds put a black hood over my head for the drive in the Humvee. But from the drive time, the turns, and my sense of how fast we were traveling, I know that I am back in Boston. Specifically, I am in the building on the site of what would be the Prudential Tower in my world. Here, I do not think the Prudential Tower exists.

There were no buildings that tall when I arrived in their Boston with James and Mr. Franklin. My sense is that it is late afternoon. I have been alone in this room a good part of the day. My stomach growls. I am starving. I have not eaten since breakfast and that was a granola bar and banana on the go.

The door opens. It is James. I start to say his name and then catch myself. I do not know if their Serenity knew who James is. I will wait and see if he says anything.

"I've read your file, and I know all about you," James says. "I know what you're capable of, but there are two guards right outside, so don't try anything."

So, he does not know their Serenity, at least not personally. And he obviously thinks that I am her.

"I brought you something to eat," he says. He places a plate of food and a bottled water on the table in the center of the room and leaves.

I do not believe they would poison or drug me at this point. At least not until they get what they want out of me. So, I immediately sit down in one of the two chairs at the table and dig in to the food. Meatloaf and mashed potatoes. It probably is not that good, but because I am so hungry, I think it tastes great. I could eat anything. I gulp down half the bottle of water at once. The question is whether I play along as their Serenity or try to convince them of who I really am.

If I play along, they will certainly want to parade me in front of the cameras as being captured and will probably want me to denounce the Resistance. And worst case, they will perform a public execution. I do not want to think about that. But playing along will buy time for the Resistance to formulate a plan and find me. And the Feds still need me—the *real* me—to program the sphere. They will

< 209 >

assume the Resistance still has me, and maybe they will even bargain me for me. How would the Resistance trade the real me for their Serenity when they do not have the real me and their Serenity is dead? That would be interesting.

If I convince the Feds of my true identity as the other Serenity, then they will not kill me, at least not until I program the sphere. That also buys time. But they will also know their Serenity is dead and will certainly show the made-up me to the public to prove it. That could harm the Resistance more than anything.

And then, there's my dad. If the Feds have the real me, they no longer need my dad. They could kill him. But if they think the Resistance still has the real me, they will probably keep my dad alive for insurance.

The riskier play for me personally is to remain the fake Serenity. But that is the best move to protect the Resistance, and it is also the safest move for my dad. So, I will continue to play the role of their Serenity for as long as I can, or until the truth will benefit the Resistance and my dad. That means rebellion, sarcasm, and rough English for me. Everything that I am not. I scoop the last of the meatloaf and potatoes into my mouth and finish the water. Then, I stand and unzip my suit to the bottom of my neck. Ah, what a relief that is.

I pace around the room. If Isaiah does not live and Danica did not believe me, the Resistance will bring Trent up to date on everything, including who I really am. And then the Feds will know the truth. I cannot think about that. I just need to play the part of their Serenity and hope that either Isaiah or Danica comes through.

I continue to pace and think. There is also Dirk Bailey. I need to find a way to warn him that the Feds know about him. They have been letting him live in order to feed him misinformation.

< 210 >

But as soon as they no longer need him, he will be dead.

The door opens. I again sit down at the table, and Mr. Franklin, wearing a three-piece suit, walks in. I know him, but does their Serenity know him? Following him is a tall bearded man in a tan camouflage military uniform and a tan beret with a red stripe around it. He carries a folding chair. The last man to enter is their Serenity's father. He looks a lot like my dad, but he is no longer made up to look exactly like him. His hair is darker and slicked back. The smug look on his face and his arrogant walk are both of their Phillip Ashdown. But he thinks that I am his daughter. I have to continue to convince him of that. Can I do so? His slip-up with me was so small—*Pumpkin* instead of *Peanut*. Will I make a similar mistake? But that is not in my control. What is in my control is my attitude.

The bearded man sets up the folding chair beside the empty chair on the other side of the table. Mr. Franklin sits in one chair and their Phillip Ashdown in the other. Phillip lays his hands on the table. "Serenity. I had hoped I would see you again under different circumstances. Where did I go wrong with you?"

I do not answer. The less I say, the better. The less likely I am to mess up.

Phillip continues. "You know Mr. Franklin." He nods toward Mr. Franklin. Mr. Franklin smiles at me and nods. "This is General Lev Ostrovsky." He turns and nods toward the tall bearded man towering behind them. General Ostrovsky does not change his expression or acknowledge me. I nonchalantly sit back in my chair and do not respond.

"Serenity," Mr. Franklin says. "General Chen told us everything that happened at the office building. That was valiant of you to give up yourself to save your comrades. We commend that. You have fought

< 211 >

long and hard for what you believe to be a just cause. But that fight is over now. It is over for you, and it will soon be over for the rest of the Resistance. I believe that is how you refer to yourselves. President Masterson is a fair man, and he wants to give you the opportunity to make things right."

"I'm listening," I say, trying to look like I have been through this type of interrogation before. But in reality, I am scared to death.

"This can go one of two ways, Serenity," Phillip says. "You can publicly renounce the Resistance. Tell the world that the Resistance is dissolving and no longer opposes the government. And convince the core of the Resistance to lay down their arms. True to his word, President Masterson will let each and every member of the Resistance return to their homes with their families, and no repercussion will come to them."

"And me?" I ask.

Phillip leans back in his chair. "We have to make an example out of someone. Otherwise, people will think they can start a revolution anytime something doesn't go their way. The president will let you live, but you'll spend the rest of your life in prison. And your friends will go free."

Seeing the conditions in which the people in this world live when they are free, I cannot imagine what the prisons are like. But if it will keep Shawn, Isaiah, and the others free, maybe it is worth it. But the President offered this in his speech, and nobody in the Resistance believed him. And the Resistance would not lay down their arms even if I did make such a public announcement because they know that it is me, not their Serenity. A public announcement would just confuse the public, and Shawn and the Resistance need the public behind them now more than ever.

< 212 >

I lean forward and rest my forearms on the table. "And if I refuse?"

Phillip leans forward as well, putting his face close to mine. He glares at me. "If you refuse, you will be executed on worldwide television, which will likewise destroy the Resistance. It'll just take a little longer to accomplish, and it will be a lot more painful for you. And we will round up each and every member of the Resistance and execute them as well." He grits his teeth and squints. "Either way, we get what we want: The Resistance eliminated and *you* out of the way. You ceased to be my daughter the minute you joined the Resistance. So, if that's your choice, we'll turn you over to General Ostrovsky right now."

General Ostrovsky looks at me with a smile on one side of his mouth.

I lean back in my chair, trying to act tough rather than scared. I keep my hands on my lap underneath the table so that they do not see them shaking.

What do I do? Then, I think.

They still need me, the real me.

I force myself to smile confidently. "Aren't you forgetting something? What about the other Serenity? You need her to program the sphere. Without her, it'll take you years to program. And there goes your precious invasion plan. By then, it'll be too late. That's right. We know all about your plan." I confidently fold my arms, hiding my shaking hands. "With either of your options, the Resistance will keep her hidden so deep, it'll take you years to find her. Again, too late for you." *Anger.* That helped me last time. I let myself feel it, for everything they have done and are threatening to do, and put myself nose-to-nose with Phillip. "Why don't you take that to your precious president and see what he has to say!"

< 213 >

Phillip leans back. Judging from his expression, I hit a nerve. Mr. Franklin does not look much calmer. Phillip leans over and whispers to Mr. Franklin.

Mr. Franklin leans toward me. "All right, we exchange you for the other Serenity. So, you go free. But first, you publicly call off the Resistance."

That seems reasonable to me. That keeps me as their Serenity alive, and it will likely get me and my dad home once I program the sphere for them. But I won't have a home for long. If I cause the Resistance to dissolve, there will be nothing to keep the Feds from following my dad and me home. I have to push for everything.

I stand up. "No! Me for the other Serenity, and I make no announcement. Just a straight trade."

In one motion, Phillip jumps to his feet, grabs the underside of the table, flips it over, and shouts, "No!" The top edge of the table smacks my shins. I feel a sharp pain and stumble backward. Mr. Franklin quickly stands. Phillip clenches his fists and glares at me. "You think you're so smart. So smug. Always dictating how things will go. Not this time! I am going to watch you die! Slowly. And I'm going to enjoy it. Get her out of my sight!" He turns his back toward me and looks at General Ostrovsky.

General Ostrovsky approaches. His figure towers above me. He snarls and grabs my upper arm, then yanks me forward. My shoulder almost feels like it rips out of its socket. He leads me from the room.

< 214 >

22

SERENITY'S MIND

They place the black hood over my head, and General Ostrovsky walks me to my new room. Although "cell" would be a better description. Just as I did when they walked me into the building, I count every step, memorize every turn left or right, and make note of every door we walk through. I also count the number of steps in the multiple stairways that we descend. Most importantly, I memorize the distinct sound of the numbers being pressed on the security keypads at each door. It must be an old building to have a security system more outdated even than the ones in my world. A numbered code on a touchtone keypad. Again, lucky for me. If I could escape from my cell and avoid the guards and anyone else I run into, I could easily walk out the door we came in. But first things first. How do I get out of this cell?

The cell is a decent size with thick glass walls on the front and sides. The back wall appears to be white-painted concrete, and the floor and ceiling are both white tile. There is a bed, and that is all. No bathroom or chairs or anything else. So, they must not expect me to be here long. At least I hope not. I do not test the glass. I am sure that people much stronger than I have already done so, by the looks of the scuff marks. I do try the metal door in the front wall, but the lock is controlled from the outside with a keypad.

The entrance door into this cellblock swings open and bumps the front glass wall of my cell. A young man in a suit walks down the hall, which is lined on one side with ten glass cells and with what appear to be offices on the other, one opposite each cell. The office walls are solid but I can see a desk, computer, and filing cabinets through the open doors of two of the offices. The man passes my cell and enters one of the office doors. As his door closes, I look through my glass wall and down the line of cells. They all look empty, except for the adjacent cell, where a man lies in the bed with his back to me.

I sit on the bed in my cell with my head in my hands. I am exhausted. What has happened to me? I am all alone in a building I do not know, in a city I do not recognize, in a country that is no longer the United States, in a world that is not my own. And I am not even *me* anymore. The bravado I showed in the interrogation melts away, and all of this finally sinks in. I start to sob. I try to hold it back, but I cannot. A sense of loneliness, hopelessness, overtakes me.

"Serenity?" The voice comes from the cell next to mine.

The sound is muffled by the glass, but the voice is familiar. I do not look up. I do not feel like talking.

< 216 >

"Peanut, it's me. Dad."

I feel like my heart skips a beat. It cannot be. A warm feeling rushes over me. I look up and there, standing next to the glass, is my dad. My real dad!

This time he is unmistakable.

I jump up, run to the glass, and smash my hands and face against it. "Dad! Dad! Oh, how I have missed you! I have been trying so hard to find you. I saw Mom. She was alive!" I ramble in my excitement, until a sadness washes over me. "She was alive. But they killed her. I tried to help get us out of here by turning myself into their version of me." I step back from the glass and wave an open palm down my body. "But now, they are going to kill me."

My dad interrupts me. "Serenity, calm down. It's okay. Everything will be okay. I know. I know everything that has happened to you. Dirk Bailey has kept me informed. The good Dirk Bailey. Serenity, I'm so sorry for getting you into this. I never intended for you to come through the sphere. And I had no idea that they were planning on using it for an invasion. Dirk filled me in on that too. He said that you figured it out."

I take another step backward. "You should have told me more about the project. You expected me to do so much, but I never knew why. You just pushed me. Maybe I could have helped—*really* helped—if I had known more."

My dad steps back from the wall. "But they had Mom. They threatened to kill her if I didn't do what they said or if I told anyone what was going on. I had to try to get her back. I wanted to tell you that she was alive. I really did. But if I couldn't save her, I didn't want you to have to go through losing her again."

I shake my head. "In the end, I had to go through it anyway."

< 217 >

I lower my head. My eyes fill with tears, and I feel a lump in my throat. "I am scared, Dad. I do not know what to do. I cannot do this anymore. I just want to go home."

My dad steps up to the wall again, leans on his hands, and presses on the glass. "Serenity, listen to me. You can do this. You *have* to do this. Dirk has told your Resistance friends where we are. They are coming for us. But first, we have to help from the inside. Dirk has a plan. He's going to explain it tonight after he talks to the Resistance."

"But Dad, the Feds know about Dirk. They know he is with the Resistance."

"What? How do you know that?"

"It does not matter how I know. We have to warn him when he comes tonight."

My dad nods. "Okay, right. We will."

"Oh no," I say. "I was not thinking. The Feds probably have these cells bugged. They probably heard everything we just said."

My dad shakes his head. "No, we're clear. Dirk works out of one of those offices sometimes, and he scans the cellblock daily so that he and I can talk. They have some pretty high-tech scanning equipment over here. They must consider it a weapon. It fits in his pocket. Nobody can tell he is scanning. And bugs are something the Feds can't hide from a scanner even if they do know about Dirk."

I relax a bit. "Oh, good."

My dad must see the doubt on my face. "Serenity, you have to stay strong. And you have to continue to play the part of their Serenity."

I lower my head. My face feels hot from crying. "If I just explain that I am the other Serenity and I will program the sphere, then they will let us go." I know that is not true. I already went through the scenarios.

< 218 >

My dad shakes his head. "Serenity, they'll use you to program the sphere, then they will kill us both. They won't need us anymore, and they won't want us around to reprogram it against them in the future. And the Resistance won't have a chance to stop the invasion. Our only chance is for you to continue convincing them that you are their Serenity. And that very well may be our world's only chance of surviving."

"I know." I move forward and lean my forehead on the glass and shake my head. A tear drips onto the floor. "But I do not think I can, Dad. I am too scared. I am not strong enough."

"Look at me, Serenity."

I lift my head.

"You are the strongest person that I have ever known. You have overcome obstacles that would finish most people. Strength doesn't have to come from muscles or weapons. Your strength comes from here." He places his hand over his heart. "And from here." He points to his forehead. "Nobody, and I mean nobody, can match your strength in those areas. Courage isn't being fearless. Courage is being scared to death but moving forward anyway."

# # # # #

I lie on my cell bed in the pitch black. In the windowless underground, there is no hint of starlight or moonlight to which my eyes can adjust. The last person left the offices across from the cells shortly before Mr. Bailey arrived, and he left my dad and me several minutes ago, just before they cut the lights. We might just be able to pull this off, keeping the Resistance strong and getting Dad and me home, but still, I cannot sleep. Tomorrow will be day eleven since I passed

< 219 >

through the sphere. It seems like an eternity since dinner at Grandma and Grandpa's in my world the day before I passed through.

I cannot believe what Mr. Bailey told us. The plan worked. It really worked. Fancy filmed everything, and it was all broadcasted, even my capture, before the Feds were able to cut Todd off. People are rallying behind the Resistance everywhere. And my capture strengthened the movement. As Mr. Bailey put it, "Seeing their Serenity alive rekindled their hope. Seeing the Feds immediately snatch you away has incited people almost to the point of riots all around the globe."

Enough thinking about that. Since I cannot sleep, I might as well run through the key parts of Mr. Bailey's escape plan one more time. Or at least the inside part that I have to pull off before we get to the exchange. "The exchange," I whisper. Mr. Bailey never explained how the Resistance convinced the Feds to exchange one Serenity for the other or how they convinced the Feds to set my dad free. Or how the Resistance plans to pull off the exchange when there is just one of me. Maybe cooler heads prevailed over the other Phillip Ashdown's hatred for me—I mean, for his daughter.

I tried to convince Mr. Bailey to call it all off. It is too risky. I told him everything I know and that his life is at risk. He needs to get out of here. He believed me but said we have to go through with it. He assured me that nothing in the plan relies on intelligence that could be misfed to him. He said Isaiah is still unconscious, but my message got through to Danica. Trent is on lockdown. The Feds will not be tipped off.

If Mr. Bailey is willing to risk his life by going through with this, then I have to make sure I do not mess it up.

I need to run through my part again in my head. The door opposite the last cell in this block does not lead to an office. Rather, it

< 220 >

opens to an elevator that provides the only access to a bunker underneath this building. Any plasma missile and antimatter bomb in the UR can be launched from that bunker. Apparently, it is one of several backup launch sites that exist in case the main sites in D.C., Moscow, and Beijing are destroyed. By whom, who knows, given the strength of the UR.

More importantly, the bunker houses the controls for the unmanned plasma machine guns, rifles, and grenade launchers that surround the site where the sphere is housed. They are all controlled by artificial intelligence, and they are the first line of defense before an intruder even gets to the site's armed guards.

I saw the elevator door when a guard escorted me to the bathroom at the far end of the cellblock. The door is controlled by the same type of touchtone keypad as the rest of the building. According to Dirk, the Feds like the old keypads because they cannot be hacked remotely. Dirk will get someone with clearance to open the door so I can hear the tones. But I need to be in the bathroom catty-corner to the door so I can hear. Once I have the tones, I will be able to open the outer door with the keypad. Dirk says there is a regular, old-fashioned elevator inside. Old-fashioned for them if it aids their weapons, but probably state of the art in my world.

After Dirk leaves, it will be up to my dad and me to create a diversion and get me out of my cell so I can get to the bunker. There, I will upload a program that Todd put on the flash drive Mr. Bailey gave me. That will allow Todd to control the AI weapons at the sphere site from his computer. According to Mr. Bailey, the room is unmanned when there is no crisis. I hope he is right. If all of that works exactly as planned, and the Resistance is able to get their Serenity back in the exchange without actually having the real me, then Todd can shut

< 221 >

down the AI defense, the Resistance can attack the site, I can program the sphere, and my dad and I can go home. Simple!

There are so many places that this plan can go wrong, terribly wrong for me, but that does not matter. In the past ten days, I have grown to hate the Feds. I will do whatever I have to in order to help the Resistance stop the Feds, to keep the Feds out of my world, and to get my dad and me home.

# # # # #

I wake up to my dad tapping the glass wall between us. I must have fallen asleep at some point.

"Dirk's going to be here soon," he says.

"Okay, right. Thanks." I sit up, rubbing my eyes, and try to shake off my grogginess. I really have to go to the bathroom.

"Hey, I have to go to the bathroom!" I shout. Usually, someone in one of the offices comes out and then calls a guard. I shout again. "I really have to go. Badly!"

A Chinese woman opens the door opposite the cell on the other side of my dad's, looks down the hall at me, and then goes back inside. A couple of minutes later, the main door to the block opens, and a guard dressed in the typical green uniform enters and leads me down the hall to the restroom. Just as I open the bathroom door, Mr. Bailey walks through the main door back at the far end of the hall. He is with General Ostrovsky.

Oh no, they are on their way to use the keypad to open the elevator door. I cannot miss it. I have to hear it. But I really do have to pee. If I go now, I may miss the keypad tones. I cannot risk it. So, I stand just inside the bathroom door, holding it in. I cross my legs

< 222 >

and half-squat. I hear them slowly walking down the hall. Could they walk any slower? I start to bob up and down, sort of dancing. But after bob-dancing for a minute, I conclude that dancing is a myth. It does not really help hold it in. As long as it is taking them to walk down the hallway, I could have gone and been back to the door.

Finally, I hear them talking to the guard outside the bathroom door. *Come on! Just open the elevator already or there is going to be a mess by the door.* Then I hear the keypad tones and a click of the latch. Good, got it.

I turn toward the stall when the guard knocks on the door. "You about finished in there?"

"Another second please," I shout back. Then, at last, I run into the stall. Of course, I have to fight my way out of this stupid bodysuit. But finally, relief.

When I leave the bathroom, I step quickly to the right and punch every key on the elevator door keypad in order. The guard grabs my arm just as I press the last key.

He yanks me back. "What do you think you're doing? You can't go in there, and why would you even try with me right here?"

I look up at him and smile. "Just testing your reflexes."

"Come on." He squeezes my arm even harder and thrusts me forward. But I got the information I needed. All of the keypads in the building work off of the same key tones—at least, all of the ones I have heard. And I have heard the tone of every door that I have been taken through, and more. But I did not know which tone matched each number.

Now I know.

< 223 >

23

THE ESCAPE

I wake up again. I must have slept for a while. My lunch sits on the floor just inside my cell door.

I do not know what Mr. Bailey said to get General Ostrovsky to take him to the bunker, and I do not know how long they were down there.

I walk over to the glass wall between my cell and my dad's. He sits on his bed eating his lunch. "When did Mr. Bailey and the General leave?"

He sets his tray down and stands up. "I don't know. They took me out for a while. Somewhere else in this building. Blindfolded, of course. I got a hot shower and a change of clothes. I don't know if they did that because they are letting me go in the exchange or planning on killing me." He grins.

"That's not funny, Dad."

I walk to the door and pick up my lunch tray. I look down at the cold lunchmeat sandwich and some sort of broth. I do not have much of an appetite. "I sure could use a shower myself and definitely a change of clothes. This suit is killing me."

"Yeah, that really doesn't look like something you would have in your wardrobe. But I do like the red hair." He grins again.

"Stop it, Dad. How can you joke when we're probably about to die?"

"Just trying to lighten the mood, Peanut."

I sit down on my bed again and try the sandwich. Stale bread and old lunchmeat. I flop it back onto the tray and set the tray on the floor.

My dad takes his tray to the door and sets the empty plate, bowl, spoon, and water bottle on the floor. Then he slides the metal tray underneath his mattress. He did this once before, and the food service person took the dishes without seeming to notice the missing tray.

"Are you ready?" he asks.

"As ready as I will ever be. As soon as the last person is leaving the offices, I will start. Just before lights out."

We sit around until the final office light goes out. A young woman exits that office. I untie my tennis shoe and wait until she walks past my cell.

She glares at me.

I do not know what the people in these offices do. Maybe they study prisoners. Or maybe they are weapons analysts. I do sometimes see them go in and out of the elevator during the day. But in any event, they are not very pleasant people.

< 225 >

"Hey," I say. "Can you please tell the guard that I have to go to the bathroom?" How many times will the bathroom trick work? Hopefully, once more.

She looks at me but has no reaction, then walks on. This plan might be over before it starts. But soon the guard walks through the door. Thankfully, it is a different guard than the one who escorted me this morning. That guard might be more on his toes, ready for me after what I tried with the elevator keypad.

The guard opens my door. I step out in front of him and take a few steps until I am right beside the keypad for my dad's door. I know the exact four digits to open it. One-four-eight-one. The four tones I heard when it was opened earlier.

I stop quickly so the guard will be right upon me. I bend at the hips to tie my shoe. Here it goes. I have only one chance at this. And I am glad that I am flexible. As soon as my shoe is tied, I look between my legs for the target, then mule kick with my right foot. *Smack!* I hit his groin perfectly. I hear the pain in his shout.

Out of instinct, I say, "Sorry," as I immediately turn to the right and punch the numbers on the keypad beside my dad's door. One-four-eight-one. The guard recovers and wraps his arms around me, but it is too late. My dad bursts through the door and smacks the guard in the face with a metal tray. I do not believe my dad has ever struck anyone before. But I guess when your life depends on it—or, more importantly, when your little girl's life depends on it—you will do just about anything.

The guard releases me as he tumbles backward, and I race to the end of the hall.

"Stop," he yells. I glance back. He ignores my dad and races after me. But I have a head start. I reach the elevator door and punch in

< 226 >

the code I heard this morning while I was in the bathroom. The door clicks.

I look back—the guard is closing in quickly. I swing the door open to reveal a set of closed elevator doors. I look again. The guard is ten yards away and sprinting. There is just one button since the elevator only goes down. I press it and the doors slowly open. "Come on. Come on," I say. I look back. The guard is five yards away. I dart inside the elevator and press the "down" button. He dives and slides his arm between the closing doors. They close on him, preventing them from shutting all the way. He pulls himself to his feet, keeping his arm in the doors, then starts to pry them open. What can I do? He is way too strong for me to push him out. The doors slowly open from his force. He grimaces and snarls.

He forces his way in further. "I've got you now, you little—"

The metal tray crashes down on the back of his head. He shrieks in pain and stumbles backward. The doors close.

"Thank you, Dad," I whisper.

The elevator goes down, and the doors open. Then I flip the elevator's kill switch to freeze it down here. I know I will eventually have to go back up. And when I do, I will face the wrath of the guard. But at least he cannot get down here to me. By the time I go back up, the program will be installed, and he will be none the wiser. Poor Dad. He is probably facing the wrath right now.

The large room is dimly lit. Many computers, all running, are lined up on built-in desks and countertops. They all face a giant wall-to-wall, floor-to-ceiling screen on the front wall. I pull out the flash drive. According to Mr. Bailey, Todd said I could use any computer. It would not matter. I move to a machine in the middle of the room in the back row. It is close. I look around for the USB drive. Before I

< 227 >

locate it, my heart skips a beat, and I jump backward. Someone is sitting at a computer two rows in front of me, off to the right. He looks down toward the monitor. I have not been quiet—he had to have heard me.

Something about him looks familiar.

I slowly move to an opening in the line of computers and walk into the next row. Then I walk down the row and come up behind the person. He still does not move. Something must be wrong with him. I reach his location, lean over the terminal in front of me, and tap him on the shoulder. His chair swivels, and he slumps forward. His body turns as his head flops onto the keyboard in front of him. I scream and jump backward. His throat is slit, and there is blood all over his shirt. It is Dirk Bailey.

"I thought I could count on you coming down here."

I jump. General Chen's voice comes from behind me.

I close my eyes and shake my head. "No, please no," I whisper. I have not installed the program. I have failed.

I turn and General Chen walks toward me. "Looks like I need to train my guards better." He grins. "But you're slipping, Miss Ashdown. I seem to keep catching you. The great Serenity Ashdown, caught again."

Okay, time to go into other Serenity mode. What would she say? How would she handle this situation? "What do you want, Chen?"

His left cheek twitches as he smiles. "That's *General* Chen."

I force a laugh. "General? Right. You're nothing but a hired two-bit murderer taking orders from a bunch of men in suits. Doing their dirty work, like a good little doggy." That was probably convincing but not very smart of me to say. I am making him angry. I will try to change the subject. "If you knew I was going to come down here, why didn't you just stop me in the first place?"

< 228 >

He continues to approach. "First, I wanted you to see for yourself what we do to traitors. And he wasn't even a very smart one. We used him quite often for our own benefit. But his usefulness ran out. Second, I wanted to see what you were up to." He finally reaches me and holds out his hand. "Hand it over. You won't be needing it."

No use trying to hide it. He would search me and take it anyway. And having his hands searching me is the last thing I want. I hand him the flash drive.

"Thank you." His tone is smug.

I look at the handgun in his holster. He follows my eyes to the gun and smiles. "Why don't you go for it, Miss Ashdown?" His smile disappears. "I would love a good excuse to take you to the exchange, bruised and broken."

I step backward.

"Aw, you're scared. You're losing it," he says. "I'm not worried. I'll still get my chance." He steps forward and leans in closer. "And as to your earlier point, I don't kill for others. I kill for myself. I enjoy it. Just like I enjoy ordering all the hits on you Resistance people. That big guy's family, your London headquarters. That was a good one."

I think about Isaiah and all the women and children who died in London. The anger that I had never felt before coming to this universe returns. My face gets hot.

"Oh, and ordering the shot on the other Ashdown's mother. That was a last-minute improvisation that worked quite well."

I feel my blood boiling. I clench my fists.

He grits his teeth. "But the kill that I am most waiting for is you. That one I'll do personally."

I lean my face toward his. "You will try!"

< 229 >

THE EXCHANGE

Two guards lead me out of my cell. One is a tall, slender African American man. The other looks Danish, light-complected and solidly built. He is the guard I kicked in the groin and my dad bashed with the metal tray last night. The first guard calls him "Franz." He glares at me as he slips the black hood over my head.

What about my dad? They did not take him. Mr. Bailey said that he is part of the deal, too. He is to be set free. What if it is a trick, like how General Chen shot my mom as soon as she was free. I stop, but I cannot say anything. They will wonder why I care so much about the other Phillip Ashdown.

The first guard yanks my arm, pulling me forward.

I hear Franz walk in the other direction. Then I hear my dad's cell door keypad. Good, maybe Franz is getting him for the exchange.

I hear my dad's voice from inside his cell. "What are you do—"

He is cut short by the sickening sound of a fist smashing flesh. And then there is a thud as someone falls to the floor. I want to shout, *Dad*. I want to turn and run to him, but I cannot. I simply stop again.

The guard yanks my arm harder.

"You got the jump on me yesterday," Franz says from inside my dad's cell. "Not this time. Now, see how it feels."

I hear what sounds like someone kicking a sack of flour over and over. My dad moans with each kick. My heart aches. Out of instinct, I try to pull away from the guard, but he is too strong. He drags me forward through the main door. The sounds disappear as it closes behind us. I stumble on the steps and stop resisting. The hood, wet with tears, sticks to my face.

I have to stay strong for my dad. I have to continue with the plan. That is what he would want. And if Franz did not kill him, getting back to the Resistance is my best shot at saving him. I pull myself together and count the steps up the stairs and down the hallways. I keep track of the turns and doors and keypad tones. The route is exactly the reverse of when they brought me in.

# # # # #

Judging from the height of the vehicle they put me in, it feels like a Humvee. From the voices and other noises, I count four people in the Humvee besides myself. Franz, the other guard, Mr. Franklin, and General Chen. We do not drive far before stopping. Based on the speed, time, and turns, we should be at the location of the COI

< 231 >

building. Why are we stopping? Surely the exchange is not happening here. The guards lead me into the building. They continue to keep me blindfolded, but I know exactly where I am since I have been to the COI building before—although, they do not realize that. We take the elevator up to the twenty-second floor. I remember the elevator from my last visit, so I know this is the top floor. After winding down two hallways, we stop.

There is one guard on either side of me. I sense that General Chen and Mr. Franklin each stand next to one of these guards.

"Take that thing off of her." The voice comes from in front of me. It sounds familiar.

As the hood comes off, I am momentarily blinded by the sunlight shining through the floor-to-ceiling window behind the desk that is in front of me. I squint and blink until my eyes focus. Sitting behind the desk is their President Masterson.

He leans back in his leather chair and swivels slightly to the left and then the right. "So, you are the young lady that has been causing me so many problems. Notwithstanding, I hope you have been treated well by these gentlemen. After all, we aren't savages."

Yeah, right, I want to tell him. But I do not say a word.

"I apologize for the cloak and dagger," he continues. "But I hope you understand the necessity of it. We can't be freeing the leader of my greatest opposition if she knows exactly where our key assets are located."

I would like to tell him that he already blew that one, but I keep my mouth shut.

President Masterson continues. "Mr. Franklin, tell me again why I must set this young lady free?"

Mr. Franklin clears his throat. "Sir, we need to exchange her for the other Serenity Ashdown. We need the other Ashdown to program

< 232 >

the sphere. Otherwise, we will have to wait for a random, lucky connection, or months—even years—to program it without her. We don't have that kind of time, sir."

President Masterson stands, casually walks to the front of his desk, and leans against it. He stares at me intently. "You know, you and I are a lot alike. We both fight for a cause that we believe in, for a people that we want to protect. The only difference is that I am willing to sacrifice a few for the good of the many." He folds his arms.

What would their Serenity say? She would not be silent for long. I do not know what she would say, but I know what I will say. "*We* are nothing alike. *You* kill, torture, and murder for the sake of money and your own power. *You* are willing to sacrifice women, children, and an entire other planet for your own petty survival. But the biggest difference between you and me is that *you* are going to lose!"

He smiles. "My, my. Everything I've heard about you is true. Quite the feisty one. I don't think I'm going to lose. You're the one in the custody of my men. And even if I do lose, you won't be around to see it." He looks at Mr. Franklin. "Have the arrangements been made?"

Mr. Franklin nods. "Yes, sir, they have."

I begin to panic. What arrangements? They are up to something. They are not going to exchange me at all.

General Chen taps on the computer notepad that he has been holding, then moves his finger across the screen. "Here it is, sir. The schematics we came up with." He stretches his arm in front of me and hands the notepad, face up, to President Masterson.

I glance at the screen. A glance is all I need. I now have the schematic in my mind. But I do not have any idea what it means. I am still afraid.

The fear must show on my face. President Masterson stands up straight and steps toward me. "Oh, does that surprise you? You didn't

< 233 >

really think that I was going to set free the one person who can destroy my life's work, did you?" He looks at General Chen and grits his teeth. "Get her out of my sight!"

#

Back in the Humvee, wearing the hood again, I follow our route in my mind. We finally stop at what would be Logan International Airport in my world. But I do not hear anything. Not the roar of jet engines, no planes landing or taking off, not even a car. We get out, and they pull the hood off of my head. Again, the sun blinds me momentarily. Then I look around.

We stand in the middle of one of the airport runways. There is nothing but open space in every direction. It would be impossible for either side to set up any type of trap or ambush. There are trees at the far end of the runway, straight ahead, but they are at least a mile away. Behind us, a little closer, are several hangars. The sign on each reads "United Republic Air." The terminal is behind the hangars. Funny, there are no planes moving anywhere, and there are only a few stationary planes. They sit in front of the closest hangar. The rest of the planes must be inside. There is no sign of the Resistance.

In my mind, I pull up the schematic on General Chen's notepad. The runway is marked with multiple X's arranged to form a U shape. If the schematic is to scale, the X's should be fifty yards down the runway from where we stand. Then there are multiple circles, each with a number inside. The circles are close together and, again, if the schematic is to scale, the numbered circles should be directly behind us. I turn my head to look. The numbered circles would be right where the closest hangar is located.

< 234 >

"Think Serenity, think," I whisper. "What does it all mean?"

"They are late," General Chen says. "I don't like it."

"Patience," Mr. Franklin says. "They will show. Is everything set?"

General Chen's left cheek twitches. "Waiting on my command."

The Feds will kill the Resistance members once they have what they want or once they figure out the Resistance does not have me.

That is it! The schematic! The X's are targets they plan to hit with explosives. The ends of the U shape point toward us. The Feds will let the Resistance cross the explosive line, then bomb or detonate along the line. The Resistance will be trapped. And the numbers must correspond with vehicles or aircraft hidden in the hangar. That's why the commercial planes are outside. However many vehicles the Resistance brings, they will be outnumbered. But surely, the Resistance will figure the Feds have something up their sleeves. I assume they will come prepared and will have a plan themselves.

Before it is visible, I hear a vehicle—just one—approaching from the far end of the runway. General Chen, Mr. Franklin, Franz, and the other guard stand behind me beside the Humvee, also looking toward the far end of the runway. Then, the white van comes into focus, the sun giving a small glare off the windshield. The van slows to a stop exactly fifty yards from where we stand. I cannot see who is inside, but two people, heavily armed, get out and start walking toward us. Shawn and Horace. What are they doing? What could their plan possibly be? They do not know they are walking into a trap. I have to do something. I have to make them leave. Otherwise, the van will be blown up, and Shawn and Horace will be shot. I have to save my friends. I have to save Shawn.

I turn to face the Feds. "Look, do not do anything. I am not who you think I am. I *am* the other Serenity. You already have me. Let

< 235 >

them go." I point toward Shawn, Horace, and the van. "Please. I will do anything you want me to do. Just let them go."

I immediately realize that I may have sold out my Earth and ended the Resistance by acknowledging their Serenity's death. What am I doing? But seeing my friends walking into a death trap, the only people who have really cared about me outside of my family, I had to do it. I could not let them die. I could not let Shawn die.

General Chen grunts. "Why would we ever believe that?"

"Because it is the truth. Look at the video of the attack where you captured me. I never shot my gun. It was filled with blanks." I step toward General Chen. "General, your left cheek twitches once every thirty-two seconds." I immediately turn toward Mr. Franklin. "Mr. Franklin, you had polio as a child. Your right leg is three-quarters of an inch shorter than your left. And when I first came into this world, we met in the COI conference room with Dirk Bailey, Gordon Conklin, Artemis Glenn, and Phillip Ashdown posing as my dad. The coordinate numbers that must be programmed into the sphere are a set of fixed numbers and one series of numbers, seventy-five to one hundred of them, repeating. You need me to recall those numbers." I step back. All four of them stare at me as if they are deciding whether to believe me. I put my finger to my eye and take out a contact lens. "And my eyes are blue."

General Chen's lips turn up in a wry smile. I think he has just realized that he killed the real Serenity. I look at Mr. Franklin. He nods. He knows that I am telling the truth. I look back at General Chen. His smile is gone. He looks toward Shawn, Horace, and the van. He is still going to kill them. I know it.

I turn and sprint toward Shawn and Horace. Their only chance is for me to warn the van and get between Shawn and Horace and any

< 236 >

shooters. The Feds will not kill me. They need me. But they *will* kill everyone else. I raise my arm as I run, motioning for the van to turn and go. Then I motion for Shawn and Horace to get down.

The van's tires squeal on the asphalt as the driver pulls into reverse. Shawn and Horace each drop to one knee and aim their weapons past me. Plasma guns fire from beside the Humvee and a plasma blast burns deep into Horace's chest. He falls backward immediately and lies motionless. Shawn fires twice, and I hear someone fall to the ground beside the Humvee. Then a second plasma blast hits the asphalt just in front of Shawn. I sprint the final few steps and dive on top of him.

Mr. Franklin shouts. "Hold your fire!"

Then General Chen says, "Go get them!"

There is an enormous explosion followed by deafness and pain shooting through my head from the concussion. I look up. U-shaped flames surround me, Shawn, and Horace's lifeless body. The smell of burning asphalt fills the air. Franz sprints toward us through the opening at the top of the U. The Feds did not use bombs or normal explosives. They have planted a chemical weapon in the asphalt, and it continues to burn. Flames at least seven feet high spew from the crumbled asphalt in a continuous U.

Shawn gets up and pulls me off the ground. "Come on!"

He grabs my hand, and I run behind him, blocking any chance for Franz or General Chen to take a shot. We race toward the flames. Vehicles come at us from the hangar, but there are no aircraft.

"Get ready!" Shawn shouts.

I reach back, unzip my collar, and pull my fireproof hood over my head as I run. I feel the heat from the flames as we approach. When we reach the edge of the fire wall, I feel like I am burning. Shawn picks

< 237 >

me up by the waist. I put my hands into my pockets and bury my head in my chest, then he throws me through the flames. There is searing heat for a second, and then I hit the asphalt and roll. I am uninjured and thankful that I am still wearing this awful suit.

I turn and see Shawn jump through the flames. His left arm catches fire, but he lands on his feet and does a somersault. As he comes out of the somersault, he spins to face the flames, drops to one knee, pulls up his weapon, and immediately fires. Franz leaps through the flames, smashes his face into the asphalt, rolls over, and lies motionless. Blood comes from a small bullet hole in his chest.

I hear vehicles approaching the flames to our left. They come closer, then circle the flames. The van has turned around and is heading to meet the onslaught of Fed military vehicles. The Resistance does not have a chance. I hear a helicopter in the direction the Resistance came from.

"Is that ours?" I ask.

"Is what ours?" Shawn replies.

"The helicopter." It comes into view as I speak.

Shawn nods. "Yeah. Our evac. But it'll never have time to get back up if it lands to get us."

He motions for the helicopter to go toward the Fed vehicles. "We have a better chance to escape if we use the chopper to hold off the Feds. Come on. We have to make it to the woods."

We sprint down the runway. My lungs burn, and I cannot feel my legs. But I have to keep going. The Resistance members in the van and helicopter are giving up their lives to get me out of here.

When I hear an explosion, I glance over my shoulder. The van is engulfed in flames. There are more explosions, and I look again. The helicopter has taken out some of the Feds' vehicles. We are almost to

< 238 >

the edge of the woods when I look one last time. Nobody is following us. The helicopter has them occupied. We run into the woods, and I collapse, gasping for air. Sweat runs down my face. My suit sticks to my skin like glue. Shawn and I both turn. All of the Feds' vehicles look to be disabled, but smoke comes from the helicopter. It starts to spin.

"They are going to crash," I say. "Can they jump out?"

Shawn shakes his head. "Too high to jump. Too low for a parachute. And they won't let themselves be taken alive anyway. They would be tortured until they give up our HQ or die."

I am sick to my stomach. Partly from the run, and partly from the thought of those poor people in the helicopter deciding between death and torture. All because of me. I vomit. My throat burns, and my stomach continues churning. I cough, choke, and vomit again. As I do, there is an explosion louder than any of the others. I do not need to look. I know that the helicopter just went down.

I turn toward Shawn and look at his face. I am exhausted. He is covered in dirt, sweat, and grime. I am sure I look the same. Then I notice his left arm. The flames burned through his jacket and into his skin. The air smells of burned flesh and vomit.

I reach for his arm but do not touch it. "Are you all right?"

He looks at me and pauses. "I am now."

I let myself fall into his arms and feel his embrace.

< 239 >

25

A CLOSE CALL

follow Shawn. We walk quickly through the ever-dying woods. Through the wilted tree leaves, I see the sun lowering. The trees should be losing their leaves by now, but they are hanging on for dear life as they fight whatever is killing them. I imagine these will be the last leaves these trees ever sprout.

"So, how did you plan on doing this exchange without having me to trade?" I ask. "What was your plan back there?"

Shawn turns his head. "The plan was to get you and run."

"That is not a plan."

"It worked." He grins. "So, are you the tactical expert now?"

I know he is joking, but he is right.

What do I know about military tactics?

"We knew they wouldn't have any military aircraft on site because we are able to monitor aircraft movement. It would have given away their plan. So, we thought our chopper would be able to get us out. I was wrong."

"Where are we going, anyway?" I ask. "The Feds will be all over this place soon."

"We need to get to the coast and find a place to hole up until dark. After dark, we can follow the coast to Belle Isle Park. That's our rendezvous point for any survivors on the ground. An evac helicopter will be there at sunrise tomorrow."

I stumble over a log but catch Shawn's good arm and keep my balance. The woods are not too thick to pass through but thick enough to hide us. The landscape around the airport is similar to that around Manchester. Mostly woods and fields with a house here and there. Such a difference from my world, where the coast is packed with houses. As I understand it from talking to Fancy, people on their Earth pack into smaller living quarters in the cities. Due to war, poor living conditions, and atmospheric and environmental problems, there are simply fewer people in this world. Life expectancy is forty years for women, fifty for men. So almost everybody's double dies sooner here than in my universe.

"Can we just call someone to pick us up?" I ask.

"No. We didn't even bring coms. As soon as we say something, the Feds will be on us. Just like in our Manchester mission, we have to maintain radio silence. The Feds monitor everything in this area."

I am starving, thirsty, and exhausted. My legs ache, too. It takes everything I have to continue putting one foot in front of the other. I make a second mental note. In addition to hitting the gym, I need

< 241 >

to hit the running track if I survive all of this. But I push on, trying to keep pace with Shawn. In the last bit of daylight, I see the trees thinning up ahead and hear the ocean coming in and rolling out. Over and over. We have hit the coast.

Not long after we start north, staying just inside the tree line, a light appears at the edge of the trees. We move toward it in the darkness until we can make out that it comes from an old farmhouse. From the best I can tell, there is a field between the house and the ocean. We stay in the cover of the trees as we approach, and I make out a barn close to the house.

"Perfect," Shawn says. "Let's hide out in the barn and get some rest. Then, we'll move on so we are near the park just before sunrise."

The thought of resting in a barn reminds me of Grandma and Grandpa's farm. I love the smell of fresh hay and the coziness of a country barn. "Sounds perfect. Besides, for as long as I have been wearing this suit and as filthy as I feel in it, I should fit right in."

Shawn chuckles.

We make our way into the barn through a side door. Once inside, Shawn closes it and turns on a small flashlight. He slowly shines it around. A few cattle stir in a pen to our right. There is an old tractor and a couple other pieces of farm machinery in the barn's main area. The wooden floor creaks as we walk. I stay close to Shawn.

"This equipment looks pretty outdated," I say.

"This is top of the line," Shawn says. "Not much research and development go into agriculture. Another reason half the people are starving. Wait here." He hands me the flashlight. "Keep the light on me so I can see."

I do as Shawn asks. He climbs to the haymow and throws down four bales of hay, then comes down and cuts the twine with his

< 242 >

penknife. The hay aroma permeates the air as I help him spread it into two long piles.

Shawn smiles. "Instant beds."

A man shouts from outside the barn door. "Who's in there?" He is older, judging from the sound of his voice.

Shawn looks through a crack between two boards and whispers. "A farmer. Not the Feds. But he has a double-barrel shotgun. I'll hide and work my way around behind him. We'll know pretty quickly what side he's on once he sees you. If he's a Fed supporter, I'll jump him. We can tie him up and move on."

I nod. Shawn still has his weapon, but I am certain that he would never shoot an innocent man.

The door creaks open. I stand in the open with the flashlight on, pointed toward the roof so the farmer can identify me. The man steps inside with the shotgun stock against his shoulder, ready to fire. He has a flashlight in the hand that holds the barrel.

I am not scared.

Maybe it is the exhaustion, or maybe it is because I have been shot at by just about everything in the past few days, or maybe it is because he reminds me of the kinder Mr. Johnson.

He moves the light around until it hits me. Blinded, I squint and cover my eyes.

"Who are you, and what are you doing in my barn, mister?" he demands. He spits tobacco juice on the wood floor.

My hands still cover my eyes. "Can you lower your light a little, please?"

He lowers it enough to take the glare out of my eyes.

"You're not a mister. You're a she!" he shouts. Then he spits again.

"Thanks. Yes, I am a girl."

< 243 >

He moves the light up and down my body. "Wait a minute. You're her. Aren't you? That rebel girl, fighting all those bureaucrat idiots that have ruined our country."

I nod. "Yes."

"And now they're giving our country to China and Russia. Darn fools!"

Good. He sounds like he is on our side. Shawn will not have to jump him and tie him up. And more importantly, we might not have to move on before we can get some rest.

He walks closer, the gun still pointed at me. He spits again. "Well, I'll be. It *is* you. What in tarnation are you doing out here in the middle of nowhere, hiding in my barn . . ." He looks at the twine and the hay on the floor. ". . . and breaking apart my hay bales?"

"Sir, I am sorry about your hay bales. We will compensate you for them." I point to his gun. "But do you think you can stop pointing the gun at me?"

He looks at the gun and then at me and quickly lowers the weapon. "Oh, yes, of course. Sorry, ma'am." He holds out his hand. "The name is Randolph. Randolph Fowler."

I shake his hand. "Serenity Ashdown."

"A pleasure to meet you, ma'am."

"I have a friend with me," I say. "Is it okay if he comes out? He is harmless."

The farmer nods his head rapidly. "Oh, of course. Any friend of yours, Miss Ashdown, is a friend of mine."

Shawn emerges from the darkness near the door with his gun pointed to the ground. "It's nice to meet you, Mr. Fowler. We've had a little run-in with the Feds today. Would it be okay if we get some rest in your barn for a bit? We'll be gone before morning."

< 244 >

"Of course that's fine," Mr. Fowler replies. "I would invite you to stay in the house, but if the government comes a-knocking, they'll surely search the house. But I can keep them out of here. I'll tell them I've had a swine flu outbreak. Everyone's scared to death of that. They won't even know I don't got pigs." He chuckles.

I look at Shawn. "They are that scared of the swine flu?"

He grins. "I'll explain later. It's a lot different in this world." He turns to Mr. Fowler. "Thank you, sir."

"That's a nasty looking arm you got there, son. Why don't I have the misses take a look at it for you?"

Shawn shakes his head. "It'll be okay until I get back to HQ. It'll get looked at then."

"Okay, suit yourself." Mr. Fowler turns to leave. "Make yourselves comfortable. I'll send the misses out with some blankets, hot soup, and water. Maybe some salve for that arm, too, no matter what you say."

"Thank you," I say. "You are a blessing, sir." I smile. He has no idea how hungry and thirsty I am. And I am sure Shawn feels the same.

Mr. Fowler stops and turns his head. "You know, I always figured you to be a giant Wonder Woman, superhero-type person. But you look no different than my little granddaughter. You are the blessing, ma'am."

It warms my heart to hear that. There are so many good people in this world. They have just been beaten down, mistreated, and led astray. If only I could do more to help them.

I collapse on the hay and lean against the tractor tire. Shawn does the same. Finally, our first moment of calm.

"Who was in the van and helicopter?" I ask.

"The only person you know was Horace."

< 245 >

I can still see, as perfect as a picture, his dead body—lying on the asphalt with his chest burned.

If only I had the ability to delete unwanted words and images from this mechanical mind of mine.

"And how is Isaiah?" That has been a burning question of mine.

"He came to. He lost a lot of blood and still has a ways to go, but Sam says he'll be fine."

I close my eyes and whisper a two-word prayer, "Thank you." That is a huge relief.

"Shawn, they killed Dirk Bailey. I saw him. General Chen did it. It was horrible." I pause for a moment. I do not want to tell Shawn who killed their Serenity, but I feel that I must. So, I continue. "And it was General Chen who killed your Serenity. He told me so."

Shawn closes his eyes, lowers his head, and is silent for a while. Then he nods and looks at me. "We figured as much about Dirk when he went silent."

He does not address my comment about their Serenity, so I let it go. "They knew about Mr. Bailey for some time, and they fed him information to throw off the Resistance."

"Yeah," Shawn says. "We figured that out, too, after Isaiah filled us in on how you figured out Trent. You know, you saved all our lives in Manchester."

I lower my head. "Not *all* your lives. If I had figured it out sooner, all of those on the other team would be alive, too."

Shawn takes my chin in his hand and tips it up. "Hey. Even if you stop right now, you have already done as much for the Resistance and the people of this world as any one of the rest of us has. We all owe you such a debt of gratitude. You have to stop beating yourself up over things that you cannot control." He lowers his hand.

< 246 >

"That is just it. I feel like I should be able to control everything because I can see so much. Because I know so much. I would rather that I could not see or know anything."

Shawn smiles. "Even Mr. Fowler said it, and he just met you. You are a blessing."

I look at his face. "Thanks." I pause for a moment. "But now I have blown everything. The Feds know who I really am and that your Serenity is dead. So now the Resistance support is going to fade, and who knows what they will do to my dad."

Shawn leans forward and turns toward me. "No, no. You have it all wrong. You have no idea the support the Resistance has gained ever since they saw you in Manchester. Once they see you freed, the support will grow even stronger. The public doesn't know about the sphere and a parallel universe. They have no idea that there were two of you. So, there is no way they'll believe a story like that even if the Feds try to tell it. And I doubt the Feds will go there because they'd likely end up losing even more credibility. And your father is safe for now. The Feds know that they'll need him to get you back, and they still really need you."

The barn door creaks open. Mr. Fowler's wife enters with blankets over her shoulders. She carries a tray with two big steaming bowls, two cups stacked together, and a pitcher of water. I can smell the soup immediately. My mouth begins to water.

# # # # #

I lay on my hay bed. The blanket feels wonderful on such a chilly night, and the soup really hit the spot. I feel like I could sleep forever, but I am exhausted past the point of sleep. There is so much

< 247 >

running through my mind, and I know we have to move again soon. Shawn is still sitting up.

I sit up, too. "I cannot sleep. I am beyond tired." Then I hear faint voices. I whisper, "Do you hear that?"

"What is it?"

"People talking. Three men and Mr. Fowler." I recognize his voice. "Sounds like they are at the house."

"Probably the Feds. Can you make out what they are saying?"

"No, too faint."

"Come on." Shawn picks up his blanket and the food tray. "Let's stuff these under the tractor and cover them with hay."

I grab my blanket and help him. Then, we walk to the crack in the wall between the boards. Three flashlights approach the barn. As they get closer, I can see the men wear military uniforms and carry plasma rifles. Shawn puts his gun to his shoulder but keeps the barrel pointed down. I know what he is thinking. He will only shoot if absolutely necessary because the sound would alert the other Feds to our position. The men stop outside the door. One says, "Didn't you hear what the old man said? He's had a swine flu outbreak in there."

The second man replies, "Yeah. Have you ever seen what that stuff does to humans? It's nasty. And there's no cure."

The third man responds. "He was probably lying so we won't go in there. He's probably hiding something . . . or someone. Let's go in."

My heart races—I feel every beat. I am certain they have orders to bring me back alive, but they will kill Shawn. And I will be back in their custody. The barn door creaks. Shawn pushes himself against the wall and pulls his weapon up, aimed at the door. I stand against the wall behind him. My hands shake, and I hold my breath as the door starts to open.

< 248 >

"Wait," the first man says. "General Chen will never know if we don't go in. Why should we risk it?"

The second man responds, "Yeah, and if they *are* in there, they'll get the swine flu and die anyway. So, our job will be finished."

The third man is right at the door. He says, "Good point. I didn't think of that. Let's move on."

I exhale and almost collapse.

Shawn turns and raises an eyebrow. "That was close." He sets his weapon on the ground and leans it against the wall. "Let's give them a chance to clear out, then we'll move out to the evac point. I don't think we're going to get any more rest here."

< 249 >

A KISS

I take Isaiah's hand in mine. I had to see him before doing anything else here at HQ. It is so odd seeing him lying in bed surrounded by monitors and with an IV in his arm. He is the strongest person I have ever met.

He opens his eyes, turns his head toward me, and smiles.

"That is one of the few times I have seen you smile," I say with a grin.

He gently squeezes my hand. "You made it back. I knew you would."

"I had to. Somebody has to take care of you."

He smiles again. "You weren't supposed to give yourself up that easily. You should have let us try to take them out."

"Then you would be dead right now, along with the rest of the team. I could not let that happen."

He nods. "I know you couldn't. That's a sign of a true leader, you know. Always putting the team first."

"Well, any leader has to have a great team to lead, so get yourself better and get back out there. I need you."

I do not want him to go back out and get shot again, but I want to encourage him.

"Don't you worry, I will."

"You know, the HQs are meeting soon to discuss what we need to do next. I think it will involve me going home and the Resistance destroying the sphere." My throat starts to feel tight.

"I heard."

"So, this might be goodbye." I stop talking as I fear I will cry.

"Hey, it's okay," Isaiah says. "You'll be fine. And, thanks to you, we'll be fine, too."

My eyes start to water. "I just want to thank you for . . ." I pause. "For everything you have done for me. You were the first person in this world, and for a long time, the only person in this world, who believed in me. And you were the first person I knew I could trust. I could not have survived over here without you."

Isaiah reaches up.

His large, rough hand gently wipes a tear from my cheek. "It's us that should be thanking you. Now, you go out there and do your thing. Get yourself and your father home. And don't take any unnecessary chances. Be safe."

"I will never forget you."

Isaiah blesses me with another rare smile. "Nor I you."

I lean down and kiss his forehead.

< 251 >

# # # # #

I feel much better after a solid meal and some sleep and, most of all, getting out of that bodysuit and taking a shower. A shower never felt so good. And while the dye is still in my hair, it feels good to be myself, even if it is temporary. My room at HQ has become familiar, relaxing. In fact, the entire HQ complex is starting to feel comfortable. And seeing all of the smiles and hearing "welcome back" and "great to see you" when Shawn and I exited the elevator into the ops room made me feel like these people are family.

The ops room is empty except for the core group sitting around a table, a flashback to the last time we sat around this table, but some things have changed. The other HQs are on the big screen, with London HQ noticeably missing.

Also noticeable is the empty spot where Horace would sit. And Isaiah is still in the infirmary.

"Thank you all for getting together on such short notice, but time is running out," Shawn says. "Todd, can you give us an update on the Feds' progress?"

"Roger, boss." The only thing missing is a salute. "The UR is growing stronger every day as more and more governments try to join. But thanks to our footage of Serenity and her capture, the public's support for the Resistance is growing just as quickly. Our ability to air it in all languages was huge. Pockets of the Resistance are popping up all over the world in places where we have never had supporters. People don't want their governments joining the UR. Or, if they're in, they want them to leave."

A woman from Beijing HQ interrupts. "We have reports that the Chinese UR officials have an enormous number of vehicles, troops,

< 252 >

and weapons in transit to Boston. We assume it is because that is where the sphere is located, where the strongest connection is. They want to protect it."

"And they're preparing for an invasion," a man from Moscow HQ says. "We are getting the same reports about the Russian UR officials."

Sheila leans forward. "Isn't that why we've been mobilizing in Massachusetts, Resistance troops and equipment from all over?"

"Yeah, preparing for World War Five," Rodney says. "To be fought right here."

"Or, more appropriately, the first real Resistance-UR war," Sheila replies.

"Either way," Shawn says, "we aren't going to get our reinforcements here before the UR's arrive. And even if we could, our reinforcements will be a drop in the bucket compared to theirs. So, we need to take action now, before any reinforcements arrive, if we are going to have any kind of chance. Agreed?"

People on screen and in the room reply in various accents.

"Yes."

"Agreed."

"We agree."

"Affirmative."

"What action are we talking about?" Fancy asks.

The Chinese woman on the screen responds. "We need to take out the sphere. That has to be our first priority. That will at least buy us some time to capitalize on growing Resistance support while the UR rebuilds the sphere, and it will stop an invasion into the other universe, at least for now. With the Feds controlling the only access point, and ample resources on the other side, that would be a disaster for both worlds."

< 253 >

"I agree," the Russian man says. "We cannot beat them in an arms war. We need the people to beat them. To overthrow their respective government leaders."

I feel like I should just be a silent observer, but I have to say something at this point.

"This sounds just like what this world has been doing for centuries. One group knocks another out of power, just to be replaced by a worse group. Or one country takes over another just to oppress the citizens even more. How are all of these pockets of the Resistance taking over going to be any different? And if the Resistance does succeed in eliminating the UR, who will step into that role?"

Shawn leans back in his chair and looks at the screen. "Well, we haven't talked about it much. We've just been focused on surviving day-to-day." He pauses, looks down, and then looks up again, at me. "But it was our Serenity's plan, and hope, that once the Resistance takes control of the UR and any other countries that support it, there would be a one-world government with a democratically elected leader. That was what her leadership was based on. Why people followed her. That's still our ultimate goal."

I am certain there is an enormous amount of thought that needs to go into structuring a single-world government, giving one person that much power, but now is not the time to continue this discussion. Anyway, I am hopeful that I will be back home by then.

"Back to the plan," the Russian man says. He laughs. "What *is* the plan?"

Shawn looks up at the screen. "We need to take out the sphere, but first, we need to send Serenity and her father back through it, for two reasons." He holds up one finger. "First, as long as Serenity is here, the Feds will be after her. And if they get her, that speeds up

< 254 >

their progress." He holds up a second finger. "Second, maybe Serenity and her father can warn their world so they can prepare in case we fail on this side."

The Russian man stands up. "Moscow is in agreement."

The Chinese woman does the same. "As is Beijing."

Every other HQ follows suit.

The Chinese woman walks to the front of the table in her conference room and looks directly into the camera. "It looks like you have the full support of the Resistance. Since you will need to act before any of our resources arrive, we will leave the planning up to Massachusetts HQ. Let us know if you need anything, and keep us posted." She pauses for a moment. "And good luck, Massachusetts."

Shawn looks around the table. "Okay, folks. We need to act quickly, before the UR reinforcements arrive. But even without them, the sphere is housed in a virtual fortress. We're going to have to deactivate the AI system prior to attacking the sphere site."

"But how?" I ask. "I was not able to install Todd's program."

"No worries," Shawn says. "Do you think you can find the building they had you in and get back to the AI system? Will you need some sort of keycard, retinal scan, or other access?"

"Yes and no. Yes, I can find the building and get to the system. And no, they use touchtone keypads for access. The whole building is outdated, especially for the technology that exists on this side."

Todd jumps in. "But remember, most of the advanced technology is in weapons. And keeping outdated systems in that building is intentional. It's harder to hack. We can't get into the systems remotely."

I lean forward and look at Shawn. "But how can I get to the AI system? You will need me at the site to program the sphere. And what about my dad?"

< 255 >

Shawn folds his hands on the table. "Your father is being kept in the same place where the AI control is located. Is that right?"

I nod.

"We'll send a team to the AI building to extract your father and shut down the AI. You'll be at the sphere, but you can remotely walk the team through the building to get to the AI computers. Todd will be good at following your directions, and then he'll be there to shut down the AI."

Todd perks up and nervously glances at Shawn, then at me, and then back at Shawn. "Uh, wait a minute, boss. Did you just say that I will be with the team? In the field? You know that's not my thing, right?"

Shawn grins. "You'll be okay, buddy. We need you. Besides, maybe it'll give you a chance to use that Colt .45 you're always carrying around."

"But that's just for show, boss. I never really use it."

Shawn ignores Todd's comment and turns to me. "We could use one more public appearance out of you. Todd already broadcasted the fact that you broke free from the Feds, but if people can actually see you free, it may just be the boost they need to make them really want to make some noise and, therefore, the big boost the Resistance needs. Will you do that?"

"You have done so much for me and are still trying to get me and my dad home. How can I say no?" I nod. "Yes, of course I will."

Max, who has been quiet during the entire meeting, perks up. "Sounds like a plan. Let's make it happen."

# # # # #

"One more time," I whisper. All the activity I've done trying to be their Serenity has made me realize how out of shape I am. I figure

< 256 >

fencing is as good of an exercise as anything. I just need to do it more. And I need to tune up, as my sabre is my only defense against the Feds. I stand in the gymnasium alone, barely able to see the entrance from my position in the middle of the sparring mat. I only turned on a couple of lights.

I take the en garde stance. Advance, advance, retreat, advance, thrust, block, retreat, advance, advance, thrust. I pause. My gray sweat suit sticks to my skin, and I reach up to wipe beads of sweat from my forehead. They keep it warm in the gymnasium.

"Do you want some competition?" The voice comes from behind me.

I turn and see Shawn dressed in street clothes, standing by the bench along the wall.

I say, "It does not look like you came prepared."

He smiles and holds out a bottled water. "I thought you might be thirsty."

"Thanks," I say.

I walk over, take the water, and sit on the bench. Shawn sits beside me.

"Tomorrow's the big day," he says. "We need to find a place along the way to film you, but after that, if all goes as planned, you'll be going home."

Ever since I walked through that sphere, those are the words I have longed to hear: *You will be going home.* But hearing them now as I sit with Shawn, in this underground home, among friends who truly care about me, I do not feel the excitement I had imagined I would. It is with mixed emotions that I will leave my friends. That I will leave Shawn. Of course, that all assumes this complex plan actually works *and* I live through it.

< 257 >

I take a drink of water. "Yeah, that will be nice. That is what I have been wanting."

Shawn rests his elbows on his knees, still looking at me. "Are you nervous?"

I chuckle. "Are you kidding? I have been nervous ever since I walked through that sphere. And I have no idea how I will make it through tomorrow."

He smiles. "But you will. Just like you always do." He pauses, looks straight ahead, and continues. "You know, the other Serenity was tough. She could fight, punch, shoot, do just about anything combat-related, and she sure could put people in their place with that mouth of hers." He grins as if he is picturing her doing just that. "You may look exactly like her, but you're so different. I've never met anyone like you. You are tough in ways that I have never seen in anybody before."

I grin. "I will take that as a compliment, I think."

"It is." He looks at me, and his voice becomes solemn. "No matter what happens tomorrow, what you have done for the Resistance and for the people of this world can never be repaid. We could never thank you enough. You have risked everything and gone so far above and beyond. I can't even imagine what you've been going through." He looks at the floor. "And what you've done for me—" His voice cracks and he wipes his eyes. When he continues speaking, I hear the tears in his voice. "What you've done for me is give me my life back."

I take his hand. I try to talk, but there is a lump in my throat. My eyes fill with water and I feel the soft trickle of a tear rolling slowly down my cheek. I want to tell him how I feel about him. How much he means to me. I want to say, "I love you." But the words will not come out. Instead, I lean my face toward his as he does the same, and we kiss. A warm glow flows through my body from head to toe. He

< 258 >

pulls back and we stare into each other's eyes. His touch is gentle as he rubs the tear from my cheek.

We sit there in the moment. Shawn starts to say something, but the silence is broken by Todd's voice and the clang of the entrance door banging against the doorstop.

"There you are, boss." Todd walks quickly toward us. "I've been looking all over for you. What are you doing in—" He stops abruptly when he reaches us. His face lights up in surprise and embarrassment. "Oh. Sorry, boss. I didn't know you were . . . I mean, I had no idea that . . ."

Shawn saves him. "It's okay, Todd. We were just talking. Why are you looking for me?"

Todd stares at me. "Sorry to interrupt, ma'am."

He just called me "ma'am," as have others. Have I grown up that much since I arrived here? I grin slightly. "It is okay, Todd."

Shawn waves his hand between me and Todd's stare. "What's so urgent?"

"Oh, right. We just received a report from Diego. Apparently, a new bunch of Resistance supporters in Haverhill, Massachusetts came across three Feds in suits. They must be higher-ups. Anyway, they caught them and have them in the Haverhill Police Department holding cells. The entire town seems to have turned on the Feds and local police. All law and order is gone. They plan on executing them in Grand Army Park tomorrow at 'high noon,' as they put it. Apparently, some country boys are in charge, and they've watched too many Westerns. I don't think the Feds know about it yet. Diego says there are no Fed troops in the area."

Shawn stands. "Tell Diego to sit tight and let us know if anything changes. Tell him we'll be there tomorrow morning with a team." He

< 259 >

turns to me. "This looks like our opportunity to get you on the air, and with a crowd." He turns back toward Todd. "Without Dirk on the inside, can you still plug in to all the stations?"

Todd nods. "Roger that. Dirk left everything in place. I had him bury our program so deep, they'll have to dig to China to find it. They aren't as smart as we are, you know."

"They aren't as smart as *you* are," Shawn says. "Good work. Make the arrangements with Fancy."

When I stand, Shawn turns to me and stares. The look on his face matches my feelings. I wish the moment before Todd interrupted could have lasted forever.

< 260 >

THE LYNCHING

After another round with Ma and Charles last night, I am back in my full "combat Serenity" look. Charles, of course, wore another loud outfit. Although, "loud" is an understatement. A fresh coat of red dye, more tanning solution, a new pair of green contact lenses, and a reapplied tattoo have me looking just like their Serenity again. I tried to talk them out of the bodysuit, to no avail. Ma said it saved me once jumping through fire, and it could do so again. Ma did add a black jacket to the ensemble, since the temperature has been dropping.

As I understand it, every possible combat personnel from this HQ, as well as all others in range and those who have arrived in or near Boston from other HQs, along with every available weapon and vehicle, will be in action today. And the Feds will still outnumber and outgun us. People have been leaving the HQ in droves. There is no secrecy. The Feds know we are coming. That is why they are trying to get reinforcements here.

Not that they really need them.

It is still dark when I exit the elevator shed and hop into a white van that Shawn drives. Sheila, Max, Takeo, and Danica are also in the van. So is Fancy with the camera. We have to swing by Haverhill while the rest of the troops organize.

The drive is smooth and uneventful. When we reach Haverhill, I turn and peer between Shawn and Danica to look through the windshield. It is still odd to me recognizing the street names and landscape in and around the towns and cities where I grew up while the buildings are so different. It does not feel like New Hampshire or Massachusetts at all.

As we move closer to the center of town, there are more and more people on the sidewalks and in the streets. We drive as close as we can to the police department. It will be about half a block from Grand Army Park, unless that has changed, too. We finally have to stop about a block away from the park. The streets are too crowded to drive any farther.

Shawn glances in the rearview mirror. "Looks like we're on foot from here, folks. If we have to separate, meet back here at o-nine-hundred. We have exactly forty-five minutes to get the footage we need and depart. We have to be at the rendezvous point on time. But do not split off alone. And again, no coms. We can't let the Feds know we're here." Shawn looks at me. "Serenity, you're with Fancy and me at all times. We need to get you on camera."

< 262 >

We all climb out of the van.

Fancy turns to Shawn. "How will Todd know when to patch in our feed?"

"Yeah, we fixed that from last time," Shawn replies. "He'll patch in our feed once you start recording. He programmed the feed to go directly to a separate computer that he is monitoring. Once he sees a picture, he'll patch the feed in live to all networks and other channels."

Fancy nods.

Takeo reaches back into the van, under the bench, and pulls out his oversized submachine gun. He looks at me and smiles. "My personal bodyguard." I do not know why he thinks he needs such a gun for this stop. These people are all friendlies, except for the three Feds. And they are in custody. But that is Takeo.

I sling my sheathed sabre over my shoulder and grab my small gun with its empty magazine from under the bench, then move out with everyone else.

I feel suffocated as we push through the crowd, trying to make our way past the park to the police station so we can see the three Feds. At least the crowd is moving in the general direction of the park, but we need to move faster. Everyone is dressed in normal street clothes. There are no Resistance fighters here except us. Just Resistance supporters. But nobody seems to notice us decked out in tactical gear and carrying guns. These people must be so used to war and fighting that they are immune to someone walking down the street with an automatic weapon.

Pain shoots through my foot as a man's heel smashes down on it through my combat boots. Not on purpose, so I do not say anything—I just push on. In some spots, I have to lift my gun above my head to squeeze through the crowd. Still, nobody seems to notice.

< 263 >

When we reach the edge of the park, we come to a standstill. I cannot see a thing except the backs of the people in front of me. There is noise everywhere. Not shouting or protesting. Just loud talking and bustling, like you hear when people file into a crowded stadium.

"What's going on?" I shout to whoever cares to answer.

Max, the tallest member of our team, cranes his neck, peering over the crowd. "Looks like something is going on in the middle of the park. There's a little clearing with just a few people in it."

"Can we get to it from another angle?" Shawn asks.

Max relaxes and turns to face the rest of us. "No, the crowd has the clearing surrounded."

"Okay," Shawn says. "Max, you and Sheila head to the police department. See what's going on there. See if the Fed guys are still there." Then he looks at Fancy and me. "Fancy, Serenity, and I will move in for a closer look and see if we can get Serenity on camera in front of the crowd." Then he turns to Takeo and Danica. "You two hang out back here in the street as a go-between so we can report to each other without coms."

Everyone nods, and we separate. Before I dive into the crowd with Shawn and Fancy, I turn and scan the town behind me. If I block out the people and noise at the park, the rest of the town is eerily still and quiet. In that moment, I realize how long my mind has been focused on other things.

How long *has* it been since I randomly counted something or uselessly calculated the outcome of a situation? But thinking about it makes me count again. Forty-two trees in sight. Thirty-one different buildings. Fifty-seven parked cars: twenty-six sedans, eleven pickup trucks, eight vans, seven SUVs, and five large box trucks. Only one moving vehicle—a black SUV.

< 264 >

"Stop it," I admonish myself. I hesitate before turning toward the crowd. I try to clear my mind by focusing on the mission of being filmed. I do not want to turn and count the people in the crowd. Focus.

I turn to follow Shawn and Fancy into the crowd, but they are gone. They could be just a few feet in front of me, but I would not know. I can only see immediately in front of me. They must have moved forward thinking I was following. So, I begin the task of pushing through the crowd. I lower my head and point my gun barrel toward the ground. Holding my gun in one hand, I use my outstretched arms to pry apart the people in front of me, stepping forward through one pair of people at a time. Sunshine in the cloudless sky warms the air to an above-average temperature for late autumn. The forecast called for a much cooler day. With little airflow among the crowd, and due to the effort it takes to make my way through, I heat up. The jacket on top of the bodysuit is uncomfortable now, and there is sweat on my back.

An elbow catches me in the cheek, hard.

"Ouch," I instinctively shout. I stop and rub my face.

A large, heavyset man turns toward me, rubbing his elbow. "Sorry," he says in a strong Boston accent. He looks away and then quickly turns back. He lowers his head, squints, and looks me up and down. Either he is the first person to wonder why a girl carrying a sabre and an automatic weapon is fighting through the crowd or he recognizes me.

"Hey, you're the Ashdown girl, aren't you? Serenity Ashdown. Everyone's been wondering if you would be here for the executions. Most people said you wouldn't. They said Haverhill is small potatoes for you. You have much more important things to do." He straightens

< 265 >

up, a proud smile on his face. "Not me. No, ma'am. I knew you would be here. I told everyone you care about every town and every situation. Yes, ma'am. That's what I said. Oh, and the name is Clarence. Clarence Shultz."

Is this what it is like for movie stars and athletes? Do they get treated like this day in and day out? I smile. I want to keep moving forward.

Then it dawns on me. He is a big man. Maybe he is my ticket to getting to the front of the crowd.

"Yes, sir. I came to oversee the proceedings. Do you think you could assist me in getting through this crowd to the clearing?"

He still wears his proud smile. "Why, it would be an honor, Miss Ashdown."

He puts a large, hairy hand on my back, turns toward the crowd, and starts to push me forward, shouting, "Make way! Clear a path! Serenity Ashdown coming through! I'm escorting the leader of the Resistance. Make way! Clear out!"

People turn to look at Clarence bellowing out commands, then they look at me. To my amazement, they nod and step aside as soon as their eyes fall on me, pushing their backs into people, forcing them to make room.

Slowly, a path opens before us. Clarence and I move toward the clearing step by step. He continues to yell commands, although unnecessarily now because the people have started a chain reaction of turning. And as soon as they are fixed on me, the noise and chatter around us stop.

As we get close to the clearing, I hear distinct voices coming over a microphone. The sound probably could reach the street if it was not drowned out by all the crowd noise.

< 266 >

"So, Bo, how should we settle this?" the first voice asks.

"Well, Jimmy, I think we oughtta vote," the second voice replies.

"Yeah, let the people vote. They have rats, you know."

"Rats?" I whisper. What is he talking about? Oh, *rights*.

We move closer. The path continues to clear.

"All right," Jimmy says. "Good idea. Let's vote. We'll go by whichever gets the loudest roar from the people. Y'all have two options to pick from."

Really? Have this many Massachusetts people gathered to listen to an address by two Southern country boys?

Bo takes the mic. "Rat Jimmy. Y'all can choose either the sword for a beheading—my personal favorite—or guns for a firing squad."

Oh, this is not simply an address. They are deciding how to kill the captured Feds. That was not supposed to happen until noon.

Finally, the path opens into the clearing. At the center, standing beside each other, are two men with a microphone, presumably Bo and Jimmy. From his voice, I can tell the tall, thin one in blue jeans and flannel is Jimmy. Bo wears bib overalls. Probably the only thing he can fit over his protruding belly.

"So, what's it going to be?" Jimmy says into the mic. He points toward a samurai sword and the three rifles sitting on a table beside them. "Death by a sword or death by guns?"

My eyes move across the table and off to the side.

Three men sit in folding chairs. Their suits are disheveled, their ties have been removed, and their hair is mussed. The men's heads are down, and their hands are behind the chairs. Two more men in denim and flannel stand behind the Feds, each holding a shotgun.

They look like they are trying to stand at attention, but both are fidgeting.

< 267 >

I look around but see no sign of Shawn and Fancy. Then, I look up at Clarence.

"I thought the executions were to be at noon?"

"They were," he replies. "But the boys moved them up to nine for fear the military would find out and get here before noon. Good thing you got here early."

The Feds then lift their heads and look toward Bo and Jimmy. I gasp. I recognize two of the Feds. One is James. And the other—the other is Phillip Ashdown. Not my dad. It is their Phillip Ashdown. These people probably do not realize how big a fish they actually caught. All three of the Feds look tired, dirty, and hopeless.

What do I do? The people will expect me to oversee the executions. Maybe even perform them. Their Serenity would probably enjoy that, after everything these men did to her. But I cannot oversee such a thing, let alone execute someone. I think about my dad. I think about what the Feds have put me through. I try to make myself angry, hoping that will help. I think about General Chen. How he killed the other Serenity. How much that hurt Shawn. And I think about the smug look on General Chen's face as he told me he had ordered the shot that killed my mom.

Anger boils inside me.

I want to see the Feds die. And yet, I also do not. Not here, not now, not like this. That is not me. And more death will just feed this community's rage. That is all they have known. Kill or be killed. There has to be another way. For these people to survive, for their planet to survive, they need an alternative to killing that does not leave them feeling helpless. Their only hope for survival has always been to destroy the enemy. They need a new hope, one that gives them a peaceful way of life.

< 268 >

Clarence brings me out of my trance. "Come on. I'll introduce you to the boys."

I look around. Still no sign of Shawn or Fancy. Clarence puts his hand on my back and moves me forward again. As we walk across the open ground toward Jimmy and Bo, I look toward the Feds. James looks at me and our eyes connect. The expression on his face says, "help us." All three of them must know who I really am. My declaration and proof to Mr. Franklin and General Chen would have made it all the way up and down the Fed ranks by now and probably the rest of the UR.

But Shawn was right. They did not try to convince the public. And that was a wise choice based on how this crowd has reacted to me. Just one crowd in one small city in one country. Any attempt to expose me would have backfired.

I continue to look at James as I move forward. He knows that I am the scared, shy girl that he drove around, got meals for, and took care of when I first arrived. I would not call James a friend, but he never did anything to harm me. Well, nothing beyond being a Fed. He was always kind.

Mr. Ashdown looks at the ground again. He hated me when he thought I was his daughter. He wanted nothing more than to kill me. I was so afraid around him. But it was not me he hated—it was his daughter. My dad and I have our differences, but how a father and daughter can grow so far apart, I will never know, but now he knows for sure that his daughter, his Serenity, is gone. He will never see her again. I wonder if his feelings have changed.

When we reach Jimmy and Bo, their eyes light up. Jimmy lays the mic on the table. "You've got to be kidding me, Clarence. Where'd you get her from?"

< 269 >

Clarence smiles and blurts out in his Boston accent, "I told you boys she'd be here. Came for the executions." He looks at my sabre. "Probably wants to perform them herself with her own sword."

Bo interrupts. "Aw, man. I wanted to do a vote."

Everyone ignores him.

Clarence holds out his hand to me, palm up, and looks at Jimmy and Bo. "Jimmy, Bo, I would like to introduce you to my good friend, Miss Serenity Ashdown."

His good friend? We just met ten minutes ago.

Then, Clarence moves his hand toward Jimmy and Bo and looks at me. "Miss Ashdown, meet Jimmy and Bo. They're in charge of things here. Well, they were until you arrived."

Jimmy holds out a hand. "Nice to meet you, Miss Ashdown. You can take over the proceedings. Just let Bo or I know if there's anything at all we can do for you." I shake his hand.

Bo throws his hands in the air. "Now all the fun's gone. She's just gonna kill 'em. There won't be no vote."

Again, Bo is ignored.

Clarence steps to the side. Jimmy picks up the microphone, flips the "on" switch, and looks out to the crowd. Word must have already spread about me, because they've already quieted down.

"Folks, we have a very special guest with us today. I give to you the one and only, the leader of our great cause, the one who will lead us to victory over our oppressors, the one who will singlehandedly destroy the Feds and bring down the entire UR." Then he shouts into the mic. "Miss Serenity Ashdown!"

The crowd erupts in a deafening roar. Never have I heard such a noise. And it is directed at me. I feel grateful and humble and terrified all at the same time. What these people expect from me, not even

< 270 >

their Serenity Ashdown could deliver. Their cause is far greater than one person. And the Feds and the UR are far more powerful than their cause. But the more immediate problem is that they expect me to execute these three men. I search the crowd. It stretches as far as I can see. I look at those in the front and see the hope in their faces as they stare at me. Then, I see Shawn and Fancy. They are in the front row. The camera is rolling. Shawn must figure this is my moment. He stays back. His gun is at the ready, but I probably couldn't be in a safer place, physically, than I am at the moment.

Jimmy hands me the mic, and I lay my gun on the table. The crowd goes silent. Time to talk like their Serenity. I do not think I have to be sarcastic and mouthy. I just cannot talk too perfectly. I do not think it will take much to keep this crowd convinced I am their Serenity.

"Wait," Bo says. In one swift motion, he grabs me by the waist with both hands and swings me up onto the table, high enough that my feet are firmly planted on it. Then he scoots the weapons to the side. "There, a stage."

I look out at the crowd. I can now see all the way to the street and beyond. I quickly survey the area, and something catches my attention. The black SUV is parked near the park. There are just as many sedans, pickups, vans, and SUVs as there were earlier, but there are now two additional box trucks. The original five are parked next to a commercial establishment. But the two new arrivals are parked in a residential section of town.

Clarence loudly clears his throat. I look, and he is staring at me. I realize the crowd has been silent, waiting for me to talk.

I put the mic to my mouth. "Ladies and gentlemen of Haverhill, it is my pleasure to be with you today. And it is so nice to meet you all."

< 271 >

The crowd mumbles. I look at Clarence, Jimmy, and Bo. They look a little puzzled. I can tell that Clarence is now forcing his smile. I look at Shawn. He motions for me to kick it up a notch. I guess my pleasantries are not suited for an execution. These people must be expecting a little more. But I am still not sure what I want to say. How do I get out of killing these Feds, yet still leave the Resistance intact and convince the people that I am their Serenity? Oh boy. But I need to say something. And use contractions.

I look at the crowd again and shout into the mic. "People of Haverhill. You've accomplished what nobody else in the Resistance has been able to do." I pause for effect. "Capture three high-ranking Feds!" The crowd cheers. "The Resistance is proud to have you as supporters, and I am honored to have you on my team!" The crowd cheers again. Then, I shout louder. "With people like you, how can we fail?"

The crowd erupts, even louder. I have them going. I have their attention. Now is the time. This may be my one and only chance to change the direction of the Resistance, to change the direction of this war, to change the direction of this planet. I am in front of an enormous crowd and on worldwide television. I now know what I have to do.

I point to the three Feds and continue. "These three men have helped the UR government cause nothing but pain and suffering to you and your children."

A man in the front yells, "Kill them!"

Another man repeats it, "Yeah, kill them!"

Then the crowd erupts, everyone yelling. "Kill them! Kill all the Feds!"

"Wait," I say into the mic. But the crowd still shouts.

< 272 >

I shout into the mic. "Silence, please! Silence. Let me speak."

The crowd quiets down, and I continue. "If we execute these men, then we are no better than the Feds. All that you have known in your lives . . ." I catch myself. "All that *we* have known in our lives—is war, fighting, death, and destruction. Look what it has done to our planet. Look what it has done to our lives. Look what it has done to us, and to our children. Our children are not dying solely because of the Feds, and they're not dying solely because of the UR. This planet started to die long before those governments ever existed. It's the culmination of war after war after war that's killing this planet, and our children." I pause.

The crowd is completely silent.

James, Mr. Ashdown, and the other Fed have raised their heads. They look at me intently.

I continue. "Even if your children survive, is this the world you want them to grow up in? Will there even *be* a world to grow up in? This planet is dying because of what we've done to it. It must change now for there to be any hope of a future. We can't keep doing what our fathers did."

I look directly at Mr. Ashdown and then back toward the crowd.

"We cannot keep doing what our grandfathers did and their fathers and grandfathers before them. It has to change. I know the Feds have promised a change. A new life that will save everyone. Well, I'm here to tell you that is not true. I've seen what the Feds are referring to, and it's not an option. It would come at a great cost of innocent lives. Your only hope . . ." I catch myself again. "*Our* only hope is this planet. This life that we have right here, right now. What you, the Resistance, and the rest of the world choose to do from this moment forward will define what that life is like. We've all suffered

< 273 >

great loss. And out of revenge, survival, or whatever reason, I, like the rest of you, have vowed to physically destroy the Feds and everyone involved with them. You've put your faith, trust, and hope in me to lead you in this quest. But now, I'm here to tell you that we must be bigger than the Feds. We must change our goals, change our quest." I shift to a louder tone. "Our quest can no longer be to destroy a nation. Our quest must be to unite a world!"

The people look at one another, nodding and smiling.

I speak softly again. "This new quest will still call for sacrifices. We'll still need arms to defend ourselves against the Feds. But that is just in the short term. What we must do as the Resistance, as a nation, and as a world, is to join hands and become one common voice. We have to unite every person in every country in every part of the world in our quest for peace, because nothing short of a world-wide effort will save this planet from the toxins that are killing it. The Feds and the UR are no more than a *thing*—a governmental structure. But without any people to govern, there can be no government. So, if the world unites under a common peaceful cause, then there can be no Feds." I shout again. "There can be no United Republic!"

The crowd erupts with cheers.

I take a few steps across the wobbly table. "And remember, the Resistance isn't one person. Our cause isn't one person. Our new quest isn't one person. It's the people. It's *you*." I pause. My eyes start to water and my throat grows tight. I truly want these people to live joyful lives. I clear my throat. "I may not always be here. A time may be coming soon when you'll have to move on without me. But I'm not your only hope." My voice cracks. I pause to gather my emotions. "*You* are your hope." People nod, and some wipe away tears. "So, I say to you again: What you choose to do at this very moment will define

< 274 >

the rest of your lives. This is your one chance to change everything. To change the world."

I point to the Feds. "These three men have hurt me as much as they have hurt any of you. But I choose to walk away. I'm not going to kill them. I choose peace. But the choice is yours. You can execute them with swords, knives, guns, however you like, and continue down the same path that you have been on for hundreds and hundreds of years. That path will certainly lead to your death by the Feds or death by the planet itself." I put both hands on the microphone. "Or, you can set an example for the rest of the world, a world watching this live right now, and walk away, choosing the path of peace, giving yourselves a chance at life, giving your children a chance at life. Giving yourselves hope."

The crowd is completely silent. I lay the microphone on the table. Clarence and Jimmy are both silent, no smiles. Just calm. Bo is crying, a little too much for a grown man.

I look at the Feds. The unknown man watches the crowd with a look of hope on his face. Mr. Ashdown's head is bowed again. He is either remorseful or planning what his next move will be if we let him go. Probably the latter.

James looks at me, tears in his eyes. I believe he truly is remorseful. I nod to him and look at the crowd again. The people have turned and are beginning to quietly disburse. Nobody comes forward toward the Feds. I look beyond the crowd again. The two box trucks have moved closer, still in a residential area. I squint. They are far away, but there is no writing or markings on their sides, like you would expect on a delivery truck.

Oh no.

I jump down, grab my gun, and run toward Shawn and Fancy.

< 275 >

Before Shawn and Fancy can say anything, I shout, "They are here! The Feds are here! You need to break radio silence. Tell the rest of the team they are in two unmarked box trucks in the residential neighborhood one block north of the park."

Shawn pulls out his radio and relays the message.

I look at Fancy. "Was I live?"

She smiles. "As live as ever, girl. You were fantastic."

Shawn interrupts. "The team is all together in the street. They are directing people to the east and west, and then they will move toward the neighborhood to intercept the Feds. We're going to go northwest, then come back east and try to flank them. We'll be outgunned and outnumbered, so that's our best shot. Let's move."

Danica and Takeo shout orders, and people move with urgency to the east and west. As we start to move out, a voice comes from behind us. "How can we help y'all?" I turn. There stand Jimmy, Bo, and Clarence, each with one of the three rifles that had been on the table. The two country boys that were standing at attention are also there with their shotguns.

I can see the wheels turning in Shawn's head. I am sure he is thinking that we can use the numbers but wonders if these guys will make it harder for us and get themselves killed.

Shawn nods. "Alright." He points to Clarence, Jimmy, and the country boys. "You four go with what's left of the crowd and make sure they go right and left. When you hit the street, join up with the rest of our team for a frontal assault." Then, he points to Bo. "You come with us."

Bo smiles from ear to ear. How can this be fun?

As we move out, I hear the first weapon fire coming from just beyond the street and the neighborhood. First plasma rifles, then

< 276 >

automatic weapons. I turn one more time. The three captive Feds have broken free of their chairs and are running across the park toward the gunfire with their hands still tied behind their backs. Nobody secured them.

I did not want them killed, but I did not intend that they be set free. At least not until all of this is over.

We run hard. I am actually starting to get in shape. I am able to keep up. A little winded, but not like before. I can see that Bo is struggling, sweating profusely in his heavy shirt and bib overalls. From the looks of him, it has probably been years since he increased his stride past a walk.

The weapon fire continues, growing louder and more frequent. The crowd races for cover now. But oddly, there is not much screaming or yelling, like people are used to this. That is good, yet in a way, it is also sad.

As we close in to flank, Danica shouts, "Take cover!" We all dive to the ground next to two vans parked along the street. First, I hear an explosion. It does not sound like the explosions I have heard on television, nor does it sound like anything that I have heard in this world. It sounds more like an implosion—softer, not deafening.

Then, I see yellow, red, and blue flashes in the large area we just came from. They probably cover the entire park and the street in front of the park. Then dirt, asphalt, debris, and tree trunks split in half fly into the air.

"Oh my," I say. "What was that?"

"Plasma grenade," Fancy answers. "There will be a crater back there a good twenty to thirty feet deep, fifty to a hundred yards across in every direction. And grenades are tiny. You don't want to see the damage from a plasma bomb or plasma missile."

< 277 >

I shake my head. "Those poor people. Some of them still had to be in that area."

Shawn looks at me. "But if you hadn't warned us, they all would have been."

Once again, I should be happy that I saved lives. But instead, I am saddened that I did not save them all.

I look at Fancy. "You guys keep saying how much more destructive the weapons are here compared to my world. Plasma grenades, plasma bombs, plasma missiles. I believe it."

Fancy looks at me. "And that's not the half of it. Antimatter bombs are the real doozies."

I remember Isaiah telling me that antimatter bombs are fifty times more destructive than nuclear bombs.

Fancy confirms. "They are much more destructive than your nuclear weapons, and they leave no after-effects, like the radiation from your nukes. So, the enemy can move right in."

Shawn crawls to the other side of the van, then crawls back. "It looks like the rest of the team has the Feds pinned down around a few of the houses on the next street. The houses are probably empty since everyone was at the park, so we should be able to go full-on. Thankfully, we got to the Feds before they could disburse." He looks at Bo. "How good are you from a distance?"

Bo smiles and spits on the ground. "I can shoot a gnat off a horse-fly at a hundred yards."

"Good," Shawn says, giving Bo a look that says, *really?* "You and Serenity stay here and cover us. Fancy and I will move up to flank."

Bo stands and leans against the front of the van with his rifle up and ready to fire.

I feel useless now.

< 278 >

I wonder if Bo questions why I, the Resistance leader, hang back, why I do not take a shooting position. But he does not seem to care. Maybe he thinks the Resistance always protects its leader like this. Or, the more likely answer is that he does not think at all.

I crawl to the back of the van and peer around it, watching Fancy and Shawn. They get into position and start firing. Soon, return fire comes at them. The Feds wear their normal green military fatigues. I watch as one of them moves to Shawn's left. It looks like he is trying to flank the flanker. If that is even a military term.

Shawn does not see him. I draw in a deep breath to shout a warning as loudly as I can, but before I do, Bo's rifle pops. The flanking Fed drops to the ground. That was at least seventy-five yards. Wow, Bo *can* shoot.

I watch as Fancy takes a shot in the leg. She is immobile as two Feds move up on her. I do not think of the consequences. I have to help my friend. I gather myself to sprint toward her.

"Cover me," I shout to Bo.

I sprint as fast as I can across the street and into the next row of houses. I look up and see one of the two Feds taking aim at me. But I cannot stop. I have to get to Fancy. I have to hope he misses. Bo's rifle pops again and the Fed drops. There is another pop, and the second Fed drops.

I dive to the ground beside Fancy. She holds her leg and grimaces. She has to be in a lot of pain. "Are you hit badly?"

She shakes her head. "Just my leg."

"Can you put a little pressure on it?"

"I think so."

I help her up and, with her arm around my neck and mine around her waist, we run-limp toward Bo. He fires beyond us. Nothing comes

< 279 >

at Fancy and I. Bo must be keeping them at bay. We dive down behind the van.

"Thank you," Fancy says.

I look around the van again. Shawn has moved forward. And I can now see the rest of the team closing in. Then, the black SUV speeds past the box trucks. One of the trucks pulls out, and the weapon fire stops. The other box truck just sits there. There are no more Feds anywhere. They must not have needed both trucks to haul themselves out. We must have really had them pinned.

Bo and I help Fancy up, and we move forward to meet the rest of the team. Except for Takeo, Jimmy, and the two country boys, everyone is there, including Diego. Max, held up by Danica, clutches his side.

Shawn looks at him. "How bad is it?"

Max grimaces. "I'll live. Just a plasma graze. It didn't burn too deep."

Sheila looks at Bo. "The two guards that were helping us. They were in the grenade blast zone. I'm sorry."

Clarence lowers his head and walks away.

Bo shakes his head. "I never knew who they was. They just come out and started guarding."

Takeo shouts from near the street where we all started. "You guys better get over here."

We hurry to him. First, I see Jimmy lying on the sidewalk, hands on his stomach. He is deeply burned and will not make it. Bo runs to him, kneels, and takes his hand. Tears run down Bo's cheeks. He does seem to be quite emotional for a big ol' country boy.

Jimmy struggles to talk. "Did you get 'em all, buddy?"

Bo nods and talks through his sobs and tears. "I did, buddy. I got 'em. We killed them Feds and ran 'em out of town."

< 280 >

Jimmy looks at Bo and nods slowly. "Good, good." His head rolls away from Bo, and he is gone.

"What happened to the captive Feds?" Shawn asks.

Takeo says, "I saw Mr. Ashdown and one of the others get in the box truck."

Then, I hear a faint voice. "Help."

I turn in the direction from which it came. One of the captive Feds lies in the grass. I walk over. It is James. He was hit in the chest by his own men. He has a plasma burn. It is not deep, but it is deep enough.

He stares straight up.

I kneel beside him. "James, I am here."

He struggles to turn his head toward me. "Serenity, I am sorry. For everything."

"Try not to talk, James. We will get help." I say that, but I know help will never arrive in time.

He slowly shakes his head. "It's too late. You didn't deserve any of this." He reaches in his pocket. Struggling, he pulls out a long metal object. It is hollow and about as wide as a pencil, but half as long. He places it in my hand. "You will need this."

I have no idea what he is talking about. "For what? What will I need it for?"

He tries to speak, but nothing comes out. He swallows hard and tries again. "For . . ." His eyes go blank, and he stops breathing.

I examine the object. There are random jagged edges inside the hollow tube. I do not know what it is for, but I put it in my jacket pocket.

I hear footsteps behind me, then Shawn's voice. "What did he say?"

< 281 >

I stand and, for the first time, notice the massive crater in front of me. Staring at the enormity of it and knowing that it was caused by one small grenade almost overwhelms me.

I answer Shawn. "I am not sure."

< 282 >

28

THE BATTLE

I peer between Shawn and Danica at the map laid out on the Jeep Wrangler's hood. Shawn moves his finger across it as he reinforces the plan.

"We, team one, are here," Shawn says as he looks at the map and points to our position. "The target site is here, about two miles east of us." He points again. "Team two is about another two miles east of the site." He looks up at the unit leaders gathered around the front of the Jeep. "We couldn't jam the Feds' signal, so teams one and two will maintain radio silence until the attack begins. Then, it doesn't matter. We go at fifteen hundred." He looks at the group, then at the map again. "We'll spread out along this perimeter and push forward." He points to a spot on the map and moves his finger. "They'll be expecting us, but our intel says their reinforcements have not yet arrived." He looks up again and clears his throat. "Still, they have us outnumbered, and they have superior weapons. We don't expect any tanks since they have the AI defense. Plus, given the terrain, tanks would be pretty useless." He pauses as a few people mumble something among themselves. "We'll have some mounted machine guns, but, again, the vehicles will have a rough go of it. And their aircraft will be useless in this forest. It's too thick, and their own troops will be too close."

We are on a dirt road in the middle of a forest. Surrounded by trees, for the first time I notice the rotting smell of the dying vegetation. "Is it like this all the way to the sphere?"

Danica nods. "Yeah, and it gets worse. The building housing the sphere sits on top of a hill. We'll be fighting uphill. The prime connection point between universes couldn't have been in a more defensible location for them. They got lucky."

"But how do they get equipment in and out?" I ask.

Shawn replies, "There is a gravel access road to the south, right here." He points to a spot on the map. "But it'll be the most fortified area. We'll try to avoid it."

Sheila steps forward. "So, what's the plan to deal with the artificial intelligence defense?"

Shawn takes a deep breath. "Okay, so here's the deal. They have plasma rifles, plasma machine guns, and plasma grenade launchers surrounding the site. They also have anti-aircraft and anti-missile AI, which is why we can't just bomb the site or drop in. There's no way to destroy the sphere from a distance." He pauses and wipes a bead of perspiration from his forehead. "Anyway, the ground AI defense units have been randomly placed anywhere from five to thirty yards

< 284 >

from the building in all directions. They are in the ground, completely buried, with motion detectors or vibration detectors or some sort of detectors. Something triggers them and they pop up and start firing. We haven't figured out what makes them choose their targets—motion, vibration, heat, something. But they are very accurate."

I step back from the Jeep. This sounds like an impossible task. Maybe I should get them to call it off. I do not want them to risk their lives in such a situation just to get my dad and me home. But I have been told time and time again that this mission is not just about getting us home. It is about preventing an invasion into my world and about getting the upper hand on the Feds, especially before their reinforcements arrive. So, I say nothing.

Shawn continues. "Team three, led by Rodney, is in Boston. They will be invading the building where the AI system is located which is also where Serenity's father is being held. Their job is to secure the building, grab Serenity's father from his cell which is on the route to the AI system controls, disarm the AI system, and evacuate Serenity's father to the site once it's secure. Todd has a program to disarm the AI system. They just need to get him to the system." He nods to the gray van parked behind the Jeep. "Serenity will be in the back of the van, which will stay right here. Far enough from the action to be safe but close enough to the site to get there once it's secure. She'll be on video and com with Todd, giving him directions and keypad codes. We were able to jam the Feds' signal in Boston, so Serenity and Todd can talk." Shawn looks at me. "You'll have a second screen in the van with a video feed from me so you can see what's going on here. If we lose coms or the Feds jam them, you can see when it's clear for you to move forward. If something happens to me or my camera, switch to channel two. Danica has a backup."

< 285 >

Danica takes over. "But the real fighting begins once the AI system is down. We have to penetrate the concrete structure that houses the sphere without blowing it up. It'll be heavily guarded by Feds, both inside and out. Once we're through that, it's up to Serenity to program the sphere."

Shawn looks at me again. "Do you have the program from Todd?"

"Yes," I answer. "Mr. Bailey made him a copy of the program the Feds were going to have me use. But Todd says he made some upgrades, so it should run much faster. I just hope I can keep up with it."

Takeo smiles. "You'll able to keep up. Zettai ni."

Danica steps back from the Jeep with a stern look of determination. "And once Serenity and her father are through, we set the charges and blow the place."

Shawn looks around at the attentive listeners. "Any questions?" It is silent. He looks at his watch. "Good. We move out in fifty-three minutes. Make sure you have plenty of ammo."

I walk to the van, sit on the ground, and lean back against the side. Fifty-three minutes. Anxiety, fear, and sadness simultaneously come over me. I am anxious to get started. The waiting is the most difficult part. Yet I am also scared to get started. So many things have to go right for the plan to work, but so many little things can go wrong and ruin it. And sadness. If all goes as planned, I will be home in a few hours. That was all I wanted when I got here. But these people have become my friends. Not like friends who are acquaintances or people who are your friends because you can do something for them. These are true friends. They are willing to lay down their lives for me. And then there is Shawn. I will never see him again. Just thinking of that breaks my heart. I do not know if he feels the same about me. His

< 286 >

feelings are surely more complicated, but he very well might. But does he feel that way because of who I remind him of, or does he feel that way because of who I really am?

Shawn plops down beside me and hands me a bottled water. He takes a drink of his. "Are you ready for this?"

I take a sip. "I think so. But ready or not, it needs to happen."

Shawn bends his knees and rests his elbows on them, still holding his water bottle in one hand. "I suppose so."

I pick up a small stick and scratch the dirt with it. "So, what happens after my dad and I are gone? I know you blow up the sphere, but what then? I'll be back in my comfy world, and you'll still be dealing with all of this."

Shawn looks out into the woods and is silent for a moment.

Then, he speaks. "Well, hopefully your speech takes hold. Best case scenario, we continue to fight the Feds and the rest of the UR for a while, but the general public slowly makes the UR government obsolete. Then there is no longer an invasion threat for your world, and we put in a democratic system, get the planet back on track, and live happily ever after."

"And the worst-case scenario?"

He looks at me. "The worst-case scenario? Your speech doesn't work, or it only works for a while, until the UR threatens and kills enough people and they start wanting a hero again instead of using the power they have themselves to change things. The Resistance is either eliminated by force or crumbles under lack of support. The Feds build and program another sphere and invade your world." Shawn picks up a stone and tosses it into the woods. "But the most likely scenario is that the fighting continues as it always has. It takes too long for the Feds to build and program another sphere, and the

< 287 >

planet and everyone on it dies. The good news is that in two of the three scenarios, your world is safe."

I put too much pressure on my stick, and it breaks. I look at the broken piece lying on the ground. "But in two of the three scenarios, you die."

He tosses another stone. "I suppose that's a possibility."

I look at him. My heart is breaking. "I do not want that to happen."

We stare at each other, and I look deep into his eyes. I want to be close to him again, like in the meadow. I want to kiss him again, like in the gymnasium. I lean toward him, and he leans toward me.

"Shawn!" someone yells from the other side of the van. Neither of us moves. Then, we move our faces closer together. "Oh, there you are." A boy, probably my age, with bright red hair and freckles, bounces around to our side of the van. "We need you," the boy says. He does not even acknowledge me or apologize for the interruption.

But I guess, this is war.

I see Todd's view on one screen, and on the other, I see Shawn's.

"How's my feed?" Shawn asks.

I press Shawn's com. "Crystal clear, but why are you on com, Shawn? We are supposed to be silent until the attack starts."

Suddenly, I hear weapon fire and implosions. The same sounds the plasma grenade made at the park. Based on the video feed, I can tell Shawn has hit the ground. There are blue, red, and yellow flashes, and then tree trunks, dirt, and debris fly into the air.

I press Todd's com. "Todd, it has started."

< 288 >

"How's the feed at the Eagle's Nest?" Todd asks.

I press the com again. "Good, Todd. It is coming in clearly."

"Affirmative. But remember, I'm Eagle One, and Shawn is Eagle Two. This will keep the Feds from tracking us."

Sometimes I wonder. For as brilliant as Todd is, he has no common sense.

"Todd . . . um . . . I mean Eagle One, we have the Feds' signal jammed in your area, so no code is necessary. And if they are able to break the jam, they know who we are. We and they are the only people who use these channels. So, I think we are long past stealth. Just saying."

"All right, all right. You have a point."

I hear Shawn on the com. "Hold your fire. It's the AI."

Someone else comes over the com. "We have heavy casualties over here."

"Back off," Shawn says. "They increased the range of the AI."

Then, more weapons fire. Plasma rifles and conventional weapons. Plasma blasts hit around Shawn. He fires. There are Fed troops among the AI weapons that have deployed, but the AI does not target them.

"What's going on?" Danica shouts over the com.

Shawn replies, "The Fed troops are pushing out from the building. We can't move any closer or the AI will activate. Stand your ground."

I can see what Danica was talking about earlier. The Fed troops have the high ground. The Resistance cannot hold at the perimeter forever. They will get picked apart. And they did not figure they would be under fire from Fed troops while they waited for the AI to be taken down.

"Todd, where are you guys at in the building?" I ask.

< 289 >

He replies, "We aren't even in the building yet. Rodney's team is still trying to secure it. I'm in the back in one of the vehicles."

"Get out and give me a look."

"What? They're shooting out there!"

"Todd, I need to see what's going on. Team one and two are under heavy fire."

I can tell the speed of Todd's movements based on the image from the video feed. He slowly climbs out of the vehicle and ever so slowly creeps around back. The target building appears on my screen. I do not recognize it as I was always blindfolded while going in and out, but I can see Rodney's team moving in.

I turn in my chair toward the freckled redheaded boy Shawn had left as my guard. "Dan. How long can teams one and two stand up against that kind of fire?"

He sits in a chair behind me and holds the barrel of his rifle with the stock resting on the floor. "They'll be okay for a while. They can dig in pretty good in that forest."

There is a knock on the double doors at the back of the van. "You guys okay in there?" It is the guard Shawn left outside. "A couple of those plasma blasts hit pretty close. We can back the van out another fifty yards."

I look at Dan and shake my head. I do not want to add to the time it will take to get to the sphere once the site is secure. If the site is ever secure.

"We're good," Dan replies.

Shawn shouts over the com, "Team one, back off about forty yards."

Then, another voice shouts, "Team two, do the same."

There are shouts, gunfire, and plasma blasts every time Shawn or someone else in the woods opens their com. There is gunfire

< 290 >

everywhere on Shawn's video. Plasma blasts burst all around him, and I see Resistance fighters go down when Shawn looks right or left. I can tell that he and the other Resistance fighters are shooting back, but very few Feds fall. Then, I see why Shawn fell back. The hill is not as steep in this spot, so they will not be fodder for target practice.

I sense Dan near my head. I turn, and his face is right beside mine, looking at the screens.

"Team three has to get the AI offline," he says, "so one and two can try to flank. They're getting killed just sitting there."

Todd's voice comes over the com. "I think we've secured the building. Rodney is motioning for me to move forward."

I watch Todd's video feed as he moves up to the building. "The outside entrance code is five-six-five-eight," I say.

Todd punches in the numbers, and the team enters. Good. At least the Feds have not changed the codes.

Rodney's voice comes over the com. On the screen, he points to three men. "You three stay out here to keep the building secure." He pauses. "Unit two in the rear, stay put."

The rest of the team enters the building.

"Straight ahead," I say. "Through a non-secured door. Then right." I watch Todd's view as he follows my directions. "At the end of the hall is a doorway to a stairwell. The code is one-one-one-three." I see men in front of Todd and hear more behind him as they descend the stairs toward another door. One of the men opens the door at the bottom of the stairwell. He is blown backward at the same time I hear the blast of a plasma rifle. His chest is burned through.

"Oh, oh! He's hit!" Todd exclaims. A Resistance fighter hugs each side of the door. Each in turn pops into the doorway and fires. One is hit, and another takes his place.

< 291 >

Rodney shouts, "Todd, get back up to the last landing!"

Todd moves up and peers over the railing at the action. Another Resistance fighter goes down, but then they move through the door. They must have cleared the hallway on the other side. I direct them down the corridors, through the secured doors, and down the stairwells until they are in the final stairwell leading to the cellblock. They have incurred no further resistance to that point.

Shawn comes over the com. "How are we coming on the AI? We're getting hammered out here!"

I respond. "They are close." Shawn's video feed still looks like a war zone. Then, I shift my attention to Todd's screen. "Okay, through that door is the cellblock. The code is eight-nine-eight-nine. My dad should be in there. And the door and elevator to the AI system will be at the end of the hall on the left." The door opens, and I immediately hear plasma rifles. The first two Resistance fighters go down. The Resistance fighters use the same tactic as they did at the bottom of the last stairwell. Two more fighters go down before I hear someone say, "All clear." Rodney and a woman I have not met enter ahead of Todd.

My anxiety builds. "Is my dad there? Look in the cells." The cellblock looks the same as it did when I was there. Todd pans along the cells—the first, the second, the third. They are all empty. The camera moves to the left. The offices are empty, too. Todd walks to the end of the hall. All cells are empty. No! Where is my dad? I cannot leave without him.

"Nobody's here," Todd says. "The entire block is empty."

Rodney looks into Todd's camera. "I'm sorry, Serenity. We'll regroup and try to figure out where he is. But right now, we need to neutralize the AI system to take the pressure off the other teams."

I know that he is right, but I do not respond.

< 292 >

Shawn breaks in. "I'm going to move up and get a closer look to see if I can figure out how many troops they have. Jackson, Sheila, cover me if I'm spotted. Serenity, I'm going to keep my com on two-way open so you can hear me and I can hear you. Tell me if you see something that I don't."

I know it's not my place, but I cannot help but respond. "That does not sound like a good idea, Shawn. Team three is almost to the AI system."

"Good, but I need some recon anyway. We're getting hit too hard, and we're all out of position. I'm moving now!"

I watch his feed. He darts and dives from cover to cover. I see a few Feds, but it does not look like they see him. Good so far. He moves farther in, then drops to the ground.

Shawn, you are going to get trapped. Get out of there. I want to tell him that, but if I know that, so does he. I see no more troops. He is behind the line and crawls forward. An AI machine gun pops up and fires a round of plasma bursts that fly just barely over Shawn's head. I see some of the other AI weapons that deployed earlier. It looks like Shawn is trying to stay clear of them. He stays down but looks around.

A gray wall of the concrete structure emerges at a distance in front of him, through the brush and wilted leaves. When he looks backward, I see a Fed troop who faces the other direction. Shawn does not shoot him, though. It would give his position away. Shawn starts to get up, and the AI machine gun fires, just missing him. He drops again, burying himself and his gun under the brush. The AI gun stops firing.

He looks behind himself. Sheila is making her way to him on the same path he took. Shawn motions for her to go back, but she ignores him. She gets to within ten yards and dives toward him. The AI

< 293 >

machine gun fires, hitting her right shoulder. A submachine gun flies out of her hand as her arm flings backward, nearly wrapping around her back. The machine gun fires again as she hits the ground, but it misses. Shawn looks at Sheila. Her arm hangs limp, probably dislocated at the shoulder, and is burned badly. She grimaces, obviously in severe pain, but she bites her lip, not making a sound. I am sure she wants to scream.

"Hang in there," Shawn says. "I'll get you back." He looks closely at her shoulder as they lie on the ground. I have to turn away. "No arteries are hit. You'll be okay. Stay low."

They belly crawl until they are out of the AI machine gun's range. Shawn slings his weapon over his shoulder to help Sheila, and they slowly make their way through the Fed line. Then, Shawn turns around. A Fed troop is at the spot where Sheila got hit. Shawn freezes as there is a clear line of sight between them. The Fed raises his plasma rifle and points it toward Shawn and Sheila. They drop to the ground. The rifle jams, and the Fed throws it down.

Shawn tries to remove his weapon from his shoulder, but it catches on something. The Fed looks around, takes two steps, picks up Sheila's discarded submachine gun, and takes aim. Shawn's weapon is still down. Even though I see what Shawn sees, I instinctively yell, "Look out, Shawn!" I hear the machine gun fire and watch for the worst. But it is not the sound of a conventional submachine gun. It is the sound of a plasma machine gun. The Fed drops to the ground dead, revealing the AI machine gun behind him. He is directly in its line of fire.

Shawn and Sheila make it back to the Resistance's line, where Shawn hands her off to another fighter. "Get her back to Doc Sam." Then, he flips his com back to general broadcast. "Team three, how are we doing on the AI system?"

< 294 >

Rodney responds. "Four of us are in the elevator now, heading down to the AI system. We can only fit four in the elevator at a time, and according to Serenity, it is the only way down."

I look at Todd's video feed from the elevator. Rodney turns to face Todd and the other two Resistance fighters. "Be ready to fire when these doors open. We have no idea who or what is down here."

I watch through Todd's camera. He is in the back of the elevator. Based on the vantage point, it looks like he is crouching. Rodney and the other two men are in front with their weapons aimed at the elevator doors. They open. Four men face the elevator, but nobody fires.

"No!" I shout into the com. General Chen has a small plasma gun to my dad's head. There are also two Feds in military uniforms with plasma rifles aimed at the elevator. Todd reaches down and opens the com one way so I can hear them but they cannot hear me.

"General Chen," Rodney says.

"I've been expecting you," General Chen says with a smile on his face. He presses a button on one of the computers, and the elevator lights go out. He has shut it down. "Now, lay down your weapons or I burn Mr. Ashdown's head. And I know his daughter would not like that."

Dan still peers over my shoulder. "Never give up your weapon," he says.

He is just talking to me since the others cannot hear us, but I still reply. "They have to or else he will shoot my dad."

"He's going to shoot your father anyway."

I know that Dan is probably right, but his honesty still irritates me. "You do not know that."

The com picks up Rodney's reply. "What will keep you from shooting us once we lay down our weapons?"

< 295 >

"Nothing," General Chen replies. "But I do need you alive to call off your attack on the sphere site. Have you ever seen what a plasma blast does to a head at point-blank range?"

Rodney holds up a hand. "All right, all right. We're laying down our weapons." He turns to the other men. "Lay them down, guys."

They do as Rodney commands.

General Chen points to the other Resistance fighters. "Shoot those two."

"No!" I shout. But only Dan hears.

Each of the Feds fires a plasma blast into one of the fighters' chests. They drop immediately. The camera jolts as Todd jumps backward. I can only see the back of Rodney's head as he lunges toward General Chen.

General Chen pushes the plasma gun against my dad's head. "Ah, ah. Stop right there or it'll be messy."

Rodney pulls up short of General Chen.

"Now, about that attack of yours," General Chen says. "I know you are in communication with your men. Call it off or he dies, as do you and the geek over there."

"That's Todd," Todd blurts. Then he backs away. I am certain he wishes he had not said that.

Rodney does not move. *Think, Serenity, think.* How can I help them?

General Chen continues. "Okay, let me help you out. I assume the *geek* is planning on doing something to the AI computer system to shut it down. Well, your Miss Ashdown, in disguise, already tried that and failed. I retrieved the flash drive. Don't you think we would have closed that loophole? You people . . . always a step behind. We centralized the controls at the sphere site. You now have to get through the AI in order to shut it down. Which, I might add, is impossible."

< 296 >

"Oh, crap," I say, again, only to Dan. "If that is true, we are finished."

General Chen continues. "Let me prove it." He looks at the other Feds. "Guys, have at it." He steps away from the computers. My dad and Rodney follow.

The Feds raise their plasma guns and open fire on the computers. They blast away. Sparks fly, some of the computers catch on fire, and others melt away. They even blast the screen on the wall.

General Chen smiles and turns toward Rodney. "See? This site is no longer connected to the AI. Now, about that com call?"

Dan flops back in his chair. "It's over."

"Wait," I say. "I have an idea."

Dan perks up. "To shut down the AI?"

"No, to get Rodney, Todd, and my dad out of there. I am working on the other, but first things first. I need to get Todd to turn off the open com so I can talk to him."

I quickly press Todd's com three times so he will hear three clicks. Hopefully, he gets the message. Nothing. He does not move. I press it four more times. The video feed quickly swivels left then right. Then the open com goes silent. He got the message. Now we are back to one-on-one communication. Todd will be able to hear me, but he must remain silent.

I press Todd's com. "Todd, I have an idea. Just give a slight nod with the camera if you understand or a slight shake if you do not."

Todd nods.

"Do you have your Colt?" I ask.

He nods.

"Okay," I continue. "Here is what you do. Slowly make your way in front of the two Fed guards. Get about three feet away. They have

< 297 >

been standing side by side the entire time, generally with their weapons pointed down ever since you guys were disarmed."

I see Rodney move toward General Chen and my dad. Good. I need Rodney to be close to General Chen when I tell Todd to make his move. Rodney and General Chen are talking, but I cannot hear what they are saying now that the open com is off.

I continue speaking to Todd. "I have watched the two guards raise their guns a couple of times. When they hurry, it takes a half second to raise their weapons to a firing position. Once you are in front of them, get your hand on your Colt and casually look at them."

The video feed turns toward Rodney and General Chen again. Rodney is still standing close to General Chen. They continue to talk. Rodney must be trying to negotiate, but he has no leverage.

I speak to Todd again. "I control the camera functions from my computer. When you are in position, I will switch the function from video to photo and turn on the flash. With your free hand, reach up and snap a photo. The flash will blind them for three seconds. That gives you three-point-five seconds to pull out your Colt and fire two shots to take out the guards. Hopefully, that also distracts General Chen just enough for Rodney to jump him. Do you understand?"

Todd shakes his head.

"Todd," I say. "If you do not try this, General Chen *will* kill you. You *will* die."

Todd does not move.

"Todd?" I say slowly.

He nods.

"I thought so," I say as I turn off the com.

Dan stands over my shoulder again. "Do you think this will work?"

< 298 >

"I have no idea, but it is the best I can come up with."

General Chen pushes the gun harder against my dad's temple as he says something to Rodney through clenched teeth.

Todd is still standing.

I flip the com back on. "Todd, move!"

He slowly makes his way to the guards. Rodney is no longer on the screen once Todd turns toward the guards. I cannot see Todd's hands, but I assume he has one on the Colt in his pocket. At least I hope so.

"Good, Todd," I say. "Just a little closer."

He steps forward nonchalantly, looking at the floor.

"Okay, look up," I say.

He does.

"Are you ready?" I ask.

No response.

"Todd, are you ready?"

He nods.

I flip the camera function to photo and flash. The flash will be a split-second before the camera takes the photo. "Go!" A moment later, a photo pops onto my screen showing the guards' faces, eyes closed, and heads jerked back. That part worked.

I immediately turn the function back to video so that I can see what is happening. Todd's arm is extended with his hand holding the Colt. The two guards are falling backwards.

Todd turns, and I see Rodney and General Chen wrestling. Neither has a weapon. They have crashed into the burned computer stations.

"What do I do?" Todd asks.

"Are the elevator lights on?"

< 299 >

"Yes."

"Good. They must have shorted out whatever program they used to shut it down. Get my dad out of there and send down the other fighters to help Rodney. And switch to two-way open com."

The camera shakes as Todd runs to the elevator with my dad in front of him. They enter the elevator, and Todd pushes the up button. As the elevator doors open at the top, I hear a plasma gun blast from the elevator shaft but can't see what happened. Either General Chen or Rodney must have gotten to one of the Feds' guns. I watch as the last four Resistance fighters enter the elevator, their conventional weapons at the ready. Todd and my dad remain in the cell block. Todd has the camera trained on the closed elevator door as the elevator descends. A few seconds later, through Todd's open com, I hear four plasma gun blasts coming from the elevator shaft. There is no conventional gunfire. It had to be General Chen who got to the plasma gun.

"Get out of there, Todd! Now!"

< 300 >

29

ARTIFICIAL INTELLIGENCE

Shawn's voice cracks over the com. "Teams one and two, it's an alternate backfire. The Feds' line is too strong. Retreat fifty yards. They have a real front. Two F R."

I look at Dan. "What is he saying? What does 'two F R' mean? From what I saw, their line looked thin."

Dan sits. "That's what Shawn thinks too."

"But he just said that the line is too strong. They have a real front."

Dan shakes his head. "It's all in code in case the Feds are monitoring our frequency. Alternate backfire means that the opposite of every other statement that he is about to make is true. So, the statement that the Feds' line is too strong means that it is weak. He wants everyone to retreat fifty yards—that's true. Probably so when they flank, they'll be out of the range of the AI. The statement that they have a real front means the Feds have a false front. 'Two F R' is a true statement of what he wants the teams to do. Unit two in each team is to flank right."

I nod. "Okay." That is a pretty genius code, but a simple "okay" is the only response I can come up with.

Shawn talks again. "Todd, Serenity, how are we on the AI? We *have* to get the system down. They'll have more troops coming. And we don't."

I look at Dan. He must have seen the question on my face. He answers me before I ask it. "No more code. He needs the AI system down."

Todd responds before I can. "Boss, we have a problem. General Chen was in the room with the AI system. You see, we hit the building with a frontal assault. We hit them hard. It took a while, but we finally got through. Then . . ."

I break in and interrupt. "Shawn, they centralized the AI controls at the sphere site! We cannot disarm the AI system until we get past the AI weapons to the sphere!"

The com is silent for a minute.

"Shawn, are you there?" I ask.

"Yeah," he says solemnly. "Are you sure?"

"Yes, positive," I say.

"Affirmative," Todd says. "Serenity, I'm about forty-five minutes out with your father."

I do not answer Todd. While I am thrilled that my dad has been set free and that I will finally see him outside of a cell, he and I are stuck here. There's no way we can get to the sphere and go home today. And once the Feds' reinforcements arrive, we will never get

< 302 >

to it. And even worse, the Feds will control the sphere without challenge. If they are able to program it, with or without me, they will invade my world, and it will be finished.

Short of me getting to the sphere, my only hope is that this planet dies before the Feds are able to program it. That's the only way my world survives. The Feds' best chance of programming the sphere is using me. I can say that I will never program it, but they have so much leverage on me. Physical pain, my dad, Shawn. I cannot say what I would do under such circumstances. So, the best hope for my world at this point is if I no longer exist. I think for a moment. The quickest and easiest way to do it is by walking into the AI's range. The AI shoots everything that moves.

Or does it? It does not shoot the Feds—except for one. I saw it. I had assumed it was shooting at Shawn and Sheila and the Fed was simply in the way. But why make such an assumption? My dad would never do that.

I turn to Dan. "Are these videos recorded? Can we rewind and play them back?"

Dan stands up. "You bet. I'm always assigned to van duty. I can run the cameras and coms in my sleep. Why? What are you looking for?"

"Go back to the first video we have of the AIs deploying and firing."

Dan punches some keys on the keyboard. The screen turns black for a moment, then comes on. It is a replay of Shawn's camera in the middle of a firefight with the Fed troops.

"Go back a little further," I say.

Dan punches the keyboard some more. The screen turns black again, then comes back on to show Shawn moving toward the site.

< 303 >

An AI grenade launcher deploys and causes the implosion that I saw. Okay, so it targeted our people. As I watch the footage, I notice that the barrels of the AI weapons make short, sudden movements once deployed and when not firing.

"Okay," I say. "Can you fast forward while I can watch it?"

Dan works the keyboard.

"There, stop! This is where the AI machine gun starts shooting at Shawn. I want to watch this sequence."

I watch as it shoots at Shawn, but it stops when he is on the ground. Same thing again, short sudden movements between firing. The video plays on. Now, Sheila is in view. She gets shot in her right shoulder and loses her weapon. I watch as it fires again but misses. It stops firing even though she is not all the way to the ground.

"What are you looking for?" Dan asks.

I do not answer. I continue to watch until the Fed takes aim at Sheila and Shawn. Before he fires, the AI machine gun hits him. "Freeze it right there!"

Dan punches a key and the screen freezes.

"Look, Dan." I run my finger across the screen. "Is the Fed standing on a straight line running from the AI to Shawn and Sheila?"

Dan shakes his head. "No."

"I do not think so either. I think I have it! I have to get out there." I jump up out of my chair.

Dan stands up as well. "What? No! You can't go out there until all weapons are neutralized."

"No, it has to be me. I have to test it. Because if I am wrong, it also has to be me."

"What are you talking about? Shawn ordered me to keep you here."

< 304 >

"I am Serenity Ashdown. I outrank Shawn."

Dan gets quiet. He has a puzzled look on his face as he processes the situation. I start to open the back door.

Dan shakes his head. "Wait, no. You can't go."

As soon as he says the last word, there is an enormous explosion outside. The van lifts off the ground, and I cannot maintain my balance. I feel like I am falling until the van slams into the ground, and my body crushes Dan against one of the walls, which now functions as the floor. I look up. Instead of the ceiling, I see the van's other wall. Outside, the Resistance fighter who was guarding the van fires his conventional rifle three, four, five times. Then, I hear multiple plasma rifles fire. Then silence.

"Are you okay?" I ask Dan.

"Yeah, but you're bleeding."

I feel a trickle on my forehead and touch it. Then, I look at my fingers. They are covered with blood. "I am okay."

Footsteps approach the van.

Dan stands, reaches up, and pulls a small handle on the floor, which is now in front of us. A hatch opens. "Quick," he says. "Get in here."

I stand and crawl in. It is difficult since I have to climb up to the hatch. It was obviously designed to step into when the van is upright. Dan starts to close the hatch, but I reach up and stop him.

"What about you?"

"It's only big enough for one. Besides, they will be expecting someone to be in here. If we are both gone, they will search much harder."

I immediately know what that means. Dan is yet one more person in this world who is giving up his life to save me. Why does

< 305 >

everybody think they are expendable, but I am not? They think they need me as a Serenity poster child, but I do not think they need that any longer. I am not special.

Dan looks at me. "You have to shut down the AI." Then, he slams the hatch shut.

I hear people right outside the van. The doors open and Dan's weapon fires once, twice, three times. Then, I hear a barrage of plasma rifles fire. The bursts hit inside the van. I feel the vibrations. And then, silence. There is a thud—Dan's body falling. I shake uncontrollably.

The van rocks. Somebody must have stepped inside. I hear a voice I do not recognize. "Clear." The van rocks again as the person steps out. I hear footsteps walk away, but I am frozen. I try to move, but I cannot. *Breathe, Serenity.* I need to breathe. I take two deep breaths and slowly exhale after each one. As I do, I slowly stop shaking. I wipe the blood-soaked sweat from my face, then I reach up and open the hatch. It takes all my effort to push it past its tipping point so it falls open. With more effort, I pull myself out. It is obvious that Dan is dead, but I check for a pulse anyway. Nothing.

My sabre and empty gun lie on the side of the van. I pick up the sabre and put it in its sheath. The van's back doors are still open. I peer out and see only the outside guard, dead, and two dead Fed troops. I hear distant weapon fire, but it is retreating. The Resistance's flanking move must be working. I climb out of the van and enter the woods. I have no com.

I move toward the weapon fire, looking for anyone from the Resistance. I cough as I inhale the air, thick with the smell of gunpowder and plasma residue. I go forward, crawling over logs and avoiding brush and fallen bodies until I see Danica. She sits with her back to a tree.

< 306 >

"Are you hit?" I ask.

Danica's eyes grow wide, and her face is stern. "What are you doing out here? Where are those two idiots that are supposed to be watching you?"

"They are dead."

Danica's face softens, and she says no more.

"Are you hit?" I ask her again.

She shakes her head. "No, I was just catching my breath. We pretty much have the place secure. But it doesn't matter. We can't get past the AI."

"I have an idea for that. Where's Shawn?"

"He's about thirty yards that way." She points to my right. "Here, I'll go with you."

By the time we get to Shawn, all weapon fire has ceased.

Shawn quickly turns when we approach. "Where are—"

Danica interrupts. "Dead. Serenity says she has an idea to get us around the AI."

Shawn looks at me.

"Not around them," I say. "Through them."

Shawn grins. "Great. Let's hear it."

By the quick change in Shawn's expression, I am sure my face reflects the grimness that I feel. "I cannot tell you. I have to show you."

The expression on Shawn's face turns from grim to puzzled. He talks slowly. "Okay then. Show us. Let's go."

I lower my head, and then I look up at Shawn. "It has to be me alone. I have to test it in case it does not work."

Shawn shakes his head hard. "No. No way. We need you. Someone else can test it. I can test it. Anybody but you."

I take Shawn's hand in mine.

< 307 >

"It has to be me. If it does not work and we cannot shut down the AI, the Feds will control the sphere. And you and I both know that they will stop at nothing to get to me and force me to program it so they can invade. I cannot let that happen. If I cannot shut down the AI, the AI has to shut down *me*."

Shawn squeezes my hand. "There has to be another way."

Danica steps up beside me. "Shawn, she's right. You have to let her do it. And we're running out of time. The Feds will have reinforcements on the way. This is our one and only shot at shutting down the sphere."

Shawn wipes a blood-tinted tear from my face. His eyes are watery as he nods, turns, and steps away.

I turn toward Danica. "If I make it through to the site, tell everyone to leave their weapons and follow."

"What?" she exclaims.

"Just do it. No conventional weapons whatsoever. You can pick up plasma weapons from the dead Feds if you want to, but leave all conventional weapons behind."

She nods. "Okay. I'll walk with you to the AI perimeter to make sure we didn't miss any Feds."

"Thanks."

We walk slowly through the woods. After hearing the weapon fire and other noise for so long, the silence is almost eerie. The closer we get to the perimeter, the tighter my stomach gets. My armpits grow damp with nervousness. There are sixteen deployed AI weapons in sight. No, do not start counting. Not now. There's too much at stake here for that little girl who struggled to save her mom and Jona eight years ago. If I start counting and calculating here and do not shut down the sphere, it will cost many more people their lives, both

< 308 >

in this world and in mine. I must stay focused. It is all right. I have thought this through. It makes perfect sense.

The AI weapon stopped shooting at Shawn every time he dove because his gun was buried underneath him and under the brush. Undetectable. It stopped firing at Sheila when she lost her weapon. It also missed the last shot it took, aiming to her right—the same direction her weapon flew. It was shooting at her weapon. And when it shot the Fed, it aimed at him instead of Shawn and Sheila because he had picked up Sheila's gun. I believe the AI weapons are programmed to target conventional weapons because the Feds do not use them and that is all the Resistance has. At least that is my analysis.

Danica stops. "This is it. We surveyed the entire building earlier. All of their exterior troops were deployed in the battle, so you'll be safe from any Feds."

I look at her and nod.

She nods back. "Good luck, soldier."

I turn to face the site, take a deep breath, exhale, and start forward. I take each step as if I might tread on a land mine. I see each type of deployed AI weapon: grenade launchers, machine guns, rifles. And there are multiples of each. They jerk and move suddenly, each at random times. First left, then up, then down, then left again, then right, and so on. I believe they are searching for a target.

In the distance, through the leaves, I make out the concrete side of the building housing the sphere. I continue to walk, targeting an AI machine gun ahead. I walk straight toward it. Its barrel jerks up, then left. My heart beats faster and faster. I am twenty yards from it and walk closer. It continues to move. The barrels on all of the AI guns continue to move in quick jerks. I stop when I am ten yards away. From this distance, I can hear a clicking noise each time a gun moves.

< 309 >

I must be safe. Surely, it would have fired on me by now if it was going to. But maybe it takes longer to sense just one person. I look down. The path between me and the barrel is clear. I close my eyes, say a prayer, and step forward. I hear the gun clicking and continue on, one short, slow, soft step at a time. I know I have covered the ten yards, so I stop. There is a loud click. I open my eyes and discover my face is inches from the gun's gigantic barrel. My entire body could fit inside it. It appears as if it is staring me in the eyes, but it does not move. I slowly reach up and touch it. Nothing happens.

My anxiety and excitement build. I am hopeful. This might be working. The Resistance might have a chance. My world might have a chance. I step to the side and run to the building.

When I reach it, I hear Danica shout. "You go, girl!"

< 310 >

THE SPHERE

I walk alongside a wall of the rectangular building. The poured concrete structure is massive up close. Now that my adrenaline has
slowed, the cool air chills me. The building is shaded by the dying
leaves of the dense forest that surrounds it.

Takeo shouts from around the corner, where the gravel road leads
up to the building. "Over here. I found it."

I walk to that side to join what is left of team one. A member of
team two trudges through the woods and away from the building to
join the rest of her team, which Shawn has spread out to guard the
perimeter. As I approach my team, I slip on the loose, golf ball-sized
stones that make up the gravel road.

I grab someone's shoulder to catch myself.

"Sorry," I say.

Takeo runs his fingers along the wall near its center and looks at Shawn. "See, there's a slight crack going up, across, and down."

I see it too. It is the shape of a door, but not as tall.

"Probably on a track system," Shawn says. "It'll slide in and over. But only accessible from the inside. I guess our intel was correct. The Feds always keep people inside and rotate them out."

While the rest of the team huddles around Shawn and Takeo, I examine the wall more closely and find another crack going upward. But it is located all the way at the corner of the building. I follow the crack as far as I can, but I lose it in the structure's second story. I walk to the other corner and find a similar crack. Takeo found the pedestrian door, and I have found a vehicle door.

That makes sense.

That is why the structure is so large. It has to house a very large sphere. It looks like the Feds are planning an invasion—not just an invasion with men, but an invasion with military vehicles as well. So, the sphere has to be large enough to drive through.

"Shawn," I say. "I think I found the vehicle entrance door."

Shawn and Takeo walk to me and examine it.

"Yep," Takeo says.

I kick at the U-shaped groove along the base of the door where it meets the ground. "This door folds down."

Shawn bends and rubs the groove with his fingers. "That makes sense. They plan on using it as a ramp to drive up and in."

Danica walks over. "Are you guys going to chitchat about the makeup of these doors or are we going to blow a hole in this house and walk in?"

< 312 >

Shawn stands up. "Right. We aren't getting in any other way." He looks at Takeo. "You checked the rest of the structure for openings?"

Takeo nods. "I did."

Shawn looks around. "Where's Hernandez with the explosives?"

Takeo holds up a hand. "How do we know the sphere is not on this end? We may blow it up too."

Danica looks at Shawn. "That would make sense to put it by the door. They wouldn't have to drive far to go through it."

I walk around the corner and along one of the building's long sides. I stay close to the wall, listening intently and wondering if I will hear anything through the concrete. It appears to be very thick. As I reach the halfway point along that side, there is a faint sound. I stop and put my ear against the building, then jerk my head back at the feel of the cold concrete against my face. I slowly put my ear against the building again. It does not help. The sound is even more muffled with my ear against the concrete. I step back and still hear it. It sounds familiar.

As I walk farther, the sound gets louder. That is it. It is a humming sound. The same humming sound that I heard in the facility's basement lab. And in the facility, the hum grew louder as I moved closer to the sphere. I walk to the end of the building where the humming is loudest.

I run back to the others. An unfamiliar man is with them holding the makings of an explosive. I assume this is Hernandez.

"The sphere is at the far end of the building."

Everyone looks at me.

Takeo looks at the pedestrian door and then at me. "How do you know?" He pauses, then shakes his head. "Never mind." He turns to Hernandez and points to the pedestrian door. "Blow it up here."

< 313 >

It is nice to finally be trusted without having to give an explanation.

Once Hernandez hooks up the explosives, he walks around the side of the building with me and two unarmed team members. Those who were able to pick up working plasma rifles stand facing the door, behind trees and just outside of the blast zone.

"Remember, make them come out to us," Shawn says. "And once we are inside, no shooting. Otherwise, we could damage the sphere." He pauses. "On my mark. Ready? Three, two, one, now!"

I put my hands over my ears and hunch my shoulders against what is coming. Hernandez presses a button on the remote in his hand. The sound of the blast pierces my ears, and I stumble backward. Concrete chunks fly past the corner of the building. I immediately hear plasma rifle blasts, both from the front of the building and from the Resistance fighters behind the trees.

Two Resistance fighters go down. I cannot see it, but I hear the telltale sign of a plasma grenade imploding in front and to the other side of the building. I stumble again from the vibration, but I catch my balance. Dirt and debris fly clear past my side of the building. Just as the grenade implodes, Shawn, Danica, and two others charge the building, firing. A man that I do not know falls. I lose them beyond my angle of sight. There is nobody left outside except me, Hernandez, and the two people we are with.

A familiar voice comes from deep inside the building. "Hold your fire! You'll hit the sphere!"

General Ostrovsky. All weapon fire ceases. Some of the charging fighters must have made it inside. Did Shawn?

The two fighters with me run toward the door, so I follow. As I turn the corner, they pull out their weapons, a sword and a knife, and

< 314 >

enter through the large hole in the concrete. I run to the opening. Everyone is engaged in hand-to-hand combat, neither side wanting to damage the sphere. I freeze when I see it. It is enormous and looks to be made exactly the same as the one in my world—same material and everything—but ten times larger.

I look at the fighting. A Fed drops from a knife slash, then a Resistance fighter is run through by a sword. The odds stay even. What can I do to help? Just as I see Takeo and Shawn, the tip of a sword barely misses my face. I jump to the side.

Danica rolls out through the hole onto the gravel outside. Blood spurts from her shoulder when she slices it on a piece of protruding, jagged concrete. She jumps to her feet as General Ostrovsky steps through the hole after her. He has a sword and Danica has a knife. He constantly strikes and thrusts. She parries his attacks but cannot counter. His sword is too long, and he has a definite advantage. I observe his moves but am too scared to do anything.

Think, Serenity, think.

I could toss Danica my sabre. No, he might turn on me next. While I am still frozen in place, Danica trips in the gravel and falls on her back. She tries to scramble to her feet, but Ostrovsky is on her. She holds herself up with one arm and blocks with her knife. He swings, she blocks. He swings, she blocks. With each blow, his sword gets closer to her face. I calculate that three more blows will shove her knife into her face, and the fourth blow will slice her throat. I have to do something.

He swings twice.

I pull out my sabre and run toward Ostrovsky. As expected, the third blow smashes the back of Danica's knife into her face. Blood spurts from her nose, and her head snaps back against the gravel. Her

< 315 >

arms drop. She is motionless. He raises his sword. This will be the killing blow.

As I reach him, I draw my sabre back to swing. He swings, too, but not at Danica. He spins as he swings, and there is a sharp sting in my stomach. I jump backward, halting my own swing. I look down. My jacket and shirt are cut and blood-stained. It stings, but it does not feel deep.

I am no longer afraid.

I am angry.

General Ostrovsky raises his sword and smiles. "You're out of your league, little girl."

I do not respond. I raise my sabre and take the en garde stance.

I am not bigger than he is. I am not faster than he is. I am not stronger than he is. I am not more skilled than he is.

But I am smarter.

He comes at me swinging. I recognize the advance and block each swing.

"Not bad," he says. "For a beginner."

He comes again. Swing, swing, and then a thrust toward my hilt—but with a twist. The twist flips my sabre out of my hand. It was the same move Takeo used. I had not seen Ostrovsky use it. But I have seen his kill swing. He always swings high and overextends. I immediately duck and dive forward into a somersault, ending up behind him. His overextension and missed contact throw him off balance just long enough for me to dive toward my sabre. The gravel digs into my bare wrists as I slide. I grab the sabre and jump to my feet, but he is on me immediately. His lip is turned up, his eyes are narrowed. He does not talk. He looks determined.

Determined to finish me off.

< 316 >

I am still not afraid. I am still angry. I feel the sweat, dirt, and dried blood on my face. My stomach stings even more as sweat seeps into the open wound. And my wrists ache from the gravel scrapes and the force of his blows against my sabre.

Stay focused, Serenity. Stay focused.

He uses the same swing combination he used to rid me of my sabre. I block, and on his next thrust, as General Ostrovsky goes for my hilt with the tip of his sword, I use the same move I used against Takeo. I pull my sabre back, catching the tip of his sword on the back of my blade. I twist in the opposite direction, and his sword flies out of his hand. He loses his balance and falls on his back. I immediately lunge forward, draw my sabre back for the killing thrust, and pause to look him in the eyes.

I grit my teeth. "This is for my mom." I bring my sabre forward for the kill, but something stops my arm mid-swing, I try to move it again, but it will not budge.

"Don't," Shawn says.

I turn to see him holding my arm.

He looks me in the eyes. "Let it go. This isn't your way."

My breathing grows shallow, and the tension slowly leaves my body. I relax to the point where I feel weak and realize what I almost just did. When I realize how close I came to dying myself, my legs start to shake. I drop my sabre, and Shawn releases my arm. I look around.

Danica sits up, shakes her head, and rubs her bloodied face. She looks at me. "That's two I owe you, Blondie."

I look back at General Ostrovsky, who still lies in the gravel. Shawn bends down to pull him up. As he does, Ostrovsky pulls a small knife from his belt.

< 317 >

"Look out!" I shout.

Ostrovsky grabs Shawn's collar with his left hand and starts to raise the knife with his right. But before the knife reaches Shawn, a sword swiftly slices Ostrovsky's throat with pinpoint accuracy.

When I look up, Takeo is wiping the blood from his weapon.

# # # # #

Excluding the large terminals near the door, which seem to control the AI system, the room contains the exact same number of computers as I saw at the facility in my world: twenty-two. They are connected to the sphere, and I start programming them with the series of numbers I saw in the facility's basement lab. If I get everything correct, I should see the same series of numbers on this sphere's screen as I saw on the one in the facility. I think about how hard my dad had to work to determine these coordinates. Years. Just to open the connection between the universes. I had been angry at him for helping the Feds and for pushing me to help him. But most of all, I had been angry at him for keeping everything from me. The project, my mom, everything. But after seeing what the Feds are capable of, what they have done to this world, and after everything I have been through here, I now know why my dad did what he did. He did what he had to do for my mom. He did what he had to do to protect Jona and I. It is as simple as that. And he needed my help, just as he will need my help when we get back in order to prepare my world for a possible invasion.

I talk to whoever is listening as I enter the numbers. "Todd said both spheres have to be programmed with these coordinates even though the spheres are located at different places in each universe. How do we know the sphere in my world is still programmed?"

< 318 >

Shawn answers. "Remember what Todd explained earlier? Even though the screens at the facility went blank, the computers and sphere are still programmed. Unless someone messes with the computers there, they will stay programmed until the ones on this side are programmed and activated. That will activate the computers at the facility and open the connection on both sides. And your Dirk Bailey will make sure that nobody touches those computers. I'm certain of that."

"But what if the Feds told him to change the programming since we took over the sphere?"

"Possible," Shawn says. "But highly unlikely. This is the only place they can communicate with him consistently. Otherwise, they would have to get lucky and find a random connection to talk to him. Also, they *want* this connection open whether they have your help or not. They wouldn't make that task even harder for themselves."

I have two more computers to program before the final one with the repeating numbers.

Then, a voice comes over Shawn's com. "This is Archer on the perimeter. We heard vehicles, so I went farther out to investigate. The Feds' reinforcements are arriving. Once they get organized, I'm afraid they're going to advance."

"How long?" Shawn replies.

"Depends on how many troops they are waiting for. I would say fifteen, twenty minutes until they have enough to get through the perimeter."

"How long can you hold them off?"

"We're spread pretty thin. I doubt that we'll even slow them down once they decide to move on us."

"Okay. Stay put until they advance. When they do, slowly retreat and circle around to the north. Maintain a small escape route for us there. Keep me posted."

< 319 >

Just then, gravel crunches as a vehicle pulls up to the building. I continue to input numbers until I hear Todd's voice outside.

I run outside. "Dad!" I shout as I see him step out of the vehicle. A sense of warmth and security fills my body. I jump into his arms and squeeze as tightly as I can.

His arms wrap around me. Then, he pulls his head back, and I look into his face.

"Serenity," he says. "I knew you could do it. My girl." He smiles.

"Dad, I was so afraid. I was afraid that I had lost you again, forever. I am so sorry I was angry at you. I know you did everything for Mom, Jona, and me."

"It's okay. You have absolutely nothing to apologize for." He steps back and looks at me. "Are you okay? You're bleeding."

"I'm fine. Hurry, we don't have much time."

We go inside. I finish the last of the fixed numbers and move toward the sphere. I look through the sphere at the concrete wall, but it looks normal. No waves. The sphere is not active. I plug Todd's flash drive into the computer nearest to the sphere, and it starts running random numbers. Suddenly, someone is standing behind me.

"Hit this key if you want to speed up the sequence," Todd says.

I tap the key, and the numbers move faster. I will have to watch until I see the entire series of numbers that I saw at the facility, in the exact sequence.

Shawn's com cracks. "Archer again. The Feds are moving in. We'll lay down fire, but it won't take them long to figure out how thin we are. Are you guys about ready to move out?"

"Roger that," Shawn says. "Hernandez, do you have the explosives in place?"

"Just finished."

< 320 >

"All right, that should give us a pretty good distraction to get away, assuming Archer's team can keep a path cleared for us." Shawn walks toward me. "How are you guys coming?"

"I don't know, boss," Todd says. "This could take a while."

I do not talk.

I just watch the screen.

Come on. Where are those numbers? We are so close. If the Feds get to us before I find this sequence, they will not only have the sphere, but they will also have the sphere almost fully programmed. My hands start to shake, and I tap the key to make the numbers move even faster. I can barely keep up. I need full concentration. I think that I can keep up with one more tap on the key. I press it, and the screen freezes. The numbers stop. My heart races.

"No! What is this? Why?" I press the key over and over until the sweat from my palms causes my finger to slip.

Todd leans in front of me and takes over the keyboard. "Let me try."

His fingers fly back and forth across the keyboard, but the screen does not change.

Todd stops. His eyes are wide as he turns to Shawn. "Boss, we have a big problem."

Shawn is already leaning over my shoulder, watching.

Todd shakes his head. "They built in a failsafe. If someone tries to hack into the system by running random numbers, the computer locks up. It thinks we're a hacker."

Shawn straightens up. "Isn't there something you can do? Override it or something?"

"Not without the password, boss. It would take hours to decode it. I would have to write a program to do it."

< 321 >

Shawn looks around. He stops when his eyes land on the AI terminal. "How about the AI system? Can you reprogram it to fire at the Feds and buy us some time?"

I feel a glimmer of hope when I hear that suggestion. But Todd shakes his head again. "Not in the amount of time we have. I would have to figure out the entire system, and I am certain that it has more than one level of security I would have to crack. We're talking days."

I drop my head. So close. I turn and look at Shawn. My dad now stands beside him.

I say, "We have to blow this place up. We can't let the Feds have it back." My heart sinks. I look at my dad. "I am sorry, Dad. I failed. I cannot get us home."

He places his hand on my shoulder and squeezes. "Serenity, you have nothing to be sorry about. I could not possibly be prouder of you. You have done what nobody else could ever do. You are my daughter, and I love you so much."

Archer's voice comes over Shawn's com. "We've held them off better than I thought, but we're retreating fast now. You have ten minutes tops to get out of there and blow the place."

Shawn presses his com button. "Roger."

Todd leans around and looks at the back of the CPU.

"What are you looking for?" Shawn asks. "We need to pack up and go."

"I had an idea," Todd answers. "But it's not going to work. Since all of their systems seem to have outdated features, I thought there might be a bypass or an override on the CPU." He pauses as he looks. "There is, but it looks like it requires a special key of some kind to turn it manually."

"What kind of key?" I ask.

< 322 >

Todd stands up straight. "It doesn't matter. We don't have it."

I raise my voice. "What kind of key?"

"It would be round and hollow, about the size of a short pencil. The key part is inside a hollow tube."

I reach into my pocket and pull out the metal object James gave me before he died.

"Like this?"

Todd's eyes light up. He almost falls over backward. "Where did you get that? Never mind." He grabs it and once again, leans around to the back of the CPU. He inserts and turns the key. The numbers take off across the screen, picking up right where they left off.

"Thank you, James," I whisper.

I watch. The sequence has to appear anytime now. I have been watching for so long.

"There!" I shout, and I hit the stop key. I move the numbers backward two digits. "That's it! Starting right there. For the next eighty-seven digits."

"Are you sure?" Todd asks.

I tip my chin down and stare at him. Of course, I am sure. But I do not say that.

He gets the message. "Right," he stammers. He takes the keyboard and does his thing. Then, he looks at the screen on the sphere. "Is that the final series?"

I look at the sphere. "It is."

Shawn's com cracks. Archer's voice is loud and nervous. I hear weapon fire through the com. "Five minutes. We're barely holding an escape route. Five minutes."

I walk toward the sphere. The center is now hazy and wavering. I see undulating trees through the haze because there is no building

< 323 >

on this spot in my universe. Trees with most of the leaves gone, like they should be this time of year. And the leaves still clinging on are beautiful shades of red, yellow, and orange. I turn around.

Shawn hands my dad a plasma rifle he confiscated from the Feds.

"This contains the basic technology on which all of this world's most powerful weapons are built. I don't have to tell you what can happen if it gets into the wrong hands, so I leave it to you as to what you do with it. But if we fail to stop the UR on this side, you will need that technology to have any chance of surviving on your side."

My dad embraces Shawn. "Thank you. I . . ." His voice trails off. Shawn nods. "I know."

I look at Todd, then Danica, then Takeo. Each grins and nods in turn.

"Take care of yourself, Blondie," Danica says. "I still owe you."

I grin. "I think we're even."

Then, I look at Shawn. My heart aches at the thought of leaving him. I run to him, pull his head down to mine, and kiss him, hard. I pull away and grab his hand, and we stare at each other. My heart aches even more, and my eyes grow blurry with tears. I try to speak. I try to say "goodbye." I try to say "I love you," but nothing comes out. He is silent as well. I want to go back to that moment in the gymnasium, and I want to stay there. But I know that I cannot. And my dad will need me, now more than ever. I release his hand and quickly turn toward the sphere. I step over to it with my dad.

My dad takes a deep breath and looks at me. "See you on the other side, Peanut." He steps into the hazy waves, and his outline is visible for a few seconds on the other side.

There is weapon fire outside. The Feds are close, very close. I look down and step through the sphere with my right leg. Then, I hear

< 324 >

more weapon fire and hesitate. If I remove my leg from the sphere—if I step back and remain in this world—I can help save it and also protect my own. I will be with my friends. And most importantly, I will be with Shawn. But I will likely die prematurely, either at the hands of the Feds or from the dying planet. And I will never see my dad or the rest of my family again.

If I step through the sphere, I will never see my friends again. I will never see Shawn again. And I will always live with the fear that the UR could invade my world at any time. But until that happens—if it even ever does happen—I will be safe and comfortable. I can help my dad prepare. I will be with my dad and grandparents and Jona— my family. And I will be home. That is where I have wanted to be ever since I stepped into this world.

I look through the sphere at the hazy, undulating trees. Then I turn to look at Shawn.

I take my final step.

THE END

< 325 >

FOR FURTHER DISCUSSION

1. What messages does this book offer about the possibility of alternate universes and parallel timelines? How are your own ideas alike or different?

2. Do you think that there is a possibility that the alternate universe described in this book could really exist?

3. What did you think about the main characters?

4. If you got the chance to ask the author of this book one question, what would it be?

5. How well do you think the author built the world in this book?

6. Did this book's pace seem too fast/too slow/just right?

7. Which parts of this book stood out to you? Why?

8. If you were making a movie of this book, who would you cast?

9. How did this book influence today's society or pop culture? Or was the book influenced by today's pop culture?

10. If you could write a sequel to this book, what would the main plot consist of?

ACKNOWLEDGMENTS

I wish to personally thank the following people for their contributions to my inspiration and knowledge and other help in creating this book.

First, I would like to thank my family for putting up with all of my long hours writing this novel. My wife, DeAnne; daughter, Lucy; and son, Luke. They supported me during the writing process and also served as my alpha readers.

In addition, I would like to thank the team at CamCat Publishing for all of their hard work and helpful advice in bringing this book to print. A special thanks to Cassandra Farrin and Helga Schier who read and reread my manuscript, edited it, and provided advice and comments. Thanks to Maryann for her fantastic cover design and to Laura Wooffitt and Gabe Schier for all of their marketing help. Thanks to Bridget McFadden for her excellent copyediting. And, of course, a thank you to Sue Arroyo for accepting this book for publishing.

I would also like to thank my beta readers and editor for this book. Jan Fisher, Debra Richards, and Leslie Richards, my beta readers, did a fantastic job giving me great feedback early on. Signe Jorgenson, my professional editor, found my typos and provided me with invaluable comments and guidance.

Finally, I would like to give thanks to my high school English teachers, Mrs. Gable and Mrs. Stocker. They were the very first people who inspired me to write.

ABOUT THE AUTHOR

Bryan Prosek is a science fiction writer and business attorney. Along with his first two novels, *The Brighter the Stars* and *A Measure of Serenity*, he has published books and articles in legal trade journals and magazines. Bryan is currently writing his third novel, *The Darker the Skies*. When he isn't writing or practicing law, you can probably find him watching science fiction movies or television shows. He loves the big screen and the small screen. There's a good chance that he'll be watching anything from the Star Trek movies to *The Conjuring*.

You can find more about Bryan at his website: www.bryankprosek.com

Taking you to new worlds.

If you've enjoyed

Bryan Prosek's *A Measure of Serenity,*

you'll enjoy

Bryan Prosek's *The Brighter the Stars.*

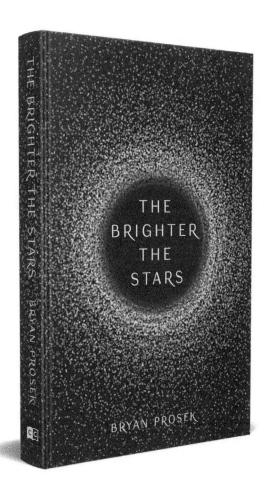

This is Nigil Diggs reporting on the history of hilaetite (pronounced hill-a-e-tight) crystals, the adoption of intergalactic Treaty 5274, and the treaty's impact on the Planet Earth. As you may know, hilaetite crystals grow similar to living organisms, like a fungus, but they are not alive in any sense.

They are classified as rock. No planet is able to reproduce them or grow them domestically, and once a crystal is picked, no new one ever grows in its place. Once removed from their host rock, they stop growing. For these reasons, fifteen years ago, in the year 2185, all known deposits of hilaetite crystals in the galaxy had been depleted.

But let's take a step backwards and give you a little history. By 2140, all diseases and cancers on Earth and throughout the galaxy had been wiped out through the discovery of hilaetite crystals. Hilaetite crystals were discovered in a small number of places throughout the galaxy and used in different forms for medicinal purposes.

These crystals were also very volatile and could cause massive explosions without being mixed with any other elements or compounds, thereby leaving behind no aftereffects, unlike the old nuclear weapons used on Earth. So planetary governments began using them in their weapons systems. The possibilities were endless. The larger the hilaetite crystal, the more power it had. It was thought that weapons could be developed that could destroy entire planets given a large enough crystal.

< 338 >

PROLOGUE

Two men stood in the blinding snow and raging, bitter cold wind. They were dressed from head to toe in saber-toothed bear hide suits from the planet Andromeda—the best and most expensive cold-weather suits in the Milky Way galaxy. Only snow goggles protruded from slits in their headpieces. Any exposed skin would be frozen solid in seconds.

From the cockpit of his spacecraft, Sloan watched the two men on the video screen. Men will put themselves through anything if the price is right, he thought. Sloan turned toward the pilot. "Will the scanners give me a video feed anywhere on the planet?"

"Anywhere that the chip goes," the pilot replied.

Sloan turned back to the screen and leaned his tall, solid frame back in his seat. The chip would go everywhere the two men went. He had inserted the audio-visual chip into the latch of the small case strapped over the shoulder of one of the men, Johnson.

Sloan leaned closer to the com. Johnson's shouts were barely audible over the howling wind.

"No wonder this planet is uninhabited," Johnson said. "They say this is the climate everywhere, year round! How far are we from the coordinates? I want to get this done and get out of here!"

Martino looked down at the transponder screen in his hand. "About half a click!" he shouted. "That way!" He motioned with his fur-clad arm.

Johnson continued to shout. "It better not be much farther! We won't last much longer out here!"

Sloan watched the men intently. If they didn't get moving, they would freeze to death before they accomplished his objective. What an inconvenience that would be; he would have to get new men and start all over.

He watched the men struggle with each step, their heavy boots weighted down in the knee-deep snow. As far as Sloan could see on the video screen in any direction, the landscape was the same, hill after hill of nothing but snow, broken up occasionally by a few mountains, also mostly covered with snow. Ice mountains, as he had heard them referred to, made of ice and rock.

That's what he was looking for.

The transponder beeped. Sloan watched as Martino scanned the landscape in front of him.

"I think that must be it!" Martino shouted, and he pointed to the faint outline of the mouth of a cave appearing through the snow.

< 340 >

It was a small opening in the side of one of the ice mountains. Perfect, Sloan thought. Its location relative to the wind was keeping it from filling up with snow, just as he had been informed. That was the only reason it was accessible.

He watched as the two men trudged the last few steps through the snow and into the cave. The opening was narrow. Once they were through it, the cave was probably ten feet tall at the highest spot, Sloan estimated. The walls looked like they were more ice than rock.

"Finally, we're getting somewhere," Sloan said, more to himself than to the pilot.

Once the men were inside the cave, the wind and blowing snow subsided. Sloan could still hear the wind through the com, but he could hear the men more clearly now, speaking in normal tones. Martino pointed down the long, dark cave tunnel. The transponder was still pointing that way. The men reached into their packs and pulled out their light cylinders. Once activated, the greenish light extended about ten feet down the tunnel.

Johnson said, "I wonder why Sloan wouldn't tell us what we're after? Just, 'You'll know it when you see it.' What's that supposed to mean?"

"He's paying us ten quads each to figure it out," Martino replied. "And I have a pretty good idea."

Sloan grinned slightly, satisfied with himself. By agreeing to pay the two men a mere fraction of what he would make, he got them to risk their lives in one of the harshest climates in the galaxy, without telling them where they were going, what they were after, or what it was for. Who else could have done that but him?

Johnson turned toward Martino. "Do you think we can trust Sloan? He gave me the creeps, the way he stared at us when we met."

< 341 >

"At this point, we don't have much choice," replied Martino. "Besides, I brought along a little insurance." He pulled a small plasma gun from inside his coat.

One side of Sloan's mouth turned up in a cold grin. "Thanks for the warning," he whispered.

Johnson said, "I don't like this at all. Something doesn't feel right."

"Come on," Martino replied. "When you're sitting in the sun spending your quads, it'll feel right."

Sloan watched the men slowly press on. Their feet slipped constantly on the uneven floor, slamming into protrusions, and they struggled to keep their balance.

After making their way deep into the cave, the men came around a bend where the tunnel opened up into a larger cavern. They held up their lights. Sloan couldn't quite see the farthest side of the cavern, but he could tell that this was probably the end of the tunnel, or at least the end of the portion of the tunnel that was large enough to walk through.

Martino looked at the transponder. "This is it. Do you see anything?"

Johnson slowly moved his light cylinder from side to side. As he moved it to his right, something glared bright against the cave wall.

Sloan leaned closer to the screen. "Can we increase the brightness? I can barely make out anything down there."

The pilot shook his head. "I'm sorry, sir. That's the best I can do."

Sloan's heart began to speed up as the men drew closer to the brightly shining object. It was a large clear crystal, about twenty-four inches in circumference, growing out of a protruding rock about two feet off the ground. It was rounded but not smooth, with many flat edges. Sloan edged his face even closer to the screen. This

< 342 >

was it. Finally, they'd found what he had come for. His latest plan was coming to fruition—a plan that would make him rich beyond imagination. But that was just the icing on the cake. Power was the real goal. In the end, he would control the two most formidable military powers in the galaxy. That would give him even more power than he now possessed, and he would use that power to control and manipulate anyone he wanted to, anywhere, beyond anything he had ever achieved. He nodded his head slightly and smiled.

Johnson spoke in an awed voice. "A hilaetite crystal. And it's huge."

Martino stared at it. "I had an idea we might be after a crystal, but I never thought it would be this big. This might be the biggest one ever found."

Johnson said, "Rumor has it that the Vernitions first uncovered some twelve- to fifteen-inch crystals way back when, but I never heard of anyone finding any even close to this size. Unbelievable! No wonder Sloan wouldn't tell us what we were after. I'd hate to think what would happen if the wrong people knew about this thing. This baby could be sold for medicinal processing for a fortune."

"And would be worth a hundred times more as a weapon," Martino added. "Can you imagine what type of weapon a crystal this size could power? No wonder Sloan's paying us each ten quads. That's chump change compared to what this thing's worth."

"But hilaetite crystals were mined out decades ago," Johnson said. "No one has found a single crystal for years. Earth, Craton, Vernius, and a half a dozen other planets have the technology to locate crystals ten times smaller than this and they haven't been able to locate any. How did Sloan find this one?"

"The less we know, the better," replied Martino.

< 343 >

"Do you suppose there's more in here?" Johnson asked. "These things usually grow in bunches, and Sloan only gave us the coordinates for this one. The rest could be ours."

"No," Martino replied. "It's not unheard of for a single one to grow, and if there were more, I'm sure Sloan would be having us snatch them up, too."

"What if we keep this one?" Johnson said. "We tell Sloan we couldn't find it. He'd never know."

Martino gave Johnson a hard stare. "Double-cross Sloan? I don't think so. You're the one that said he gave you the creeps. The man looked as fit as a Cratonite, and I'm sure he's packing the latest weaponry. If half the stories about him are true, I don't want to be the one who crosses him. Let's be happy with our ten quads."

"Good decision," Sloan whispered. He knew that his ability to manipulate came most often through fear. He liked how he could use his reputation to instill fear into those he needed to use, and when necessary, he didn't mind setting a new example.

Johnson set down the case. "Sloan said everything we need is in here."

Martino removed his mittens, flipped the latch, and slowly opened the case. It was empty, except for heavy padding on all sides and a small, separate compartment in the front. Martino reached into the front compartment and pulled out a thin, pencil-sized laser cutter. He examined it critically. "This looks like new technology since my last job, but I believe it will work just fine. You hold the crystal steady, and I'll cut it off. Whatever you do, don't drop it."

Johnson took off his mittens, blew into his cupped hands, and then placed both hands on the crystal. Martino twisted the end of the laser cutter, and a red beam shot out. He slowly worked the beam

< 344 >

around the crystal in precise strokes. With every stroke, he cut deeper into the ice and rock.

Sloan watched intently, but his sources had been right—the man knew what he was doing. He could see the skill in Martino's workmanship.

If Martino so much as nicked the crystal, that would be the end of him, and if it was more than a nick, the end of the entire planet, with a crystal that size.

Sloan turned toward the pilot. "You better take us up another couple hundred feet."

"Are you sure you know what you're doing? Is this safe?" Johnson was asking. "I've heard plenty of stories of hilaetite crystal miners being blown sky-high. This thing's big enough to take out the entire planet. One wrong move and we're finished."

Martino didn't look up, but kept on working the laser. "Why do you think Sloan hired me for this job? I used to be a hilaetite crystal precision miner. When the machinery couldn't remove a crystal, they called people like me in to take care of it. Risky business, but it paid well."

"Not as well as this job's going to pay," replied Johnson. "If we live through it."

"Shut up and pay attention to the crystal," Martino said. "Why did Sloan hire you?"

Johnson replied, "Maybe he hired me to keep an eye on you."

Martino, finishing the final few cuts, did not respond. The crystal fell free into Johnson's hands. Sloan again leaned close to the screen as Johnson very slowly and gently placed the crystal in the case. It fit snugly in the padding. Martino closed the lid, which had the same padding on the underside, and latched the case. Sloan sat back in his seat, folded his arms and smiled.

< 345 >

Martino straightened up, picked up the transponder, and punched a few buttons. "That should reverse the coordinates and direct us back to the evacuation point. Sloan will be waiting for us."

"I hope," added Johnson.

Martino picked up the case. "With this baby on the line? He'll be there."

As the two men started walking toward the narrow tunnel that would lead them out of the cave, the picture on the screen began to vibrate. Sloan tried adjusting the screen, but then he saw the two men holding their lights up and slowly turning completely around, as if looking for the source of the vibration. It must have been something in the cave. Sloan could see nothing within the range of the light. After a few seconds, the picture vibrated a second time, and a few seconds later, a third time. With each vibration, he could see the floor and walls shake harder.

"Let's get out of here!" Martino said.

Both men bolted for the tunnel.

Just as they reached the opening, a huge hairy creature crashed through the back wall of the cavern. Among the flying ice and rock, Sloan could make out a rat-like head and a mouth full of teeth. It let out a hissing sound that caused the cavern to shake even more, bringing down more ice and rock.

With that, the men broke into a lumbering run. Sloan's eyes widened and he pulled back from the screen. His heart began to race, not out of fear for the men, but for fear of losing the crystal. He could hear a low growl mixed in with vibration after vibration, faster and faster. The beast was closing the gap. The picture on the screen shook. The vibrations gave way to thuds, as the weight of each step drew the beast closer and closer. Flying chunks of rock and ice filled the screen,

< 346 >

with intermittent glimpses of the creature crashing through the sides of the tunnel.

"Faster! Faster, you fools!" Sloan shouted at the screen.

"Should I take us in closer to prepare for evacuation, sir?" the pilot asked.

"No, not yet." Sloan's eyes never left the screen. "It's still too risky. They're bouncing that case around like it's a rubber ball. At least Martino has the box and is in the lead. He just needs to outrun Johnson."

The picture on the screen began to steady. Sloan could see some daylight. They must be approaching the entrance, where the tunnel floor was smoother and wider.

Sloan kept his eyes fixed on the screen. "Okay, move us down one hundred feet, but keep us a hundred yards or so from the cave. She could still blow. That distance should give us enough time."

Johnson's foot caught hard between two rocks, and he fell face first. Sloan grimaced. He could hear Johnson's ankle snap. Martino, who was starting to open up some distance between himself and Johnson, paused and looked back.

"Don't stop!" Sloan snapped, still looking at the screen. "This is your chance to get away while that thing has a meal."

Johnson lifted his hand toward Martino. "Help me," he pleaded.

The creature bore down on Johnson, and Sloan got a full view of it for the first time. It had a long tube-like body covered with coarse, dirty white hair. It ran on ten stubby legs, each ending with paws containing four or five very long and sharp claws.

The creature's head looked like that of a giant rat, with a long snout. Large, crooked teeth protruded from its open mouth, dripping with saliva.

< 347 >

Martino pulled out his plasma gun, aimed it at the beast, and squeezed. Nothing happened. He looked at it, made an adjustment, aimed, and squeezed again. Still nothing.

Johnson shouted, "It's too cold for a plasma gun. Help me up! Quick!"

Johnson scarcely finished the sentence before the jaws of the beast clamped down on him. The scream that came from Johnson made the hair on the back of Sloan's neck stand up. He had heard a lot of dying screams, but this was one of the most hideous.

Martino turned and ran out of the cave. Sloan knew Martino had little time. At the pace the creature was devouring Johnson, it wouldn't take long for it to finish off its appetizer and go after the second course.

When Martino exited the cave, he had to slow to almost a walk. Sloan shook his head in disappointment, but he knew that was probably Martino's only option. The snow was still knee deep and blowing as fiercely as when the two men had entered the cave. Sloan watched intently. Martino made his way through the snow, glancing down at the transponder.

The creature was finished with Johnson and was now chasing Martino.

With its short stubby legs, it was just as slow in the deep snow as Martino. He might have a chance, Sloan thought. That thing isn't built for wandering outside.

Sloan turned toward the pilot. "He's clear. Take us in for evacuation."

The pilot replied, "Yes sir, but the wind is too strong to land. We'll have to make it a hover-evac. Fifty feet's about as close as I can get."

"All right," Sloan said. "Make it so."

< 348 >

Sloan made his way rapidly down to the cargo bay, zipping up his heavy coat. He looked down at Martino through the open door and lowered the ladder. Everywhere he looked it was white. White snow on the ground, white snow on the mountains, white snow in the air. The ladder was swinging wildly in the wind. As it whipped by, Martino leaped up and grabbed it. He pulled himself up until his feet could rest on the lowest rung.

He turned his head.

The beast was no more than ten yards from him now, growling and occasionally letting out its hideous hiss.

Sloan watched Martino climb toward the open hatch, the wind still whipping the ladder. The beast raised the upper half of its body and lunged for the ladder. The spacecraft rose ten feet just in time, and the beast missed, its head crashing down into the snow. It let out a vicious hiss and stared up at Martino, mouth open. Never had Sloan seen teeth like that—large, jagged, almost stacked on top of one another.

The wind continued to blow and swirl. Sloan thought, Hang on, Martino. Hang on. I've come so far. One slip and you'll be the next meal for that creature, if the crystal doesn't blow us all up.

As Martino reached the top, Sloan bent down on one knee. He leaned over the open hatch, held out a gloved hand, and shouted, "Let me take the case?"

"Go ahead," Martino replied. Martino lowered his head and lifted one hand off the ladder to allow Sloan to remove the case from over his shoulder. Sloan watched as Martino reached for the handholds on the floor of the cargo bay. He grasped, but nothing was there.

Sloan stood up, staring at Martino and shaking his head. He had removed the handholds earlier.

< 349 >

Martino looked up at Sloan and his eyes widened. "Give me a hand."

Instead, Sloan turned and knelt by the case. He flipped open the latch and slowly and gently opened the lid, then reached in and touched the crystal. "Well done." He closed the lid and moved the case away from the open hatch.

"Now pull me up," Martino said, "and we can finish the transaction."

Sloan stood and walked over to the open hatch. Martino was still hanging onto the last rung of the ladder with one hand, his feet a few rungs down. His other hand reached up to Sloan.

Sloan bent one leg as if he was starting to kneel down to lift up Martino. Then, with a quick solid thrust, Sloan smashed his boot squarely into Martino's face. Martino's head snapped back, blood pouring from his nose. His free arm flailed and both feet slipped off the ladder. Sloan watched. He'd thought that one good kick would do it, but Martino was a little tougher than he had expected. Martino swung out over empty air, clinging to the ladder with one hand. Before he could swing himself back, Sloan stomped on the hand holding the ladder. Martino's finger bones crunched. Martino lost his grip. He snatched at the ladder one last time with his good hand, but all he caught was air. Sloan leaned out over the opening and watched Martino get smaller and smaller, falling through the white snow, falling toward the snow-covered ground, falling into the waiting jaws of the creature below.

Sloan flipped a switch on the side of the hatch. The ladder ascended up into the spacecraft, and the hatch door closed. Sloan then pressed the com button on the cargo bay wall. The spacecraft's pilot came on. "Yes, Mr. Sloan?"

< 350 >

Sloan replied, "Take us out of here."

"Where to, sir?" the pilot responded.

Sloan paused for a moment and then replied, "Earth."

# # # # #

The Planet Earth is no longer divided into countries, but rather into five geographic regions, called sectors. Scientific advances have enabled space travel to all parts of the Milky Way galaxy. Many of the stars in the galaxy were found to contain solar systems similar to the solar system of the Earth's own Sun, with inhabited planets. The inhabitants of some of those planets were hostile and had developed weapon systems far beyond those of Earth. As a result, the world leaders of Earth agreed to set aside all religious and political differences in order to protect their planet. By 2145, through the development of a new planetary defense system, Earth had avoided any takeover by other planets and developed a united society.

< 351 >

1 | SURPRISE!

Fourteen-year-old Jake Saunders flattened himself against his bedroom wall, next to the auto-furnish console. He could hear Cal coming down the hall, slow and cautious. That was Cal, always the cautious one, the thinker, the planner. But this time, Jake had the plan. Not one of his spur-of-the-moment, just-wing-it decisions. Keep coming, Cal. Just a few more seconds . . . there. Cal was just outside the door. Jake made a small, deliberate noise to give away his position. As soon as he heard Cal move, Jake punched the "armchair" button on the console and dropped to the floor.

Cal swung into the room, his mock-plasma gun pointed in Jake's direction. The fake laser beam aimed straight ahead. It was powered by the latest in ion capacitor technology. "Surrender, Earthling, or face the wrath of Romalor. Your Earth Legion is no match for the Cratonites."

The armchair module slid out of its wall cavity and mushroomed to full size, right into Cal's line of fire. Jake rose to one knee and, using the armchair for cover, shot Cal with his sepder gun replica, powered by the same technology as Cal's plasma gun. Cal twisted at the last minute, and the fake plasma beam from the sepder clipped his shoulder instead of hitting his chest.

Cal glanced at his shoulder. His black game vest lit up yellow where the beam had hit. "It's not red," he said. "Just a minor flesh wound."

Jake flipped the lever on his mock sepder and the sword blade extended, just like a real sepder. Time for hand-to-hand combat. "Die, then, Romalor!" he shouted and dived over the chair. His foot caught on the arm, and he crashed into Cal, sending both of them to the floor. Each vest lite up red where the other's weapon had poked it.

"Ow!" Cal said. "You big lug. You trying to kill me for real?"

Jake's Aunt Jane called up the stairs, "Jacob Saunders, are you trying to knock the house down? Your uncle will be here any minute. Have you finished wrapping his birthday present?"

Jake forgot about his game with Cal immediately. He had been waiting forever to give Uncle Ben his present. Jake had lived with the Walkers in the Sector Four Legion headquarters, in the Owami Desert in former Nigeria, ever since his dad was killed in a quantum fighter explosion. His mom had died when he was born, so Uncle Ben and Aunt Jane were like parents to him. He called back, "I'm sorry. I was taking a break. I'll finish up and be right down."

Jake finished wrapping Uncle Ben's present and raced Cal down the steps. As they hit the landing at the bottom and saw the house

< 354 >

full of guests, he grabbed Cal and came to a sudden halt. He hadn't realized how long he and Cal had been playing, but he could never resist the chance for a make-believe battle with his mock sepder. He searched the crowded room for Aunt Jane. There she was, over by the gift table. Jake made his way through the crowd to her.

< 355 >

CamCat Books

VISIT US ONLINE FOR
MORE BOOKS TO LIVE IN:
CAMCATBOOKS.COM

FOLLOW US

CamCatBooks   @CamCatBooks   @CamCat_Books